Aftershocks

by Natalie J. Damschroder

For all the readers who crave something just a little different. You're my people.

Huge thanks to Misty Simon and Ava Quinn for your insights and recommendations on this book.

Prologue

Zoe Smith huddled against the wall of the tiny, dingy room, arms wrapped around her legs. Not in the corner, which was a trap, but next to the room's door, so she'd have a few seconds before anyone coming in saw her.

She'd learned a few things in the past year.

Like how to pretend to take pills and then act like they'd worked. How to pay attention to what was around her. How to never assume that the way things looked was the way they really were.

She sniffed and rubbed at the dry, tight skin next to her eye. She hadn't been able to wash since last night, after what they'd done to Jordie. The tears had run into her hair and made it stick out funny. Freddie had squawked about it. She hated when Zoe's hair wasn't perfect—by her crazy, messed-up definition, anyway. But Pat hadn't let her brush it before they left. He'd been in too much of a hurry.

The guy standing guard outside her door coughed and shifted, his foot scraping on the floor. Zoe didn't move, but her insides jolted and flipped, her heart racing until she knew he wasn't coming inside. Not yet.

Someone *would* be coming in, she knew that. The odd leather bag on the floor several feet away guaranteed it would be sooner rather than later. She watched the bag, a lump of shadows in the room's dimness, as screams echoed in her head.

No. She pressed her forehead to her knees and held her breath, forcing the horrors back. She was thirteen now. Closer to an adult than to a child. Her birthday had passed without her even knowing it, but they'd mentioned the date last night, a shock to her after so many months of just surviving. Drifting. *Allowing.*

But after whatever they'd done to Jordie, Zoe knew she couldn't keep going like that. Things were about to get worse, she knew it, and if she was going to escape, this was her only chance.

A voice echoed from somewhere else in the building. She froze, straining to listen, so mad at herself for locking up in that tiny ball against the wall. *Do it.*

Her gaze darted from the bag to the file cabinets crowded against the side wall, blocking the frosted windows. She could just make out a faint crack along the wall between two of them. It was too straight to be damage. But there wasn't much space over there, and if she made noise, the guy guarding the door would hear.

She didn't know his name. He was new to Pat and Freddie's family, but he had the coldest eyes. They were almost worse than Freddie's crazy ones. He wouldn't care how much he hurt her to keep her from getting away.

In a few minutes, Pat and Freddie would have what they wanted and there would be no more delay. Zoe had worked very hard at not imagining what was coming next. There was no choice here. This was it.

So just go!

She lurched to her bare feet and raced across the small room, swallowing a grunt at the weight of the bag she grabbed on her way by. The totems inside were metal, but wrapped in cloth so they didn't clink. They were heavier than they'd looked last night, when Pat was lovingly examining them and talking about what he believed they could do. She squeezed between the cabinets and slid her fingertips along the crack. It went all the way to the floor and up a few feet, and yes, there was another one at the top, running sideways. Flattening her hand, she swept it across the plaster, looking for a latch. *Please don't need a key. Please don't need a key.*

Her fingers crumpled against a square of metal and she almost yelped. She couldn't see it. The room had darkened even more. The sun must have set. That was good, but she needed to figure out how to open... She contorted her face as she fumbled, trying to keep listening for voices or movement outside the tiny room.

And then there was a click. She pulled at the square latch, and the door rasped open a few inches. Cool air swept in, bringing with it the slow *chunka-chugga-chunk* of train wheels turning and the sting of metal and smoke in her nose. From somewhere on the other side of the train yard, brakes squealed.

Zoe carefully pried the door open as far as it would go. She had no idea what this little access door was used for, back in the olden days of the train station. But now it was her salvation.

Thank God Pat and Freddie practically starved her. A year ago, she'd never have gotten through the narrow gap. But now she squeezed through easily, barely noticing the way the rough wood scraped her arm and the back of her head, yanking hair out of her scalp. A breeze brushed over her face, opening her lungs. But her shoulders hunched and burned. Someone was about to grab her, she knew it. She wrestled the heavy bag through the panel. She couldn't leave it here. Not after all the things Pat had said about "rituals" and power. If he didn't have them, he wouldn't have a reason to have her or any other girl. She had to make them disappear.

And then she was free.

She hadn't forgotten how to run, all those months tied to a bed frame or table leg, all the days when she could move no more than a few feet. Gravel dug into her soles, but who cared about bruises and cuts? Concentrate on breathing—too loud, and they'd hear her—and the slow-moving train several yards away. One of the car doors was open. Only a couple of feet, but it was enough. She ran straight for it, eyes locked on the dark interior, arm cocked. The light over her shoulder illuminated the interior as it zoomed past, searing the image into her brain. She flung the hateful bag and it went right through the gap.

The heavy thud was the best sound she'd ever heard. No, the train whistle was, as the train took those things far away from her, where Pat could never find them.

But her exhilaration didn't last. The totems were gone, but she wasn't yet. They could see her if they looked, even in the shadows. Panic seized her muscles and made her stumble. She got her balance back, then pushed herself to run harder, along the length of the train, begging it to go faster so she could get across the tracks and away from the station house.

After forever, the train passed, iron creaking and rattling. Zoe leaped over the tracks and around a single car sitting by itself. Then down an aisle between trains. But it wasn't far enough. They could still find her. She ran up and down, climbing over couplings—*oh, god, don't move, don't crush me*—and counting sets of tracks—four…seven…eight—until she reached a train that had just released its brakes with a hiss. She halted, swaying, and looked to the left. The engine was so far down she couldn't see it. To the right, dozens more cars stretched as far as she could see. The train lurched, and she could tell it was going to go the other way—in the opposite direction as the way the totems were going.

She had to get on that train.

She ran again, telling herself it wasn't much further as her sides blazed with pain and her legs grew heavier and weaker. Her head spun, and she sucked in air, no longer able to keep quiet. But there. Another open door. The metal step just below it chilled her foot for the second before she grabbed the handle and swung herself inside.

She lay on the floor, panting, waiting for the train to move. *One one thousand, two one thousand, three…* She counted four hundred and twenty-two seconds before the train lurched, then eased into motion. Held her breath until the rail yard slid out of sight, and all she could see now was dark fields and the occasional farmhouse or road with a pickup truck driving down it.

It's over.

No, it wasn't. She had to get to a town, a real town, and get off the train without getting hurt. Then find someone safe to help her. They could do it. They were smart. And crazy. And if they found her…

A sob spasmed in her chest and she fingered her earlobe, remembering what they'd done to Jordie's brother to make Jordie do what they wanted. And then they'd killed Jordie anyway. His screams and the others' laughter echoed in her head again. She shuddered. No, she wasn't out of danger.

The clackity-clack of the train's wheels lulled her, though, and soon her breathing had steadied, her heart no longer slamming against her chest bone. How many miles had they traveled? The train seemed really fast, the little bit visible outside speeding by. They wouldn't know which train she got on, right? They wouldn't know where to look. Maybe it was okay to start thinking about what came next.

She stretched out on her stomach, chin balanced on her stacked hands, and thought about going home. Her parents would be happy—wouldn't they? Her mother had to have freaked when Zoe disappeared, and she'd freak again when she had her back. Probably she'd never let Zoe out of her sight. That would be awesome in a way, but part of her felt dread, too. She didn't want to be a prisoner again. And it wasn't like they'd let her make her own choices. She was only thirteen.

She smiled a little. *Thirteen*. Maybe they'd let her have a party. For sure her mother would make a cake. Freddie never baked, so it wouldn't be creepy and awful. Zoe could handle that.

Maybe Jordie's brother would come. What was his name? She closed her eyes, remembering how he'd cried in her arms after they'd cut him and thrown him into her room. She'd helped him stop the bleeding and hugged him, rocking him the way her mom used to rock her when she had a nightmare. They hadn't talked much, but she'd asked his name. *Grant*. That was it. She'd resented him for a long time, because Jordie had been able to sneak him out. Pat hadn't cared. He didn't need Grant for anything. He'd just been a tool to get Jordie to do what Pat wanted. But that wasn't Grant's fault. Zoe hoped she'd get to see him again. She had to tell him…well, not what had happened, but that Jordie had loved him. Yeah, that was all she had to say. *Jordie loved you.* Grant would get it.

The train whistle sounded, faint, and the clacking slowed. Zoe pushed herself to her feet and leaned out the door, looking to see what was ahead. Bright lights reflected off the clouds, and a red glow suddenly flashed to green. Her heart rate picked up again. This was it. This was where she would get off. Find some help. Try to explain who she was and where she'd been.

The thought made her want to cry. She could just stay on the train. Go miles and miles, hundreds of miles, where Pat and Freddie could never find her.

But then no one would find Pat and Freddie. Jordie needed justice. So did Grant. And Zoe needed them to be in jail, so there was no chance they'd come after her again. If she went too far away, the police would never find them. And she'd never be safe.

The brakes squealed, piercing Zoe's eardrums and burying the reassuring rhythm of the wheels on the rails. The whistle sounded again. She watched the ground, and when the train slowed enough that she could make out individual ties, she braced herself, said a quick prayer, and jumped.

Chapter One

Sixteen Years Later

Zoe Ardmore was about to step into the grand ballroom when her purse buzzed. She hesitated, the faint chamber music and low murmur of voices calling to her, but she knew Kell wasn't here yet, so she moved aside to check the call. It could be the office, or one of the charity's committee members needing her somewhere behind the scenes.

But when she slipped the phone out of the clutch enough to check the screen, she frowned. The number wasn't in her contacts, coming up as "unknown." But it had an Ohio area code.

She shivered and dropped the phone back beside her tiny wallet and hairbrush. Ignoring the call wouldn't hurt anything. They'd leave a message if they were legit.

Laughter drew her to the main room's entrance again, and she smiled. Not too many years ago, she would have been one of the tuxedo-uniformed wait staff offering around trays of champagne. She wouldn't have even entertained the idea of arriving here as a guest.

"Kellen Stone!" a voice boomed behind her. She glanced over her shoulder to see Kell shaking hands with a state senator. He stood tall and graceful in his tux, his curly dark hair tamed and gleaming under the chandelier. The image of sleek success. But anyone really looking would see the interest in his eyes as he listened to the senator's story, take notice of the sincere friendliness with which he greeted the senator's wife as she emerged from the anteroom. People mattered to Kell, and it was one of the things Zoe loved most about him.

He said a few more words and then strode across the plush carpet to her side.

Zoe smiled up at him. "Looks gorgeous, doesn't it?" She doubted he cared about the light shimmering on the silky ribbons adorning the tables, or the lace cloths and curtains draped everywhere. He'd grown up in this world, and he was a guy. But she'd earned her way here, had worked hard to make the money that had paid for her ticket to this benefit. She reveled in every detail.

"The committee did a nice job," he acknowledged, his gaze sweeping the room in a second but resting longer on her face. "But this is the real beauty." He bent and kissed her softly.

Zoe leaned into the kiss, as happy to be with him as she was to be here at all.

Her purse vibrated again. *Ohio.*

She broke away, goose bumps rising over every

inch of exposed skin. Urgency prodded her forward, though it had nothing to do with taking their places inside the ballroom. She hid her confusion by looking around, pretending to seek their table.

"This way, Zoe!" Olivia, Kell's younger sister, bounced up to Zoe and grabbed her hand. "We're at table ten. You're with us!"

"Hey, squirt. You look nice."

Olivia made a face at her brother, then beamed. "Right? Mom didn't want me to get this dress, but I talked her into it." She swirled the long, flowing skirt, the action more typical of a five-year-old than a thirteen-year-old. But the dress's snug but unrevealing bodice and her dyed-to-match heels were just right for her age and the occasion. Zoe suspected Elise, Olivia's mother, had played her daughter into selecting the dress.

"Anyway, come on. We're all together." She tugged Zoe along. Zoe reached back with her free hand to snag Kell, forming a chain.

"Perfect," Kell murmured.

Zoe looked up as they crossed the room. He hadn't sounded sarcastic, though given his relationship with his parents, there was an even chance he was pleased or annoyed. His expression was smooth, open, so she couldn't tell.

Kell's mother held out her hands to Zoe, her polite smile spreading when she realized what Zoe was wearing.

"You got the Valentino."

They exchanged cheek kisses. "I did. The purple

seemed like a good choice for this event." She backed up a step, and they spent a moment admiring each other. Elise wore an ivory lace dress with a cobalt jacket that showed off her fit curviness without being inappropriate for her age. Zoe had decided on a more dramatic dress, a dark purple flat satin that crisscrossed around her waist and left her shoulders bare. It had been a hard decision, spending that amount of money on something she might not wear again. But it was another symbol of how far she'd come, and she allowed herself just a touch more pride.

A mellow tone signaled that dinner was about to be served, and they took their seats, Kell's father, Robert, breaking briefly from his conversation with the man next to him to greet Zoe. She smiled at the man to her left, someone she didn't know.

They chatted pleasantly throughout the meal, shifting topics and participants among the others at the table. Zoe enjoyed her chicken, portobello polenta, and baby asparagus. She enjoyed even more the sense that she belonged here. It wasn't just that she was with people who accepted her for who she was now rather than looking down on her for where she'd come from. All the people at the table, from Kell's family to the southern gentleman and his wife and the young lawyers across from them, treated the wait staff with grace and respect. This wasn't the world she'd read about as a kid.

They were halfway through dessert and a few minutes from the introduction of the guest speaker when Kell cleared his throat and the rest of the table fell silent. He lifted his glass of champagne, and Zoe realized everyone at their table now had one.

"I have something to say." Kell cleared his throat again. Zoe gave him her attention, and he seemed to expand to fill her world. They'd been together two years, and it still overwhelmed her whenever she thought of him as hers. His dark hair was slightly rumpled over his blue eyes, but his tux was impeccable. He gave off an energy that compelled people to look at him, but in a way that never cried arrogance or self-centeredness. The words "I love you" welled in her throat, but he was already speaking.

"I really wanted to do this differently," he began, his eyes on the bubbling liquid in his glass. "I considered and discarded a dozen different plans. I wanted your family here, Zoe."

She frowned a little. Why would he want that?

"I wanted to be a little more private, and I apologize to those of you who don't know us."

The others at the table smiled Mona Lisa or cat-canary smiles, and Zoe began to feel left out of the joke.

"But my parents are about to embark on a three-week business trip to Europe, and Zoe herself is heading for a conference tomorrow. When she returns, I'll be embroiled in a merger that will take sixteen hours of every day, and frankly, I can't wait until all of that is over. I can't wait another minute." He turned to Zoe. His mother placed her fingers over her mouth, tears springing to her eyes, and suddenly, Zoe knew. She pressed her own lips together so they wouldn't tremble.

"For two years, you've been my light and my foundation. You've shown me what it is to love with my entire being, to not only share all of my life, but to *want* to share it. You make me see the world differently, and that's a much better thing than I ever would have imagined possible. No one will ever fit me like you do."

"Kell," she breathed as he reached into his pocket with his free hand. When he pulled it out, a beautifully proportioned, clear white diamond ring held between his finger and thumb, his hand shook.

"Zoe Ardmore, will you marry me?"

She almost ran.

For a few seconds, she stopped being Zoe Ardmore and reverted to Zoe Smith, kidnap victim. A terrified, lost, angry girl forever trying to escape her past.

A past Kell knew nothing about.

What had she done? How could she be Kell's foundation when her own had so many holes? His light, when she was full of darkness? She couldn't marry him without telling him the truth, and that would forever change the way he saw her. The way he saw them.

Bullshit.

She blinked, shocked at her own voice barking at her inside her head.

You earned this. You made *it. It's real and strong and beautiful, and you don't have to destroy it with pain and sorrow.*

Calm seeped into her, creeping down from head to toe. Calm borne of certainty. She'd had no idea he was thinking about this, had barely even considered it herself, so engrossed was she, always, in the *now*. But it was right. Nothing had to be ruined.

"Kell, please put down your glass."

She could hear him swallow as he complied. As soon as the glass touched the lace tablecloth, she launched herself into his arms.

"Yes!" It was a whisper and a scream at the same time. Kell's arms wrapped around her and he buried his face in her neck, his relief palpable. Zoe was dimly aware of the applause around them. A few nearby tables had caught wind of what was happening and joined in. "I love you," she whispered, and he murmured it back.

"Here." Kell leaned away a little. "Before I drop it." He slipped the ring onto her finger, and of course it fit perfectly. "Man, that was the scariest five minutes of my life," he muttered.

Regret soured in her mouth. That she'd hesitated, and hurt him even for just a few seconds. *If you tell him the truth, it will hurt him forever.*

She shoved that aside. The soul-searching would wait. "How could you not know I'd say yes?" She laid her hand on his cheek and tilted his head up so she could see his eyes. "I love you so much." It filled her chest, swelled her throat, made her eyes burn with the sheer intensity of it.

"That's not always the point," he answered, and then his parents and Olivia were crowding them, wanting hugs, and the charity spokesperson was at the podium to introduce the evening's speaker. Zoe had to content herself with sitting close to Kell and holding his hand while they listened, when a million other things crowded her mind.

He'd wanted her parents to be here, but she was so glad they weren't. She'd deliberately kept them away over the two years she and Kell had been together. He'd met them, of course, but they lived in Kentucky now, and the distance between them and Zoe was further than those nine hundred miles. As independent as she was of her past, they were driven by it.

They'd promised never to mention it to Kell, eagerly on board with whatever they thought would help her. But the possibility of an offhand reference was another good reason for her tell him about her abduction.

She watched him watching the speaker, a half smile on his clear, open, guileless face. He always treated her as if she were something to cherish, but never something fragile. He'd mentioned more than once how attracted he'd been to her strength of purpose, her determination and sheer will. Would that change? Would he now be awed at what she'd overcome, put her on a pedestal she'd topple off of repeatedly? Or worse, see her as damaged? Something to be fixed.

Two relationships in college had been enough to cure her of baring her soul. It changed *everything*, in ways it shouldn't. And the more she'd tried to convince them to stop thinking about it, the more it seemed to matter. No relationship was so strong it couldn't be broken. But would this break her and Kell?

You'd have to tell him about Grant, too. This time the

voice in her head was her younger self. The eighteen-year-old who'd mapped out the rest of her life and was ready to launch it when she'd made the most difficult choice she'd ever faced. Most difficult until this one.

Her eyes stung. She leaned over and whispered, "I'll be right back." Kell nodded and kissed her hand as she grabbed her purse and wove between tables, making her way to the blessedly empty restroom.

She closed herself in a stall and pressed her palms to the cold metal, inhaling deeply to stave off the memories. It was inevitable, she supposed, that nostalgia would encroach. Almost nothing about that night ten years ago was like this one. Grant had proposed to her outside. They'd been wearing cutoff shorts, and the most enduring detail was the smell of fish bait.

Well, not *the* most enduring detail.

Go *away*.

She wouldn't let the past affect this night any more than she'd let it affect any other important event. If it took her over now, even for a moment, how could she stop it from encroaching on everything else? That was *not* how she wanted her marriage to be.

Her stupid phone buzzed again. Grumbling, she snapped open the clutch and yanked it out, scowling at the screen. The unknown number again. From Ohio. There had been five calls while they'd dined, all from the same number. No voice mail messages had been left.

She swept her thumb over the first listing, deleting it, then each one more fiercely than the last. "Stupid

telemarketers," she muttered before flinging the phone
back into her bag and slamming out of the stall. They
called and called and it didn't matter if the number
obviously didn't belong to their target. Jerks. Wasting
people's time and causing unnecessary tension. She
hated Ohio.

When she returned to the ballroom, the speaker
was making his closing remarks. A small band began
playing, and Kell met her halfway to draw her onto the
dance floor. She nestled into his arms and sighed. His
broad chest was strong under her cheek, and she
smoothed her hand down the satin of his lapel.
Drakkar Noir—common, maybe, even cliché, but her
favorite of his colognes—banished the memory of fish
and everything else. She closed her eyes and sank into
the moment, the *now*, as she'd become so expert at
doing. Her body slowly relaxed as they swayed.

Kell's voice rumbled through his chest, breaking
the spell. "I'm sorry."

She looked up in surprise. "For what?"

"This didn't work out like I'd imagined. I timed it
wrong. It was rushed, and you were pressured—"

Zoe released his hand to press her fingers over his
mouth. "It was perfect."

Tension lines on his face eased. "You're just saying
that."

His lips rubbing against her fingers sent a zing to
her core. She tried to keep her smile from becoming a
grin. "My only regret is that I can't"—she leaned closer
and tilted her mouth toward his ear—"strip you out of
that tux and show you just how damned happy you've

made me."

Kell chuckled, capturing her hand again and pulling her tight against his body while he whirled her around the floor.

Later, after accepting toast after toast from Kell's parents and sister, their friends, and various groups of acquaintances who wanted to wish them well, Zoe and Kell went back to their apartment, and she did show him just how happy she was.

She was moments from sleep, wrapped in his arms, everything she ever wanted just inches from her grasp, when the phone in her purse, abandoned on the floor, buzzed. And she had to fight the feeling that she was about to lose it all.

* * *

"Congratulations, Zoe!"

"Thanks, Sherry." Zoe swung through the half door next to the reception desk and smiled at the admin assistant as she went by. "Sorry I'm late. My flight got delayed." This was the first day she'd been in the office since Kell proposed. She'd left the next morning for a three-day conference in California and taken the red-eye back, even though Kell was already at work when she got in and she still had to wait until tonight to see him. She smiled at the ring on her hand, its weight unfamiliar yet already reassuring, and headed for the coffee pot behind the reception desk.

"Ms. Ardmore?"

The unfamiliar voice froze Zoe mid-step. Sherry, twenty-two and dressed like it, nervously smoothed her micro-mini and tilted her head at the dark-suited man who'd just risen in the guest area. Zoe didn't know him, but he was still familiar. Her body seemed to vibrate with denial, and she zeroed in on three vases of flowers on the polished wood counter. She opened her mouth to ask Sherry where they'd come from, but that was a stall tactic. A defense mechanism against the sheer terror that began screaming in her brain as soon as she spotted the FBI agent.

"Yes. I'm Zoe Ardmore," she added, since half a minute had gone by. "You are?"

"Special Agent Henricksen. May I have a minute of your time, please?"

Absolutely not. "Certainly." She led Henricksen down the brick-walled hallway and let curses fly through her brain. Everything had been fine while she was on her trip. No more momentary senses of doom or phone calls from unknown numbers in any state, including Ohio. She'd decided not to tell Kell about the abduction. Why mess with things when they were so perfect?

And now this.

Maybe it has nothing to do with you. The FBI could be investigating some other thing. Maybe he wanted her cooperation in gathering information on one of her clients. Or they'd inadvertently been connected to someone running a porn site, though she worked very hard to make sure that didn't happen. There were dozens of reasons the FBI could have sent an agent to her office.

But Zoe had learned a long time ago about the futility of denial. She was an expert at facing reality, and it was about to hit her in the face. Hard, since that was the only way reality hit.

"This is a cool office," Henricksen complimented as they passed through the main area.

"Thank you." Instead of cubicles, she'd let her design staff separate their work areas in any way they wanted. The converted warehouse, with its polished hardwood floors and high ceilings, echoed wildly when too many people were talking. Throw rugs, curtains hanging from rods suspended from the ceiling a story above, and thick screens divided the spaces. She'd had acoustic panels hung, which helped muffle the noise, and the art on the walls had all been created by her staff.

When she launched her web design and hosting company several years ago, it had been a typical home-based enterprise. She'd built it at a steady pace from herself and one freelance designer to a million-dollar company with fourteen employees. They created websites and e-commerce portals for businesses all over the world. The thought that whatever had brought Agent Henricksen here could jeopardize what she'd built made her want to throw her body over the whole thing and protect it with her life.

She unlocked her office door, a tall panel of maple set between glass walls, and ushered the agent inside. He stood patiently in front of her desk while she stowed her briefcase and jacket. She almost offered him coffee, but that was another delaying tactic. When she motioned for him to sit, he waited until she'd done so before sinking tensely into the well-padded guest chair in front of her desk.

"I'm not sure if you're aware of the reason for my visit," Henricksen started.

"How would I be?" she asked.

"A notice would have been sent to you."

Her gaze landed on the three-day pile of mail on the corner of her desk. It wasn't large, as Sherry would have sorted out the junk. Sure enough, when Zoe flipped through it, she found a thin envelope with an official-looking seal in the corner. She fingered the edge but didn't move to open it.

"I guess you should start at the beginning," she told the agent. Her heartbeat slowed, her breath taking longer to drag in and push out.

"Of course," he said graciously.

His voice sounded deeper, stretched. She knew what was coming. Not the details, but the essence. And she really, really didn't want to hear it.

"Patron Rhomney and Fredricka Thomashunis have been granted parole."

Everything rushed back toward her, a rage of noise and color and light. Heels tapped on the floor as they passed her door. One of the designers laughed. A phone rang. The red snapdragons and orange lilies in the flower arrangement on her desk tore at her eyes. And her voice, when she managed to work it up through the despair closing her throat, sounded weak and groggy.

"Would you close the door, please? And the blinds," she added. No one was looking through the windows, but she couldn't take the movement out there. Nor did she want to have to explain to anyone later what had happened. She was sure her devastation showed on her face.

"Ms. Ardmore?" Henricksen returned to the desk and hovered uncertainly. "Are you all right?"

"Give me a moment." She managed a deep inhale, and the bombardment receded somewhat. "I'm sorry. I should have been expecting it."

"It's understandable." He waited while she breathed a few more times, trying to keep memory and emotion at bay. Finally, he must have deemed her composed enough, because he went on.

"Mr. Rhomney and Ms. Thomashunis underwent their sixth parole hearings last month. The parole board found no reason to deny either one. Rhomney has obtained employment in Delaware County, north of Columbus, Ohio, while Thomashunis is in a halfway house in Marion."

Zoe nodded. She unfortunately knew that area well, despite having moved away so many years ago.

"They are far away from Boston," he assured her, "and the terms of their parole require them to remain in Ohio and check in with their respective parole officers once a week, in person."

"Yet here you are, notifying me of what is no doubt already in this letter." Zoe held the envelope a few inches off the desk and dropped it. But she couldn't look away from it. Henricksen remained still and silent while she fought a rush of rage and despair, forced herself to remain in the present, that off-white rectangle a bizarre center point holding her in place.

She wasn't as divorced from her past as she'd believed. It wasn't going to stay where it belonged.

And she'd been getting phone calls from Ohio.

She straightened and looked at Henricksen. "So why *are* you here? What's happened? The FBI doesn't do courtesy calls and hand-holding."

"No. Nothing has happened that anyone is concerned about." For the first time, he shifted in his chair and looked uncomfortable. "I was a junior agent at the time of your abduction. You haven't left my mind since."

She noticed that he referred to her, not her case. That warmed her, but she didn't understand. "The bad guys were caught. I was fine. It's not like the unsolved case that haunts a career. So why…"

"You were brave and fierce, and your escape gave me hope that I could actually make a difference in this job. But that's rare. Most cases do the opposite." He cleared his throat and tugged his suit jacket forward. "I've kept tabs on Rhomney and Thomashunis and knew you'd be getting a notification letter." He eyed the envelope. "It's a pretty cold way to learn something like this."

Zoe didn't tell him that might be a good thing. Acting like something was a big deal sometimes made it one. "Is there reason to believe I'm in any danger?" She was pleased with the steadiness of her voice, but swiveled her engagement ring into her palm and clenched her fist around it. A reminder that she was an adult, not a powerless child.

Henricksen didn't sigh, but he might as well have.

"Not officially, no. Reports indicate your abductors had no apparent contact during their incarceration, and those who followed them but escaped prosecution have dispersed."

Zoe felt her mouth twist and consciously relaxed it. It wasn't Henricksen's fault that prosecutors had let so many of Pat and Freddie's people go for lack of evidence. Most of them hadn't done anything bad to Zoe. Some had even been kind. But they knew she didn't belong there, and they did nothing.

Pat and Freddie had both pled out on Zoe's abduction to avoid a trial, which was what enabled their parole now. Zoe's fury that the DA had been unable to prosecute for Jordie's murder had compromised her recovery for a long time. No body, no weapons, no evidence, no eyewitness testimony except the word of two young teenagers who had never actually seen anything—the prosecutors had just gone with what they had, assuring Zoe's and Grant's families that it would be enough.

It wasn't.

But that was out of her control, and she'd finally accepted that. Or at least some part of her had.

Dragging herself back to the topic at hand, she said, "So the FBI didn't send you here."

"No. I'm here on my own. I have a bad feeling about their intentions, but bad feelings aren't actionable." He smiled a little. "Not in real life." He spread a hand toward her. "You should have someone you can come to if it becomes necessary. Someone you know and can trust."

Zoe nodded. "I understand. And I appreciate it." She told him about the phone calls she'd gotten but hadn't answered. "Is that actionable?"

He slipped a small notebook out of the inside pocket of his jacket. "If you give me the number, I'll look into it. Thomashunis made a call to Rhomney the day after he was released. I can at least find out if it's the same number, or if the one you have is connected to either of them."

Zoe pulled up the last call, glad she hadn't deleted that one like the others. "They're going to want the totems," she said. "Were they ever found?"

"No. But they weren't listed stolen property and weren't necessary to the prosecution of the case, so no one looked for them." He cocked his head, his brown eyes kind in his dark, impassive face. "Do you know where to find them?"

God, she wished she did. When she'd tossed them onto that train car, she'd been so naïve, believing their disappearance would eliminate Pat and Freddie's obsession. But she knew better now. That kind of psychotic fixation didn't fade. To them, the totems were a treasure of immense value. There was no way they'd given up their quest for the power they believed the totems would provide them.

"Would it matter if I did?"

He shook his head. "The bureau has no interest in the totems. But if you knew, we could find a way to feed that information to Rhomney. Keep him off your trail."

Zoe wasn't sure that would be enough. The

totems—according to Pat—needed a key. And they needed someone to "activate" them. Sixteen years ago, that person had been Zoe. She didn't know if, in Pat's mind, it still was.

She tried to remember everyone who had been arrested that night. The train yard now seemed an odd place to meet someone, but it had been off the beaten path, for sure. They were supposed to meet the person who had the key, something that explained the totems' significance and how to unlock their so-called mystical powers. But they'd all still been at the rail yard when the police showed up, and as far as Zoe knew, the person with the key hadn't been one of them. She asked Henricksen, but he had no more information than she did.

He rose and handed her a business card. "As I said, there's no open investigation, so I'm limited in what I can do for you. But that doesn't mean my hands are completely tied. Keep me informed of anything that might connect. Anything that makes you nervous. Even if it seems like coincidence."

Zoe understood. Every detail could be used to build a case, could combine for enough reason to investigate or act. If she did become a target, this man was on her side.

It was as reassuring as he probably meant it to be.

"Thank you." She accepted the card and slipped it into a sleeve in her planner. "And the phone number?"

"If it amounts to anything, I'll let you know." He raised a shoulder. "Honestly, it's probably—"

"A burner phone. I realize that. But I appreciate

your help."

"Good luck to you, Zoe." He closed the door behind him on the way out.

Zoe dropped into her desk chair and stared at nothing. Amazing how much things could change in three short days. She had the career, the love, the life she'd always wanted. Her happiness seemed solid. Grounded.

But it was so much more delicate than she'd thought. A few words—from her to Kell, from Pat to Zoe, even from the media to her mother—could blow it all away like smoke in front of a fan.

If Henricksen's gut feeling was right, if Pat and Freddie came after Zoe, whether for the totems or for herself, she wouldn't be the only one in danger. She thought of Kell. Of Olivia. And knew, with growing nausea, what she would have to do.

Maybe not. A tiny kernel of hope remained that nothing would happen. That her captors had changed, or moved on to other obsessions. She'd look back someday not with laughter, but at least with relief and amazement at how lucky she was. She could still live the life she'd designed.

But if she was wrong, it wouldn't matter if she told Kell the truth or not. She'd lose everything.

Chapter Two

Two days passed. Nothing happened. No phone calls. No weird e-mails or text messages or anything sent in the mail. Zoe spent far too much of her time poring over news reports. There'd been brief mentions in some Ohio papers and on the Internet, but no announcements by major news outlets of Pat's and Freddie's release.

Zoe had talked to her parents, who had talked to friends back home. Their old local station had done a more in-depth bit on the history of the case, but as they'd all changed their names and moved to a new state shortly after Zoe's escape, reporters had struck out in finding anything new to report.

Her parents were more focused on her mental state than any present danger. It had been a shock to her, returning home and finding them so different from the parents she remembered. They'd seemed simple to her, naïve, and she'd tried to keep them that way. It made things easier for her, and it also felt good to know that even after the tragedy they'd been through, they could still be that way. That anyone out there could.

She thought she managed to hide her distraction and anxiety, but Kell noticed.

"Are those carrots, or carrot-sauce?"

Zoe stared at him blankly. "What?"

He motioned with his knife at her cutting board. She looked down and saw she'd minced the carrots to mush. "Damn. I'm sorry."

"It's fine." He laid filleted chicken breasts on the broiling pan and started to baste them. "We have more. But you want to talk about what's bothering you?"

She shrugged and scraped the mess into a little bowl. "Just work stuff. Same old kind of thing. No big." She felt Kell's eyes on her and kept her gaze down, focused on chopping a new set of carrots to the proper consistency. She glanced up at the ironwork clock on the ivory-painted wall. "James and Sonya will be here soon. I don't want to get into a rant. It's fine."

He didn't look convinced, but the reminder of the time put him off. Zoe spent the rest of the evening studying Kell and their friends, listening to them discuss people in the firm where he and James both worked, and to Sonya's gossip about the spouses in their circle and their "scandalous" escapades.

Zoe and Sonya weren't close, but they had a fun, carefree friendship. How would that change if Sonya learned about the kidnapping? Would it automatically make things more awkward? Would Sonya feel like she had to be careful with what she said, afraid to trigger a traumatic reaction in Zoe? Then everything would be awkward and uncomfortable, and Sonya would withdraw. People avoided what they didn't know how to handle. Zoe had dealt with that over and over again, until she just stopped telling. It was so much easier to be friends with people who didn't know.

And what about James and Kell? They'd been best friends since prep school. Kell had commented how glad he was that Zoe and Sonya enjoyed each other's company. If that changed, the couples' dynamic would change. He'd hate that.

Telling Kell the truth didn't have to mean anyone else would know. But he'd probably tell his family. They had been slow to warm to Zoe anyway, as they would be to anyone not already part of their crowd. They respected her blue-collar upbringing and the way she'd worked her way through college and built her business so successfully. But they weren't without their prejudices. They would worry about the effect the "criminal element" had had on her, being around them for so long. They'd wonder what else they didn't know, what else she'd hidden. She would have to earn their trust all over again.

By the time James and Sonya went home, Zoe had a blistering headache.

"Come on, sweetheart." Kell turned her after closing the door behind James and eased her down the hall toward their bedroom. "We'll clean up tomorrow. You've been tense all evening." His fingers dug gently into the tendons of her shoulders and she moaned.

"Just a headache. I'll be okay." At his urging, she lay down on the bed. He perched beside her and worked on the tense muscles, applying just the right amount of pressure to loosen them. He didn't speak, just slowly worked out all the tightness until her headache eased and she relaxed.

But she had to press her face into the pillow so he couldn't see her tears. She lay motionless when the stroking slowed to a pet, his fingers pulling slowly through her hair. Probably assuming she'd fallen asleep, he went into the bathroom and closed the door with barely a click.

It was incredibly selfish, but she couldn't tell him. He'd soothed her pain away without question, without any concern that her excuse hid anything deeper. Once he knew her secrets, how she'd lied to him, he could no longer see her with such clarity. He'd always wonder if she was hiding something more.

He would touch her differently, in case something triggered a memory or caused her pain. He'd imagine the horrors she'd lived through, encourage her to talk about them. Because he was an attorney who often had to spin and twist facts and hide truths, he was adamant about being open in his personal life. She loved that about him, about the freedom it gave her as long as they lived in the *now*. When he found out she'd held back, he'd never trust her again.

Before her parents agreed to move and change their last name, everyone knew about Zoe's kidnapping, and everyone wanted to talk about it. Her teachers spoke to her in hushed voices and gave her too much leeway with her schoolwork. She didn't want to be different like that. The other kids at school asked awful questions, full of morbid curiosity. Her old friends didn't know how to talk to her anymore. They assumed she wouldn't want to do the things they used to do, that she would want to stay safe and close to home. No one believed her when she said they were wrong. Confinement of any kind was the last thing she wanted. But at first, it was all that was offered to her.

Once they'd moved and started fresh, she'd refused to tell anyone about it, with two exceptions: whoever her therapist was at any given time, and Grant. He was the only one who *only* knew her from the abduction, so the way they interacted felt normal. No one understood them like they did each other. It was her fault that relationship failed, but it was because that past drove them in different directions.

It still took too long to learn her lesson. The first guy she'd told in college had been completely freaked out. The questions were never-ending and usually out of the blue. He barely touched her and when he did, acted as if she were made of tissue. He worried about how much damage had been done. When she found herself unable to escape the tension or frustration, she'd broken up with him. His relief had hurt far more than his concern had ever soothed.

The second guy, she waited until she knew it was serious. That had been her senior year, and they'd been seeing each other for nine months. His reaction had been completely different. He'd withdrawn, wary about everything she said to him. Suspicion colored more and more of their time together, and he'd talked Zoe into attending therapy with his psychologist sister. No part of her wanted to do such a thing, except the part that thought she loved him. Until they got into session and it became clear he couldn't believe anything she said. His sister declared their trust destroyed, and he'd decided not to try to rebuild it.

After that disaster, Zoe vowed not to take the risk again. Her relationship with Kell took her by surprise, going deep slowly. There would always be some point in the future that would be perfect to tell him the truth. Except there never was. And then it was too late. She'd passed the point when telling him would do more damage than not telling him. Still, she'd believed it wouldn't matter. She was simply the woman he was in love with. He didn't have to know what or who had made her that way.

So stupid.

She rolled onto her back and glared at the ceiling. This was ridiculous. Her secret didn't have to destroy their relationship. Wallowing in it was setting that up quite nicely. She had to forget about Pat and Freddie and Agent Henricksen and just live her life like normal.

If only it were that easy. A week passed. Work was fine, and with the merger Kell wasn't around to notice her continued preoccupation. But no matter how hard she tried, she couldn't stop waiting for something to happen. For Pat or Freddie to contact her, or an ambitious reporter to pick up the story on a slow news day, or even for the FBI to uncover some disruptive detail to turn everything upside down. As they'd expected, the phone number was a burner. After Henricksen sent her an e-mail saying so, she didn't hear from him again.

During it all, she came to realize something she never would have admitted before.

As much as she loved her life, it was an exceedingly lonely one. She was surrounded by acquaintances, a few women she considered friends. People she'd go shopping with, or ask to be attendants in her wedding, and even share the minor frustrations that were part of any relationship. But she didn't have a single person she could tell about what she was going through.

Somehow, in trying to keep the past in its place, she'd avoided making true connections that might bring it to light. She'd always thought that was a good thing, but now she knew she was fooling herself. If she wanted to tell someone, there was no one to tell.

Except Kell. And that never-ending roller coaster of indecision was driving her insane.

* * *

To compensate, she spent more time at the company, solidifying operations and building their customer base, as well as shifting more responsibility to her two managers. By Sunday, when she was the only person in the office except the two off-shift web maintenance staff, she knew she couldn't continue like this.

Olivia had been complaining about not seeing them, so Kell had cleared an hour for dinner tonight at their favorite restaurant. Zoe decided to walk. It was several blocks from her office, but the late-September night was lovely, and it was after tourist traffic had dissipated and before nightlife started rocking the city.

She took her time, thinking maybe the cool air or post-sunset peace would help her de-stress.

And it worked. The gentle light, soft breeze and smiles of passersby gave her reasons to smile. As her body responded, she told herself if nothing had happened yet, nothing *was* going to happen. She couldn't keep living with the anticipation of something that would never come.

A cab pulled up to the curb slightly ahead of her. She kept walking, assuming the person opening the back door would cross the sidewalk and go into the apartment building on her left. Instead, he put himself in her path. When she swerved, he grabbed her arm.

"Hey!" Surprised, she leaned forward and then jerked her arm up and out of his grasp. "Leave me alone!" she yelled at the top of her lungs. She expected the cab driver to get out, but he didn't even turn. She realized the cab wasn't legit—just a black car with random numbers and the word "taxi" painted on its side.

No one was nearby on this side of the street. Some people a couple of blocks down had turned at her shout, then kept walking. She'd never be able to outrun him in the heels she was wearing, so she didn't try. She backed off a few steps and let her briefcase fall off her shoulder, catching the strap and wrapping it around her arm.

The man, a sandy-blond, tall, skinny guy she'd never seen before, dressed in cargo pants and a hooded sweatshirt, held up his hands in a placating gesture. He held a small manila envelope in one.

"Hey, sorry. I didn't mean to startle you. Just trying to get your attention."

"Why?" She took another couple of steps back to give herself room to swing. Her case had a stack of files and a book in it. It would hurt if she hit him right.

"I think you know why." He sketched a shape in the air, and because she'd been dwelling on them so much, she recognized the shape of the totems. Her eyes began to widen before she caught herself, not wanting to let on that she understood.

His eyebrows went up, questioning. "I have something for you," he said when she didn't respond. "I think you'll find it enlightening." He wiggled the envelope.

She didn't move. She didn't know this guy, but she recognized his type. Charming, confident that he could get anyone to do anything. A watered-down version of Pat. He'd be one of his more trusted followers, at least until he was no longer needed. Pat's "gang" had been too small and disorganized to be considered a cult, but he'd had the kind of charisma that got people to do what he wanted. A fervor, a belief, that made people think that if they stuck with him, he'd get them the power and riches they thought they deserved.

Her breathing was getting too fast, too obvious. *You're an adult. Not a kid. They have no power over you. You can walk away.*

The tight band around her lungs eased. She just had to act like this was a normal thing. Decline his offer. "No, thank you."

The guy scowled. "You don't have a choice." He

shoved the envelope at her. Zoe didn't take it, and it fell to the ground at her feet.

A bicycle glided up behind the cab, and a cop climbed off.

"Is there a problem here?" He removed his helmet and hung it from the handlebars, his demeanor relaxed but his gaze shrewd.

"No, sir, no problem." The blond sauntered back to the cab and got in. The vehicle began to move almost before the door closed.

"Are you all right? I heard someone yell. Was that you?" The cop came closer and pulled a leather folio off his belt.

She took a deep breath but was already steadier. "I'm fine. He didn't hurt me. Just grabbed my arm."

"Did you know him?" The officer started taking notes.

"No, I've never seen him before."

"Did he say anything to you?"

"He didn't really have a chance." Her arm started shaking, and she unwound the leather strap of her case and put it back up on her shoulder.

The officer looked up. "Do you want to file a report?"

Definitely not. This would still be on his incident log or whatever kind of records the police department kept, but a report with her name on it would be public information.

"No, I don't think so. There was no harm done, and I'm late to meet someone. Thank you."

"If you're sure." He flipped his pad closed and

reclipped it to his belt. As Zoe shifted to begin walking again, he held up a hand. "Hold on." He bent and picked up the envelope she'd almost stepped on. "Is this yours?"

The refusal lodged in her throat. Her hand twitched but stayed at her side. She didn't want it, dreaded seeing what was inside. But if she didn't take it, he'd probably open it to find out who it belonged to. Information made her stronger. Hiding made her weaker. So she took the packet and shoved it into a pocket on her bag.

"Thank you," she said again. He smiled and gave her a semi-salute as he got back on his bike, and Zoe continued down the sidewalk.

Now what?

The little foyer of the restaurant was crowded when she entered. She made her way to the podium and smiled at the host.

"Hi, Todd."

The young man smiled back and lifted three menus from their holder. "Ms. Ardmore. Your table is ready."

"Thank you." She gave an apologetic glance at the grumbling people waiting and followed him toward the corner where they usually sat. "Has Kell been here long?"

"Mr. Stone hasn't arrived yet." He pulled out her chair and seated her, then handed her the menu and laid two more on the place settings next to and across from her. "I'll send him back as soon as he does."

Zoe thanked him again and checked her watch. She was ten minutes late, just inside the restaurant's grace period. Kell usually arrived before her, but he was getting Olivia first, and thirteen-year-olds weren't known for their punctuality.

She braced her elbows on the table and her hands against her forehead, inhaling and letting it out slowly, determined not to tremble. If Kell or Olivia noticed she was shaken, she'd have to explain why. Which meant lying. Worse than omission—yeah, she might be able to convince herself of that if she tried hard enough.

But where were they? Relief at her reprieve disappeared when she thought about some other guy accosting them on their way to the restaurant. She sent a short text that was answered almost immediately. *Ten min. Sorry!*

At least they were okay. After a moment's hesitation, she pulled the envelope from her bag. A six-by-nine size, it felt like it held a stack of photographs. Nothing was written on either side, and the flap wasn't sealed. She pried open the clasp and slid out the pictures.

On top was one of her, entering the building her company was in. It looked like every surveillance photo in every movie she'd ever seen. Her face was even turned toward the camera, as if she'd heard a noise just before she opened the door.

She was being watched.

"Oh, no." The next photo was Kell walking down the street, obviously on a workday because he wore a navy suit and carried his briefcase. The camera had caught him twisting sideways to check traffic. His torso was turned toward the camera, the white shirt a target that filled the shot, and his vulnerability struck her hard.

Conscious of how little time she had, she dropped photo after photo of her loved ones onto the table. Kell's parents, her parents, Kell again, employees coming into or leaving the building.

Olivia.

All innocuous, in public, appearing to be routine surveillance photos shot by a PI. Finally, between the last two photos—one of her mother talking to a friend outside the grocery store and one of Zoe and Kell going into their apartment—she found a folded piece of torn paper. Her fingers trembled as she opened it. The handwriting was amazingly familiar after all these years. The ballpoint pen had dug into the thick paper, carving the words into it and filling the lines with black ink. It made her think of the spiders in the corners of an old house they'd held her in, and her skin crawled.

The words were almost as benign as the photos themselves. *Our family is incomplete without you, dear Zoe. Once you have regained our lost assets, we will give you the reunion details. Hurry, so no one is left out!*

"Jesus Christ." The paper fell from numbed fingers. She fumbled for her phone. She had to call Henricksen. This was a threat, to her and everyone she loved. They could do something now. This was a parole violation, wasn't it?

Well, no. She stared at the words and knew the FBI would find this worthless. No names, no addresses, delivered by a guy she didn't know and could barely describe, and written in friendly words that no one else would ever consider a threat. All the photos were in public. No way to tell who'd taken them, no proof who'd sent them. There would be nothing the FBI or anyone else could do.

She shoved everything back into the envelope and then her briefcase. She'd still tell Henricksen. This was exactly the kind of thing he'd wanted to know about. But he couldn't do anything about it.

Only Zoe could.

She had two options. The first was to tell Kell everything, and then together they could take steps to protect his family and hers. Then they'd wait for Pat to escalate his tactics until there was something the FBI could do. That could take years. He was smart, and maybe in prison he'd learned patience. He probably wouldn't rely on Zoe's obedience, either. He could find the totems himself, and then still come after her or her family, either in retaliation or because he believed he needed her.

"Zoe!"

Olivia tackle-hugged her from behind, shooting her adrenaline and blood pressure into the stratosphere.

"Oh my God, kid! Where did you come from?" Zoe forced a laugh and hugged her, looking up to see Kell coming across the large room, an indulgent smile on his face. She'd sat facing the entrance so no one would sneak up on her. Apparently, she sucked at this.

"I circled around so I could 'boo' you." Olivia slid into a seat and snatched a thin, crunchy breadstick from the holder in the center of the table. "Guess what?

Colin? My friend in algebra?" She launched into a story as her brother kissed Zoe and sat down across from her. Zoe concentrated on listening and tried not to think about the picture of Kell's sister in the packet burning a hole in the briefcase at her side.

Olivia was dressed today much as she had been in the photo, in snug, low-rise jeans and an equally snug cami under a cardigan that tied around her waist. She was now talking about which of her friends were hooking up, but she looked way too young for that. Kell seemed to agree, because he frowned and asked if *she* was hooking up with anyone. Olivia laughed and rolled her eyes. "As if," was all she said.

Zoe had to do anything she could to protect this girl. She just wished she knew which decision would do that.

The server materialized to take their orders. Zoe watched Kell as he explained how he wanted his steak cooked. He had shadows under his eyes, and his face seemed paler than normal under the stubble. His dark hair was never perfectly neat, but tonight it stuck up in odd places. His suit wasn't rumpled, but since he didn't take off his jacket, she guessed he had sweat stains on his shirt. When he handed his menu to the server, his smile barely flickered.

"What happened?" she asked as soon as the woman had walked away.

Kell sighed and opened his napkin to lay across his lap. "The merger isn't going well, that's all. Complications keep arising, things that should have been discovered during due diligence. I think one of the parties was pushed into agreeing to this by his partners and is sabotaging the process. I don't know." He ran his hands over his face. "It doesn't matter. Let's just have a nice dinner." He smiled at Olivia and plucked a breadstick to brandish at her. *"En garde."*

They dueled until the sticks broke into pieces, and Zoe got winners. Through dinner, Olivia guided the conversation, but Kell's rally was brief, exhaustion dragging him to one-word answers until even the kid with the never-ending energy became subdued.

"I'm sorry," Kell said to his sister as they all shared a giant chocolate chip lava cookie. "This wasn't what you wanted tonight."

Olivia shrugged and dug her spoon through whipped cream and cookie. "It's fine. I just wanted to spend time with you guys. You could have canceled because of all this work crap."

"Olivia," Kell scolded. She rolled her eyes again.

"But you didn't. I wish I could do something to help. But that's what you've got Zoe for now."

Zoe propped her chin on her hand, dipping a bite of cookie in the molten chocolate. "If he didn't have me, if he were going home with you, what would you do?"

Olivia didn't hesitate. "I'd fill the Jacuzzi tub—he'd scoff and call it girly, but he really likes relaxing in it—and get one of the books on his pleasure-reading stack that he hasn't touched in so long it's all dusty. I'd light Mom's relaxation candle because even guys like pretty smells, even if they won't admit it. And I'd pour him a whiskey with one ice cube and lock him in the bathroom for at least an hour."

Zoe smiled at her. "You nailed it."

"Good." The look Olivia gave her was shrewd and protective. "You need to know this stuff if you're going to take care of him. I know there's other stuff you can do to, you know, 'relax' him." She put down her spoon to make quotey fingers. "But I don't need to know about that."

They laughed and finished dessert, and after dropping off Olivia, Zoe insisted on taking Kell home and forcing Olivia's prescription on him. She ended it with a massage—and more—and was well satisfied when he dropped into a deep, comfortable sleep.

And then she eased out of the bed and into the bathroom, where she threw up the cookie and most of her dinner.

Olivia had more than nailed it. Zoe was supposed to take care of her fiancé. Her *husband*. Passively hoping Pat left them alone was stupid. She had to act now, whether or not she told Kell.

But how much more could he handle? She'd never seen him the way he was tonight, so stressed and exhausted. She couldn't add worse to it. And the photos told her she couldn't wait until things got better. There had to be a middle ground.

She threw water on her face and rinsed her mouth, then dried with a hand towel and stared at herself in the mirror. She looked worse than Kell had. Believably sick, and that was how she'd play it to start. She had to handle this right, or it would backfire and not only would she lose everything—he would, too.

* * *

"Stone, are you even listening to me?"

Kell stared blankly at his friend. "What?"

James sighed. "Apparently not. Maybe I should just work with Tanicia on this case. Your super-assistant can contribute more than you are."

"I'm sorry." He rubbed his forehead and realized he hadn't taken a single note, and this meeting had started half an hour ago. "I'm worried about Zoe."

James dropped his exasperation. "She okay?"

"She's been sick." She'd stayed home from work yesterday and today, and last night when he got home he'd found her in bed, buried under a pile of blankets, her eyes red like she'd been crying. He wanted to take her to a doctor, but she insisted this morning that she was better. He knew she was lying.

"Anything I can do to help, man?" James looked concerned, and Kell shook his head.

"Not yet, thanks. If she's no better tonight, though, I may need to ask you to cover a couple of things for me tomorrow while I take her to the doctor."

"Sure, anything." James tapped his pen twice. "You want to go now?"

Kell eyed the phone, then forced himself to concentrate. "No, I can get through today. Let's start this again." He slipped on his reading glasses and studied the report James had brought him. "What's their market share?"

Though he managed to work the rest of the afternoon, distraction plagued him. He couldn't shake a sense of foreboding about Zoe's illness. He couldn't remember her ever being sick in the two years they'd been together. That alone was no big deal, but she'd been acting odd for a while before they had dinner with Olivia, and even that night, she'd only seemed half there.

Had she been told something about her health? Was it more serious than a simple flu? Possibilities kept popping into his head, compelling him to look up symptoms online. He almost called her parents about their medical history but stopped himself just in time. He'd only met them a couple of times, and they were very protective of Zoe, very clingy. She told him they'd had a scare when she was a child—he couldn't remember what—and never got over it. So indicating to them that there was something wrong with their daughter, when he had no idea what it was, would be a mistake.

He gave in and called the apartment twice, but there was no answer. Sherry said she hadn't seen Zoe all day, which, knowing her, didn't mean she wasn't there. But short of running over there, Kell was powerless. And he had a client meeting he couldn't miss that afternoon.

By four o'clock, when he walked the client out to the lobby, he couldn't stand it anymore.

"Tanicia, what's left on my schedule?"

She smiled up at him. "You're clear."

"Good. I'm taking off."

"All right. Take care of Zoe." She smiled again and turned back to the brief she was reviewing.

The anxiety that had grown all day had him

swallowing acid by the time he pulled into the parking garage of their building. Zoe's Civic was parked in its spot, but facing in. She usually backed it in, so she'd gone out today. Kell got out of his BMW and beeped the lock, frowning at her car. The back seat was full of...bedding? That looked like the quilt her mother had made.

He swallowed back panic and hurried to the elevator, cursing internally every time it stopped at a floor, hating that they'd chosen view over convenience. Two floors up, then a ding. One floor. Three more. Why the hell didn't they have an express elevator? The doors opened again and he shoved his hand through his hair, trying to keep a shout of frustration inside.

"Kellen! How lovely to see you!"

He smiled tightly at Mrs. Ridgebottom, an elderly woman who lived on their floor. She swung a tennis racket at his rump as she stepped onto the elevator and turned to face front.

"Gladys and I just got back from the club. She pulled her hamstring showing off for the new tennis pro, so I helped her to her apartment."

"I hope she's okay." He wasn't really listening. His whole body was tense. He needed to be in his apartment *now*. Something was going on. Something far worse than a pulled hamstring.

Mrs. Ridgebottom chattered at him all the way to the twentieth floor, then waved a cheery goodbye, hardly seeming to notice his rudeness. A lifetime of "good breeding" was all that kept him from running down the hall. He unlocked the deadbolt and handle and shoved open the door, shouting Zoe's name.

But she was right there. Waiting for him. Standing in the middle of their perfect apartment, dressed in perfect-fitting jeans and the sweater he'd gotten her for Christmas.

"Kell, I'm sorry."

With three words, she shattered their perfect life.

Natalie J. Damschroder

Chapter Three

Zoe almost couldn't do it. When Kell burst through the door and saw her, when his face crumpled before she finished the apology she'd promised she wouldn't make, she almost took it back. Told him everything.

But then she thought of the pictures, of Olivia. She really had only one plan of action that would keep them safe, and Kell wouldn't allow it. He'd try to protect her, and that would increase the danger for all of them. The only way to keep him out of this was to be brutal and sharp, cut clean. So he could heal and move on with minimal damage while she did what Pat wanted and kept everyone safe.

"What the hell...?" Kell's voice came out a rasp. "Are you—you're not—*leaving* me?"

Zoe nodded and swallowed hard. Her eyes burned. "I have to."

"Why?" He rushed forward and wrapped his hands hard around her upper arms. "Are you sick?"

She shook her head. "Not like that. No. I just realized that I don't belong here. With you, in this life. I love you, Kell." She knew she couldn't lie to him about that and didn't even try. "But we can't be together. It won't work, and if I let it go on even a day longer, it will hurt you more in the end."

He shook his head, the pain and confusion in his eyes cracking her heart in two. "It couldn't."

He was wrong, but she couldn't explain. Couldn't tell him that her past had invaded their present and would shred their future. Pat could insidiously destroy everything, and Kell just wouldn't understand. He'd want to make things right, and only she could do that.

"I think you're being selfish." He dropped his hands and backed up a step.

She folded her arms against herself and nodded. Of course she was. She would rather he hated her for breaking their engagement than for her secrets. At least his memories of their time together would be whole. Better he find someone else to take her place than be carved up by Pat and Freddie.

"I left the ring on the dresser. In a box." She ignored his flinch, the way he rubbed his chest with the heel of his hand. "I didn't take anything we got together. Just my clothes, some of the things from my childhood…"

"Your quilt."

"What?"

"I saw your quilt in your car."

So he'd known, or suspected, when he came in. "I wanted to be ready to go. I didn't think you'd want me to stick around after I told you."

"Told me what?" He spread his arms. "You haven't told me shit."

It was her turn to flinch.

"What have I done?" His voice broke. "Why do you think we can't be together?"

"It's not you." A tear spilled out of each eye. "I know the phrase is a big joke, but it's me. I can't stay. I would rather do anything else but hurt you, and I don't have a choice. This will hurt you less."

"Less than what?"

She shook her head and blinked back more tears.

"You owe me an explanation."

"I know." She took a deep breath and tried to envision ice encasing her heart. It didn't work very well. "But I can't give you one."

"Why?"

If he pushed any more she'd break. She had to leave. "I'm sorry, Kell." She reached into her pocket and pulled out the keys to the apartment. He wouldn't take them when she held them out, so she laid them on the small marble-topped table behind the cream-colored sofa. "Goodbye."

She expected him to let her go, pride and defiance and pain holding him immobile, but he didn't. He jumped in front of her to block her progress to the door.

"No way. If you think I'm a quitter—"

"I don't think you're a quitter!" Fear sparked to life, burning away her sorrow. Why wouldn't he react like he was supposed to? "I told you, this has nothing to do with you!"

"But you expect me to just stand here and let you go."

She stared at him, no longer sure what to say to push him away. "I *need* you to let me go."

"Are you late for something?"

"What?" She frowned, the determined clench of his jaw increasing her fear. "No. I'm not late for anything."

"Then you've got to convince me."

"I do not! It's my decision!"

"You can decide to leave, but you can't control what I do about it." He studied her, the lawyer taking over. "You weren't really sick. You were packing."

"And finding a new place, yes."

"In a two-day period. Not a lot of planning time."

"You—you don't know that." *No, Kell, please don't figure it out.*

But he was smart, and analytical, and she hadn't done enough to hide.

"Something was off the night we went out to dinner with my sister. You'd been distracted before that, but things got much worse that night. So something happened two days ago to make you do this."

"No," she insisted. "It's been coming on for a long time."

"We've only been engaged two weeks."

"That was it." Why hadn't she thought this through better? "I'm not ready. I thought I was," she added, knowing she couldn't convince him that her happiness that night hadn't been real. "But it's a much harder thing to do than I thought it was. The commitment. To you." She was botching this. Kell's expression was shrewd. He knew her too well and was seeing right through all the haphazard reasons she dug up.

"Goodbye, Kell," she tried again. And again he got in front of her.

"You're not afraid of anything." He put his hand on her chest to hold her away from the door. "Definitely not something as easy as lifelong commitment. What else is going on, Zoe?"

"Nothing!" She knocked his arm away and tried to push him aside. "You don't know me as well as you think you do, Kellen Stone, and I'm not going to drag this out and make it worse for both of us!"

"Worse for you, you mean." He didn't budge.

"No, worse for both of us. It will be much better if you just forget about me. Move on." She blinked back more tears and stood, defeated. She remembered staunching Grant's blood with a filthy towel. It was all too easy to imagine Kell shackled and bloody, with a gleeful Pat and sickly delighted Freddie standing over him, others forcing her to watch as Kell was tortured. She would do everything in her power to make sure it didn't happen. *Please, Kell, let it go. Let me go.*

"Getting engaged made me look at us differently. At myself, and what I wanted. I'm not ready for this." God, she hated herself. "I take too much from this relationship and don't give enough back. That's not right. And I can't be happy that way."

He was braced to argue, she could see it, until the last words. His defeat broke her. Something inside her cracked wide and filled with pain.

"If that's what you want," he said quietly. "I love you. I want you to be happy." He stepped aside.

Zoe dashed the few feet to the door and wrenched it open, desperate to get away before she overrode herself and ruined everything. Once she was gone, everything would be okay. Kell would be safe, his family wouldn't be targeted—and she could focus on fixing her situation.

She avoided looking back over her shoulder, not wanting to see him letting her go.

* * *

"Grant. Tank. Gotta job. Tunisia. Call me." *Beeeep*.

Grant Neely didn't look up from the printouts he was reading. When he didn't call Tank back, the mercenary would call someone else on his list. Next time he needed someone with Grant's skills, he'd call again. It was a nice way to work. Simple. No politics, no games.

Unlike that other world. He gave a derisive snort and tossed aside the engagement announcement his mother had faxed him while he was in Russia. No matter how many times he told her he wasn't interested, that he didn't care about the New Life and Ambitions of Zoe Ardmore, she still kept sending him this crap.

He shoved to his feet and walked away from the rest of the papers stacked on the scarred wood table, carrying his beer bottle to the rail of his beach-side shack to look out over the calm water. He hadn't needed his mother's unofficial clipping service to keep him up to date on the Rhomney/Thomashunis situation. Because Grant had never been called to testify, he wasn't on the official notification list. But through his work contacts, he'd known when they made parole, where they were now, and what they wanted.

It was the last that was keeping him from sleeping as well as he normally did. He took a pull from his bottle and watched a windsailer down the beach teeter and fall, her laughter drifting to him on the breeze. He could easily imagine Zoe doing that, helped, as this woman now was, by her fancy fiancé. People without a care, their pedigrees and their money insulating them from the harsh realities he dealt with regularly.

He blew out a breath. That wasn't fair. Zoe hadn't grown up pampered and spoiled, and he doubted that was how she was now. He also knew money didn't insulate, and some who had it were good people. He was just in a bad mood.

The phone in the little shack rang again, the machine picking up immediately.

"Grant, honey, it's Mom. You said you'd be home today, so please—"

Grant got inside and picked up, wincing at the squeal made by the interrupted answering machine.

"Hey, Mom. I just got in."

"Okay, good. I don't mean to be pushy, you know, I just—"

"I know." He carried the cordless handset outside and dropped into his sling chair, propping his feet on the splintered rail. "I'm fine. No injuries on this gig."

"Good." She moved on briskly, but he could still hear the relief in her voice. "Did you get my package? And Zoe's announcement?"

"Of course." He refrained from mentioning that she could just e-mail him links, instead. That would just encourage her. "But I keep telling you, I don't need them."

"You say that, but I know better." She paused, and he heard the telltale puff of a cigarette.

"You said you quit."

"I'm working on it." A faint stubbing noise followed, and he smiled.

"You like when I catch you. It makes you feel guilty."

"Yes, and then I don't smoke again for at least a week. You're adding months to my life. Congratulations."

Grant laughed. A couple of girls in bikinis walking by peered at him from under their hair, but he didn't spare them more than a glance.

"Anyway, honey, about Zoe. Shut up," she interrupted before he'd done more than open his mouth. "I'm tired of your protests. If you don't care what's happening, why haven't you had a serious girlfriend since Amanda?"

"God, Mom." He dropped his head back over the top of the chair. "How many times do we have to not have this conversation?" His corrugated tin roof was pulling away from the wall. He'd have to fix that. "I wasn't serious about Amanda. We were together so long because it was convenient. Then it wasn't. I haven't told you about other women I've dated because they weren't important. When I meet someone worth telling you about, I will. And I am *not. Pining.*

For Zoe."

His mother clicked her tongue from the roof of her mouth. "Well, whatever you say, I know you still feel strongly about her, even if it's only as a friend. And I'm sure you're concerned about her current situation."

He dragged his head upright and downed the rest of his beer, setting the bottle on the planks next to him. "What do you know about her current situation?" It couldn't be more than they'd been showing on TV, the same stuff she'd faxed him, and that had already died down. Zoe hadn't even been mentioned by name in the public stuff he'd seen.

But his mother was capable of putting six and eight together and getting fourteen.

"She's in trouble, Grant. Those people are out, and they're after her, I know it. For whatever she did that got them caught, or whatever unfinished business there is." She paused. "That's why I sent you that stuff. Unfinished business."

Grant was probably the only person on Zoe's side who knew exactly what that unfinished business was. But she wasn't his responsibility. Never had been, really. They'd taken care of each other, after she'd gotten away and Pat and Freddie had been captured. He'd believed they'd take care of each other forever, until Zoe discovered her dreams weren't compatible with his.

"She needs help, Grant. You can reach out to her."

"You're the one who sent me the engagement announcement, Mom. She doesn't need me." Even after all these years, the words sent a pang of regret through him.

"You don't know that."

"Well, if she does, I'm not that hard to find." That was a blatant lie. He didn't come up in Google or Yahoo, his phone was unlisted, and his contacts weren't the kind of people Zoe would know. Not in her current world. But his mother wouldn't think about that, and hopefully she'd be reassured enough to lay off.

"So if she comes to you, you'll help her?" she asked.

"Of course. I'm not cold-hearted."

"No, dear, quite the opposite."

He didn't dignify that one with a response.

* * *

Whatever Zoe hoped would happen after she left Kell, the reality didn't measure up.

She'd known it would hurt. But she hadn't anticipated the constantly sharp digging in her chest, like the love she'd cut off was trying desperately to find its connection again. Now she understood why people drank. Not that she dared try it. It might take the edge off, but she couldn't afford the vulnerability.

Henricksen had agreed that the photos and letter were frightening, but still not actionable. He'd added them to his unofficial file and told Zoe to be careful, even recommended a bodyguard. But she couldn't reconcile that logic. She was working hard to make sure no one got hurt because of her. Paying someone to get hurt in her place? No way.

The phone calls had started again. She never

answered them, and they never left messages, but text messages followed. Their cheery tone was downright sinister, the words still mundane but clearly demanding the totems. Her stomach churning, she responded to one of those. Just one word. *Patience.* Enough to keep them at bay, and even that made her feel grimy and worthless, once again under their control.

She had no idea if they'd sent anything to Kell or his family, because when you cut yourself off from someone, that meant no communication. She couldn't risk trying to check. If Pat was watching closely enough, any contact would still paint them as viable targets. But surely someone would have told her if they were hurt. James, maybe.

She hadn't felt this helpless since she'd gotten free.

The general buzz of conversation outside her office door changed, and tension zinged up her spine. There were gasps and high, excited voices. Zoe hurried to the door and found half the staff surrounding their filing clerk, Trish, all talking at once. The girl's face was flushed, her eyes bright but half glazed, as if something unexpected had happened.

"What's going on?" Zoe strode forward, and the group parted.

"She was mugged," Sherry explained, her arm around Trish.

"Are you all right?"

Trish nodded. "I'm fine. They took my wallet, but it only had my driver's license and a few dollars."

Zoe frowned and touched the back of her hand to

the girl's forehead. "You look like you're in shock."

"Well, it was shocking." She giggled. "It's never happened to me before. In broad daylight! I was paying for a latte and he just ran by, snatching it right out of my hand. He shoved me into the stand. That's why it's a mugging." She rubbed her elbow. "Right? It sounds better if I call it a mugging."

Zoe's shoulders loosened and she managed a smile. "It was definitely a mugging. Here." She nodded her chin at Sherry. "Give her some money from petty cash for a cab. Trish, hon, take the day off. Go deal with your license, or just go home and rest." She walked her to the door, reassuring her that she'd still get paid, but half her mind was on herself instead of her employee. She was sure the mugging had nothing to do with her own situation. But it reinforced that she didn't need to love someone for them to be close to her. In danger.

One phone call to her attorney sped up the next step in her plan. It didn't get her any closer to the totems she had to find, and she knew damned well she was reacting as Pat wanted her to, cutting herself off from everyone in her support system as completely as he had the day he'd snatched her. But she didn't see any other way.

The next day, she arrived at the office to find a box on her desk, unmarked and sealed with tape. She lifted the phone and buzzed Sherry.

"Yeah?"

"Did you put this box on my desk?"

"Yep."

"When?"

"When I got in. It was on the floor outside the door."

Zoe spun it, checking for a postmark or label of any kind. "How did you know it was for me?"

She could almost hear Sherry shrug. "I don't. But it's your company. Who else is it going to be for?"

"Okay, thanks." She hung up and thought about calling downstairs to ask security who'd signed in last night or early this morning, but the building housed a dozen businesses. If this was what she feared it was, they would have been innocuous and signed in with a fake name.

Just do it. She used her letter opener to slit the tape and opened the box. On top was a small envelope, thin, with one photo inside. Olivia, laughing on the sidewalk outside her school. Printed across the bottom in red marker was one word. "PERFECTION."

Zoe squeaked and dropped the photo, covering her mouth with one hand. The other already fumbled with her office phone, but she froze before she dialed. If someone saw her company number on the caller ID, it would ruin everything.

It took only a few seconds to look up the code to block caller ID, but she couldn't breathe and that made it feel like forever. Quickly, she keyed in the code, then dialed Olivia's cell phone number. She'd be on her way to school, probably, not already there with it off, and —

"Hello?" Her bright, cheery voice was backed by other young voices. Someone said, "Ooh, look what Zach's doing," and Olivia's second "hello?" was far more distracted. She giggled, then disconnected the call.

Zoe let out the dry sobs she'd been holding back and set the phone rattling into its cradle. *She's fine, they haven't done anything, she's fine.* Her hands shook, pissing her off, as she dragged a bottle of water from her bag and uncapped it. The coolness moistened her mouth and throat, but she eyed the box that sat so patiently on her desk. She wasn't done. Their message wasn't complete.

Inside was a cheap clock, unwound. Obviously to tell her to move faster. Next to it was a smaller box, the kind that held jewelry or figurines or ornaments. It all looked like a friendly gift, surrounded by white tissue paper. But Zoe's chest squeezed until she could barely breathe again. What was in here was going to be bad.

The box was so light it could have been empty, but something shifted when she tilted it to pry open the lid. What was inside was so odd, her confusion took away the dread. She peered more closely at it, then picked up the letter opener again to poke at it. Whatever it was, it was leathery and stiff. Mostly flat, about a quarter inch thick. Kind of round on one side, a little pointed on the other end, and with a tiny hole, like a...

Like a piercing. She gagged and shoved the lid closed, almost throwing the box across the room. That was an *earlobe* in there. Grant's earlobe.

God. She swallowed bile and swallowed again. Her head swam, her vision fuzzing around the edges, hot saliva a warning to partner her cramping stomach. She had to sit. Her chair had skidded backwards when she jumped. She carefully pulled it to her and lowered herself into it. She wanted to bend over, head between her knees, until the nausea subsided. But she hadn't closed her blinds. Anyone could see her.

Think. Think. She forced herself to breathe and ignore the dizziness, the instinct of her body to escape. What were they trying to say? They'd cut off Grant's earlobe to force his brother Jordie to do their bidding. They could do anything to anyone—to Olivia—to get the same results from Zoe. That was the message here.

A half second of panic lit inside her, but she quickly squashed it. She'd just heard Olivia's voice. She was fine. And that wasn't how Pat worked. All the therapy she'd been through had given her a more thorough understanding of him than she'd ever wanted. He believed in incentive. He'd only hurt Grant because Jordie wouldn't do what he wanted. They wouldn't hurt anyone yet. She still had a chance to make sure they never did.

With nausea rising again, she pulled out her phone and sent another response to the text messages. Three words this time, her hands shaking so badly she had to undo autocorrect twice before she could hit send. They'd have to be enough.

I'll find them.

* * *

It took too long to execute her plan, even though she pushed everything through impossibly fast. The final meeting with the attorney that would erase the life she'd built occurred late in the day on a Friday. When she finally walked into the office, her shoulder briefcase dragging her down and slowing her steps, Sherry pounced on her as usual.

"Zoe, I have your messages!" Sherry jumped up and trotted after Zoe toward her office.

"Can you give me a second?" She tried not to snap at the admin, but her hovering as Zoe hung up her jacket and stowed her shoulder bag set her teeth on edge. "Okay, fine, go ahead."

"Okay." The young woman planted her feet and shot one hip, holding up the little slips of paper like they were Oscar envelopes. "Agent Henricksen called twice. The first time was at ten, and he said he'd call back. Which he did. Half an hour ago. This time, he said it was urgent that he talk to you." With a flourish she held out the slips.

"Thank you." Zoe took them and picked up her coffee mug.

"Wait! There's more."

"I was sure there would be."

Sherry ignored or didn't notice her sarcasm. "Mrs. Stone called this morning. She'd like to meet you for tea, and please don't ignore her message this time because that's rude and she knows you have better manners than that."

Zoe stifled a sigh and took that slip, too. Kell hadn't called her once, but his mom had called no less than six times. If this had been a normal breakup, Zoe would have gladly had tea with her so they could do the postmortem and wish each other well, perhaps even pledge to remain friends. She hated to consider what they all thought of her right now.

"Anything else?"

"One more. A woman who called herself Fred called. How weird is that?"

Zoe's blood ran cold, and she couldn't get the breath to reply. This was the first time anyone had made direct contact with someone other than her.

"Anyway, she said to remind you of the earring, and the"—she squinted at the paper—"um, oh, the keys to the idol guys. Does she mean Billy Idol? He's so last century."

Despite her deep-seated terror, Zoe managed to fake a laugh at Sherry's joke. The younger woman beamed.

"Anyway. She said—and this part she made me repeat—'Our perfect delicacy shan't attend the reunion should you bring our party favors on time.' " She held out the paper to Zoe, who indicated the pile of slips on the desk. Sherry balanced it on top. "She giggled when she said 'shan't.' Didn't leave a number, but said you'd know what she meant, and she'd be in touch. Do you?"

Zoe glanced up. "What?"

"Know what she meant?"

"Oh. No clue." She put her coffee mug back down, no longer able to pretend there was any normalcy to be maintained. "Thanks, Sherry."

"No problem. Anything you need?"

"Please call a staff meeting for half an hour." It was late in the day, and not when she'd planned to do this, but after Freddie's call she couldn't wait any longer. "Make sure the off-shift staff will be here, at least by conference call. I'll pay overtime, but this is mandatory. If anyone has any problems, tell them to come see me."

Sherry stopped beaming. "All right." She studied Zoe's face, but apparently decided not to ask. "I'll do that right now. Do you need any equipment or anything?"

"No. Thanks."

Zoe collapsed into her chair when the admin left, propping her forehead on her hand and staring at Freddie's message in Sherry's loopy, cheerful handwriting. She detested that woman, hated her with every fiber in her being. Hated what she and Pat were driving Zoe to do to good people. It didn't matter that she was protecting them from far worse things. What she was doing might not be enough, if Pat and Freddie assumed she cared about the company's employees whether they were hers or not. Just like breaking the engagement with Kell didn't necessarily protect him from them. It wasn't like she could go tell them, "Hey, that guy I was engaged to? Don't like him anymore. Or his sister. Don't care what you do. So let's just keep this between us, hey?" They were canny people. That was why this was just the first step, but would *any* step prevent the worst?

The sun had set by the time she entered the conference room. The brick and plaster walls bounced laughter and jeering back at her before the staff noticed she was there and subsided. She did a mental count. Everyone was there, though a couple of programmers in the back corner didn't look too happy. Well, what she had to say would cheer them up. Or not.

"I appreciate that you all stayed late. This won't take long." She waited for the final bits of whispering and shifting to settle. "There's no easy way to say this, and I don't have an explanation to lead up to it." She braced her fingertips on the shiny surface of the giant table she'd refinished herself, when she'd first leased the space here. It hurt almost as much to leave it behind as it did to leave the people.

"I have some personal issues I must attend to. As of tomorrow morning at nine a.m., I am no longer the owner of this company."

Gasps went around the room, with a couple of audible cries all accompanied by stricken looks. Her two managers shifted closer together, both frowning. She should have told them first, but hadn't been able to face explaining more than once.

"Nothing is going to change. All of your jobs are safe. Janice and Zandra will be in charge of the day-to-day business, and the new owner will be arranging some meetings next week. I'm sure he'll be as joyful to work with as I've been." She tried to smile, but no one responded, and the stony stares brought tears prickling to her eyelids. "I—" She choked, and squeezed out, "I'll miss you all." Then she had to get out of there. She heard Sherry's hurrying stilettos behind her, but closed her office door before the woman could catch up. A few minutes later she had gathered the few things she had left in the office and walked out, silently begging everyone not to approach her or she'd break down. Probably all in shock, they left her alone. Voices clamored in the main room before the outside door had closed.

Once in the elevator, Zoe slumped, not caring if anyone in security might be watching the monitor. She dashed away a couple of tears that escaped, but refused to allow more than that.

The company wasn't actually sold yet. She couldn't make it happen that fast. But her role as president would cease tomorrow morning, and the sale would go through officially in a few weeks. She hadn't met the owner, didn't even know his name as he'd used a business front for the sale. Her lawyer—not someone from Kell's firm—had power of attorney to make everything happen when it was time. The money would go into escrow, and in a fit of hope, she'd gotten the buyer to agree to a six-month buy-back clause. If she didn't have everything solved by then, she never would.

She drew in a deep breath and straightened as the elevator reached the lobby. That hope would disappear quickly if she didn't move fast. One thing left to do today, and then phase one was over. Tomorrow morning she was flying south, to the Florida Keys, to a man she'd never intended to see again.

Who frightened her almost as much as Pat and Freddie did.

Chapter Four

Kell wished he'd realized how little he knew about the woman he loved.

For example, if he were to go in to the office of his newly acquired web design company and talk to the employees, how many of them, and which ones, would be likely to contact her and tell her he was her buyer? Would they close ranks against him, loyal to the woman who'd created the company? Or would they be eager to leap to his side against the person who'd betrayed them?

How could he not know what kind of leader Zoe had been?

Was, he corrected. What kind of leader Zoe still was. Even if she had no one to lead at the moment.

"I think you're insane," James said as they jogged along the park trail.

"You said that five times already. Three on this lap alone."

"It bears repeating. I just don't get it, Kell. Are you a masochist, or what?"

"Maybe." He shifted to the right, behind James, as

a stream of speedwalkers came down the other side of the path, their arms flailing. When they'd passed he moved up next to his friend again. "You're the one who told me she was selling."

"Which I regret to the same degree that you are insane."

A few days after Zoe had left Kell, James had hurried to his office. His broker had learned of a highly profitable local business up for quick sale, which meant a great price, and he'd called to see if James had any clients who might be interested. James had, of course, recognized the name of the company and rushed to tell Kell, who hadn't thought twice. He'd called his own broker, obtained an attorney who wasn't in his firm, set up a shell company to make the offer, and within a week, he was on his way to owning his ex-fiancée's company.

"She wanted a buy-back clause," he told James. Again. "If she wants the company back, maybe she'll want me back. After."

"After what?"

"I have no fucking idea." He blew out a few breaths, pushing harder as they went up a small, steep hill. They slowed to normal pace again at the top. "Something is happening, James. She was lying to me, and she seemed panicked. And I can't believe she'd ever sell her company unless she needed to."

"Maybe she does. I mean, financially." James smiled at a woman with a baby stroller. She smiled back, ducking her head.

"Seducing young moms now, huh?" Kell panted.

"She's a nanny. Lives in Sonya's building. Not seducing. Or flirting," he warned, casting a look out of the corner of his eye.

"Don't look at me. I'm no tattler. But no, she had plenty of money. We didn't have a joint account, but we were open about our personal finances. It's something else."

They pushed a little harder as they came around the bend and into the open area near the parking lot. Neither spoke until they'd reached their end point and walked around a little, catching their breath and stretching. Then they walked over to Kell's car, where he had a cooler of water bottles in the trunk. He handed one to his friend and leaned against the car's bumper.

"What are you going to do now, then?" James poured a third of the bottle over his head and down his neck and torso, making his shirt cling to his chest. Kell shook his head when two women crossing the parking lot turned to ogle him.

"You're shameless."

"It's fun. Oops." One of the women had tripped over a cement parking barrier. "Well, it's fun until someone gets hurt." He grinned, but sobered when Kell didn't grin back. "Come on, buddy. Aren't you better off?" He sat on the bumper next to him and drank some of his water.

"No."

"Are you sure that's not just ego talking? Because the way she left has got to sting, but maybe—"

"No. I'm not better off." He couldn't even describe

how much better off he wasn't. He hadn't told James how hard it was to get to sleep, wondering where Zoe was and whether she was okay. His friend—as well as his paralegal, the filing staff, and his boss—had noticed how distracted he was. He'd even been pulled from the merger as the lead counsel. James had taken over, Kell relegated to grunt work. And he hadn't even protested. All he could think about was Zoe.

He didn't bother to describe the hole in his chest. James would confuse it with the hole in his life and tell him he just needed time to adjust. He hadn't loved like this, lost like this. He wouldn't understand. Hell, Kell wasn't sure he even did.

His watch beeped. "I gotta go." He tossed the empty water bottle into the trunk, closing it after James stood and did the same. "I have to have lunch with my mother."

"Ouch. On your one day off?"

Kell shrugged. "What else do I have to do? You want a ride?" He only lived a couple of blocks away, but Kell always offered, anyway.

"Nah. Don't want to deprive all the local lovelies of this sight." He motioned to his damp shirt. "I'll see you at work tomorrow."

"Sure." James frowned, and Kell knew he hadn't sounded convincing. "I'll be there."

"You know, you're treading—"

"I know. You don't have to tell me."

"Just so you know."

Kell lowered himself into the driver's seat with care, feeling like an old man. An old, achy man.

Everything had grown heavier since Zoe left. Harder to move around.

He wasn't really in danger of losing his job. He brought way too much cash to the firm. But they wouldn't just give him slack, either. Soon his boss would be calling him in to his office, feeling him out, trying to determine if they needed to activate the EAP for counseling or medical care, treatment for depression or substance abuse. If things kept getting worse, which Kell couldn't imagine happening, they'd make him go part time or take a leave of absence to get his head together. Floating around the apartment he'd shared with Zoe, the one still chock full of her presence, without a place to escape to, someplace that had always just been his, wouldn't heal him.

Hell, he wasn't sure what would.

After getting a quick shower at home, he dressed in khaki shorts and a polo and met his mother on the terrace at his parents' club.

"Hello, dear." She gave him an appropriately grave smile and offered her cheek for his kiss before he sat in the white iron chair beside her.

"Hi, Mom. No Dad today?" He picked up the menu and glanced over it.

"No, he's taking a lesson with the pro. He has a game with Landers this week, and he's determined to shave two strokes before then. I took the liberty of ordering you a drink," she added just before a female server—never "waitress" in a place like this—set a glass of Scotch on the glass table.

"Mom, it's too early for that."

"Nonsense, it's after noon on a Sunday. It's not like you're going to get drunk." She draped her linen napkin across her lap and smoothed it, looking up at him from under her lashes. "Are you?"

"No, Mother, I'm not going to get drunk."

"Well, you don't have to say it like that. Many men in your position would be eager to do just that."

Kell had to laugh. She made it sound like a desirable thing.

The server hovered discreetly, so they placed their orders for *salade niçoise*. Then his mother set her chin delicately on her fist, her elbow on the edge of the table, and gave him a conspiratorial smile.

"Tell me, dear, how you're really doing."

He shook his head. "Mom, you have your elbow on the table."

She blinked. "So? The food's not here. It's not unmannerly."

"You don't have to put on the act. I'll believe you're interested, I promise." He sighed when she sat back and looked down to fuss at her napkin to hide the hurt he'd glimpsed in her eyes. "I'm sorry."

"It's all right." She refolded the napkin and reached for her mimosa. "Old habits."

Kell had always believed his mother loved him. But when he went away to college and saw how parents acted with other kids—kids who hadn't gone to prep schools and been raised by nannies or parents for whom propriety was the golden rule—he realized she had a whole repertoire of roles. She *acted* like she cared about his interests. It had led to a big blow-up one

Christmas, when she insisted the feelings were real even if her way of expressing them was…designed. Her term.

Things had changed slightly when Olivia was born. The world was different. Parenting—especially parenting among those who cared what the world thought of them—was different. Elise softened when it came to her daughter, but that didn't always extend to how she interacted with her son. Most of the time Kell accepted what she was and took her at face value, but sometimes he wondered what result she was going for. And sometimes he just didn't have patience for the role-playing.

"Kell? Are you okay?"

He'd been staring off across the golf course. "Yeah. I'm fine. Well, not fine," he amended. "I'm coping."

"I imagine it's difficult to cope passively. It's easier when there's some action to take."

Kell lifted his glass and stared at the way the light moved through the amber liquid. "Yeah, that's true." Then the note in her voice had him setting down the glass abruptly. "What action? Like what?"

"You haven't told me what happened. What she told you when she left."

He couldn't stop a scowl. "Did *she* tell you?"

"No. She had other things to say."

Electricity rocketed up his spine. "When? I thought she was refusing to answer any of your phone calls."

"She was, at first."

He raised his eyebrows. "You kept calling her?"

"Certainly."

He left the eyebrows up.

"Oh, come on, Kellen, you can't be surprised. I love Zoe. I think she's a perfect match for you, and I think this breakup is a mistake. I wanted to talk to her about it."

"So, not just to find out why she did it. You think you can change things." He hated the sudden spark of hope. There was no way his mother could talk Zoe into returning to him. Even if the breakup had been more straightforward, he doubted she could do it. But straightforward wasn't even at the table. "When did you talk to her?"

"We spoke Friday. In confidence." She sipped her drink and didn't look at him.

He gritted his teeth, wanting to demand she tell him but knowing she never would. His mother was the lead-lined vault of secret-keeping. "There's something going on with her. It's not just about our engagement not being 'right.' "

She cocked her head and studied him. "Something like what? Another man?"

He stared at her, shock like cold water freezing his nerve endings. Then he laughed. "Can you believe that thought hadn't even occurred to me?"

"A bit naïve, aren't you, dear?" She smiled up at the server, who placed their fancy salads on the table with hardly a clink.

"No, not naïve. There's something else going on. She sold her company."

She gaped, her fork in mid-stab. "No."

That was genuine surprise, which meant whatever

Zoe might have told her, it wasn't everything. "See?"

"You can't let that happen, Kellen! You must—"

"Mom." He laid a hand on her arm to stop her. "Don't worry. I'm buying it."

She beamed with pride. "That's my boy. Oh, sweetheart." The smile faded and she set her fork down, her posture a little slumped. "There is something very wrong."

"I know."

"You need to find out what it is and help her."

"I want to, but it's hard to do when she won't let me. I have no idea where to start."

"Do you know where she is?"

He nodded, feeling a little guilty. He was using one of the firm's investigators to keep track of her. She was staying in a hotel, which didn't make sense to him. "But she doesn't want me anywhere near her."

His mother straightened and picked up her fork again, digging into her salad. "She's trying to protect you." The word "dumbass" was implied.

"It occurred to me." He forced a tomato between semi-clenched teeth. "I don't exactly like the notion."

"No man would. Any idea what she could be afraid of?"

"Not really." He'd had some wild theories, but dismissed them as being farfetched. The stuff of television dramas. But now here was his mother, hinting, nudging him as if she knew there was something to figure out. It was fact that Zoe had started acting strange the night she got "sick." *Something* had happened. Something she hadn't trusted him with. Why? And why would she tell his mother?

"Do you still love her?" his mother asked.

He didn't even have to think about it. "Of course."

"Are there circumstances under which you wouldn't want to be with her?"

"Probably." He shrugged at his mother's glare. "I'm a lawyer, Mom. There are always circumstances. But, no, there's nothing I can think of that would make me want her to stay away." He gave her his best courtroom glare and question-that's-really-a-demand. "What do you know."

She shook her head and stuffed lettuce into her mouth.

He gripped her wrist. "Mom. Please. If she told you something, you have to tell me."

With a gentle flick, she pulled free and dabbed at her mouth with her napkin. "She just wants us all to be safe. I promised her I wouldn't divulge her secrets to anyone." She took a deep breath and squared her shoulders. "Honestly, at first, I thought it was best to let her go. If she's gotten involved in something that suggests people close to her take security precautions, then perhaps we're all better off staying away."

He stared at her, heart hammering, adrenaline flooding him with nowhere to go. "What are you talking about?"

"I'm talking about things you two have to work out between yourselves. I thought it best for you to let her go and work things out later, when she's ready. But after speaking with you…" She shook her head, lips pursed. "I changed my mind."

"So tell me."

"No. That's still up to her. And I don't have details, anyway. It would be tantamount to gossip." She rested her hand on his shoulder and leaned closer. "Think about this carefully, Kellen. Pursuing this, pursuing her, could lead you to worse pain than you're feeling now."

"Not possible," he shot back.

"Then you know what you have to do."

He nodded sharply, all the agitation setting into a steady hum of intention. "Yeah."

Except even though he did, he really didn't.

* * *

Grant saw her before she'd even approached his shack. She rode down the worn asphalt road on a battered rental mountain bike, her blonde hair pulled tightly back but bursting out behind its holder in a bushy fluff. When she got close enough, he saw she was wearing cargo shorts and a plain t-shirt with a pair of sneakers. Her legs almost glowed in the sun, they were so white, and her arms were only slightly tanned. All in all, not the picture he'd have expected to see, given the things he'd been reading about her. Charity balls, a million-dollar company, and engagement to a corporate lawyer had him expecting a shiny convertible and designer clothes.

He wouldn't have been expecting anything at all if his mother had been a little cagier. He'd realized—a couple of hours after he'd hung up the phone, not that he'd ever admit that—that she was planning to tell Zoe how to find him. His first reaction had been to stop her. But part of him didn't want to, and he'd given in to that part.

From the time they were fourteen, he and Zoe had spent time together. Every waking minute during the summers, when they weren't working. And sometimes, when they had the same shift, when they were. So even though he didn't see her much during the school year, and hadn't seen her at all since they were in college, he'd recognized her a hundred yards down the road. The way she pedaled, he supposed, or the way she held her head, looking up at her destination, not down at the street watching for stones.

The bike disappeared behind his shack and he heard the crunch of tires on crushed shell. He waited. There was no "front" door on the driveway side of the shack, so she'd be circling around any moment…

And there she was. Despite having watched her come down the road that ran parallel to the beach, despite having expected her for a few days now, Grant felt like someone had slammed a wall at his face.

Maybe his memories had shaded his view a little, because the woman standing in front of him didn't look like the one he'd just watched. Her hair didn't bush out behind her head. It hung from its ponytail holder in silky waves. Her shorts and shirt were definitely not Walmart purchases, and the purse she'd slung across her body was true designer. Not a knockoff.

Her face, arms, and chest above the veed curve of her shirt were as creamy white as her legs. But it was a vibrant paleness, one that came from pampering and high-end skin care products.

In short, her appearance proved the hype. She'd achieved her dreams. He could be glad for her—and still resent how those dreams had taken her away from him.

Judging by the look in her eyes, the achievement had only been temporary.

Grant slumped a little lower in his sling chair, propped his beer bottle on his stomach, and looked at her from under lazy lids. "What do you want?"

Zoe's heart had started beating a triple-speed pattern even before she'd landed on the island. She couldn't believe she was standing in front of Grant. It was so surreal, the fresh, breezy beach location compared to the memories that had filled her on the flight to Florida. At first it had been the good ones. The friendship they'd built after her escape, taking comfort in each other that first summer when no one else understood what they'd been through or what the aftermath was like. The romantic summers after that, when they'd worked together at the lake, lying under the stars every night, exploring each other physically and emotionally. The last summer before she went to college, when Grant had seemed so happy for her, so optimistic about his own future.

But then the bad ones had crowded in. The way it had all fallen apart. No one's fault, really, but how the hell had they misunderstood each other so much, for so long? Had such opposing expectations?

The bad memories from the end had brought back the bad memories from the beginning. How she'd spot him across the boathouse parking lot and flash back to her time in captivity. How he'd hated her for being part of the mess that had led to his brother's death. That had made him a freak with a gross ear.

Now she stood in front of him, his harsh question ringing in her ears, and wondered why she'd thought she could get any help here.

"I'm not used to that." She schooled her expression as she stepped up onto the low deck where he sat looking so deceptively relaxed.

"To what?" He didn't move, but his lazy eyes tracked her across the wide planks to the rail, where she leaned a few feet from his stretched-out legs. The skin on her shins tingled, sending a shiver up through her body and over her scalp. The kind of shiver that came with intense scrutiny you weren't sure you wanted.

"Cutting right to the chase, no preliminaries." He didn't say anything, so she continued, "You know, greetings. 'Hi, Grant.' 'Hi, Zoey, so nice to see you.' " He snorted, and she continued. " 'You're looking well. Mercenary work has kept you fit.' 'Why thank you, how kind of you to notice.' "

This time Grant laughed outright and he stood, the tightness easing from his muscles and his wary expression fading to pleasure. He pulled her into a hug, and she breathed in his familiar yet far-more-masculine scent. Tears pricked her eyes and she hugged him hard.

"Jerk."

Grant leaned back a little, his arms still around her.

"Hey, you can't blame me for wanting a little payback."

Zoe shook her head. "If you wanted payback, you'd have gotten it ten years ago. What I wouldn't blame you for is holding a real grudge." She swallowed hard, the triple-time beat starting up again. So he didn't hold a grudge. That didn't mean he'd want to help her, or that he would even if he wanted to.

She stepped away, stalling by approaching the sliding door into the shack. It was the only thing she could call it. The weathered wooden walls had been warped by the ocean air, and the tin roof, while not rusted, still didn't quite meet the walls in places. She shuddered to think what might crawl inside. The whole place could fit into the bathroom of the Stones' summer cottage at the Cape. Twice.

Not relevant. She peered through the door, surprised. "I like what you've done with the place." She wasn't joking. A heavy wooden table centered the left side, where the kitchen counter and small refrigerator were, while a narrow, almost-double bed sat against the far wall, covered in a quilt she recognized. It was a mirror of her own, made by her mother the summer he turned sixteen. A lump formed in her throat and she tightened her arms around herself.

"You don't seem like someone who appreciates bush-beating." She turned back to find him leaning against the rail, watching her, his beer bottle back in hand.

"Nope."

"So you probably want me to tell you why I'm here."

He shrugged and lifted the bottle to his mouth. For the first time, Zoe let herself fully register his presence. He was tall, bleached blond, wearing ragged clothes, the quintessential beach bum. But appearance wasn't presence. Looking slightly deeper showed a body too well-developed for someone who hung out all day, even for someone who surfed or ran on the beach or played sand volleyball. And deeper than that was the waiting, watching, training that made him dangerous.

Made him exactly what she needed. What she'd always needed.

Crap. She didn't mean that. Maybe she'd had a need for Grant-the-man eight, ten years ago. Now it was just a need for Grant-the-mercenary. It was a job. She still loved Kell. Her heart turned itself inside out with missing him whenever she thought his name. He was the reason she was here. The reason she had to try to find the totems and turn them in, so everyone could just leave her alone.

She realized he hadn't answered her and tuned back in to the present. He saw the shift and finally spoke.

"I know why you're here."

She lifted her right eyebrow, and he curled one side of his mouth up. The crooked grin was familiar and tempting. She almost relaxed enough to step forward and kiss him. Horror followed, so cold and intense it was several seconds before she was sure she hadn't actually done so.

This was such a mistake.

"My mother sent me press clippings," he told her, seemingly oblivious to what had just happened. "Congratulations on your engagement, by the way. And your business is doing well."

He was fishing. She responded anyway. She'd have to be completely open with him or he'd never help her. The irony was like a poker in her belly.

"I broke the engagement and sold my business. If you know why I'm here, you probably know why I did that."

He didn't look surprised, only nodded approvingly. "You were separating yourself from people who could be used to manipulate you."

"That wasn't quite how I was thinking of it, but essentially, yes."

"So what's your plan?"

She shifted her weight and Grant pushed away from the rail.

"Sorry, let's go inside. I only have one chair out here."

Zoe followed him through the sliding door and took the seat he offered at the table. He detoured past the refrigerator before sitting in the matching wooden chair, offering her a can of cream soda.

"I didn't know if you still drank it," he said.

"I don't." She popped the top and sipped, unable to help the grin that followed. "I'm not sure why, now. Thank you." Then she frowned. "You knew I was coming?" He hated cream soda.

"I knew what my mother planned. She didn't tell me, but she's not that sneaky. She told me I should help you, and I said I would if you asked for it."

"She sent me a letter. You know, like those Christmas letters people send, all chatty and recapping the year?"

He shrugged, clearly not a recipient of such letters.

"Anyway, she told me what you've been doing and included your address." Her lips twitched. "She sent it via FedEx."

He rolled his eyes. "She sends me faxes."

"I'm glad she did it, because you're the only one I know who could maybe help me get out of this." She told him everything that had happened—Henricksen's visit and attempts to stay on top of things, despite his tied hands, the calls from Freddie, the guy from the cab who gave her the photos.

"What was in them?"

She took a deep breath. This was the hard part. "Me. My employees. My parents." She swallowed, her throat dry, and took a swig of the soda. It didn't help. "My...ex-fiancé and his parents. And his thirteen-year-old sister."

"Shit." Grant rubbed a hand over his face before fingering his scarred ear. "I thought for sure they'd want you."

Another mouthful of soda did nothing to ease her nausea. "I'm hoping they still do. The note with the pictures told me to get the totems and rejoin the 'family.' " She gagged and gripped the back of her neck, closing her eyes as if that would hold off the flashes of memory. Freddie brushing her hair. Pat reading her the old, brutal fairy tales and laughing when she cried. The way his people would touch and cuddle her.

Grant's hand rested against her back, warm between her shoulder blades. It anchored her in the now, and the flashes slowly faded.

"What was the trigger?" he asked. "What made you leave everything and come here?"

He was good. His insight validated her decision, and one of the million coils of tension slid away. "I had some stupid idea that once I isolated myself and everyone was safe..." She trailed off. "I had no ideas. I have to find the totems, and I texted back to indicate I knew what they wanted and would comply. But I don't *have* them. Distancing myself from the people who could be targeted was a no-brainer. But then they sent me a real warning." She swallowed hard again, her eyes on his ear, which he was still rubbing. "They sent me your earlobe."

His hand immediately came down to the table. "How do you know it was mine?"

She blinked. "I guess I don't." Why would they still have it? *How* would they have it? She hadn't thought about that before. "It doesn't matter if it was yours or not. It sends the same message." The horror of that day screamed into her mind. The light, the glistening blood, the screams. The sobs of Grant's brother, Jordie. She blinked again, and again, rapidly, until the visions faded. "They sent another photo of Olivia. Kell's little sister. With the word 'perfection' across it."

Grant hissed out a long curse. "They obviously thought that would be enough to send you to them with the totems."

"They don't know I don't have them. And they don't know me," she added quietly. Grant's head jerked up. She kept her gaze steady on him as she said, "They only think they do. I am not the compliant twelve-year-old they abducted, or the terrified thirteen-year-old who escaped them. I'm not doing their bidding, no matter what they try to do to me or anyone else. But I want them to think I am."

Admiration flashed in Grant's blue-green eyes. "Have they given you any instructions?"

"Just this." She reached for her bag on the back of her chair and removed the note that had come with the stack of pictures, handing it to Grant. "And Freddie called my office on Friday. She gave my assistant a cryptic message reminding me what they'd done to you and demanding the key as well as the idols. She also said 'Our perfect delicacy shan't attend the reunion should you bring our party favors on time.' I think the point is that they'll leave Olivia alone as long as I'm doing what they want." She rubbed her temples, overwhelmed by how everything just kept piling on. "I hope that's what she meant, anyway."

A deep breath helped her focus again. "Henricksen—the FBI agent I told you about?" After Grant nodded, she said, "He's been reviewing all the old records, everything Pat's people said about what they were doing. He found something that references a special blood moon being the most powerful to unlock the power of the totems."

Grant snorted. "Bullshit."

"Doesn't matter." Her bag was still on her lap, and her hand tightened hard enough around the strap to bruise her palm. "Not if Pat believes it."

He inclined his head. "Good point. So what makes it special?"

"It's a supermoon—"

"Close to the earth."

"Right. And fourth in a tetrad, a grouping of eclipses. And the timing corresponds to some religious holy day." She shook out her hand. "I didn't pay attention to that part, because the details don't really matter. That's all just crap Pat feeds his followers to keep them zealous. He's going to believe in the timing, though, and the full moon is in less than two weeks."

"So what's your plan, and where do I fit into it?"

She flushed. "I don't exactly have a plan. I don't know where to start. I was hoping, given your profession, you'd have some ideas."

"You might not have details figured out, but you have to have some broad goals."

"Well, yeah. Get the totems, destroy them, prove they're destroyed so Pat gives up completely and has no need for Olivia or any other thirteen-year-old girl. Then go back to my life."

Grant's expression didn't change, but the feeling in the room did. She realized he'd been holding himself back, treating her with wariness. But instead of sensing it because he stopped, like when white noise gets shut off, she sensed it because it deepened. Grew colder.

"Was this a bad idea?" she asked quietly. "Coming here?"

"No." He stood and removed a paper-wrapped packet from the small refrigerator. "I'm glad you came to me. I can help." But he didn't look at her while he set a cast-iron skillet on the stove and gathered ingredients for pan-fried fish.

Zoe waited in silence, wondering if she should continue the topic or follow his lead. He didn't say anything or look at her. The tension in the silence reminded her of the last time she'd seen him. He was wrong. Coming here *was* a bad idea. But pushing him would probably make it worse, so she changed the subject.

"How is your mother? She sent me that letter, but didn't talk about herself much."

"She's good." The tension eased subtly. "Still smoking and pretending it's a one-time stress thing. Still working at the mill, though she's been a supervisor for years, so that's a bit easier on her physically."

"Don't underestimate the power of mental stress," Zoe said.

Grant chuckled. "She says the same thing. Gripes that things were simpler when she was on the floor. But I don't know, *my* stress level is a lot lower."

She considered offering to help him cook, but there wasn't really room, and he dipped, coated, and fried with practiced efficiency.

"Is she seeing anyone?"

"Not that I'm aware of. But she wouldn't tell me."

"Because you'd do such a thorough check on them, you could tell her what their favorite food was when they were five?"

She could see his crooked smile in profile, though he still didn't look at her.

"Pretty much."

They kept the chatter light, about his mother's hobbies and Zoe's family and her web company. He finished with the fish and dumped a bag of lettuce in a bowl, and they ate in silence that was only slightly tense.

"That was pretty fantastic." Zoe sat back and patted her stomach.

"Thanks. About all I can make." He waved a hand when she started to rise and gather the dishes. "It can wait."

"Okay." She settled back into her chair. His tone told her he was ready to talk business.

"Tell me what you're really doing here."

Natalie J. Damschroder

Chapter Five

Zoe's dinner settled heavily. "I did."

But Grant shook his head. "Stone's family has money. Why aren't you holed up in some high-security compound with all of them?"

The nausea returned, bringing a churning bitterness with it. She leaned to take his plate and set it on hers, adding their silverware. "They're not like that. I mean, yes, they have money, but no high-security compound or anything. They're just people."

He cocked his head. "So they're vulnerable."

This time the nausea didn't just churn. She stood abruptly, hoping her fish would stay down, and carried the dishes to the sink. "My intent is for them not to be. I sent Freddie a return text that I was getting the totems. They won't do anything as long as they think their threat is working. I sent Henricksen the...package. That was enough for him to say he'll keep an eye on Olivia and her family, but he can only do so much within the resources of the bureau. So I talked to Olivia's mom and told her they should hire some security, just in case."

The air temperature increased and the skin on her legs prickled. She knew Grant was standing behind her now.

"Interesting," he said.

She turned on the water and stretched for the dish soap to put a couple of inches between them. "What is?"

"You didn't tell mention telling your fiancé." He turned and leaned back against the counter so he could watch her, arms folded.

"Ex-fiancé. But no, I didn't." She poured soap into the filling basin and watched the bubbles forming.

"Why not?"

It was none of his business. Not that part of it, anyway.

When she didn't answer, he said, "Do you realize that Pat and Freddie probably want you for this, not Olivia?"

An odd note in his voice made her look up at him, and the look in his eyes swept her back. Instead of warm salt air, the breeze carried the heavier scent of lake water. The light went from golden to twilight green. And Grant became everything that was good in her world. For a moment, she drowned in the depth of love in his eyes, the dragging swirl of desperation that almost made her change her mind. How could they live without each other?

And then she blinked, and eighteen-year-old Grant disappeared. If there had been any emotion there, anything showing that he felt similarly to how he had ten years ago, it was gone. One eyebrow lifted as he waited for her to answer his question.

"Of course I realize that. Why do you think I'm doing this?" She dropped the silverware into the sink and added the stack of plates. "But he's not going to get me."

"Not if I can help it," Grant muttered. He stuck the frying pan into the water and tugged her elbow. "Let that stuff soak."

She dried her hands and rejoined him at the table. He'd grabbed a pad and pen. "Start at the beginning. Did you see the totems?"

Zoe started to speak, but found her throat clogged. She hadn't talked about this since she finished therapy. She nodded instead.

"Do you remember what they look like?"

"Kind of. It was sixteen years ago!" she protested when he grimaced. "And memorizing the details wasn't exactly my priority at the time."

"Whatever you can remember." He pushed the pad over. "Want a pencil?"

"No, this is fine." She accepted the felt-tip pen and hovered it over the pad, trying to picture the small golden idols. "They were all different, but…" She started sketching the basic rectangular shape, with a wide base and cap and an animal near the top. One had been cat-like, maybe a mountain lion. Another had been a bear. The carvings on the bottom half had seemed artistic, but the one at the top was a symbol.

"Why do you call them totems?" Grant asked her, watching the pen stroke across the paper.

She shrugged. "That's what they called them.

Why?"

"Totems are symbolic. Usually relating to ancestry. They represent unity for a group, like a tribe or clan."

"Well, that fits what I remember." She described them as she drew, jotting notes alongside the picture as memory built on memory. She'd retained more than she thought she had, given her state of mind back then and the elapsed time. Not to mention all her efforts to pretend none of it had ever happened.

Her pen faltered and she lifted it with a sigh.

"What's wrong?"

"It's just…I worked so hard to get past all this. I went to therapy for ten years. When my parents' guilt and pain made me repress my own feelings, the therapist made me vent them to her. When I finally felt like it was over enough to look ahead, like I had enough control of my own life, I set it aside. I made sure it wouldn't hold me back from getting what I wanted." A wave of shock went over her at the words. She couldn't believe she had said that to him. "Grant, I—"

"It's okay." But he didn't look like it was okay. For a man with a classic poker face, he was having trouble hiding what the words had done to him.

"It's not okay. Shit, Grant, I didn't mean…I meant…I didn't mean you," she finished with a whisper. It didn't matter what she said. The truth was, at the time, it *had* meant him.

The breeze shifted, and she could swear it carried the scent of dead fish through the sliding screen door and out the window on the other side of the shack.

"I know what you meant," Grant finally said. "And now, despite all your hard work and careful planning, here you are. Right back in the thick of it."

Zoe hated his bitterness, barely heard beneath the words of understanding. She stood and went to the doorway to look out on the beach.

"This probably wasn't a good idea," she murmured, mainly because she had to. Her fingers found the delicate chain around her neck, the sand dollar charm that was usually tucked under her shirt. Kell had never asked her where it came from, why she never took it off. Now, she wished he had.

"Depends on your perspective."

He'd shoved back whatever he was feeling, because any hint of emotion was gone from his voice. Zoe half turned back to him. "And your perspective is?"

"The right one." He picked up the pen from where it lay on the table and tossed it onto the pad. "Come back here and finish drawing."

She went back to the table and sat to study the picture. "I don't know. I think this is as close as I can get."

He studied the sketch. "And there were four of them?"

"Yep. About ten inches tall, I guess? Narrow enough to wrap my hand around. Not very big."

He sat back again. "Tell me what you did with them the day you escaped."

"You know what I did."

"It was almost sixteen years ago. Tell me again."

She rubbed her eyes and dredged up that awful day. "Jordie showed up with them at two in the morning. The whooping and hollering woke me up, and the guy who usually sat in my room while I slept must have gone out to see what was going on. I peeked out the curtain over my doorway and watched for a little while. They passed around the totems, toasting them and Jordie. They drank. A lot. Probably did drugs, too, but I stopped watching. Then—" Her throat closed. Grant knew what had happened then. She didn't have to say it.

Jordie had come through, after he'd been threatened with his younger brother's death, after he'd had to watch them cut off Grant's earlobe. He'd snuck Grant out a few hours after that, when everyone was asleep, to take him home. He'd whispered apologies to Zoe that he couldn't take her, too. She hadn't really understood until later. He'd been able to sneak Grant out because they didn't care about him. He'd been blindfolded the entire time he was at the house, and she'd heard Pat saying they could pick him up again at any time. They didn't need him. He was just motivation.

But they did need her.

Jordie was supposed to get the totems from someone within two days. He did it, and they "celebrated" by torturing him. When the memories surged, her brain attached images to them based on the sounds she remembered, sounds she didn't really understand at the time. The reality had to be even more horrifying. But she and Grant hadn't talked about that part, not in detail, and if he didn't know, she couldn't tell him. There was no reason to.

"It took hours, but eventually they fell asleep. I knew things were about to get much worse." From the moment Freddie had grabbed Zoe from the grocery store parking lot, she and Pat had acted like she was their daughter. At first they'd hit her when she didn't do something they wanted, and she figured out pretty quickly that to humor them, to pretend to go along, would keep her safe until she could escape. But then they'd added more and more members to their gang. They'd moved from ramshackle cabin to abandoned house to tent city in the woods, keeping her disoriented and off balance, so that she didn't know where to run if she did manage to get away. And they'd kept a guard on her at all times, usually a big guy or someone really scary, who acted like he'd go off any minute and start killing everyone.

Remembering how many nights she'd lain helpless, inert, terrified, still angered her. Her last therapist had told her she was reviewing that time with the perspective of an adult, and she had to forgive herself for not doing what she couldn't have done. Zoe understood that, even agreed with it, but she couldn't banish the ugly glide of disgust and resentment that she'd never managed to find the right combination of opportunity and courage.

Not until that night. After they got the totems, they'd all been jubilant and relaxed. The person with the key was meeting them in a rail yard that evening, and then they'd have everything they'd been working toward for a year.

"I hoped they'd leave me at the cabin, but they dragged me to the rail yard and left me and the totems in a little room in the old station building, with one of their biggest, meanest guys outside the door. But they got sloppy and didn't notice there was another door behind a row of file cabinets. It took a while, but I managed to shift them just enough to get through to the door and get out. I took the bag of totems with me."

"What was outside that door?"

She closed her eyes, calling up the squealing brakes, the chugs and clatters of moving steel. All she could see was the strip of gravel in front of her, the dark cavern behind a half-open door, her one chance to get rid of the hateful things.

"A freight train. It was moving slowly, but I have no idea in which direction. I threw the totems into an open car."

Her moistened palms slipped across the top of the table. The wooden chair was solid under her legs. But her breathing was harsh and shallow, and her heart pounded in her ears, blocking out any possible sounds of pursuit. She couldn't see anything but the giant metal canyon she ran in. "The door was open on another train going in the opposite direction, so I got on it."

A warm hand settled on top of hers, doing more to ground her in two seconds than everything else she'd tried. Slowly, the rail yard faded and the orange glow of the lowering sun filled the shack. She eased her breathing and forced her shoulders to ease down. Grant was watching it happen, his gaze steady with patience.

"Sorry," she murmured. "Hard to go back there and not get stuck."

He nodded and withdrew his hand. "Unfortunately, what you did is going to make them damned near impossible to track down. Even if we can determine the train they were on, they could have wound up anywhere along the line."

"I know." She slumped, bowing under the weight of possibilities. It could take years to explore them all. And she had less than two weeks.

"Have you done any research on them?"

Another unwelcome wave of heat washed over her. This one was shame. "No, I haven't. I mean, I have what Henricksen found, but it's vague and mostly comes from the interviews they did back then. I didn't even think about—" She pressed her lips together, refusing to overapologize. "I haven't had time."

Grant nodded. "We could track down Pat and Freddie's gang members, the ones who aren't still working for them. Find out what they know and remember."

"Yeah," she said slowly, "but I don't know who they are or if Henricksen will give me a list or anything. He can only do so much."

"I can get it. Tracking people down is time-consuming, though. That might not be the most expedient path. But first, we need the history. We need to know exactly what we're going after and why it's so important."

"It was like a bedtime story to Pat. He told me the legend of the totems over and over again."

"I know the story. Jordie told me before he died."

"Oh." She twisted her fingers together. That had to be the last time he saw him. Even when she and Grant were together, during those high-school summers, he didn't talk much about all that. One of Pat's gang had grabbed him after school. He'd been so freaked out he couldn't remember, later, all the details. Just that they'd used him to get Jordie to do what they wanted, Jordie had caved, somehow gotten Grant out and home, and then died anyway.

Why had Jordie told Grant the legend? Was it to distract him from everything else? Jordie was several years older than Grant, so they hadn't been close, but she knew they'd loved each other.

Grant cleared his throat. Pointedly. "That's not the part we need. We don't know what details in Pat's version are real and what are legend."

"I'm pretty sure the part about immortality is legend," she joked. Grant just stared at her, unamused. "What? You can't tell me you think we should take that part seriously?"

"I don't think we should discount anything. And you're the one who pointed out that what Pat believes matters the most."

There was something he wasn't saying, but he rose and started cleaning up the rest of the stuff from their dinner, so Zoe joined him.

"But you think there's a logical reason that's part of

the story, right? Not that they can actually all be brought together to make the holder immortal. Like a vampire or something. Right?"

"Right."

He sounded amused, and she scowled at him.

"Something in that sentence had to be right," he said.

Zoe rolled her eyes and backhanded his upper arm, then had to pretend to bobble the glasses she held to hide her surprise. The man was rock solid. Not tight and wiry like he'd been back when they were barely not-teenagers. Not even "mmm, muscles" as one would imagine just to look at him. But very, very hard.

And, of course, that made her think of the possibility that he was hard all over.

And that made her knees weak.

History, she reminded herself. That was all it was. All it was ever going to be.

She thought of the sand dollar, and shivered.

* * *

Forty-caliber ammunition. Lines of sight. Uzbekistan. Orange alert. Wheels up. Paid-up life insurance. Beach bunnies.

It wasn't working. No matter what anti-Zoe things Grant tried to think of, she filled his senses and his brain.

When she'd said it had been a mistake to come, he wanted to agree with her. He had enough adventure in his paying job. A job that didn't dredge up the worst of his past.

But he couldn't hurt her like that, which proved he

was too far gone. This wasn't just about nostalgia and scent memories. At some point since she arrived—hell, maybe the minute he'd seen her on that bike, coming down the road—he'd known he'd lied to his mother. The reason he'd never had a long-term relationship was because none of the women was Zoe.

He handed her a dripping glass and watched her dry it. She did it the same way she'd done when they were kids, washing dishes at the yacht club every night. She dried the bottom, then the sides, turning the glass around and around until she could see no external moisture. Then she tucked the towel down deep into the glass and spun it until it was dry. Then she placed it in the open cupboard over the sink.

She was lost in thought, or pretending to be, no longer putting any expectations on him, neither for retrieving the totems or over their shared history.

Over. It really wasn't. Didn't matter that she wanted to go back to her life. Nothing was over between them. What was more, he knew it was mutual. She'd thought because her back was to him, he couldn't see her movements. But the angle of the sun on the glass door had cast her reflection, and he'd seen what was in her hand.

His sand dollar.

The realization had wrenched something inside him, twisting him back to the day she'd refused him. She didn't know she'd turned his life to shrapnel that day. In some ways, for the good. She'd made him evaluate his intentions and whether his willingness to settle for a certain kind of life was a disservice.

He and Jordie hadn't been close, being years apart and very different. Jordie always seemed to make the wrong decisions, getting himself into trouble no matter what he did. Grant had been a good student with decent friends and disgust for thoughtless, destructive behavior. Jordie's death had added a dark weight to his family's lives, but in some ways, nothing changed. In others, they even got better.

Still, Grant had been prepared to lead a solid, blue-collar life the way his parents had until Zoe challenged him. When he strove for more, he'd wound up fighting against the consequences of the types of choices Jordie had made, as well as the kind of people—like Pat and Freddie—who pushed others in the wrong direction. That was how he'd wound up here, with the skill set and connections Zoe needed. Full circle, indeed.

The sun was setting by the time they finished the dishes and went out on the deck with a couple of bottles of beer. Grant let Zoe have the sling chair, and he dragged one of the kitchen chairs outside. They watched the seagulls wheel and dive, looking for scraps the beachgoers had left behind, and waited for the dim glow of the sun to fade. It was intimate, and Grant was content to let it be.

But it didn't last.

"I want to ask what's next," she said, "but I'm afraid I already know."

"Research."

"Yep, that's what made me afraid."

He held back a sigh. Fine. They could focus on business. "There's an Internet café at the other end of the island. Same street as the hotel, which doesn't offer access." He paused, but she didn't say anything, which meant she expected to stay there. "You find out whatever you can on the history of the totems, what the story is. We know they wanted you for a ritual. What's the goal?"

Zoe cringed, and he almost reached out a comforting hand. But that wasn't what she wanted from him.

"You don't have Internet here?" She frowned skeptically.

"I have a wired connection. One jack, no WiFi." He hid his grin at her sigh behind his beer. When she didn't say anything else, he went on, "Legends like that tend to splinter the more they're told. So digging down to the base story can help us know what we're facing."

She tipped up her beer, swallowing audibly. "They could be a guide to treasure," she said. "Because of the key."

The key. He hadn't known anything about a key. He forced himself to remember his last moments with his brother. The endless, over-in-a-second trip back to their house. Jordie had told him a story about magical totems that gave great power, including the power to heal. Grant had been too terrified and in too much pain to focus on the meaning, even as the words burned into his brain.

But Jordie hadn't mentioned a key. That had only been part of the record because of Zoe's testimony. "You have no idea what the key is?"

"No."

"See if you can find mention of that, too."

"There's a problem," she said. Grant waited. "I'm on a cash basis from here on."

"You need money?" he asked automatically, then felt foolish. Of course she didn't need money.

"No, I have enough cash to cover at least a couple of weeks. But Internet cafés usually want a credit card to charge for your time on the computer."

And there it was. The first disconnect between the kinds of lives they lived.

"Probably in the chi-chi cafés in Boston and Europe and wherever else you might have used them, they do. But in places like here, they don't cater to the rich or comfortable. Their customers are like me. They take cash."

Zoe didn't take the bait. "Okay. You're right, I didn't realize that would be the case. So it will be fine." She stood and set her half-empty bottle on the rail. "I'd better head down there. It's getting dark."

"You want me to go with you?"

"Of course not. I rode down here, I can ride back." She stepped down to the sand, and Grant followed her to the bike she'd propped against the wall of the shack.

"Did you check it over when you rented it?" He squinted at the tires and gauged the straightness of the handlebars. "Chain okay? Enough air in the tires?"

"I checked it over fine." She pulled it out of his way. "It's fine. With no cars allowed at this end of the island, a business like that would keep its rentals in good shape. Accidents due to lack of maintenance aren't good marketing."

Grant shook his head. "We're not a tourist destination, Zo. You're thinking too much like a consumer."

She shrugged but didn't argue.

"Call me when you get down there, all right?" He caught her hand and scrawled his number on her palm with the pen he'd tucked behind his ear, somehow managing not to react when a connection zinged between them, warmth seeping from the point of contact, the same sense of rightness he felt when he returned home from a mission.

He released her hand slowly, careful not to scratch the soft skin with his battered ones. "Be careful."

Zoe's eyes glittered in the twilight, and a few seconds passed before she said, "I will," and rode off.

Grant knew she'd felt the same thing he had. She'd deny it, or dismiss it, but he knew what it was.

And he started to question how noble he was going to be able to be.

* * *

Zoe pedaled steadily until the first curve in the road took her behind a stand of mangroves. The back tire skidded a little when she braked on the shoulder, and she hopped to keep her balance. Her breathing echoed in the still air, as if she'd pedaled up a hill instead of across completely flat land.

This wasn't going to work.

"Kellen," she whispered, squeezing her eyes shut and trying to pull up his image. It didn't want to come. She couldn't get the stupid smell of dead fish out of her nostrils, and she could feel Grant all around her. Her hands tightened on the handlebars until they ached, but she couldn't change it.

"Shit."

She pushed off, hard, and pedaled as fast as she could to the other, more populated end of the island. She had to dodge kids and couples coming off the beach and out of the restaurants as they geared up for the nightly parties. Grant had said this wasn't a tourist island, but the people here followed the same patterns as one. Soon there would be music pounding out of the open-air bars and people dancing on the sand. Tonight, it was too similar to the way Pat's gang had acted so many nights, and her skin tried to crawl away with her inside it.

She turned in the bike and retrieved her tote from the locker she'd stowed it in, then headed straight for the two-story hotel that dominated the end of the beach. She hoped they had a room. She hadn't wanted to check in before seeing Grant in case he was out on a job or refused to talk to her. If that had been the case, she wouldn't have stayed. She didn't know what she'd have done.

The lobby of the hotel was bright and airy, decorated with palms and ferns that hid the places where the paint chipped off the stucco. A bucket near one wall caught a drip of water every few seconds. Zoe paused, disconcerted. The lobby was on the first floor, presumably under guest rooms. One of which was apparently leaking.

There were no other hotels on the island, so she

approached the smiling man at the counter.

"I'd like a room for tonight, please."

"Certainly, ma'am. Just one night?"

"No. Indefinite."

His smile faded a little and he squinted at the screen. "I can give you four nights. After that we are full for three."

"It's fine." Zoe would deal with that later. She couldn't really plan more than a day ahead at this point, anyway. She paid for all four nights in cash, since she didn't want to give a credit card and risk her location being traced. The clerk assured her she could get a refund if she checked out early.

The room he assigned her was on the beach side of the building, but she didn't bother to check the view. Dropping her tote onto the desk chair, she fell onto the surprisingly plush bed and buried her face in her arms. Then she let go.

The memory leading the swarm was the worst one. The source of the phantom dead fish odor that kept plaguing her.

It was the end of their final summer at the lake. Grant had just turned nineteen, a birthday she faced two months later, and he'd told her a few days before that he was about to make all their dreams come true. She hadn't really thought about what that meant. Her dreams were already coming true. She was leaving for Amherst College in Massachusetts in two days and had scored enough scholarships, grants, and financial aid to get her through two years there. More, if she didn't eat a lot and got a second job in addition to the on-campus work program. She was in love with a great guy, her best friend, and while they were parting for a while, she knew that wouldn't hurt their relationship. They'd shared too much.

Their last night at the lake, Grant had picked her up at the girls' bunkhouse and they'd gone down to the deserted dock, where they ate the picnic dinner he'd scored from the yacht club kitchen. Someone had left a bait bucket and remnants nearby, but the odor hadn't bothered her. Not at first.

"I'm gonna miss this place," Grant had said.

"Not me." Zoe grimaced and ate a carrot stick from the vegetable plate. "Being ordered around by rich guys who have no idea how to take care of the boats they had their assistants buy for them? Treated like trash when those 'assistants' don't need me for something? I'm glad to say goodbye to it."

"Yeah, me, too, but the rest of it. The water, the sailing. You." He threaded his hand through hers and she smiled.

"We don't need the lake. We just need each other."

Grant nodded, but she watched his Adam's apple bob.

"What's the matter?"

"Nothing." He cleared his throat and sat up. "Um. Did you…find out about your roommate yet?"

Zoe didn't think that was what he'd been about to say, but she answered, describing the letter she'd received the day before, forwarded with a last care package from her mother.

"Did you save me some of those cookies?"

"Of course." She rummaged in her patchwork shoulder bag and pulled out the plastic-wrapped pile. "The other girls saw the package, so I had to share, but Mom always has a batch wrapped up separately for you."

Grant grinned and snatched one of the cookies. "Your mom is so cool."

"Yeah." Mention of her mom, as always, dredged up feelings of failure and regret. "She comes through." With cookies, anyway. Zoe bit into one, letting the vanilla and chocolate ease away the sourness.

"You going home first, before you go to Amherst?"

She sighed. "I guess. I don't want to, but there's stuff there I need, and it will break their hearts if I don't."

Grant nodded and swallowed his third cookie. Zoe watched him feel his pocket, and her stomach went cold. Her breath caught, and she wasn't sure if it was from anxiety or anticipation.

"Zoe," Grant began, and now she found it hard to swallow.

"Yeah?"

"I, um, have something for you."

Her breath waited in her lungs. He didn't move for several seconds, then suddenly shoved his hand into the pocket of his cargo shorts and pulled out something small, something she couldn't see. She touched the small gold sand dollar at her throat. He'd given her the necklace last year, with money he'd saved all summer, something to remind her of him during the long, cold midwest winter when they would be lucky to see each other once or twice. This separation would be longer and more difficult, since he'd be doing ROTC at Wright State in Dayton, Ohio, hundreds of miles away from her. So maybe he had—

Grant cleared his throat, interrupting her thoughts, but kept his gaze on the water lapping below their feet. Zoe couldn't see his eyes.

"I've been thinking about this all summer," he said. "Longer. It's like…the end of something, and the beginning of something else, and I'm afraid we'll be doing two different something elses."

She went cold and pulled her hand free to wrap her arms around herself. What was wrong with that?

Grant turned his body to face her, sitting cross-legged, whatever he was holding still hidden in his fingers.

"I love you, Zoe." He glanced up expectantly. It wasn't the first time they'd said it, not by a long shot, but she dutifully replied, meaning it, but suddenly not sure what "meaning it" meant.

"You're, like, the other half of me. And even though we're going to be in different places, learning different things, we'll be together. You know, in spirit or whatever."

He'd never sounded so awkward. Tears pricked her eyes. She blinked hard, not wanting him to see.

He took a deep breath, straightened his spine again, and held out a tiny diamond ring. "Zoe Ardmore, will you marry me?"

She didn't take the ring. "When?"

His face fell, and part of her, buried under the

coldness, knew she'd crushed him and was sorry.

"What?"

"When do you want me to marry you?"

"I don't know." He spread his hands out, realized that put the ring over the water, and swung them back into his lap fast. "Whenever."

He looked confused. Of course he did. Because she didn't mean *when*, she meant *why*, but couldn't seem to ask that properly. He would just say because he loved her, and that wasn't the point.

Something was squeezing her lungs, tighter and tighter, the way it used to be when her parents tried to keep her "safe."

"Whenever, like when I'm done with college and you're doing your stint in the Army? Or whenever, like over the holidays, so you can freeze me in place?"

He gaped at her. "Not— I don't know. I figured we'd decide that together." He looked down at the ring and held it toward her again. She ignored it.

"I don't think you want to marry me for the right reasons."

He gaped more. "I want to marry you because I love you!"

Yep, there it was. "No. I think you want to marry me because you're afraid. You think you might lose me."

"Never."

He said it fast enough, with enough confidence, to give her pause. Maybe she'd read him wrong. But…

"What are your plans, Grant?"

"You know my plans."

"No, I don't. I know you're going to Wright State and then you have to be in the Army, and if you don't die in some stupid war, what next? What kind of career do you want?"

He shrugged and gazed toward the sailboat marina. "Something like this, I guess. You know, on the water. Maybe fishing charters or tours somewhere."

"That's all?" The words sounded funny because her throat had swollen and now burned. She tightened her arms. "You really don't want more than you have now?"

"Why would I?" He leaned to touch her arm and she tried not to flinch away.

"Because it's not good enough!" He was too close. She scrambled to her feet. A splinter dug into her bare foot, but she didn't cry out. It wasn't important. What they were saying was. "Grant, I don't want to live like that."

His face went stony. "You don't."

"How could you not know that?" She shoved back her hair and tried not to feel like everything was falling apart. There was a reason they hadn't talked about this before. She'd known, without thinking about it, that their goals were too incompatible.

"I don't have to do that. I can do whatever you want me to do."

"No. That's not what I want." The tears that had threatened earlier gave no such warning now, just started streaming. "I want you to do what makes you happy."

"*You* make me happy, dammit."

"But I don't think that will last. I want—I want more. A lot more."

"Like what?" he burst out, exasperated. "One of those?" He pointed at the yacht marina. "You want to become one of the people you just complained about?"

"Yes. No." She paced along the pier, limping with her splintered foot. "I don't want to be spoiled and treat others like crap. But I want to have my own business, a really successful one. I want to go to charity balls and write big checks that will help kids. I want beautiful clothes and a car I *choose,* not the cheapest one on the lot."

"None of that stuff is important, Zoe."

He was right. She just didn't know how to explain. To most people, those were superficial trappings that had little to do with relationships and personal satisfaction and all that. To her, they represented so much more. A life that she created, that was hers from top to bottom. That had never been touched in any way by her past. By Pat's power trip and Freddie's crazy idea of motherhood, her mother's fears and her father's desperate rules that trapped more than they protected.

But she didn't hear that from him. What she heard, that he probably didn't intend, was "your dreams aren't important."

And that was it, the moment it had broken forever.

Chapter Six

Zoe realized the bedspread under her had grown damp with her tears and that she really, really needed a tissue. She shoved herself up and off the bed to find one. The light on the desk hurt her eyes, and when she blinked, her eyelids were so swollen they didn't seem to fit together right. She had no idea how long she'd lain there, crying, immersed in the past.

She'd still been in therapy when Grant proposed, the second of a series of sessions with empowered and empowering people who'd helped her get past the residual effects of the abduction. One of those effects had been her need for control. When she first got home after her escape, that need manifested in screaming fits about what her mother tried to feed her at mealtimes. Once she adapted to a "normal" daily life and came to terms with her parents' limitations, the things she tried to control grew more complicated and important. Deciding what classes to take, working at the lake, being with Grant, choosing a college—and planning the rest of her life. The therapist had encouraged the planning, as long as she recognized her need for control and worked to balance it against the needs of others.

That last part had been harder, and her relationship with Grant had been the first casualty.

He hadn't understood. He had a typical poor-kid view of the rich and hadn't wanted anything to do with that world. Zoe's opinions weren't all that different, but her goals had nothing to do with fitting in with "people like that." He couldn't see it. All he could see was that she was greedy and selfish, and now, from a ten-year vantage point, she knew she had been. Not necessarily about what she wanted, but how she treated his plans and dreams. They'd argued for hours, Grant intent on convincing her that he could do anything, go anywhere, that he just wanted to be with her, and Zoe just as intent on not believing him. She hadn't simply wanted him to want his own things without making her the center of his existence. She wanted her new life so much she couldn't understand why he'd be willing to give up his own. She was afraid that if he made sacrifices, it would force her to do the same.

And maybe it would have. Even in retrospect, she couldn't see any easy path for them. They'd have been at different schools, so far apart. They'd have grown in different directions, made new friends, met hot new guys and girls. How many *normal* long-distance relationships survived? Once she was able to get real distance from the past, Grant would have been the only tie remaining. How strong would have been the need to cut that tie? Eventually, hurting him—hurting each other—would have become inevitable.

She threw her soggy tissues in the wicker trash can and looked around for an ice bucket. She needed some water. She spotted the ugly yellow plastic bucket on a table by the window and stood to get it, making sure she had her key card before she went out to find the ice machine.

The problem was, even though they'd ended things that day, it hadn't been over. She had gone back to the bunkhouse and cried herself to sleep, because after her initial reaction to the *way* Grant had proposed came her reaction to the *fact* of the proposal.

She found the vending nook and grimaced at the puddle under the ice machine. This must be the source of the leak to the lobby. When she lifted the cover to the bin, she found small cubes swimming in a pool of water. There was no scoop, and she couldn't bring herself to dip the bucket into that mess. She bought a bottle of Coke instead and headed back to her room.

Grant had loved her so much he wanted to commit to her, to make her commit to him, believing that would keep them together through anything that happened. And she'd loved him that much, too. The realization that they weren't going to be part of each other's lives anymore had felt like glass shattering, slicing every part of her that could feel pain.

She'd moved on, the only thing she could do. They saw each other one more time, at church during the holidays, when Zoe's town held a vigil for missing children. Her mother had started the event and made it kind of in Zoe's honor, or in recognition of the rarity of her escape, or something like that. And even though Grant's family lived a few towns away, they always came for the vigil. After all, they'd lost a son to the same people who'd had Zoe, even though he'd been an adult and involved with them by his own choice.

That night, while everyone stood praying and singing with their candles, Zoe and Grant had snuck away and made desperate, powerful love in the graveyard behind the church. Neither one of them had really said anything to the other. Grant had looked at her with promises in his eyes, and Zoe figured he saw nothing but regret in hers. But she was already looking forward.

She drank her soda while she got ready for bed, changing and brushing her teeth by autopilot, still rolling through her past. She'd transferred from Amherst to Suffolk University once she decided on her career in graphic design and computer science. Then came internships, summer jobs in the city, every choice made to forward her goals. Every man she dated qualified as a rebound guy. Eventually, she'd managed to stifle all her feelings for Grant and start having real relationships, though all failed miserably before Kell. She'd met him a few months after she got a loan, quit her job at a major web company, and launched her business. He'd embodied everything she wanted and more. Despite the reputation of his profession, he was a core-deep good man, someone who made her feel as safe emotionally as physically, without being tethered by his dreams and expectations.

She missed him.

But now here she was, back with Grant. And things were far more complicated than she'd expected them to be.

Their mothers had kept contact. Zoe always thought that was weird, even when her therapist explained they had a connection beyond Zoe's relationship with Grant. They'd both been through hell and "survived," even if that word was as fragile as Zoe's mother. They updated each other on their kids' progress, and in turn told Zoe and Grant. That was how she knew about his stint in Special Forces before he took an honorable discharge and went private sector—the polite way to say mercenary—and that he hadn't ever married. The Grant she'd put together from these updates and stories seemed so different from the man she'd loved, she'd hoped seeing him wouldn't dredge up the past she'd put to rest. He was different, she was different, and there'd be no connection anymore.

She was so wrong.

Every movement he made was pure Grant, exactly how she remembered him, but now with the power and masculinity that had only been potential ten years ago. He smelled the same, smiled the same, and when she looked into his eyes—which she'd tried to avoid the entire time she was there, a mistake given the impact when she finally did it right before she left—whatever had made them perfect for each other as teenagers was still there.

She turned off the light and climbed into bed with a soul-deep sigh. She wished their connection was just because they'd shared something horrific, but it wasn't. They *knew* each other in a way most people never did, a way she now understood she had never allowed with Kell.

All of that was bad enough on its own. Then it had to be compounded by attraction. Zoe had been attracted to other men. A faint buzz, a little *mmm, delicious* and mutual, silent acknowledgment of possibilities. That was all easily dismissed, even when the man was a client or colleague and she had to be around him more than in passing. This was different. Uncontrollable, raw, and if given any toehold, possibly her ruination. If she was smart, she'd send Grant a "thank you, but never mind" note and leave. But if she left, she might never get her life back.

So much for control.

* * *

Zoe had been drifting into sleep for only moments when her phone rang. She shot upright with a sharp gasp and whipped to look at the clock. Music and voices drifted in from outside her window. She snatched the phone off the nightstand and squinted at the display, heart still racing. The number on the screen didn't match any of the ones in her contacts list. That meant it wasn't someone from back home or Boston, so everyone was okay. She calmed enough to recognize the area code as Florida, which meant it was probably Grant.

And dammit, she'd forgotten to call him. Hadn't even thought about the number inked on her hand when she washed up.

She stabbed the button to accept the call. "Hello?"

"So you're okay." His voice was as stony as his expression could be.

"Yeah. I'm sorry." She took a deep breath, a little shaky from the adrenaline rush. "I totally forgot to call you."

"I hoped that was it."

Zoe realized she could hear music in the background on the other end of the line. The same music she heard outside her window.

"Where are you?"

A few beats went by before he answered. "Outside the hotel."

"Why? Why didn't you call me first?"

He didn't answer, and Zoe had a feeling the reason was a lot like the reason she'd forgotten. He, too, felt what was between them and didn't want to acknowledge it. So he'd avoided talking to her.

"The bike place said you'd returned the bike, but the hotel clerk wouldn't confirm you'd checked in, so… Sorry I bothered you."

"It's no bother, Grant." The words came out husky and gentle, and she cursed herself. That was the last signal she wanted to send. She tried to sound more businesslike when she continued, "I'm sorry I made you worry. I'll talk to you tomorrow, right?"

"Right."

"Night."

"Night."

The line stayed open for several seconds, the music playing in stereo, before Zoe finally ended the call.

* * *

The next two days weren't exactly the torture she'd dreaded. She spent most of the next day in the café, nursing lattes and blowing too much of her cash reserves on the Internet, trying to find information about the totems as well as Pat and Freddie. She'd never realized how much her perspective was still that of a twelve-year-old. Her therapy had always focused on herself, healing, building a safe future. Now she could review that time as an adult and see them as human, with goals and motivations that made sense, twisted as it was. Freddie thought Pat had given Zoe to her as a present, a "baby" to mother. But it was clear now that he'd used Zoe to distract his wife, to keep her satisfied and happy while he strove to achieve the kind of power that didn't really exist.

Thank God for Henricksen. His access to the old records, including interviews with Pat's associates, and his preliminary research when all this first started had saved her a lot of time. There was no easy place to begin looking if she didn't have the links he'd provided as a jumping-off point.

She and Grant talked on the phone a few times. He was using his contacts to track their nemeses and try to pinpoint where the totems had gone after she threw them on the train, using copies of the schedules from the FBI file—again, thanks to Henricksen. She remembered little about it, but the location of the rail yard and track number, plus the time of year and time of day, had helped Grant determine the likely chain of cars.

They agreed to meet the third morning to compare notes and try to come up with a plan of action. Zoe rented a bike again and rode down to Grant's shack, a bag of food from the restaurant next to the hotel tied above the back wheel.

Their phone conversations hadn't been awkward or tense, but Grant stood on the deck waiting for her, his posture a study in wariness. Zoe wheeled up the crushed-shell walkway and hopped off, propping the bike against the wall. He wore a ball cap today, his blond hair sticking out the sides and back, but even though it shadowed his eyes, she could still feel his laser stare.

"I brought lunch," she offered, raising the bag in the air.

"Good." Grant turned and went into the shack. When Zoe rounded the corner and stepped up onto the deck, she saw he'd left the door open for her.

"Thoughtful," she muttered. Maybe all her worries the other night had been for naught. One-sided attraction was much easier to handle than the mutual kind. On the other hand, maybe she'd pissed him off about something. When she stepped inside, he was standing next to the paper-strewn table. His arms were folded, his stance wide, and the beach bum was nowhere to be seen. She wasn't sure it was a good trade. He seemed like he'd be scary when he was pissed off.

"Do you want to eat, or should I put it in the fridge?" She waved the bag at the papers on the table.

"Put it on the counter. We'll eat in a minute."

She complied, then hung her sling bag over the back of one of the chairs. She scanned the papers, half recognizing some as charts or maps, but couldn't see enough of any of the rest to tell what they were.

"Is there a problem?" she finally asked when the silence dragged on.

Grant seemed to do battle with himself, but finally dropped his arms and the tension he was holding onto like a security blanket.

Zoe's optimism popped. He'd gone mercenary on her as a self-protective barrier, and there was only one reason he'd do that. Her hope that things would be easier, that the attraction was all on her side, dried up.

Focus on business. She struggled to think of a good opener, but all the information she'd gathered swam in her head, and she didn't know how to make the shift.

But Grant took over. "I didn't know you'd bring lunch. These are laid out in a kind of order, so let's eat on the deck."

"Okay." She grabbed the bag and two beers and followed him out. He dragged a beat-up plastic table over from the far corner of the deck, set two plates, forks, and napkins on it, then went inside for another chair. When he came back out, Zoe had balanced the plates side by side and was laying out the sandwiches she'd gotten.

"I hope you still like turkey and smoked cheddar."

He didn't smile, but she thought he wanted to. "Yeah. Zinger's has good stuff. Thanks for picking it up."

"No problem." She pried the top off a tub of three-bean salad and forked some onto each plate. "I ate there last night and thought it was the least I could do—" A thought struck her and she jerked her head up. "Um...I didn't ask before. About your fees."

He smirked. "If I cared about fees, I'd have brought that up first thing." He picked up his plate and sat in the deck chair. Zoe got up from her crouch by the table and settled on the hard-back chair, crossing her feet up under her so she could cradle the plate in her lap.

He eyed her position. "Sorry. Not the most comfortable arrangement."

"No, it's fine." She bit into her ham-and-cheese pretzel sandwich and watched the small waves rolling in, far away at low tide. "I think I'll go for a swim later." She'd worn her bathing suit out of a craving for normality and escape. If she was going to be in such a gorgeous place, she might as well take a few minutes to enjoy it. Who knew when, or if, she could again? The beach down here was far less crowded than the other end of the island.

When Grant didn't say anything, she started to turn to look at him. "Is that okay? Do you want to join—me?"

He was staring at her as if trying to see her bikini through her t-shirt. A wave of heat loosened her body, and she fought not to smile. Dammit. She wasn't supposed to be pleased at his appreciation. He wasn't some construction worker whistling at her as she walked down the street. She took another bite of her sandwich and chewed, watching the endless ocean.

"No, thanks," he said long enough later that it took

her a second to remember what he was responding to.

"Okay."

They finished eating in silence, Grant well before Zoe. He stood as soon as she forked up the last bean, and took their plates to the sink. She dragged the chair back inside and sat.

"Did you find anything about the totems?" he asked immediately. "Their origin?"

"Boy, did I." She grinned. "Henricksen's stuff was a fraction of what's out there. There's a buttload of information, considering these things are far from famous or anything."

Grant raised his eyebrows. Zoe paused in reaching for the notes in her bag. "What?"

"Buttload?"

She shrugged. "I guess I'm regressing a little."

"Gee, thanks."

"Is plethora better?"

He just rolled his eyes.

"Anyway." She pulled the folder out and set it on the table, dropping her bag to the floor. "There really isn't much historical value. They're not ancient. Antique, I guess. What's the age limit? A hundred years?"

"That's your world's thing, not mine."

The words could have stung if he hadn't said them so matter-of-factly and if they weren't so basically true. "I haven't exactly gotten into that part of 'my world.' Anyway, they were made by a metallurgist-slash-artist in the late eighteen hundreds. They're not solid gold or even an alloy, but gold molded over iron."

"Cuts the monetary value, then."

"Right. So Pat and Freddie are all about the mystical stuff."

"What did you find on that?"

She flipped open the folder. "Tons of different things. The guy who made them—Jacob Farmer—was an American mutt. He had ancestry from a couple of Native American tribes, a powerful Gypsy clan, and even what his mother claimed was an African shaman, though he wouldn't have been called that. He had some bland Caucasian blood, too, but that's less significant. One legend said he was obsessed with his heritage, with uniting it, and that he created the totems as a way to do that. He supposedly infused the totems with power that gave strength to whoever brought them together and unlocked their secrets."

"As opposed to just sticking them in the same bag."

"Right. They do nothing by themselves. There are a few different stories about how they work, most telling the same basics but with different outcomes. Shapeshifting, magical power, control over the elements, a wide range."

"Do they all say they need the key?"

"Yes." She flipped through her printed pages. "I only found one description of the key itself." She found the page and flipped it around for Grant to see the picture on it. It was a hand-drawn rendition of what looked like a diagram painted on leather. Four squares connected in a diamond pattern by filigree-style chains, with a few symbols in the center.

"So you'd obviously put the totems on each of the

squares." He pointed with a long finger. "Any idea what the symbols mean?"

"None at the moment. We should talk to someone who's expert in pictorial languages."

"Or magical arts."

He said it with such a straight face she thought he meant it. Then she glimpsed the twinkle in his eye. She said, "There are plenty of people who claim to be. Never know who might help."

"If you say so. Where the hell will we find someone like that?"

"I have some leads. Which one we follow depends on what you found."

"We'll get to that. Anything else?"

"Yeah." Zoe hadn't been thinking about this part, but when she remembered, a spot in the pit of her stomach went cold. It explained a lot she hadn't understood of the situation she'd been pulled into so long ago. "One source I found cited a set of rituals to do with the totems. I don't think they have any connection to the original maker. Anything that mentions his name talks about power of different sorts, but not…this kind of thing."

"What kind of thing?" His voice was kind, as if he'd guessed already.

"Sacrifices. Rape. Carving the symbols into living flesh. I think with Jordie…" She couldn't say it, not to Grant. But he had no qualms.

"They were practicing." It came out flat and emotionless, but Zoe recognized the pain behind his blue eyes.

"Right," she whispered. "And I was probably going to be part of the final ritual. That one required purity and innocence. Me at twelve…or Olivia now." She cleared her throat. "That's why they didn't abuse me—much."

Grant's jaw flexed, but he didn't show any emotion. Stone face, again. "What's this ritual supposed to get them?"

"Access to all kinds of things. Knowledge of true history, which will help them find lost objects."

"Treasure."

"A window to the spirit world, which can cloak them in darkness and stealth."

"To steal treasure."

"And a portal to other dimensions. Not to travel to, but to summon from."

"Summon what?"

She shrugged. The ridiculousness of it all didn't diminish her anxiety over the stupid things. "It was a little vague, but it sounded like, I don't know, weapons of some sort? Ways to kill without risk. Something like that."

Grant shoved to his feet. The chair scraped harshly across the floor. He kicked it back under the table as he started to pace the wide room.

"So basically, this set of rituals would make them all-powerful." He glared at her. "If the story is true."

"Hey, don't look at me like that," she protested. "I'm not going mystical on you. I'm just reporting what some people believe. As far as I'm concerned, the end result they're going for is irrelevant. It's the killing and raping people part I want to stop."

"And the forcing-you-to-help part."

She shook her head but couldn't meet his eyes. As she'd read about this stuff and it clicked more and more with what she remembered, the harder it had been not to slip back there. So many years fighting to be strong, decisive, balanced—so ridiculously easy to lose what she'd gained. It was fine during the day, but at night, in the dark hotel room, with people whooping and hollering outside her window, the past had pushed its way out. Every set of footsteps past her door had been someone coming to drag her somewhere she didn't want to be, and her dreams had been swirling nightmares of anxiety and helplessness. Worse were the ones where Olivia was the girl in the dirty bedroom, curled into a ball, frantic breaths puffing into sobs. Zoe always tried to reach her and could never move. Tried to scream for help, the sound no bigger than a high rasp.

Warm hands pulled her to her feet. Strong arms wrapped around her, and Grant's deep voice rumbled through his chest and into her ear. "You're not that person anymore," he assured her. His shirt felt damp, but when Zoe lifted her cheek she found the moisture was on her face. She was crying and didn't even know it.

"Dammit."

She tried to pull back but he held her tighter, cradling her and even rocking a little.

"I hate that they can reduce me to this. That they can make me afraid again. If they get their hands on—"

She was going to say "Olivia," but Grant apparently assumed she was going to say "me" and interrupted.

"They'll be sorry they ever tried." From reassuring to hard in a heartbeat, his voice actually stiffened her spine. "You are *not* the same person," he repeated. "You haven't been since about six months after you got home, when you made the decision to keep your parents out of your recovery."

She sighed and settled back into his arms, almost forgetting where she was. He was right. The first, awful therapist her parents got for her had made her feel ashamed, as if everything was her fault. He'd told her mother to smother her with love and caring, which to her mother meant feeding her endlessly, following her around the house, and sleeping on an air mattress in her room. He'd told her father she needed discipline, so whenever she lashed out or covered her fear with anger, he'd tried to lock her in her room, the only way he really knew *how* to apply discipline. Some might say it was better than physical, but to someone who had been abducted, chained, and locked away for a year, it was like she'd never escaped. So she did every night, climbing out her bedroom window like so many normal teenagers, yet not knowing what to do with the "freedom." When spring hit, bringing sunshine, warmth, and hope, she had demanded a new therapist. This one had supported her need to break from her parents emotionally and follow her own path of healing. She'd started reassuring her mother and behaving for her father, ensuring their guilt was appeased and allowing them to "put the past behind them" while she dealt, every day, with the remnants of her fears.

She sighed, loosening her grip from Grant's waist. "It's getting harder to be the person I've tried to become. I *hate* them," she said fiercely. "I hate that they can still make me feel like this."

"That's okay." He smoothed her cheek dry with his thumb. "Your strength is not about being fearless."

"It's about facing those fears. I know." She smiled up at him. "I remember the therapy. But it's not just about me…"

The words and her voice faded away. His mouth quirked a little, but he wasn't really looking at her. Or rather, he wasn't looking at her the same way she was looking at him. He swept his hand under her hair to push it back off her face, and his fingers trailed along the side of her neck, to the nape, where she'd always been sensitive. Her breath caught, his eyes met hers, and it was like someone turned on a brilliant flashlight in a dark room. *No!* yelled her brain, but her lips parted a yes, and Grant's head began to lower.

He stopped halfway to her mouth, his fingers now tight on the back of her head. "You're not committed to anyone right now. You broke your engagement."

Yes, but I love Kell and I'm still committed in my heart lined itself up in her brain, but only the "Yes" came out of her mouth.

"Good." He dropped the rest of the way, covering her lips with his, parting them immediately and diving in, tangling his tongue with hers, so much for finding their way back slowly, and dear lord, he was hot, and tasted the same, and smelled the same, except so much better, and his body felt the same against hers, except so much harder, driving desire into her from the bottom up, filling her with need, craving, desperation to banish the loneliness that had filled her in the weeks since she'd left Kell, and she kissed him back, God help her, as if she were dying and this was the last time she'd ever touch anyone, ever again.

Eventually, somehow, common sense tapped one of them on the shoulder. She wasn't sure which of them had stopped, only that he wasn't holding her anymore, and she was very, very sorry about that.

No! her brain yelled at her again. *You are not! You're sorry it* happened! *What do you think you're doing?*

The truth? She had no freaking clue.

* * *

Grant could barely stand to face Zoe. She stood there, unmoving, her eyes a deep green, wide, shocked. He didn't know what to say to her, didn't want to know what she was thinking. He couldn't apologize, couldn't walk away in this stupid excuse for a house that didn't even have a proper bathroom she could hide in.

"I think I'll go for that swim now," she said in a very small voice.

Relief infused every muscle. "Okay."

"I think it's best if you don't join me."

"Absolutely."

"I'll be back in…soon."

"Fine."

He didn't watch her leave the shack or cross the

sand. Witnessing the removal of her shirt and shorts would have killed him. But he could only restrain himself so long and moved to the sliding door to see what she was doing.

She stood hip deep in the small waves, sweeping her hands through the water and looking out into the ocean. He pushed the door open to lean against the jamb. She was too far away for him to see details, but the red-and-white two-piece was too modest to be called a bikini. Still, when she bent to splash water up her arms and across her torso, he could see how well it curved around her breasts and ass. She'd always had a well-proportioned body, not one shaped to perfection but not too skinny, either, with softness where a guy wanted it and no pokey sharp angles. She pushed out deeper into the water and dove under, coming up in a freestyle stroke that took her out twenty feet before she turned parallel to shore and swam down the beach a ways. Her body was like her personality—strong but yielding in the best ways.

The common sense that had stopped them in that mind-bending kiss told him to stop watching her now, to forget the kiss had happened. She didn't want him. He'd had his chance ten years ago and blown it. Or she had. Either way, they weren't together and weren't going to be.

But he didn't operate a lot on common sense. For the guys he worked against and with, common sense was just another rule to break. He operated on instinct and gut-level belief, and both told him that he and Zoe belonged together. He was going to fight for her.

Rightness surged through him. It didn't matter that the other party in the fight, whatever-his-name-was Stone, had no clue there even was one. Whatever honor Grant had was unique and didn't extend to fighting fair.

He was going to win her back.

Natalie J. Damschroder

Chapter Seven

Zoe didn't swim far, just a couple hundred yards down the beach, before flipping onto her back and letting the water float her in to a deserted stretch of shore. She just needed to be away from Grant. The situation. If she could get away from herself, she would.

Don't compare, she warned, but too late. Grant's passionate devouring of her was nothing like Kell's usual kisses. His need and desire were always apparent, but tempered by time, affection, tenderness. There was nothing tender about her old flame. Her body shuddered at the memory just before her head scraped sand.

She sat up in the shallows and wrapped her arms loosely around her knees, not seeing the sparkle of sunlight on the gentle water or the wheeling of the gulls overhead. The breeze cooled her wet skin, but she didn't feel cold. She didn't feel here at all.

Déjà vu hit like a thunderstorm. She'd felt like this before, when she first got back to her parents after her escape. Not part of the world she'd just been living in, but even less a part of her normal world.

She didn't want Grant. She wanted Kell. She didn't fit into a life where a shack was an acceptable way station between dangerous jobs—yet she felt so comfortable here. If things were different, she could see taking the next step with Grant, as easy as breathing. Her old life—her *real* life—seemed so far away.

Yet not so far away that she couldn't dredge it up. It was like being on vacation, sitting here with sand in her suit, tasting the salt water on her lips, and thinking about her company and employees and what she would likely face when she got back, and how Kell wouldn't have changed anything in the apartment, and being with him would feel safe and right.

How could two men both feel safe and right in two such totally different ways?

Sitting here was getting her exactly nowhere. But instead of rising and walking down the beach, she just pushed back out of the water and sat on the sand, letting her skin air dry. Letting her brain empty.

Trying not to think about the one deep truth that separated Grant from Kell. He *knew* her. Knew all of her. She'd never hidden anything from him like she'd hidden herself from Kell.

"You okay?"

She let a sigh through her lips. It figured Grant would follow her. At least he'd given her a *few* minutes to herself.

She didn't turn. "Fine."

A ragged, red-striped beach towel landed on the sand.

"Thanks."

When she didn't move, Grant said, "We didn't discuss what I found yet."

Right. The totems. The reason she was here, in this whirling confusion. And on this island. She sighed and stood, the towel in one hand. She was already mostly dry so she whisked the towel over her back and legs to get the sand off, then wrapped it around her waist for the walk back to Grant's shack. He fell into step beside her, about a foot away, and gave no sign that the kiss had meant anything to him.

You are not disgruntled about that.

"What did you find out, then?" she asked about halfway back.

"Not a heck of a lot, but enough, hopefully. I put out a lot of feelers that might still net something. It's amazing how much data is computerized now. Old rail routes, for one thing."

"Online?"

"No. I worked with a guy not too long ago who's one of those insane railway hobbyists. You know, the ones who take photos of every car that ever passes a certain spot, and go on road trips just to watch them, stuff like that. They keep records like birdwatchers do."

"I think we watched something about that on TV once."

"Yeah. Anyway, he doesn't have any business connection to the railroads, but he knows tons of people from his hobby research. God help us if the terrorists ever find out about him." He shook his head.

"Did you figure out what train I was on?" The

water rushed up over her feet, the tide coming in. Grant angled away from it, then back to her as it receded.

"That was easy. The FBI had already noted it in your file."

"What? You have my file?" She looked up at him. "The whole thing? How?"

"I worked with the feebs on my last job. An agent owed me a favor and gave it to me when I said it was personal."

"Great." Zoe tossed up her hands. "He's going to tell Henricksen. He will not be happy that we called attention to this."

"He's not going to tell Henricksen. As far as my friend knows, this is just an old case. And I didn't tell him why it was personal. It was pretty obvious."

"Oh." Of course. Grant and his brother would both be named in the file. "I'm sorry. I'm so self-centered."

"Nah. Self-focused, maybe."

She smiled at his attempt to soothe her but had to look away quickly when he smiled back, a full smile, not the half-quirk he usually gave.

"But knowing what train you got off of helped the FBI narrow down where you probably got on it, which helped me and my hobbyist friend figure out which train you put the totems on, and where that was going."

"And where was that?" She held her breath, hoping it had been near the end of its run.

"California."

"Shit."

"No kidding."

"So it's hopeless."

"No, it's never hopeless." He caught her hand on the backswing and gave it a quick squeeze, then released it. "It's a lot of ground to cover. But we have a narrow corridor to start in, at least."

"But it could have fallen out, been picked up…anything, anywhere along the line."

"We'll narrow it down more."

"How?"

She was getting agitated, because it seemed so fruitless. If she couldn't find them, knowing the most of anyone about where they'd gone, Pat and Freddie would have even less chance. Which meant they'd never find them, which meant they'd never stop trying. This would never end.

"My friend doesn't work for a railroad, but he has friends who do. They can check around, find out if anyone ever talked about finding something like the totems."

It was too much. Zoe stopped and spun down to the sand, slumping against her towel-covered legs.

Grant sank to a knee beside her. "What's wrong?"

"I was foolish to think we could get anywhere. That could take years, and it's so haphazard. *If* some guy was checking cars and found the bag and brought it home…*if* he still works there after a decade and a half, or *if* someone remembers him."

"It's not as hopeless as it seems." He stroked a hand down her damp hair. "They have employment records, schedules. We can do a targeted investigation.

If something's going to come up, it won't take long to do so."

"Another if," she sighed. "And what if it didn't get taken off the train?" She concentrated on the details, because the consequences were too much. If she spit out enough variables, they might hit on something they could act on. They had so little time. "What if it stayed in that car for a long time? Where did it go next? Where is it now?"

Grant's expression changed. Before it had been semi-stony, not revealing much but a hint of reassurance. Now it cleared—still stonyish, but more resolved, less like it was hiding something.

"You're right."

"I know."

"No, I mean about the rail car. Where it is now." He rose and pulled her to her feet, tugging her along behind him as he trudged toward the shack.

"That's not relevant. It's been too long. Hasn't it?" She tried to trot in the soft sand to keep up but twisted her foot. It didn't hurt, but she said, "Ow." Grant didn't slow. Apparently, he was skilled at assessing other people's injuries on the run, without even a glance. "I need to get my clothes."

He released her hand, which tingled as if its circulation had been cut off. Zoe shook it.

"Get them. I have a few things to look up, calls to make."

She detoured toward the water, hoping the incoming tide hadn't soaked her clothes. It was still a foot away, but closing in fast. She snatched up the shorts and shirt and hesitated. Did she want to put them on out here, where anyone could watch her reverse striptease, or take them inside where the lack of privacy was more intimate?

The question provided its own answer. She stepped into the shorts and pulled them up under the towel, then yanked the shirt over her head and pulled it down, grabbing the towel as it fell. She was going to be very uncomfortable the rest of the day, with the sand and salt and damp bathing suit. But hopefully the day wouldn't be that long.

When she got inside Grant was on the phone, his index finger pinning one of the maps on the table. Energy swirled in the air, but Zoe couldn't tell what kind. She circled around to stand next to him, leaning over to try to figure out the map. It covered the western half of the U.S., showing contour elevations and way more rail lines than she'd ever imagined possible. One set of rails in Wyoming looked like they formed a pentagram. Grant's finger was mostly covering a symbol in lower Utah, and he was making grunting sounds of assent or disagreement. After a minute, he thanked whoever it was and hung up.

"It's in Utah."

"The rail car."

"Yep."

The energy was excitement, and it slipped into her, tempered by the hopelessness that had taken up residence. "How do you know it's the right one?"

"The color, the placement on the train, its destination. You were able to open the door—that limits the possibilities."

"So who has it?"

He shrugged and started to gather up the papers. "Some guy who lives off the end of an old spur, which was close enough to make it affordable to get the car to his property. No idea what he did with it when he got it there, though." He glanced at her. "Why don't you go back and check out of the hotel. I'll find out about flights to Utah and meet you at the boat dock."

For some reason, his orders raised her hackles. "Wait a minute. You're not my boss."

"Yeah, and?"

"And you're suddenly in mission mode, ordering me around."

He looked ready to argue, but closed his mouth and nodded. "Okay. You're right. Input?"

"I'm going back to the hotel. Stop smirking." She smacked his shoulder. "I'm going to shower and pack before I check out, and *then* I'll meet you at the boat dock."

Grant nodded, his face mock grave, his eyes twinkling. "Much better plan."

Zoe rolled her eyes and stuffed her own papers into her bag. She didn't care what he thought. Being part of the plan, even if it only meant a minor modification, made her feel miles better. Her therapist—at least half of them—would have said she was asserting herself to combat any loss of control that would flash her back to the past. Some would call it healthy, others would have made her talk and talk to try to eliminate it.

Okay, enough. They'd earned their money. They didn't need to take up residence in her head. It was crowded enough in there as it was.

She slung the bag over her shoulder and headed out to her bike, taking her time as she rolled along the beach road. She had a feeling these would be the last moments of peace and lack of urgency for a long time. She wished she'd fished her hat out of her bag, though, because the sun beat down on her, and she was far enough from the water that the breeze had stilled. But she didn't think Grant was going to allow her a leisurely amount of time; she'd rather be waiting for him at the dock than the other way around. So she pedaled faster, both to ensure that and to get out of the sun.

She'd just crossed from the open beach-and-marsh area into the town when the back of her neck started to prickle.

The sensation threw her into the past again. While Pat and Freddie's prisoner, she had grown so used to near-constant watch that when she got home she'd always felt like it was still happening. She hadn't expected to ever stop feeling that way, but somewhere along the line she had, without even noticing it. Until now, when it was back.

She forced herself not to look around, but whenever she turned her head to check for traffic on a cross street, she scanned the groups of people clustered around storefronts and bar entrances and individuals walking up and down the street. She didn't see anyone she recognized, but that wasn't surprising and didn't mean someone wasn't there.

A few ideas for giving them the slip flitted through her mind, but she discarded them. There was no time. So she stuck to the original plan and returned the bike, crossed over to the hotel, and went up to her room, where she quickly showered and packed. She checked out and left the hotel only twenty minutes after she came in, about forty minutes after she'd left Grant's.

Zoe was chagrined to find him standing halfway down the boat dock, negotiating with one of the captains for passage to the nearest island with an airstrip.

"Hey." Grant handed the captain some money and turned to her while the captain hopped onto his boat and started prepping it. "Joaquin's going to take us— what's wrong?"

"Quiet." It was a struggle not to look over her shoulder. "I think someone's following me."

Grant narrowed his eyes at Joaquin. "Hey, amigo!" He stepped closer to the boat and asked the man a question in Spanish. The guy shrugged and shook his head, then rattled something back. Grant said "*sí*" and turned to lounge casually against the tie-post.

"What was that?" Zoe watched him scanning the dock from under his hat.

"With you thinking you were being watched, it seemed a little too easy that this guy was ready and eager to take us over. But I don't think he's lying."

"About what? What did you ask him?"

"If anyone paid him already to take us."

"And he said? Besides no."

"He asked if we still wanted to go over. Said his cousin had a boat further down the dock if we didn't like his."

She nodded and waited. Joaquin disappeared below decks, and a minute later the engines powered up. Smoke floated out of the hatch.

"That's encouraging," she muttered.

Grant twisted to look. "Just oil burning off."

"Like I said."

He grinned. "I don't see anyone who's paying you extra attention. What made you think they were? You see someone?"

She shook her head and rubbed the back of her neck. "No. Just a feeling."

He looked up at the second-story windows of the buildings flanking the dock. "Couple of kids up there might have eyes on you."

Zoe wandered in a random pattern, like someone bored with waiting, until she could see who he was talking about. Two dark-haired, white-shirted young boys leaned against a wrought-iron railing across a doorway above a fish shop. They saw her looking and immediately straightened, but instead of disappearing inside, they called to her and waved their arms. She caught the words "pretty lady" in Spanish and winced.

"If they're watching me, they don't care that I noticed." She waved back, sending them into spine-bending swoons.

"They could just be sophisticated about it. Pat and Freddie didn't mind using kids," he pointed out.

"True." She watched the boys for a minute. They

put on a show for her, calling compliments, hooting, jeering down at a group of slightly older teens on the sidewalk below, who ignored them. It was a nice diversion until Joaquin told them he was ready, but when she turned, her instincts screamed at her that someone was close. A threat.

She spun, but her conscious and subconscious definitions of "close" apparently didn't match. No one was within ten feet of them.

"Come on, hon." Grant patiently held his hand out to help her onto the boat. She glared at it for a second, really wanting to climb on herself, but he was setting up a cover. Being argumentative would call attention to them, and that was the last thing they needed.

No, she thought a moment later. The last thing they needed was company.

They'd barely settled onto the cushion-covered aft bench when two guys lightly leaped from the dock to the rail of the boat, then onto the deck.

"Howdy!" The taller one tipped an actual cowboy hat. His boots clicked as he crossed the planks to them, and one thumb hooked through the belt loop of his jeans, as if out of habit. "You folks taking the tour?"

Grant gave him the stone face. "No."

"Too bad. We love just motorin' around these islands. The uninhabited ones are really cool."

Zoe tuned him out, leaving him to Grant, and watched his buddy. This guy seemed less out of place, wearing a tank top under an unbuttoned, short-sleeved shirt and board shorts. He said something to Joaquin, handed him some money, and wandered over to join his friend.

"Hey, sweetie. Wanna go up front and watch for dolphins?" he asked the cowboy.

Zoe waited until they'd done so before she murmured, "We're in trouble."

"Yeah. If they're gay, so am I."

She eyed the dock. The boat was slowly rotating away from it. "We could jump back."

"Not a good idea."

She didn't argue. They'd already missed the short window. "Now what?"

"We lose them later."

"What's the plan? The original one," she added.

"Boat to the next key, small plane to Miami, flight out of there tonight to Salt Lake City. Layover in Atlanta, though, so I can work with that if we don't shake them on the way."

They watched the "couple" lean against the port-side bow rail, beach-boy leaning on his elbow and facing aft, where he'd have a better view of Grant and Zoe than of any sea life.

"I'm guessing you haven't seen them before." Grant kept his voice low, though Zoe could barely hear him and didn't think the other guys had any chance at all.

"No, never saw them. They don't seem like Pat and Freddie's kind of crew."

"Ex-cons, cons, or soon-to-be cons."

"Well, yeah, but more than that. Zealots. These guys don't have that weird light in their eyes." She tipped her head back to enjoy the sun but left her eyes slit to watch the two.

"Maybe Pat met them in prison or something."

"Maybe." He was resourceful. And who knew? Maybe he'd branched out. "Are they a danger to us?"

"I don't think anyone is a danger right now. If these guys know you're on the trail of the totems, there won't be any reason to hurt you or anyone else."

She wanted to believe that, but was afraid it was too simple. "Do you think that would change if they lose track of us? Would they try to grab someone as insurance?"

She appreciated that Grant didn't give her the easy, expected answer. He was silent as the boat reached open water and picked up speed. She grabbed at her hat as the wind caught the brim and tightened the strap at the back.

"They might," he finally said. "They'd go for the most vulnerable, the one you care about the most."

Her involuntary whimper shouldn't have been audible, but Grant's head turned slightly toward her and his hand twitched, as if he'd arrested the instinct to comfort.

"I have someone on her," he said.

Her lips parted, her eyebrows rising. "On who?"

"Olivia. An old partner agreed to be extra eyes."

Tears welled and she gripped his forearm in relief and gratitude. "When did you do that?"

He shrugged and folded his arms, removing her grip. "The day you got here. I know you said you told her parents so they could take steps, but this is added insurance. Just in case."

"Thank you." Her voice cracked, and a little of the tension left Grant's body.

"So it doesn't matter at this point if they keep track of us. We'll play it by ear, okay?"

She nodded and settled back on the bench, closing her eyes and shifting her hat to cover the expressions she couldn't hide.

"You worried about your parents?"

"A little." They were pretty innocent, considering. Not child-like, but someone she'd want to protect. "I should call them."

"When did you last talk to them?"

"The day I came down here."

"How'd they sound?"

"Normal. I don't think anyone had contacted them. They were relieved it was off TV and didn't have anything more to say about it."

"Did you tell them about your broken engagement?"

"I didn't tell them I was engaged in the first place."

"Oh, really?" He said it like that was a telling statement, and she bristled.

"Yes, really. I didn't have a chance. I got engaged and went to a conference the next day. When I got back, the FBI was in my office. I didn't want to mar something so happy when something so distracting was going on." Kell's mother hadn't wasted any time putting the announcement in the paper, but by the time Zoe realized she was doing it, it was already out. Luckily, her own mother stuck to the crime section of the Boston papers and hadn't seen it.

Grant nodded, but she saw something in his expression that she didn't like.

"What?"

"Nothing. Heads up." The cowboy and beachy guy were heading back toward them.

"Getting choppy." The cowboy dropped to the bench next to Zoe and crossed his ankles way out in front of him. As he folded his arms and tilted his hat down over his face, his friend settled next to Grant.

"So," said Beachy, "If you're not taking the tour, where ya headin'?"

Zoe leaned forward to smile at him. "You know how honeymooners are. We just go where the wind takes us."

Beachy's smile dropped a millimeter. "Sure, sure. Sorry to bother you guys."

"Not at all." She smiled wider. "What about you two? Intimate vacation?"

She'd have sworn Beachy barely restrained himself from grimacing. But he managed. "Sure thing."

She turned to the cowboy and started to ask where they were from, but a snore drifted out from under the hat, barely heard over the rumble of the boat's engines. Barely, but still heard, which made her suspect he wasn't really sleeping.

She hoped Grant was planning behind that granite face, because she wasn't sure if they'd decided to string their followers along or ditch them. And her parents…she pulled her phone out of her pocket and checked for a signal. She actually had one, which surprised her, but the engine was too noisy to call her parents now, even if they didn't have eavesdroppers.

Half an hour passed. The exhaust and noise started to give her a headache. She stood and moved to the bow, staying to the left of the bridge window. The fresher breeze there helped. She closed her eyes and let her mind phase out. Even floating in that state of non-awareness, she knew when someone approached, and she knew that someone was Grant.

It was enough to make her question everything about her life.

He came up close behind her, half trapping her with one hand on the rail. "So what do you want to do?" he said an inch from her ear. His scent, salty and hot, surrounded her. Images flashed into her mind that had nothing to do with the totems.

She had to turn her head so he'd be able to hear her response. "You mean about letting them follow us?"

His two-day beard growth scratched against her cheek as he nodded.

"Let's pretend we haven't guessed for a little while. They probably won't step up their game then. And I can check on my parents. Make sure they're okay." She wasn't sure what she'd tell them, but somehow she'd get them to safety. Just to simplify the equation, in case Pat got frustrated that Olivia was protected.

"The plane we're taking to Miami is owned by a friend of mine," Grant said. "Do you want me to change that, get something public so they can stick with us?"

She shook her head. "We don't have to make it too easy. We'll just mention Miami where they can hear us."

He nodded again, his breath feathering her hair, and she forced herself not to move away and cast doubt on their honeymooner story. Yeah, like that was hard. Her body was certainly happy where it was, with her shoulder pressed against Grant's chest and his leg brushing hers whenever the boat bounced into the trough of a wave.

It was the best and worst kind of torture she could imagine. Relief warred with disappointment, both coated with self-disgust, when their destination loomed ahead. They watched the captain expertly dock the boat, then headed back to the gate to disembark. Cowboy and Beachy joined them, making room for the captain to toss the tie-off ropes to a couple of guys on the dock.

"I'm hungry, honey," Zoe told Grant. "Is there a place to eat on this island?"

"No, I've got a surprise for you in Miami," he told her. "A sweet little place. You'll love it."

She beamed at him, hoping it looked real. "I hope it won't take long to get there."

"Nah. Short flight. Private plane." He waggled his eyebrows. "So we can get going right away."

"Excellent."

Out of the corner of her eye, she glimpsed the "couple" sharing a look. It had worked.

They didn't see the duo after that, not in Miami or on the plane. When Grant caught her looking over her shoulder for the eighth time since they'd disembarked in Atlanta, he assured her it was okay that they hadn't.

"They don't want to make us suspicious, and running into them here would do that."

"I suppose." But she couldn't stop looking. Not just for Cowboy and Beachy, but for anyone who looked like they were too casual, or watching them too carefully, or following them, or even, hell, speaking too animatedly—or not animatedly enough—into their cell phones.

"I'm turning paranoid," she complained. They were at their gate, surrounded by people, and she couldn't look in every direction at once. She moved to a seat that was angled around a center table, putting her forty-five degrees to Grant. It let her look out the window without moving her away from where he could see the whole concourse. "When is our next flight again?" She was having trouble holding on to details.

"We board in half an hour."

She sat for a few minutes, not looking around, not looking at Grant, but also not able to stop her knee from bouncing and her mind from racing in a hundred different directions. What if they'd lost their followers completely? She'd used her credit card to buy their plane tickets to give them something to trace, but maybe that was a step too far. What if they got someone to Utah first? Not that there was going to be anything in that train car for them to find. But if not, that meant they were wasting time and money, themselves.

God. She shot to her feet. "I'm going to call my parents." She pulled out her phone and started to move away.

"Don't go far." Grant continued to recline in his seat, still sporting the beach bum look. He'd changed into relaxed-fit jeans worn to holes in places and a loose, short-sleeved button-down shirt over a t-shirt. The baseball hat was turned backwards, the brim scrunched down over his wavy hair. He hadn't shaved in a couple of days. In short, he looked delicious. If Zoe had just spotted him as she walked down the concourse, she'd have tripped over someone's suitcase because she'd be unable to look away from him.

Just like that woman there. Well, she didn't trip over a suitcase so much as walk into a TSA agent. He didn't look very happy.

Zoe sighed and leaned against a pillar while she speed-dialed her parents' house. The phone only rang once before her mother answered. She was never very far from it.

"Zoe?"

She grimaced. Yay for caller ID. "Yeah, Mom, it's me. How are you?"

"Oh, darling, it's so good to hear your voice. We haven't talked to you in days."

She didn't point out that they usually went a couple of weeks between calls. "I know. I'm—I've been busy." She'd almost said she was traveling, but caught herself. She wanted the bad guys to know where she was, but it wouldn't benefit her parents. It would open up questions and make them vulnerable if someone decided they had information. "Work's been crazy," she added. "How are you?"

Again, her mother avoided the question. "Sadie Milner asked about you on Monday. No, wait. It had to be Sunday, because your father skipped church. Yes, I saw her on the steps there, not the grocery store. I ran into Barbara in the grocery store. She asked about you, too."

Zoe let her mother ramble on and tried to determine if something was wrong or if she was projecting. It was hard to tell. Her mother had a nervous demeanor in the best of times, which they hadn't had in sixteen years. It had gotten worse as she progressed into her sixties.

"And how's Dad?" she asked when her mother took a breath.

"A touch of a cold, actually, dear, and you know, at his age, that can get serious." Her father had just turned seventy. "He's taking his vitamin C and echinacea like a good boy, though, and Sally at the pharmacy said zinc and…oh, what was it…?"

"Garlic?"

"Right! Garlic can help, too. More as a preventive, she said, but maybe it could shorten how long he has his symptoms this time. So, you know."

Okay. Time to dig a little. "So, who else have you talked to, Mom? Anyone calling that doesn't normally? I hope you're not getting strange phone calls. Like pranksters."

"Are you?" Her voice quavered. "How dare they! You should get an unlisted number. I swear, the nerve of—"

"No, no, Mom, I'm not getting prank calls." That

was the truth, though having a new, unlisted number helped. She hoped Kell wasn't getting any, though. Crap. She hadn't thought of that. "I was just hoping you weren't. You know, they didn't really give my name on the national news, just locally, back in Ohio." The small town they'd moved to in Kentucky was far enough away from their old town that her parents didn't get those local broadcasts.

"Oh, good." She heaved a sigh. "Well, we did have some calls in the beginning, you know, some well-wishers, and some people who pretended to be."

"I know, you told me that last week." She couldn't keep the impatience out of her voice. "I mean, is anyone bothering you *now*."

"Oh, no, dear, no one has called in a while. Except, you know, friends." Suddenly, her tone turned cagey. It was a tone Zoe hadn't heard in a while. "You know, what makes it all easier is having your father here. You can get through anything with the right man at your side."

Zoe gritted her teeth. "Remember Kell, Mom? You don't need to worry about me."

Her mother was silent for a few seconds. "You haven't talked about Kellen in a few weeks. I thought maybe something had happened."

She swallowed back hysterical laughter. "So you were hinting? Doing a little subtle digging?"

"I am your mother. It's what we do." Zoe could hear the smile in her voice and relaxed.

"Okay. No, nothing's happened." She managed to get the lie out without her voice going all tight and squeaky. Everything seemed to be normal at her mother's end. If someone had approached her, she wouldn't be able to hide it. Not even behind subtle digging. Zoe chatted with her until Grant signaled that it was time to board, and rang off feeling much better about that end of things.

For now, anyway.

Natalie J. Damschroder

Chapter Eight

The four-hour flight passed uneventfully. Grant slept. Zoe tried to, but had trouble turning off her awareness of him. It wasn't throat-drying need or muscle-inspired lust, only a sensation down the right side of her body that he was close. A tuning in when he shifted or made a noise in his sleep. Just enough to keep her brain from drifting away.

So when they landed and got off the plane at the Salt Lake City terminal, she was slightly on edge and in need of a few moments to herself.

"Hey! Some of us don't have camel humps," she called after Grant when he headed straight for the main entrance. He turned, frowning at her.

"I have to go the bathroom?" She waved a hand in that direction. He nodded, and she grumbled all the way into the stall. "Thanks ever so much for your gracious permission."

She was glad he couldn't hear her griping. She wouldn't have gotten even this far without him, and it wasn't his fault she couldn't turn off this awareness.

It wasn't hers, either. She straightened and stared

at herself in the mirror. It wasn't her fault. Chemistry was natural. Uncontrollable. The side of her mouth quirked up in her reflection. For once, not being able to control something made her feel better.

So all she had to do was ignore it. Pretend it didn't exist.

When she came out of the bathroom a few minutes later, Grant was leaning against the wall, his expression lazy under the brim of his cap, but his eyes sharp. Her pulse picked up speed at the sight of him. She ignored it.

"See anyone?" she asked.

He shook his head, pushed off the wall, and started walking. "Do you want to get a hotel room first, rest a bit?"

"You mean hotel *rooms*, don't you?" She emphasized the S, then kicked herself. She sucked at pretending.

"Whatever. Do you? You didn't sleep much on the plane."

"How do you know? You did."

He just slanted a look at her.

"No, I'm fine. Let's just find this rail car."

"Pushing yourself isn't going to do anybody any good."

Zoe walked faster. She didn't want to argue, but the clock was ticking. "I'm fine," she repeated.

"Hey." Grant grabbed her arm and yanked her to a halt.

Before he could say anything, a man charged at them from the right, roaring. "Get your hands off of her!"

Zoe cried out as the man body-slammed Grant, ripping his hand off her arm. He blocked the attacker's swing, but before he could throw a punch, she yelled, "No! Stop!"

Both men actually froze. Kell looked at her, but Grant didn't take his eyes off the other man. She stood panting, even though she hadn't been the one fighting, and stared at the sudden collision of her two worlds.

"It's okay," she said, not knowing what else to do. "He's with me."

"Who?" both men asked.

"I guess...both of you." She blew out a frustrated breath. Joy twisted with shock and fear in a queasy tangle. "Kell, what are you doing here?" She hated how harsh it sounded, but they were being tracked, if not outright watched. His appearance could undo everything. She had to get rid of him, fast.

Grant dropped his arm from where it was braced against Kell's. "This is your fiancé?" He eyed Kell speculatively.

"Ex-fiancé." For a second, Zoe tried to see him through Grant's eyes. He looked like the lawyer he was, in khakis and a polo and Italian loafers. An expensive travel tote lay on its side a few feet away. Even after his lunge at Grant, his hair was perfectly combed and expertly cut. He was the antithesis of Grant's scruffiness.

"I'm obviously at a disadvantage." Kell, too, had dropped his arms, but he glowered at Grant. "Who is this guy, and why was he manhandling you?"

"Grant Neely," he growled, "also ex-fiancé, and I was just stopping her from running off. She's cranky right now."

"Oh, for cripes sake." She stomped over to them. "Grant and I knew each other when we were teenagers. I never accepted your proposal," she reminded him. "He's helping me with…something." It was probably too late to keep Kell out of this, but she had to try. "Here's a tip: don't tell a cranky woman that she's cranky."

Grant grinned, but Kell still glowered.

"What's going on?" He used his courtroom voice. Zoe took a deep breath to keep fear from coming out as annoyance, then decided to let it fly. Maybe she could argue him into leaving.

"What's going on is none of your business. We're not engaged anymore."

"Are you with this guy?" He gestured toward Grant without looking at him, somehow managing to be dismissive but not losing the tension in his body. His tone made clear that he meant *with*, not just "with."

The earlier kiss flashed through her brain. "Not romantically," she said, not sure if it qualified as a lie. She could have said yes, because hurting Kell would make things simpler, but she'd done enough of that. "He's just an old friend who has the connections and skills I need to solve a problem."

"And I don't."

"No." The word came out softer than she'd intended.

"Are you in danger?" He moved closer to her.

"She could be," Grant answered. Kell didn't look at him until he continued, "She doesn't want you to be part of this."

"You tell me she could be in danger and then to stay out of it? What kind of man do you think I am?"

"I didn't tell you to stay out of it," Grant corrected. "It's her call. And I'm waiting for you to show me."

She didn't get it. "Show you what?"

Kell did. "What kind of a man I am." He shoved his hand through his hair. "Zoe, you owe me an explanation."

"No, I don't." She really did, but... Hell, she might as well be honest. "You're in more danger than I am." She swallowed Olivia's name, unsure if that would send him away or make him more determined to stay.

His brows knitted. "From whom?"

Grant rolled his eyes at the grammar, or maybe at his cluelessness, but it wasn't Kell's fault he didn't know anything.

"It's a long story," she tried.

But Kell just nodded. "Okay, then. Let's go somewhere we can talk." He turned and walked over to his bag, bent to grab the strap—

—and something zoomed past, right where his head had been.

Grant didn't give them time to react. Before Zoe was done gasping, he'd grabbed her arm and pulled her behind him as he pushed at Kell.

"Run."

Kell hesitated long enough for them to pass him, putting himself between Zoe and whoever was behind them. Grant led the way, and they dashed past the baggage claim area and toward the exit. She strained to hear running feet while fighting not to look back and slow them all down.

They rushed through the automatic doors. Grant paused a split second to look both ways, then led them right, past the cars dropping off and picking up people. They leapt over a low pile of luggage—one, two, three, Zoe holding her breath but clearing it without a stumble—and ran past a line of people lumbering toward the cab line.

Grant ignored the attendant who approached and yanked open the first taxi's door, shoving Zoe in and sliding in after her. Through the window, she watched Kell hand the attendant some money before he climbed quickly into the front seat.

"Downtown," Grant barked at the driver. A seasoned older woman, she put the vehicle in gear and pulled out without looking, cutting off a shuttle. Horns blared behind them. Zoe drew a deep breath, afraid to consider them safe. Grant studied the traffic behind them through the back window.

"Two men, average-looking, kinda brown hair, one darker than the other," the driver said. He turned and met her eyes in the rearview mirror. She continued, "They ran down the sidewalk after you. One kicked someone's suitcase when we pulled away. Said a few bad words, too. Wanna hear them?"

"No, thanks." Grant gave her his crooked grin. "What were they wearing?"

"Jeans, normal shirts, you know. Nondescript. One

blue, one gray shirt. No hats or glasses."

He laughed. "Impressive. You get people on the run often?"

"You'd be surprised." Her eyes crinkled as she smiled back at him in the mirror.

"Did they get a cab?"

"Nope. Georgie made them get in line."

"We were lucky," Zoe murmured. Her body eased into the seat behind her as the tension drained out of Grant.

"Not lucky," he said. "Smooth. Thanks," he told Kell. "Quick thinking, paying Georgie to intercept. You okay? Did it hit you?"

Kell half turned to look at them, but his gaze was mostly on Zoe. "Fine. It missed. You see what it was?"

Grant shook his head. "Something heavy. It thudded, then clattered as it went across the floor. I didn't see who threw it, so don't bother asking."

Zoe closed her mouth and looked out the window. She'd never seen the Rockies from the ground, only flying over, and the way these towered over the city ahead of them, practically glowing in the setting sun, put a feeling in her chest she couldn't describe. Awe, probably. She'd have to come back here someday, for vacation or business. It deserved to be enjoyed, not careened through.

"We're nearing downtown," the driver broke the silence. "Where to?"

"Any hotel will be fine," Grant told her.

"Something with suites," Kell added, then murmured something Zoe couldn't hear.

Zoe bit her lower lip and concentrated on the mountains. She had a ton of questions for Kell, including how he'd found her and what he was doing there. But she didn't want to ask them because if he answered, she'd have to give him answers to his own questions. Questions that would take a lot longer to answer, and hurt more. And probably some about Grant that she didn't know the answers to, anyway.

She remained subdued until the car pulled into a driveway in front of a gorgeous marble building. A doorman in a tan uniform opened her door and handed her out. She smiled uneasily. She wasn't dressed for this place, and neither was Grant. Kell must have given the driver the name of this hotel, but how he knew about it, she had no idea.

Worse than their appearance was how much the rooms would cost. She couldn't let either man pay for his own space. They were both here because of her. But more than one night here would severely deplete her cash, and though she had plenty of savings she could access, doing so would leave too much of a trail. They wanted to make their pursuers feel like they had tabs on them, not point neon arrows at themselves.

Kell paid the driver and closed his door, then turned to Zoe. He must have read what she was thinking, because he stepped closer and murmured, "I had a reservation here already. Tanicia made it for me when I left. We can register under the firm, not in your name. Okay?"

She reluctantly nodded. She didn't know if the people following them would know it was Kell who'd joined them. If they did, the firm registration gave them something to track that was connected to her, but distant enough to maybe take a little time to nail down.

"After you, then." Grant motioned at the doors, waving away a staff member who reached for their bags. Kell narrowed his eyes at Grant but, apparently deciding there was no downside, spun and led the way. Grant and Zoe stood back from the desk while Kell registered. They headed for the elevators before he did, so it wasn't obvious they were together. Grant guided Zoe the whole way, telling her in a very low voice what Kell was doing. The precaution should have made her feel better—his outwardly casual touches on her arms and back and the motion of his lips near her ear had a dual effect that was far from calming. Part of her felt warm and zingy, enjoying the intimacy. The rest of her looked in from outside, knowing the whole charade had to be driving Kell insane.

When they got in the elevator Kell handed Grant a key card. "You have the room next to us."

"I thought we were doing a suite," Zoe protested. "I can't afford two rooms."

"You're not paying," the men said together.

"I decided a suite isn't practical," Kell explained. "These rooms are spacious, with sitting areas. We can still talk comfortably, and this way, no one has to sleep on the couch."

She couldn't really argue. Not without using words like "sexual tension" and "complicated feelings" and "damn, I'm horny." She thought about taking a room for herself, pictured the two men sharing a bed, and snickered.

"Okay, fine." She sounded so ungrateful. "Thank you for doing this."

"Don't thank me." He waited as the doors opened and Grant leaned out first to check the hallway. "Just tell me what the hell is going on."

She sighed. "It's a long story," she repeated.

"I'm not going anywhere."

Grant stopped at the third door on the right. "This is me. I'm running out to pick up a few things. You'll have about an hour, then we need to plan."

Zoe thanked him and followed Kell into their room. How the hell was she going to handle this? Sharing a bed with him, when she'd broken their engagement and not too long ago had been involved in a steamy kiss with Grant, didn't seem like the best idea. Then they cleared the entryway and she halted at the sight of two double beds.

"I thought that's what you'd want," Kell said. He set the keycard envelope on a small table and motioned into the room. "Do you need to do anything before we start?"

She could shower to give herself time to think about what to say, but they didn't have time for stalling. "No."

"Okay, then." He walked across the room and dropped onto the love seat under the window. "Why don't you start at the beginning?"

She didn't move. "You shouldn't sit in front of the window."

"We're ten stories up."

"There's another tall hotel across the street." They hadn't gotten the mountain view side.

He didn't move, and she heaved yet another sigh. "It's a *very* long story."

"Then you'd better sit down."

She chose a chair on his right and closed her eyes. "I never wanted you involved in this. I thought it was long past, something that couldn't touch us. I'm sorry."

He didn't respond. Afraid to see what he was feeling on his face, she looked down at the rich wool carpet and began.

"I was abducted when I was twelve years old."

Kell didn't move, but the absolute stillness of his body told her of his shock. He didn't say anything, though, and she wasn't sure if she was relieved or disappointed.

She shifted on the seat, crossing her legs, but they immediately uncrossed, setting her feet flat on the floor. "A woman, Fredricka Thomashunis — Freddie — saw me outside the grocery store. I'd run out to get something from the car. She dragged me into a van and drugged me so I couldn't fight or get away." She jerked to her feet and paced in the archway between the bedroom and the sitting area. It was so similar to when she was in therapy, she almost expected Kell to be taking notes when she glanced at him.

"The woman who took me was married, kind of. Not legally, and not in any recognized religion, but it was a marriage to them. They kept me tied or chained, usually with a chemical camping toilet and a bowl of water in the room." It was odd what details came out, her mouth working ahead of her brain. She'd never told her story like this, to someone who knew absolutely nothing about it. She'd always thought knives would carve chunks out of the adult she'd created, but it was more like a melting, as past and present began to shift and merge. The idea could have been frightening, but instead she felt…a hint of peace.

"How long?" The question was low, raw, and pulled her out of her head and back into the lush room.

"They took me just after my twelfth birthday and I escaped just after my thirteenth." Memories began to reel out ahead of her, surrounding her, so that she could almost smell the rags that made up her bed and hear Freddie's cold laughter. She had to get through this faster. "During that time they had kind of a gang. They were after something important to them. These…totems. One of their people tried to get out of it, but they grabbed his little brother and cut off his earlobe."

"Grant's earlobe."

She nodded, unsurprised. Even though Grant kept his hair long enough to hide the damage, it wasn't completely invisible. And Kell was a smart guy. He'd probably made all kinds of connections already.

"He lived a town over from me. We'd never met until that night, and then only for a few minutes before they showed Jordie what they'd do." She told him that Jordie somehow got the totems, and the horrors of the celebration that night.

"I couldn't stay there anymore, but I was scared to

try to leave. I'd tried a few times in the beginning, and they always caught me." Her arm twitched, the skin burning as if the rough ropes they'd bound her with had materialized. They'd kept them tight for weeks, until finally, when they gradually loosened them to give her a little freedom of movement, to use the toilet and wash up and eat her own food, she stopped trying to get away.

"The next day, we went to a rail yard where they were going to meet someone who had a key of some kind, something to do with the totems. They left me in a room with the totems in a bag. They thought I was woozy from the drugs they gave me whenever we moved. But Pat loved action-adventure movies. I'd watched a ton of them over the year, and read a lot of adventure novels too. There was nothing else for me to do, and they didn't care because it kept me quiet, when Freddie wasn't indulging her twisted idea of motherhood." She suppressed a shudder and hoped Kell didn't ask. Describing the ways Freddie twisted normal things like hair-brushing and breakfast-making wouldn't do it justice. She'd never been able to articulate the awful feelings in the pit of her stomach, the absolute wrongness that went beyond the falsity.

"The movies and books gave me ideas. About how to pretend I was taking pills without taking them. About hidden exits and how to hide. So I sucked up all the courage I could and found an access door behind some file cabinets. I managed to squeeze through, tossed the totems into an open rail car, and hopped on another one on a different train that was just getting ready to move. A few hours later, I found a police officer in a town, and blah blah blah." She stopped and faced him, bracing for his questions. But instead of asking them right away, he stood and reached for her. Without thinking about it, she jerked back. Hurt flashed through his eyes.

"I'm sorry! It was—"

"No, it's okay." He sat back down. "This is hard for you, sharing something you kept secret for so long."

Was that a dig? He had to be hurt and angry that she'd lied to him, and had every right to be. But she knew they'd get to that and simply nodded.

"Why did they take you specifically? Do you know?"

Her lips twitched. He was starting with the lawerly questions. "Freddie—the 'wife'—was kind of obsessive about being a mother." She swallowed hard. "She home schooled me. Kind of. Pretended she was teaching me. They were pretty messed-up people. Are. *Are* messed-up people." She folded her arms and paced again, more slowly. "We figured out that they had plans with the totems that required—well, a sacrifice. I think I was supposed to be for that."

"God, Zoe." He sat forward and rubbed his hands over his face. "Why didn't you ever tell me about this? It's been two years. We're *engaged*."

"Because it was past!" She tossed up her hands and sat back down on the chair next to the love seat. "I worked very hard to get through it, to make sure it didn't ruin my whole life. I was afraid it would change us, when it had nothing to do with what we have."

Kell raised his head. "And neither did Grant?"

She flushed, but forced herself to meet his gaze. "No."

"But you left me and went to him."

She'd known it would come to that, as soon as she'd seen him at the airport, but hadn't thought he'd go there so fast. "That's not the way it is." But of course she thought of the kiss, of the way Grant had touched her and talked to her and stayed near her, maintaining a kind of casual intimacy, ever since. And she was sure Kell could see some of that on her face. She owed him the truth, or at least as much of it as she understood.

"You were engaged to him."

She explained about their summers, how they'd helped each other through the aftermath and fell in love. And that it just didn't work out.

"That was then," he pointed out. "I can see what's happening now, Zoe."

She shook her head. "It's not like that. I mean…" *Truth, Zoe.* "Okay, yes, there's still some attraction between us, and the history will always be there. But it doesn't mean anything. It's pretty clear we live in different worlds."

Kell's brow furrowed. "I don't know, you seem to fit together okay."

She drew in a short breath, stunned by how that felt like a little needle to her heart. "Are you saying I don't fit in our world?"

"Of course not. I don't even know what you mean by that. I'm just saying you seem comfortable together."

"Oh." She shrugged and looked back at the floor. "Time out of time, and all that. This isn't my real life." So why did her voice lack conviction?

"Is anything?" He shifted toward the end of the love seat, closer to her, and let his wrists dangle off his knees so his fingers were a scant inch from her tightly folded hands. "Our life wasn't real. Your work life wasn't. Did you know—" He cut himself off and shook his head. "You can't break yourself into parts like that and have what you share be complete."

A week ago, she wouldn't have agreed. She'd have said she'd done it quite successfully. But now that she'd seen what happened when those compartment walls came down, she couldn't deny the truth of it.

Complete. The word felt foreign in her brain, but the melting she'd started when she began her story whispered to her that it wasn't impossible. She could find it, maybe. It wasn't too late.

But it was a faint hope, one that couldn't grow under the weight of what she still had to do. However Kell reacted to all this, nothing could be repaired until she got Pat and Freddie out of her life once and for all.

He let the silence roll for a moment, then asked, "Why did you leave me? Why didn't you trust me?"

Another crack in her heart. She managed to explain, through a throat that kept tightening with tears she refused to release. She told him about the stories behind the totems, hinted at the rituals she suspected they had planned with her at the center. Disgust carved itself into his face, and she quickly moved on, explaining the messages she kept getting from Freddie as well as the photos and the threats that didn't sound like threats, trying to make her do what they wanted.

"So you're doing it anyway. What they want."

"No!" She turned at a knock on the door. "I'm trying to finish it." She saw Grant through the peephole and released the chain and bar lock so he could come in. "Pat and Freddie want me to lead them to the totems. They have awful intentions." Her throat tightened as she let Grant lock the door behind himself and went back to stand near Kell. *Tell him about Olivia.* But her brain balked, and instead she said, "They could bring attention to me, to us, and the attention, the scandal…"

"You can't be that stupid."

Zoe reeled. Kell stood, his fists clenched. He didn't even nod at Grant, who hovered in the small foyer.

"What did you just say?" But the protest was so weak it squeaked. Inside, everything was red, frantic, fluttering at the edges, obliterating any hopes she'd had that she could go back to her life. As soon as she told him Olivia was a target, and that she'd kept it to herself, it would be over. He'd walk, and he'd never forgive her.

So she just kept being stupid.

Kell came around the coffee table and stalked to her. "You don't honestly think I'd rather lose you than have people *talk* about us."

"It would be more than that!"

"Like what?" he scoffed.

"Like losing clients at your law firm. Maybe losing

your job. Being in the papers. Your parents shunned at the club."

"That's not what you really think," he said in a softer tone. "You know none of that would happen, and that I couldn't care less about reputation. That isn't the real reason you left me." His eyes flicked to Grant and back to her, clearly expecting her former fiancé to be the reason.

"No, that's not—"

"Your inability to trust me isn't important right now." The softness was gone. His blue eyes were so dark, so intense, and pinned her so hard her restless legs went still. "I know you're keeping something else from me."

She tried to swallow, and her dry throat spasmed. Why hadn't Grant left? Why did he have to witness this? Her hand shook when she pushed back her hair, and that was enough to piss her off. All of her mistakes were crystal clear now, but cowering was not acceptable.

She lifted her chin and rested a hand on one hip. "I left you because I was afraid they'd do something to you. I left Boston because I was afraid they'd do something to Olivia."

All the air seemed to go out of Kell at once. He braced a hand on the back of a chair and stared at her. "My sister?"

Zoe blinked back the tears that stung her eyes. "She's the age I was. The age they think is ideal for the ritual."

"Oh, God." His face had gone white. "They can get

her. They could have her right now. I have to—"

"She's okay." Grant stepped forward, his hand out. "I checked right before I came in here. Your parents hired a security service, and I have a team watching all of them, too. And for what it's worth, I think Zoe's plan will work. Just hear her out."

"Zoe's plan?" Kell straightened, and red flared into his cheekbones. His eyes seemed to flash as he stared at Grant. "Her plan where she thinks it's safer *not* to tell me my sister's a target of a group of freaks? The plan where I do *nothing* to protect the most important person in my life?"

Zoe clamped down on the stab of pain she had no right to. She rushed into the silence, "I know. It's unforgivable. I told your mother so they could take precautions. I just…couldn't face telling you," she admitted in a whisper. Before Kell could respond, she hurried on. "As long as Pat thinks I'm doing what he wants, that I'm going to bring the totems to him, he won't do anything. And once I find them, I'll destroy them, and then he won't have reason to want Olivia."

"*Or* Zoe," Grant added, and Zoe frowned at him. She didn't matter. Not in the big picture, and not to Kell. Not after what she'd done.

It was obvious in the way Kell refused to look at her, at the rigidity of his expression as he glared at Grant. And that was fine. She deserved nothing less, and there was no time to dwell on personal pain.

Apparently, Kell agreed. He faced in her general direction and folded his arms. "Do you know where the totems are?"

"No, but we're working on finding them."

"And the fact that you're using your credit card means you want them to know that. You want to be visible."

"That's the whole idea." That must be how he'd found her, too. He had access to a dozen private detectives through the law firm, and she bet there were a few who could access her financial records.

"In order to keep me safe."

She frowned. "You and everyone—"

"He's talking about the airport," Grant broke in. He pushed away from the wall and walked into the room, dropping onto the end of one of the beds. "Whoever threw that thing at him had a different goal."

Zoe said, "At him?"

Grant nodded. "Yes, at him. It was luck that he bent to get his bag and it missed him. I don't know why he was targeted, but it definitely was him and not us."

"Why would someone try to hit me?" Kell asked. "Why wouldn't they go for you first? You're clearly the stronger threat. Taking out the biggest obstacle is SOP."

Grant looked at her. "He knows his stuff."

"He's a lawyer," she grumbled. And apparently was going to leap whole hog into this mess. Now he was analyzing and stuff. Instead of leaving, storming out and going back to Boston to protect Olivia, he was talking to Grant like they were old friends. No, war buddies.

"They might not have tactical training," Grant said.

"Where'd you get yours?"

Kell grinned, and Zoe's stomach swirled. There was a fierce glee there, covering the anger and pain.

"Courtroom. Different kind of battlefield."

Grant nodded. "So maybe this person didn't have tactical training, or they could have judged you as a multi-faceted threat. I look like a street fighter, and the kind of guy who'd take on an attacker. You look equally likely to call security or use martial arts, or even to have bodyguards nearby."

Zoe felt left out. "Or it could have been a cull-from-the-herd kind of thing. He'd moved away. Singular target. And then, while we rushed to help him, they'd get us?"

Grant shook his head. "No, I think they were uncomfortable with a playing field that includes him, and they acted to take him out of the picture." He shrugged. "But that's just speculation. We won't know unless they keep trying."

"But there won't be any reason to try," Zoe said firmly, "if he goes back to Boston." She didn't have quite enough courage to say it directly at Kell.

"I'm not going anywhere." Kell dropped back onto the love seat, leaning to brace his forearms on his knees. "You've just worked hard to convince me that Olivia is safest if you finish the job you started. The more help you have, the faster you can do that. Isn't there a ticking clock here?"

"Blood moon," Grant confirmed. He checked his watch and headed for the door. "I'm sure you two have more to talk about. We'll meet for breakfast downstairs at seven-thirty and then head out to the ranch with the rail car."

"I think you need to explain that," Kell said to Zoe.

"Don't stay up all night," was Grant's parting shot. She didn't miss his double meaning.

Chapter Nine

"Are you sure this is it?" Zoe leaned between the seats of the SUV Grant had rented the previous afternoon. He clenched his jaw against the smell of her skin blended with the expensive body wash the hotel supplied. This was harder than yesterday's flight had been. Even four hours right next to her wasn't the torture sharing her with Kellen Stone was.

The other man had been in the room when she showered. Maybe he'd showered with her. At breakfast, Grant had been brought up short when he automatically moved to seat Zoe and Stone cut him off. The other man had shot him a knowing look, but Zoe hadn't noticed. Grant's hand kept reaching for her back or elbow to guide her, and once he'd even started to wrap her hair around his fingers, something he'd done when they were together over a decade ago.

He had to keep fighting the urge to claim her, and it was making him irritable.

"I'm sure," he growled belatedly. Zoe shifted away from him. His jaw throbbed from the clenching.

"What are we expecting to find here, after all this

time?" Stone asked.

Grant kept silent. He knew he was being childish, but he'd probably continue until Zoe called him on it. At least it would get her attention.

"Expecting? Nothing," Zoe answered. "It's just the best lead we have. Only lead."

"Does the owner know we're coming?"

"No."

Now Stone was silent, and Grant read disapproval at the way they were handling this. Too bad. Zoe had come to him for his expertise, so his way would be the way they handled it. At least this part. Stone was smart and not without ability, and Grant wasn't so immature that he'd fail to use an important asset if it would help their mission. But for now, the plan was his.

He turned left off the main road onto a dirt lane and pointed to the right, where an overgrown railroad track was visible. "See?"

"Okay, so we're in the right place." She leaned forward again, her shoulder brushing his. Probably Stone's, too. "Any idea where the car would be?" Before either man could answer, they reached the main house. Partially visible to the right, about fifty feet behind the house, was a bright orange rail car. Tall grass grew up around the edges and in front of the side door. The ladder at one end looked rusted, and the part that connected to the next car in line supported a row of cracked wooden flower pots, only two of which sported blooming fall flowers. It obviously hadn't been opened in a long time.

"So what do we do first?" Stone asked.

Grant shoved open his door. "Knock." He strode up to the ramshackle farmhouse. Silence reigned around them, the kind of silence that went with abandonment, even temporary absence. There was no movement at the windows as they climbed the steps, no sound from within. But the porch was swept clean, the panes of glass in the top of the door intact. The screen had no holes.

Grant rapped on the side of the screen door and half turned so he could watch for dust on the drive. As their own dust cloud settled lower and lower, sparkling in the sunshine, no sound came from inside. Zoe knocked again, impatiently, while Stone strolled to the end of the porch and peered around the side of the house.

"No one's here," Zoe said after a minute.

"Doesn't look like it."

"So what now?"

"Grab the crowbar from the back of the truck."

"Thank God." She hopped down the steps and hurried to the vehicle.

Grant joined Stone at the porch's far rail. The visible portion of yard was barren, no tire tracks in the scrubby grass.

"We need a lookout," Grant said.

Stone didn't turn. "You're the expert. I'll go in with her."

Figured. "Not sure we *can* get in."

Stone straightened. "We'll have to play it by ear, then." He turned and crossed to the steps, meeting Zoe at the bottom and saying something Grant couldn't hear. He had to give the guy credit. Most guys would assume the worst in a situation like this, and act blustery and territorial if not downright hostile at the threat Grant posed—real or not. But not Stone. He was civil, accepted that Grant knew more than he did about some things, and acted like they all had the same goals. And maybe they did, at least as far as getting the totems went. But that wasn't the only goal Grant had.

He braced a hand on the rail and leaped over it to the ground below, landing lightly next to Zoe. She ignored him, all her attention on the rail car.

"What do you think?"

She moved forward slowly, zipping up her hooded sweatshirt and pushing her hands into the pockets. "It's not the same color."

"No." Grant scanned the ground between them and the car, then moved forward. "It's been painted. A few times." When he reached the side of the hunk of steel, he flicked a bit of peeling paint. Green patches showed through the orange, and a few scratches revealed brown underneath.

Zoe took a deep breath and tilted her head up at the door. "It doesn't look locked."

Stone tested it. It didn't budge. "Rusted."

"That's what this is for." Grant lifted the crowbar from Zoe's hand and stepped to Stone's side. "Look out." Stone backed up a few steps. Grant raised the bar and jammed the end between the door and the main wall. When he put pressure on it, paint and rust showered the grass below. Stone tried the door again. This time the metal groaned.

"Zoe, watch the road." She frowned, but turned to look down the lane while Grant moved the bar higher and pried again. This time, when Stone shoved at the door, it moved a few inches.

"There's no one coming," Zoe insisted. "Let me help." After Grant did one more jam-and-pull as high as he could reach, she ducked under Stone's arm and pushed with him. With an eardrum-shearing protest, the door slowly slid sideways.

"If anyone's in the house, that'll wake 'em up." Grant caught Zoe's arm to keep her from clambering immediately into the big box. "Let me check first."

"Why you?" For the first time, Stone sounded like a threatened fiancé.

"Because I have this." Grant slipped his pistol from the clip holster under his loose shirt and showed them. "Arguments?"

Zoe folded her arms, but let him pass. "I think the rusted-shut door already made one, but go right ahead, Mr. Macho."

She was right, but it never paid to make assumptions.

"How'd you get that, anyway?" Stone asked as Grant hefted himself into the opening and peered around, the gun held ready. "You couldn't take it on the airplane."

"I have my ways." He'd gotten it while he was out arranging for the SUV, but it was none of Stone's business how.

He moved into the empty car, hoping there'd be something in the shadows that they could at least look through, but there was nothing. The unit was completely empty.

Shit. This was going to crush Zoe.

"Well?" she called from outside.

He reholstered his weapon and hung his head for a second before going back to the opening. "It's empty."

Disappointment flickered over her face, but she didn't hold on to it. "Let me see." She reached for him to pull her up. He grabbed her wrist as she braced her foot and pulled, aided by Stone lifting her from behind. Then Grant was obligated to boost the other guy in, too. He jumped down instead of lingering with them in the gloomy space. The need to keep watch wasn't stronger than the need to be ready to comfort Zoe, but it was more urgent. He stood outside and listened to their conversation.

"I don't know what I expected." Her low voice echoed against the metal. "Storage, maybe. Boxes we could move around and dig through."

"Look around anyway," Stone told her. "Maybe there's something crammed into a corner or something."

Footsteps clattered across the floor. "No. I tossed the bag inside, to the right. Here." Grant could hear scraping, like she moved debris with her foot. "It's not like there's anywhere for it to be hidden." She huffed an exasperated laugh. "What, did we think someone had left a note? 'If you forgot a bag of metal things in here, call me.' This is so ridiculous."

"Maybe it's not the right car."

"It is." Her voice caught and changed. "See that

graffiti over there?"

"The skull and dagger? Or the profanity?" Stone said it with amusement, but Zoe wasn't ready for that.

"The skull. I described it for the FBI after I escaped. It was in the file." Her voice slowed with despondence. "I don't know why they didn't paint over that, but this is the same car. There's just nothing here. It was a wasted trip."

"It was worth a try," Stone soothed. Grant imagined he pulled Zoe into his arms and rubbed her back. She probably rested her head on his shoulder.

Dust appeared down the lane. A car was coming.

"We have company!" he called over his shoulder. "Book it!"

Zoe jumped out. Stone followed, and the three of them shoved the door closed. Zoe and Stone raced toward their parked SUV. Grant stayed behind to make sure they hadn't jammed the long grass in the door. If someone looked closely, they'd see the paint on the ground and even notice the fresh marks from the crowbar. He hoped they could be gone before the owner looked that carefully.

He joined the others at the SUV. When he brushed his hands off, paint fell. "Check your hands," he told the others. They swiped at flecks of paint while he circled them, making sure none of them had paint on their clothes. Stone scuffed dust over the flakes on the ground.

Then they stood still as the dust cloud down the lane resolved into a pickup truck barreling toward them. The men flanked Zoe, who stepped forward when the truck slid to a stop and a fat, balding man in sagging jeans and a Denver Broncos jersey got out.

"What can I do you folks for?" he called across the drive, hitching his pants before striding toward them.

"Hello!" Zoe called back. "We're railroad hobbyists." She walked toward him, a convincing grin spreading across her face. "We're so glad you're here. We were checking out your car"—she motioned behind them—"and hoped the owner could give us some history of it. Are you the owner?"

"That I am. Rudy Rumbolt." He smiled as he shook her hand, then stretched to shake Stone's and then Grant's. "You were just passing through and spotted my rail car?"

It was a testing question, Grant knew. You couldn't see the rail car from the road. He spoke up before Zoe could lie and get them in trouble. "No. Zo here tracks down cars sold to private individuals and seeks them out. She likes to track where they end up and stuff."

Rudy nodded like that made perfect sense. Maybe some of those railroad nuts really did that. "Well, I'm happy to share what I know."

"Do you have time now?" Zoe asked eagerly. "It's an old car, isn't it?"

"Sweetheart, I have all the time in the world!" He hitched his pants again and checked his watch. "Well, all the time there is until noon. Gotta lunch meetin' at noon."

Grant had a feeling that was more of a social thing than a "meeting," but so what? There were nearly two hours until then. He hoped Rudy had a lot to tell them.

* * *

Kell was having a hard time keeping his attention on the conversation.

It wasn't that Rudy was boring. Any other time, Kell would have been engrossed in his stories of working the railroad and the characters he ran into. Zoe was far from unique in stowing away on a freight train, even in modern times. And Rudy'd found a mess of cool and not-so-cool items both on and off the trains.

But bits of last night kept coming to mind, alternating between the horrors of Zoe's abduction, the surrealness of their current situation, and the confusion of being back with her, close to her, with everything different. He couldn't believe less than a month had gone by since she left him. Nothing was what he'd thought it to be, not before she left, not after.

Last night he'd gotten her to talk more about the past, and she'd shared things with him that she'd never even hinted at before. "Why didn't you ever tell me?" he asked her more than once, trying to get past her shields. "Why did you decide leaving me was the only option?"

She'd looked at him with haunted eyes. "It wasn't who I wanted to be," she'd finally said, but Kell knew it was more than that. It wasn't who she wanted him to see. To her, the Zoe Ardmore who ran a successful business and charmed high society at charity balls was completely different from the Zoe Smith who'd been abducted and held for a year. She hadn't said it, not like that, but he could see it. Hear it in her tone when she talked about the past. As far as he could tell, she didn't hold back details of what had happened. But she did hold herself apart from it, and from him.

The fear of losing her—really losing her this time— kept him awake almost all night.

Everything he knew was different now. Last week, he'd walked into her company and introduced himself, sending a shockwave through the room. Every person there knew who he was. But not a single one of them approached him about Zoe. Though he sensed the grapevine humming after the initial meeting, he didn't think any of them were in contact with her. There'd been a definite division between employer and employees.

It made him sad, because he realized all Zoe's friends were their friends jointly. James and Sonya. People from the social circuit, or his law firm. If she had friends from college, she didn't stay in touch with them, or at least, he didn't know about it. That all fit now, with the deep chasm she imagined between her past and present. A chasm she'd been pulled back across, leaving him—and everyone else in her life—on the other side.

As much as it had sent him reeling, he could have gotten over it. Could have convinced her to come back to him. It would take time to rebuild their relationship. He had to get over the feeling that he didn't really know her. Everything she said or did, he couldn't take at face value. But eventually, it would have worked out.

Except for Olivia.

He'd called his sister while Zoe was in the shower

last night. She sounded fine. Happy and chatty, as usual. She'd asked him if he'd heard from Zoe, and he lied and told her no. *Lied* to his baby sister for the first time in his life. Zoe had done that. But she'd also, through her silence, put Liv in danger. It just made no sense. If he'd known about Zoe's past from the beginning, none of this would be happening now. Even if she'd told him a few weeks ago, when she learned her abductors were out on parole, they could have taken steps to protect both of them. He would have hired someone to search for the totems so they could have stayed safely in Boston.

How had Zoe trusted him *so* little? And how could he have been so oblivious to all of it? He couldn't love someone he didn't know. Couldn't marry someone he didn't trust. But none of that kept him from longing to be next to her. Touching her. Dragging her away from Grant's side.

He'd also done some digging on Grant last night. If the men he'd asked to watch Olivia were as good at their jobs as Grant appeared to be at his, then Kell would try not to worry about her. And there was logic to Zoe's plan, even if it was far from the path he would have chosen.

So last night had been tense and awkward. Zoe had gotten into the bed closest to the door, as if she was still trying to protect him. She'd turned her back to him, but hadn't slept. Not until well into the dark hours of the morning. He knew, because he'd lain there listening to her stillness, unable to get over the shock of what they'd become.

And trying not to think about how Grant Neely fit into it all.

Kell dragged himself back to the conversation. Rudy was answering something Grant had asked.

"Sure, sure, we had a tradition, even. Once a month, at the Salty Chicken, we'd get together and do a trade." Rudy pushed himself out of his ratty armchair and walked to a set of dusty shelves on one wall. "Got some of it here." He lifted an Alabama license plate that said 4TI2DE. "One of the guys on the overnight found this stuck to an engine. Weren't any reports of crashes on that line, so it must've gotten kicked up off the tracks somehow." He pondered the plate for a minute, then set it back on the shelf. "I got 'bout fifty a those, out in the barn. That's what I collect. Stuff with state markings. Few keychains, mugs, clothes. Don't wear the clothes, of course." He chuckled and sat back down. "Never been outta Utah, if you can believe it. That's why I like getting stuff that has."

"So does everyone specialize?" Zoe asked. "Like, when you find stuff, do you know who might collect that kind of thing?"

Rudy narrowed his eyes at her. "You're gettin' at something specific."

She opened her mouth, half closed it, then leaned forward, clearly unsure what to say.

Kell jumped in. This was his forte. "Did any of your colleagues collect curios? Dustcatchers. Statues and figurines and stuff like that."

"Oh, yeah, that'd be Ozzie." He turned his shrewd

gaze on Kell now. "He was the sucker of the group. Liked that stuff so much he'd give ya anything for it, 'specially if it was unusual. One time, he gave me three plates and a hubcap with a Texas star on it just for a coupla hunks of brass." He chuckled and shook his head. "Worth at least a one-for-one trade, but you know, how much you want something's always going to dictate how much you pay for it. Ain't always about value."

Rudy was right. At some point, it always came to money. Kell was prepared to pay whatever he needed to, to get Zoe out of this and back home with him. But Rudy didn't have to know that. He could guess, but Kell would never let him be sure.

"So?" Rudy barked. "What is it you're lookin' for?"

Grant described the totems in basic terms. Rudy's eyebrows puckered, rose, fell, and scrunched together. Finally, he said, "Don't ring a bell. But definitely, Ozzie'd want something like that. He'd have bartered for 'em."

"Do you know how we can reach him?" Grant asked, pulling out a small pad and pen. Kell discreetly typed the phone number Rudy rattled off into his phone, then, while Zoe asked Rudy again if there'd been anything in the rail car he owned, he pulled up the number on the Internet, found the corresponding address, and mapped the quickest route to get there.

"Sorry, sweetheart, the thing was empty as my stomach at supper time. Speaking of." He looked at his watch. "I've got to get goin' if I'm gonna make my meeting."

Zoe and Grant rose from the sofa they'd been sitting on and thanked Rudy, Zoe going so far as to give him a kiss on the cheek. Kell slipped his phone back into its holder on his belt and stepped forward to shake Rudy's hand.

"We appreciate your time."

"Hell, it goes both ways." They made their way to the front door. "Old men like me always like having someone new to tell stories to, you know." He clapped Kell on the shoulder and nudged him through the screen door. "You kids good luck findin' them things."

He was kicking up dust, barreling down the long drive in his truck, before the three of them had finished getting into the SUV.

"So let's call Ozzie," Zoe said immediately, leaning forward between the seats again. "Find out where he lives."

"I already know." Kell showed them the GPS route on his phone. "We can be there in half an hour. But the question is, should we call ahead or just show up?"

"If someone else has already gotten to him," Zoe said, "our call could spook him."

Kell turned in the seat to see her better as Grant started the vehicle and put it in gear. "How would anyone have gotten to him? Rudy gave no sign he's talked to anyone besides us."

"No, but they could have talked to someone else, following the railroad connection. That's kind of a no-brainer, isn't it? I just don't want to alert him. Or anyone." She took a deep breath. "I feel like Pat's people are on our tails, just waiting to do their damage."

"You're not wrong."

"What?" Kell and Zoe said together, staring at Grant, who was frowning into the rearview mirror.

"We've got company."

They craned their necks to look behind the truck.

"How can you tell?" Zoe asked. "That could be Rudy's dust."

In a few more seconds, however, it was clear the dust cloud was building toward them, not settling away. And it was moving fast.

"That's a one-lane drive," Kell reminded Grant.

"I know." His jaw set, Grant stepped slowly on the gas, moving the truck at a crawl around the side of the house, stirring as little dust as possible.

"It might be no one," Zoe said, but her tone was anxious.

"Might be." Grant stopped the truck and surveyed the land in front of them. "Do you want to take that chance?"

The road was about a mile and a half straight ahead, but it was open ground. The SUV was built for off road, not just to look like it, but there was no cover. Their dust cloud would reveal them the same way it revealed whoever was approaching the house now. Kell looked over his shoulder, but the terrain was identical in all directions, and any roads back that way would be further than the one they'd come in on.

Still, they sat.

"What are we waiting for?" Zoe asked.

"Timing," Grant bit out.

Kell touched Zoe's hand where it rested on the center console. "Better sit back and buckle up," he said in a low voice. "This won't be smooth."

"Damn right," Grant muttered. His gaze burned straight ahead, his hands loose on the wheel but his arms tight with tension. He seemed to be counting in his head, probably trying to calculate when the car would be at the best point to give them an advantage.

"What if they know something that could help us?" Zoe suggested. "We could stay and find out."

"They're behind us, Zoe. We know more than they do."

"She doesn't want to run," Kell told him. He could tell that Zoe was going to push, and Grant wasn't the kind of guy who took well to pushing. He didn't really care what kind of guy Grant was, but he was the one driving. "She hates being ruled by fear." And now he understood why.

"I get that," Grant responded. "But it's tactical. She's going to—"

"Stop talking about me!" Zoe yelled at them both. "It's not about fear *or* running!"

"Good." Grant slammed his foot down on the accelerator. The SUV bounded across the dry, not-so-flat ground. Zoe put her hand up to brace against the ceiling when she bounced.

"I told you to put—"

"Oh, shut up." She tried to glare at Kell, but they were all moving around too much for it to be effective. After a struggle, she managed to click the seatbelt into place. It helped a little.

"So you got that address plugged in?" Grant asked Kell. "Would be helpful right about now."

"Yeah." He thumbed his phone on. It was recalibrating based on the direction they were going. "Hang on."

"We're hanging."

"Literally." Zoe clung to the handle over her door.

"See if you can see them behind us," Grant ordered.

After a moment, she said, "I can't tell. The dust cloud's too thick."

The GPS program was having difficulty plotting them. Kell tried to skim ahead on the three-D route, but it didn't show which way to go.

"Left or right?" The racing engine slowed as a hard bounce took Grant's foot off the accelerator. A few seconds later, they lurched forward again. "Left or right?" he said louder when Kell didn't answer.

"I'm trying to figure that out!" He switched the view to overhead and zoomed out. "Left," he managed just before they hit the road. Grant spun the wheel, the vehicle skidded in a quarter circle, and before it had settled, he was mashing down the accelerator again.

"Why are you in such a—" Zoe cut herself off when she looked ahead. They had to pass the entrance to Rudy's property, and there was a monster pickup truck sitting there at the end of the drive. Their pursuers—assuming they'd been after them and not just visiting Rudy—hadn't been stupid enough to try to follow them off road. They were just going to wait to see which way they went on the blacktop.

"What are they—" Again, she cut herself off, this time adding a curse.

"Brace yourselves." Grant muttered something Kell couldn't hear, his right knee rising but his foot not letting up on the gas. His gaze stayed fixed on the truck.

"Which pieces?" Zoe quipped.

Kell braced his feet against the floor, not sure what was coming, but knowing it was coming soon.

He didn't know how Grant did it. How he anticipated so perfectly. How he even knew what the bastards were planning. But as they sped down the road, at the instant the waiting truck jumped forward to smash into them, Grant slammed on the brakes and cranked the wheel left. The truck whipped across the road in front of them, and Grant hit the gas again. Kell twisted to look out the side window and watched the truck spin, trying too soon to follow the SUV. They'd been going too fast, and the truck teetered on two wheels.

Then they were too far down the road for Kell to see any more.

"Everyone all right?" Grant asked.

"Yeah." Kell spun back the other way to check Zoe. She was hanging over the back seat, trying to see through the rear window. "Zoe?"

"I don't see them." By the clarity of her voice, she was okay, too.

"They're coming." Grant was alternating between watching the flat road ahead of them and checking the rearview mirror.

"You see them?" Zoe asked.

"Not yet." He waved at the phone clutched tight in Kell's hand. "Route?"

"Oh. Right." He wiped away the sweat that smeared the screen and tapped the display back on.

"Checking for traffic," the musical voice told him. He bounced his knee, impatient, and glanced in the side mirror. He couldn't see the truck behind them.

"Go straight…four point two miles…and then…turn right." The name of the road to turn on appeared at the bottom of the screen.

Grant sped up even more. Kell had thought they were at top speed already, but the engine growled and the tires whirred and holy shit, if they hit a pothole they were dead.

The road curved gradually to the right, and the mountains loomed ahead of them once more.

"It will be easier to lose these guys in the foothills," Grant told them.

"Good." Zoe stayed in her seat, raising her voice so they could hear her over the road noise. "I don't think we want them *this* close."

"No."

"Why are they coming after us?" Kell checked the distance to the turn. "Don't they just want to keep track of you? That was pretty aggressive."

"They might think we found the totems at Rudy's," Grant said.

"Or someone doesn't want the totems found at all," Kell countered.

Zoe made a noise but cut herself off.

"What?"

"Nothing."

He twisted back again, thinking he was going to need a chiropractor after this was all over. "If you thought of something or had an idea, tell us."

"No, nothing like that. I just—it was stupid."

Grant gave her a steady look in the mirror, and she relented, annoying Kell.

"What he said reminded me of that movie, *The Mummy*. You know, with Brendan Fraser?"

Kell exchanged a "whatever" look with Grant. She blew out a breath.

"Anyway, they were in a secret city, looking for an ancient book. And they were attacked, but they found out the people attacking them were protecting the book so no one would wake the mummy."

"So?" Kell wasn't sure where she was going with that. "It doesn't matter what these people's motive is. They're not trying to reason with us. That move—"

"I know! That's why I said it was stupid. I mean, I thought, if they know where the totems are and don't want us to get close, maybe they'd help us. Maybe we could find some common ground. But they can't listen to us if we're dead."

"Go one mile… and then…turn right," said the GPS.

Kell faced forward and prepared to navigate for Grant. And tried not to think about the possibility that the people behind them would catch up before they got to their destination.

Chapter Ten

"Sure, I remember those!"

Zoe stared at the grizzled old man in the doorway in front of them, hardly daring to believe her ears.

"You do?" Then the word he'd used clicked, and her heart sank as low as it had just leaped. "You don't have them anymore."

Ozzie shook his head. "I have some other nice things you might want to look at."

"No, thank you, it's just these particular statues." She fought to control her disappointment and think of what to ask next, but Kell took over for her.

"Mr. Cocalico, can you tell us a little about the statues and what you did with them? Where you found them? We're historians." He didn't jump to an explanation when Ozzie skeptically eyed the dust that coated their clothing. Zoe folded her hands so she wouldn't compulsively brush it off.

Finally, Ozzie backed up and let them in. "Sure. Can't hurt."

Thank goodness for old men who loved to talk. Ozzie led them into the living room of his spacious house, and Zoe gaped. Built-in shelves filled the walls on three sides. Rather than the eclectic, cluttered display in Rudy's house, Ozzie had carefully grouped his finds and even installed special lighting on some of them. They ranged from what looked like handmade rag dolls to gleaming porcelain. There was a lot of gold, both fake and real.

"I can't believe you find so much stuff along the railroad tracks!"

"Oh, well, it's not just that. It's a combination."

Zoe followed him around the room as he pointed out his favorites and told the stories behind each acquisition. The man had a steel-trap mind, which gave her hope. She waited for an appropriate moment while the guys hovered at the foyer entrance.

"Mr. Cocalico," she began.

"Please, call me Ozzie." He replaced a tattered book on its stand and smiled at her.

"Thank you, Ozzie. I was just wondering if you remember who you gave those statues to. The ones we were interested in."

"The ones made by Jacob Farmer."

Kell jerked forward at the name. Grant had more control, but Zoe felt him tense and knew he was ready for action. Luckily Ozzie was turned away from them and didn't notice. Zoe held them back with a flick of her hand. Ozzie couldn't see her racing heart, but she knew her eyes gleamed. Hopefully he had cataracts.

"You know their history?" she asked. She couldn't believe they'd actually tracked the things down. A day ago, less, she'd been certain there was no way. They didn't have them yet, but they were a million miles closer.

He shrugged, but his own eyes glinted. "The basics. You have to know the background to charge what they're worth."

"So you sold them." A guy like this would keep records. But would he tell them who the buyer was?

"Sure did." He abandoned their tour and crossed to a small rolltop desk in the corner of the room. "A few years ago, to a collector. I do that every so often. eBay." He hefted a large ledger-style book and grinned. "Best invention ever."

She smiled back. Her heart slammed so hard she pressed her hand to her ribcage. "And you kept records?"

"Of course. The IRS, you know." He slipped on a pair of reading glasses and peered at the first page of the ledger, then flipped several other pages. "William Carling is the collector." He paused and looked over the silver frames at her. "Are you familiar with him?"

She was, but only as a name. Someone with money, a man who gave a lot of it away. She made eye contact with Kell, who nodded slightly, and with Grant, who shrugged.

"I didn't know he lived in Utah." She felt stupid as soon as she said it. He'd learned about the totems on eBay. He could be anywhere.

"Nah, California." Ozzie found the entry he was looking for and scribbled something down on a piece of scrap paper. "Here you go."

She went closer to take the paper, a little

disbelieving that it was this easy. "Thank you."

Ozzie didn't release it right away. He'd dropped the affability. "I hope these give you what you're looking for."

She thanked him again, but he still didn't let go. "You know the legends?"

"I'm familiar with them," she admitted after a moment. If she said no, he'd probably regale her with them all day, and she was antsy about the people in that truck catching up with them. Finding Ozzie. She didn't want anything to happen to him or to Rudy, simply for being nice and helping them out.

"Are they the reason you're looking for them?"

"No." She said it swiftly and surely, and he relaxed and let her have his note.

"That's good. Because whatever's causing the panic you're trying so valiantly to hide, those things aren't the solution."

God, she hoped he was wrong.

* * *

"What now?" Zoe asked when they were back in the SUV, heading for the hotel, with no nasty black truck in sight.

"Research," Grant said. "We find out what we can about William Carling and determine the best way to get to him." He glanced at Kell. "What do you know?"

Zoe leaned forward. She hadn't thought Kell knew more than she did. His family wasn't at Carling's level, but they probably kept their eyes on people like him.

But Kell was shaking his head. "Just what's public. He's not east coast society, so my parents don't talk about him, and my firm's not that high-powered."

They rode in silence until they got to the hotel. The lobby staff shot them multiple veiled glares for entering their fancy establishment looking so rough and dirty, but Zoe didn't care. And wasn't that interesting? A few weeks ago, she'd have checked into a cheap hotel, showered, and changed into nicer clothes before daring to come back here.

Of course, a few weeks ago, she wouldn't have needed the shower. Or the subterfuge. She couldn't fool herself anymore. She'd changed. She could never go back to the life she'd worked so hard for. It remained to be seen if Kell could or would move forward with her. If he wasn't considering it, why was he still here?

Right now she was too worn out to lament the changes or fret about the future. She followed the men onto the elevator and turned to lean against the back wall, her mind flicking through Google searches and magazine archives, and what kind of information she should look for regarding William Carling. Did she have time to shower first? She needed to knock off the grime and sweat before hunkering in front of a computer.

The indicator had just dinged the fourth floor when she became aware of the tension in the car. She didn't know what had caused it, only sensed it creeping over her as it rose. She glanced at Grant and saw he was looking steadily over her head at Kell. She turned the other way and found Kell staring back. Their expressions were intense but not hostile. Both stood tall, yet casually leaning against the side rails, as if trying to convey supremacy in both power and ease at the same time.

They were posturing over her.

The ridiculousness of it burst a giggle out of her and she faced forward again quickly, though probably both of them knew she'd been looking. Then fear trickled in. She couldn't be annoyed that they were acting like this, like either currently had a claim over her. They both had reason to think they did. If Kell wasn't at least a little open to taking her back, he wouldn't still be here. She knew there would be a long, long row for her to hoe to earn back his trust and try to prove worthy of his love.

But that wasn't where the fear came from.

Because she had kissed Grant. Kissed him in a way that not only called up old passion, but told them both it was still there. They hadn't talked about it. And when Kell showed up, she'd clarified that he was her ex. More than once.

All of which added up to one thing: She didn't know what she wanted.

Well, not in the long run, anyway. Not beyond the next half hour. She knew exactly what she wanted right now.

She marched ahead of them when the elevator finally stopped on their floor, ignoring Grant as she passed his room, ignoring Kell when he followed her into theirs. She went straight for the phone but halted shy of it. That wasn't fair. She had to say something to him first.

When she turned, he stood warily by the foyer, his hands in his pockets, shirt untucked, head dipped. Waiting.

"I'm going to get my own room," she told him.

He didn't move. "Why?"

Though the question was obvious, she hadn't prepared an answer.

"I just...think it would be best," she tried, knowing it was lame.

"Because..." When she didn't elaborate, he pushed off the wall with his shoulder and wandered a few steps into the room. "Because you caught me and Neely staking claims."

"Is that what you were doing?" If only that would generate some anger in her. Anger would make everything easier. But it wouldn't come, probably because she had no right to it.

"Can you please be open about this?" He moved closer, and she could see his hands in his pockets were fisted. "Do I have a claim to stake? Or has Neely taken over?"

"I didn't think you'd want one."

"I don't know if I do."

Tears surged into her eyes, and she turned quickly away to hide them. It took several slow breaths before she could speak evenly. "He hasn't taken over anything."

"Maybe he doesn't have to. You two have a powerful history."

"Yes, *history*." She sank onto the far bed and swiped at the moisture on her face. "I only came to him because I didn't know anyone else who could help me. And I couldn't do this alone."

"I understand that." He sighed and sat on the bed across from her. "I understand all of it, which makes everything a lot more difficult. Even with the parts of it that should make it simple."

She knew he was talking about Olivia. When they'd talked last night, he'd asked plenty of questions but said very little in return.

"You're being too tolerant." She sniffled, and he pulled a tissue from the box on the nightstand and handed it to her. "Why aren't you raging at me?"

"These aren't exactly normal events," he said. "Not for you and me, anyway. Maybe this is normal for Grant."

She managed a smile and tossed the tissue in the wastebasket. "I'm pretty sure it is. Half of his normal, anyway."

"He wants you."

Her head came up and her mouth opened to protest, but the words didn't come out. Though he had every reason to see things that weren't there, she knew damned well he wasn't. He nodded, and she stood and moved around the bed, needing distance from his pain.

"Just be open. Be real." He stood but didn't follow her. "You've kept secrets from me, but you've always been more real than anyone else in my life. That's all I want from you now."

It was the least she could give him. "I—I love you, Kell." His body relaxed at her words, but she could tell he knew there was a but. "I—Grant kissed me. I let him. And I'm confused, because working with him reminds me of why I fell in love with him so long ago, and he's a good, caring man—"

"Who's also a warrior," Kell broke in, scowling. "I get the appeal. I don't need it spelled out for me."

She swallowed, a little frightened. Openness was a minefield. But he'd asked for it and he deserved it, so she pressed on. "He's like you. He is," she insisted when he didn't seem to like hearing it. "You're a warrior, too, you just fight with words instead of guns. You're both smart, and protective without being patronizing. You treat me like *I'm* smart and have something of value to contribute. But like you said." She huffed and held out her arms. "This isn't normal. Things will be very different when it's over, even if I'm not dead."

She choked on the last words, and Kell quickly came around to her, wrapping her against his chest. "You're not going to die."

"You don't know that." She closed her eyes and pressed her face into him. He smelled so good, like home and heat. "But if I do, that's okay. It will be worse…" She couldn't say it. "I will die before I let anything happen to her."

"I know." It was almost a whisper.

"But if you two are helping me— It would be worse if you died." She meant "one of you," and he got it.

"We won't die, either." He loosened his hold but didn't let her go. When she didn't lift her face he did it for her, holding her chin with his forefinger and thumb. "Neely's too good, and I'm too determined."

Zoe didn't bother protesting anymore. His reassurances were flat, but he meant them. They had other things to think about. Things they could control. She started to move away, but Kell kept her close.

"I'm not going to pressure you right now," he said. "You broke up with me, so I have no real claim and no right to ask anything of you."

"You have a right to ask a lot of me."

His lips curved. "I meant, to dictate your decisions."

As far as she was concerned, he still had some rights. "I didn't break up with you because I don't care anymore. I did it to protect you and your family."

His look recalled his accusations from the night before. "Would you have told me any of this if Olivia wasn't part of the equation?"

Her mouth opened, but she couldn't answer—which was, of course, answer enough.

"Yeah. You did it because you were scared. Because you thought I wouldn't want you the same way if I knew about your past. And because you didn't want to admit you'd lied to me."

The truth had barbs as well as spines. She pulled free of him and backed up a few steps, as if that would stop the ripping, tearing honesty. "Maybe. Sure. I was scared. But I'm not a coward. I didn't run and hide from everything. I'm confronting it head-on, and that's because…because I still had hope we could rebuild our future." She hadn't dared focus on that hope or that it would have required telling him everything, anyway.

It seemed easier to consider as a vague, future possibility once it was all over.

He stared at her. "Well. Kinda backfired, didn't it?"

"Because of Grant, or because—"

"Yeah, because of Grant. Whatever old feelings exist between you, he cares about you *now*. And so do I. Look, I'm not pretending I don't feel betrayed by what you did. And I can't say how I'll feel if they do stop using Olivia as a threat and turn her into a tool. But I'm not flying home in a snit, or picking a fight with the guy helping you. And I'm not trying to take you away from this. But I won't stand back and let him steal you from me, either. I'm going to fight for you."

Zoe's eyes welled again. "Oh, Kell."

"He's going to fight, too." She shook her head, but he stepped forward again. "Don't be naïve. He's not backing off. You saw that in the elevator. He considers you fair game."

"Doesn't that make you mad?"

To her shock, he grinned. "Nope. I've got a few aces. One of which is ownership of your company."

It didn't sink in right away. She was still processing the guilt and the reality of being wanted by both men, but his words slowly penetrated. "You…what?"

"I'm your buyer."

She bit back the anger that finally, inappropriately, swelled. He'd bought her company and was just now telling her? "How?"

"I found out you were selling and swooped in. It was actually my first clue that something was wrong. Something more than emotional craziness."

"Nice." She glared at him, then shoved her hands into her hair and left them there. "I can't believe you did that."

"You wouldn't have sold it if something wasn't really wrong. I wanted to save it for you."

That he would do something so monumental floored her. He'd have needed a loan, fast, and a smarter financial advisor than the one they'd been working with as a couple, in order to hide his identity from her.

"I don't know what to say."

He smiled gently and cupped her face in his hands. "You don't have to say anything."

"Thank you?"

"That'll do. When this is all over, I'll sell it back to you." He leaned forward and kissed her gently. It wasn't hungry or demanding, just telling her he loved her, still.

And confusing her all the more.

Kell hovered while she called the front desk to arrange for another room, glad for the hotel's high rating that allowed her to give them her credit card over the phone and have staff bring her the key card and carry her bag to her new room down the hall. She was so tired and overwhelmed. She couldn't see the next step, never mind down the road to dealing with her romantic mess. Food and sleep were all she wanted to face for the next nine hours.

But she'd just hung up from ordering room service when there was a knock on the door. Heart in her throat but too weary for adrenaline, she peered through the peephole. Great. Grant.

She opened the door. "How did you know what room I'm in? They're not supposed to give out that information."

He pressed past her into the room. "They didn't. I followed you."

She rolled her eyes and walked away to the sitting area, wanting some distance. He didn't give it to her. When she sat on the love seat he sat on the chair beside her, his long legs trapping her in. She shifted to her right, toward the gap at the other end of the coffee table.

"This isn't smart, Zoe."

"It's fine."

"You're vulnerable. You used your own credit card."

She passed her hand over her eyes. "They know where we are already, but they're not going to attack here. It's too secure and too obvious. They'll wait until we're on the move again."

"It depends on what they want. Killing you would be a lot easier if you were asleep rather than barreling down the highway."

She dropped her head against the back of the love seat. "Fine. They can kill me. It'll be easier."

She'd never known silence could be alarmed. She tipped her head to the left to see Grant's face. No, not alarm, something stronger. Something amazing. She doubted he'd have felt much more than a vague sorrow had she died last week, before she had gone down to the Keys, but now...

"You don't go for easy," he said softly.

"Not usually."

"You're just tired."

"Definitely a factor."

"And you're getting a rush out of having two guys on the hook."

She lurched upright, appalled. "I am not! I— Shit." He was laughing. "There, you finally got a rise out of me. Happy?"

"Happier than when I thought you were ready to die." He reached out and caught her hand, tugging her back. "Everything will work out. Don't worry."

She couldn't believe him, no matter how confident he sounded. But her mouth didn't heed her desire to avoid any more relationship talk. "I don't have two men on the hook."

He eased back in his chair, wrapping an elbow over the ornate corner of it. "Oh? Did you tell Stone you're done with him?"

"No! I'm not—" She growled. "Stop doing that." It took a couple of deep breaths before she sorted out what she wanted to say. "Kell thinks you're staking a claim to me."

"He's a smart guy. Not that it takes a lot of brains to figure that out."

"You don't have a right to do that."

"That kiss the other day says differently."

"It was—" She couldn't say meaningless. He'd know she was lying. "An aberration."

"Then I vote we have more of them."

"Seriously, Grant."

"Okay." He went earnest, unhooking his arm and leaning forward, elbows on knees. "If you can tell me, one hundred percent honestly, that I have no chance with you, that you have no romantic feelings for me, then I'll back off."

"I have no romantic feelings for you. You have no chance."

"Nice try." He stood, grinning, and actually patted her on the head. If she hadn't been too weak to do so, she'd have ripped his hand off.

"*Grant.*"

"I said it had to be honest. Your eyes flicked to the left."

She rolled them, knowing he was right. James had pointed out the tell during a charity poker game a year ago and never stopped teasing her about it.

"We do not need this right now," she warned as he headed for the door.

"Don't worry. I'm not going to seduce you or anything. I'll just be myself, and at the end of the game, you won't be able to resist me." He said it lightly, but with an undertone of steel, and Zoe knew he was right. At least, had a chance to be right. She couldn't imagine picking him over Kell, but she couldn't imagine telling him no, either. Not at the moment.

"Oh, by the way." He stopped at the door. "We're heading for the airport at five tomorrow. Our guy is in San Francisco. Stone's magic paralegal is getting us tickets to a benefit he's attending. We should be able to talk to him there."

And with that he was gone, leaving Zoe with a

helluva lot of thinking to do.

* * *

They didn't make it to five a.m.

Zoe hadn't slept the night before, so she went to bed early and fell into deep slumber, shocked awake by a sharp noise outside her room. In normal circumstances she'd have lain still, listening, trying to determine if she'd heard something real or dreamed it.

Tonight, she knew and was out of bed and dressed before her brain could even process that she'd moved. She grabbed her bag and stood on tiptoe at the peephole. The hall was empty, but she was at the end of a short arm and couldn't see the main hall, where Grant's and Kell's rooms were.

Shit. She couldn't see to either side of her door, either. Stepping outside could make her a target, but she couldn't stay trapped in here.

Her cell phone buzzed in her pocket. She struggled to get it free, cursing. The mini display showed Grant's name. She answered and pressed her eye to the door again.

"What's going on?" she asked. The hall was still empty.

"Get down here to my room. Fast." The line went dead.

"Fuck." She shoved her phone back in her pocket, took a deep breath, and gripped her bag in one hand, ready to swing it or use it as a shield. She unlocked the door, wincing at the loud *snick* it made, and eased it open, staying to the left. The hall outside, the part not in her blind spot, was clear. No one pushed the door open, and silence rang. She quickly spun around the jamb, and when no one attacked her from the left, she dashed down the hall, the untied laces on her sneakers clicking where they swung against her shoes.

Turning the corner, she skidded to a halt for half a second, arrested by the sight of a room's door busted in. Debris littered the floor, the doorjamb destroyed where the lock had been.

She'd moved on toward Grant's before she realized this was her former room. Kell's room. Horror welled in her throat, burning with fear, but then Grant and Kell emerged into the hall ahead of her, carrying their own bags.

"Are you all right?" Zoe gasped as she reached them. She touched Kell's arm, reached for his chest, but he brushed her aside.

"I'm fine. I was down here."

That he was in Grant's room instead of his own was weird enough to make her pause again, but they were pulling her toward the stairwell so she held her questions in and kept moving. A few minutes later, they were in a cab—which was faster than getting their vehicle from the valet—heading for God knew where. She had to bite her tongue hard to keep from asking questions that she knew the cabbie shouldn't hear. They sat, all three cramped into the back seat, Zoe in the middle as if they wanted to protect her even though this was the second time Kell had been in the line of fire.

Finally, the cab dropped them at a twenty-four-hour diner close enough to the airport that Zoe could see flashing lights on circling planes. As they walked up to the glass door, she asked about the SUV.

"Rental company will pick it up," Grant answered. "I'll call them later."

They went inside and paused to survey the place. It had a basic fifties-era construction, with booths lined up along huge windows and spinny stools at the Formica counter. Chrome shone everywhere—on table and stool edges and legs, the side of the counter and booths, and around mirrors and framed Elvis posters mounted on the little bit of plain wall space. Though the place was empty of customers, Zoe could smell bacon and fresh coffee. Her stomach growled.

A waitress came through the swinging door from the kitchen, toweling off her hands. "Sit anywhere, hons. I'll be right with you."

Grant led them to a booth on the far right, the last one along the side of the room. It was against the wall instead of the window, which looked out on a chain-link fence rather than the front parking lot. He made Zoe slide in first, then Kell, and he took the window side.

The waitress arrived immediately at their table with a coffeepot in one hand and menus in the other. She doled them out and poured coffee without asking, her expression light and friendly. "I'll be right back to take your orders. You need me faster, just holler for Fay."

They thanked her and flipped open the menus, pretending to look at them until she'd disappeared into the kitchen. Zoe dug into the bag scrunched between her and the wall and found the watch she'd tucked into it the night before. It was four a.m.

Kell was watching her. "How did you have time to gather your things?"

"They were already gathered." She looked up to find Grant eying her with approval, Kell with surprise. "What? I've been doing that since I left home." Their regard strengthened, and she huffed. "I've known for weeks that I was being watched. It's not such a big thing that I'm ready to flee at a moment's notice. Kind of cowardly, if you think about it."

"Yeah, well, I'd have appreciated the advice," Kell said wryly. "I got out with nothing." He lifted the coffee cup to his mouth and winced at the heat or the taste. Zoe decided not to drink any. She'd get good stuff at the airport.

"Why? What happened?" She leaned forward and lowered her voice. "What were you doing in Grant's room at that hour, anyway?"

Kell glanced at Grant. He ignored them, perusing the menu.

"We were strategizing."

Zoe scowled. "At three-thirty in the morning? About what?"

"The benefit that William Carling will be attending."

"Without me."

"You needed your sleep."

She didn't think he was telling the whole truth, but pushing it would probably go back into the romantic territory she'd gotten her own room to escape, so she let it go.

"So what happened?"

Grant flipped his menu closed. "Someone busted in the door to Stone's room."

"I saw that." She flattened her palm on the table and reined in her frustration. "How? They're all reinforced and stuff to prevent that kind of thing."

He shrugged. "We didn't see it. By the time I got to the hall, they'd apparently determined the room was empty and retreated. They made enough noise to get security up there."

"Why did we book it out so quickly if the threat was gone?"

"Because retreated means backed off, not left. They could have been watching for us."

"And could be watching us now."

Grant shook his head. "The car that followed us kept going when we stopped here. They'll probably pick us up again when we leave, just to make sure we're going to the airport."

"So we have no idea who it was." She leaned back as Fay approached again, pad at the ready.

"What can I get you folks?" She eyed Zoe's and Kell's open menus. "Need a few more minutes?"

"No, we're ready," Zoe told her. She ordered a short stack with bacon. Grant and Kell both got the special, a traditional platter loaded with fat and cholesterol. It surprised her, because Grant was the kind of fit that meant he ate healthy, and she knew for certain that Kell didn't usually eat like this. But it was expedient, she supposed, and when you'd narrowly escaped an attack, it probably didn't seem like such a big deal to eat real eggs cooked in bacon grease.

"This'll just take a few minutes." Fay smiled again and moved away to greet a couple of trucker types who'd just entered and were settling at the counter.

Zoe leaned forward again, keeping her voice low enough to make Kell and Grant lean in, too. "We don't know who they are or what they want, but we can be sure that they're targeting Kell."

Grant shook his head while Kell said, "No, we can't."

"Why not? That's twice now. Three if we count the truck."

"Can't count the truck," Grant said. "We were all in it."

"You're a more likely target," Kell argued. "You were only a few feet away at the airport, and this was your room, too."

"But not in my name. Why would they assume I was in your room and not Grant's, or in a separate room under an alias, like I actually was?"

"It depends how they got their information and who they are."

"And it doesn't matter." Grant's statement effectively halted the debate. "We're together and we have the same goal. No matter who the target is, we're all equally vulnerable. We have to focus on getting the totems."

"And you guys have decided how to do that."

"Next step, anyway," Kell said. "Grant did the research on Carling."

That Zoe had been planning to do but hadn't gotten around to. "And?"

"He's not reclusive, exactly, but he is reserved." Grant stopped to let Fay drop their food on the table. She offered ketchup, which Kell accepted, and quickly left.

"He's the top guy at a huge business money-wise, but small in every other way," Kell explained. "They develop proprietary technology for a niche market. So approaching him at work would be difficult."

"High security?" She slid the butter across her pancakes and set the giant pat on the edge of her bacon plate before drizzling syrup over the stack.

"We assume so." Grant dipped toast into his egg yolks. "And finding his home is turning out to require less-than-legal means."

"Even if we found his address, showing up there would put him on edge." Zoe watched the waitress steer a weary-looking couple to a booth on the other side of the building. She was good. Paid attention to her customers' needs. They'd have to tip her well.

"Right. Hence, the benefit. It's definitely the best way to approach."

"When is it?" She bit into her crisp bacon, amazed at how hungry she was. It seemed like her body shouldn't care about food, it had so much to dwell on. "How much time do we have?"

Kell grimaced and stabbed a piece of sausage with his fork. "It's tonight."

Chapter Eleven

For all that San Francisco was unique on the outside, different from all the cities Zoe had visited on the East Coast and in the Midwest, everything in the ballroom was exactly the same.

Tanicia, Kell's super-assistant who never asked questions, had scored three tickets to the benefit and managed to get them rooms in the same hotel *and* clothes for tonight. They'd all split up to make phone calls and sleep a little. Then, while Kell worked with Tanicia to arrange what they needed—including some regular clothes and toiletries for him—and Grant settled things with the hotel and car rental they'd abandoned in Atlanta, Zoe'd been dealing with the FBI.

She accepted a glass of champagne from a server and drifted through the ballroom, looking for people she knew and wondering if Carling was here yet. She'd left messages for both Grant and Kell that she was coming down here. They had probably been in the shower, as guys tended to wait until the last minute to get ready. Sitting in her room would have been hell on her nerves, so she'd decided to brave their annoyance at her for not waiting.

A figure appeared in the wide entryway. Zoe paused and sipped her champagne as cover while she checked him out. He surveyed the crowd while he shot his cuffs, his stance wide and confident but not too arrogant. The five-button tux was blacker than black, with a white Euro-style tie and satin vest that fit the lean, muscled body like it had been tailor-made. Her eyes rose, noticing the slight skew of the tie at his neck and the smooth sweep of overlong hair that had been tamed without being slicked.

Then she met his eyes.

And realized it was Grant.

And he was *pissed*.

It didn't show on his face, only in the eyes that had probably turned dark green. She was chagrined that she remembered they did that. But then, it was the color she'd stared into when she refused to marry him.

He made his way to her with an elegant stride, hiding his purposefulness. Three people stopped him with greetings, and he paused, clasped hands and gave warm smiles, and moved on, probably leaving them trying to remember where they'd seen him before. More than a few women watched him walk away, and even a couple of gay men, one of whom couldn't take his eyes off Grant's ass. To Zoe's amazement, when Grant caught him looking, he actually winked at him!

But her amusement was gone by the time he reached her side, and she could feel how tightly he was holding himself.

"Don't say it."

He looked down at her. "Say what?"

"Don't ask what the hell I think I'm doing."

"You shouldn't have done something to make me ask it."

She sighed. "I waited until another couple was coming down. I wasn't alone in the elevator. I stayed near groups until I handed off my invitation outside. Safe as houses."

He scowled. "What does that mean?"

"No idea."

"Being part of a couple doesn't make someone safe. Pat and Freddie are a couple."

She nodded toward the stage, where an elderly man and woman laughed at something a younger man was telling them. "That's them. See? Harmless."

Grant's eyebrows went up. "That's him."

"Yes, and his wife. They like to stay in the hotel for these benefits so they don't have to drive so far in the evenings. We chatted in the elevator."

"No, I mean *him*."

"Oh!" Zoe realized he meant that the younger man was Carling and started to turn and look. But two more men entering the ballroom caught her attention. Kell looked familiar and comforting in a traditional one-button tux with a dark blue bow tie and cummerbund. Tanicia was crafty, because the blue matched Zoe's long, slinky satin gown and gloves. He spotted them and started across the room.

Agent Henricksen followed him.

"Shit." It was under her breath, but Grant heard

her and followed her gaze. "What? He looks good." He flicked back to her, then zeroed in on Carling again. "You guys match."

Zoe kept quiet, too much roiling through her brain to trust what would come out. She'd expected to match Kell. Not in clothing, necessarily, but in demeanor or whatever. She'd assumed they'd take the lead together, with Grant like a…a bodyguard or something equally out of place, yet not. The way he always was. Yet here they stood, and it felt natural, and she hadn't even been thinking about Kell until he walked in the door, equally as intrusive as the taller, wider, much-less-comfortable-looking agent behind him.

Henricksen's tux didn't fit as well as Grant's or Kell's, even though they were all off the rack. The way the fabric reflected the light in places it shouldn't told her it was cheaper than theirs. But then, the FBI probably didn't have the budget of a top corporate attorney.

Henricksen's approach had destroyed all that natural comfort she'd been feeling, though. She hadn't had a chance to explain to Grant and Kell why she called him. She'd slept on the plane all the way to San Francisco, and then there were always people around. Grant had been intent on making sure they weren't followed, while Kell constantly texted Tanicia to tell her what they needed. Once they were in the hotel she had little time to put her plan in motion, and the guys needed their sleep. She'd gotten some last night and on the plane, while she was pretty sure neither of them had.

But she hadn't expected the agent to come here, and so quickly. She'd thought she had more time.

Kell stopped next to them, already clued in to Grant's target. "Excellent. Those two are moving away. He'll be alone. Shall we approach him?"

"Not just yet." The smooth, deep voice came from behind Kell and surprised both men. Zoe couldn't believe it. Grant had missed tagging a Fed?

"Ms. Ardmore." Henricksen inclined his head at her.

"Agent Henricksen." She warily introduced Kell and Grant. He shook both their hands, taking their measure as he did and being measured in return.

"We need to do this now," Grant murmured to Zoe, his hand on the small of her back. She almost heard Kell's teeth grind.

"I know. Shaun." She used the agent's first name instead of repeating his title, as the room was filling more rapidly now and they didn't have as much space between them and other people. "Please excuse us for just a moment. I'll explain everything. Just—trust me."

He didn't look happy but nodded, surprising her. She nodded back, took a deep breath, and turned to approach the guy who held their future in his hands.

* * *

"What the hell are we doing?" Kell scowled across the empty table between him and the one where Zoe sat alone with Carling, who was apparently the funniest man in California.

"Hell if I know." Grant swallowed a mouthful of champagne. "My plan wasn't to be useless tonight."

Shaun-the-agent-Zoe-hadn't-told-them-about fiddled with an extra fork that had been left on the table. "She was supposed to be back in a few minutes. I shouldn't let this go on."

Grant ignored the Fed. He had nothing against him, of course, he worked with federal agents all the time. But until Zoe explained why she'd called him in—which was what the agent claimed she'd done— Grant wasn't giving him anything. The agent hadn't been very forthcoming, either. Grant didn't know how much Zoe had told him about their plan, and he didn't want to answer questions while they were surrounded by several hundred unknown people.

Carling had locked onto Zoe as soon as she approached him. Grant hadn't been able to hear what they said, but it didn't look like Zoe had needed to manufacture any pretext. They'd gone through the dessert line together, then sat to listen to the various speakers extol the virtues of the project they were raising money for. He, Stone, and Henricksen had been left to find their own table and watch, useless.

The original plan had the three of them approaching Carling as a team from a high-end magazine and arranging a private interview about his art collection. But Zoe had glided off looking so little like a journalist that Grant had held Stone back, letting her take point. It was her gig, after all.

But it had been two hours since Carling handed off a check to one of the runners. Half the crowd had gone, but the two of them sat, cozy and rapt—and holding hands, goddamn it.

He wondered if Stone was as roilingly jealous as he was.

"Why doesn't she just ask him about the damned totems already?" Stone grumbled. He shifted in his seat for about the hundredth time, flinging his elbow over the back of the fancy-covered folding chair.

"Looks like they hit it off," Henricksen observed.

Grant found that one difficult to ignore. His head jerked toward the agent, irritated words on his lips. Then he saw the twinkle in the guy's eyes and stood down. Henricksen had read them and thought he had an idea of what was going on. And he was probably right. Grant wouldn't give him the satisfaction of taking the bait.

That he almost had was disconcerting. *He* was the mercenary, the tough guy, trained to be in control at all times. Stone knew it, too. He could feel him smirking on his left, smug that he'd seen through the agent's ploy before Grant had. If he didn't like the guy so much, he'd lock him in a utility closet.

"I suppose you two know that Carling is one of the ten richest men in the state of California."

Henricksen must be bored, Grant thought. The big man eased back in his seat, faking relaxation, and kept talking casually.

"When Ms. Ardmore called me, I did some research on him. I'd heard of him but hadn't realized how much money he's actually made with his little gizmo things. It's amazing he's avoided getting married. Probably tired of all the gold diggers clamoring after him. A guy like that, he'd have good radar for a woman with guile. So it looks like Zoe's either hidden her intentions well, or she's been honest with him."

Grant said nothing. Clocking a Fed was never a smart idea, even when deliberately provoked. Even for fun.

Stone didn't seem to be reading Henricksen the same way. "Zoe knows how to be captivating. She's been to a hundred of these things."

Or maybe he was trying to make a point to Grant. He hid a grin and swallowed more—ugh, warm— champagne. He was getting somewhere if Stone felt threatened.

Except now he wasn't sure where it was he wanted to get. He watched Zoe laugh yet again, her face practically glowing with her interest in the man. She had her arms draped on the table and her body angled toward Carling, who kept threading his fingers through hers. If Grant didn't know better, he'd think they already knew each other. He kept imagining getting up, striding over there, and gently but easily drawing Zoe away from the guy in a way that left no uncertainty about whose she was.

Of course, she wasn't Grant's. Deciding he was going to make her his was easier when he'd thought Stone was a Carling type, unworthy of her. But his expectations had been shredded almost as soon as he met him. It wasn't his habit to make assumptions about people, and it galled him that he'd applied stereotypes to Stone just because he had money, was an attorney, and was born into high society. But he kept a cool head in a crisis. He put Zoe's safety and happiness above anything else, but didn't go alpha on her—which would have been to Grant's advantage, because Zoe wouldn't stand for someone else taking control.

Stone even had good ideas, for someone not in the business. Despite his fatigue, Grant hadn't been able to sleep last night. He'd worried about Zoe and patrolled the hallway several times, each time forcing himself not to knock on her door. On his third trip he'd caught Stone doing the same thing. They started talking about the situation and what Zoe should do, and next thing Grant knew, they were strategizing over tiny bottles of Scotch from the minibar.

And Grant found himself wondering if fighting him for Zoe was right. Her happiness was the important thing. Which one of them could make her happier? He didn't know anymore.

The ballroom was nearly empty now, with only a few pockets of lingering attendees scattered around. The staff had started to clear tables and collect chairs. Zoe and Carling leaned in very close to each other, then stood and headed for the doorway. Zoe didn't look back once.

The three men rose to their feet simultaneously, all stepping forward, all used to being in the lead. Grant glowered at Stone, who gave him a mocking smile and stepped back. He didn't bother to look at Henricksen. The agent was at a disadvantage, not knowing the plan. He'd defer to Grant.

Who didn't know the plan anymore, either. That was okay. He was good at improvising. He followed

Zoe and Carling into the lobby, where they paused halfway between the elevators and the front door. Grant crossed to the concierge stand and stood behind a guy making arrangements for theater tickets. He caught a glimpse of Henricksen lingering in the ballroom doorway, half obscured by a conveniently placed potted plant, and Stone lifting the house phone in an alcove near the main desk.

Carling sandwiched Zoe's hand between both of his. She nodded, smiling still. Was she ever going to stop smiling? He bent and kissed her on the cheek, then the back of her hand. He slipped his hands into his pockets and watched as Zoe got into the elevator. She waved with her fingertips. As the doors closed, Carling headed for the front door. The professional in Grant saw his smile and ambling gait as belonging to someone who'd just had a nice time. The jealous lion saw self-satisfaction and sleazy intentions.

When Carling had disappeared outside, Grant turned to find the other guys. Stone already stood at the elevator, stabbing repeatedly at the button and looking at the digital numbers above the doors. Henricksen, grinning, joined Grant as he walked toward the alcove.

"I hope he's smart enough not to confront her like that."

"I guess we'll see."

Zoe's ex got on an empty elevator and scowled through the closing doors, not bothering to hold it for them. Pissed, Grant mashed the button with his thumb. They didn't have to wait long. When they reached their floor, Zoe's door was open. She'd known they would be right behind Stone, but Grant would scold her anyway for the safety breach.

No almost-loud voices filtered into the hallway. When Grant and Henricksen entered Zoe's room, they found her lying on her stomach across her bed, one hand propping up her chin, and Stone leaning against the dresser, his arms folded, his expression set. He looked up when they entered.

"She wouldn't talk until you got here."

Henricksen closed the door and took up position beside it, so Grant moved into the room and sat on the bed next to Zoe. Stone's deepening scowl made him smirk.

"What happened to the plan?" he asked her.

She smiled. "I ditched it."

"Why?"

"Because as soon as I walked up to him and saw the pin on his lapel, I knew there was a better way to connect."

Grant hadn't been close enough to detail the guy's jewelry. "And?"

"He belonged to the same honor society I did. In college. He went to a different school, but we knew some of the same people from the alumni organization."

"So that's what you talked about for so long?" Stone demanded.

"Of course not. From there we talked about professors and then bars in Boston we went to while we were in school, and that led to telling stories about some of the geeks we knew. We weren't in the same field, but both were geeky. And I told him about my web design business and he told me how he admired anyone who could mesh technology and art." Her eyes started to shine as her enthusiasm picked up. "I asked if he had an extracurricular interest in art, and that launched him on a lecture about his collection, which I barely held my own on, but he seemed to appreciate anyway."

"You seduced him," Henricksen observed.

She shrugged, a move that shifted her breasts up in the bodice of her dress, drawing Grant's eyes. He'd sat next to her in an attempt to avoid looking there, but the way she was lying on the bed… He dragged his gaze back up to her face as she maneuvered up to sit, her legs draped to one side. The movement sent her perfume drifting toward him. It was the same perfume she'd worn their last summer together. Had to be. It threw him back in time, filled him with the kind of longing only horny teens who thought they were in love felt. He stood up and leaned on the wall, his hands in his pockets, and tried not to look at the breasts squished up by her twisted bodice or the long leg now exposed by the slit of her skirt.

"The bottom line is that he invited me to his home tomorrow before I fly back to Boston. We're having brunch and he'll show me his collection."

"Hell, no," all three men said.

"Look, we need to back up." Henricksen stepped forward. "You need to tell me, Ms. Ardmore, what you're doing and why you called me."

Her eyes were wide and pleading as she gazed up at him. "I'm sorry, Agent Henricksen, I didn't know you'd come out here. I didn't mean to be disruptive."

His smooth skin didn't wrinkle, nor did his body language indicate frustration, but Grant still sensed it.

"Disruptive? Ms. Ardmore, what do you think I've been doing for the last few weeks?"

She frowned a little, some of her animation fading. "I don't know. Going after bad guys?"

"Going after the bad guys who are after *you*." He moved away from the door and clasped his hands behind his back, pacing a little as if giving a speech in front of the rookies. "Since you sent me the photos and notes you received, I was able to initiate a watch on known associates of Patron Rhomney and Fredricka Thomashunis. Under that aegis, we've spoken with half a dozen people regarding the search for the Farmer totems. All of those people were tracking you."

"Who are they?"

"Treasure seekers, mostly," he said, surprising Grant. "Rhomney is smart. He's no doubt keeping his zealous followers close while he hires those with other interests to operate in the field. These are people with some damned good investigating skills who've been able to keep watch on your activities, determined to get their cut when you find the totems."

Zoe exchanged a look with Grant. That explained the guys on the boat.

"So far, we haven't talked to anyone who cared about the totems before they were approached by Rhomney, or anyone who seems to have been ordered to harm or detain you."

Stone spoke up for the first time. "I can't believe this *nobody* could convince so many people to work for free. That's what you meant, right? If they get their cut when Zoe finds the totems, that means they're not getting paid now?"

Henricksen nodded.

"He's charming." Zoe's voice was so low Grant could barely hear it. "He's awful, but he has that charisma. And he's an expert manipulator, whether he's using fear or enticement as incentive."

"Still." Stone didn't look convinced. "Didn't you say these are mostly iron?"

"Do you have any idea what William Carling paid for them?" Henricksen asked. They all stared at him.

"Do you?" Zoe said.

"We do now." He named a figure that was easily a hundred times what Grant would have expected. He automatically eased closer to Zoe. It was the kind of money desperate people would kill for.

"How do you know?" Zoe pressed the agent. "You didn't know where they were a few weeks ago. And you said you couldn't open an investigation."

"I still don't have enough to do that. And I'm not here today in an official capacity. After you called me and mentioned your visit to Mr. Cocalico, we dug into his history and found the transaction with Carling."

Now apparently too anxious to sit still, Zoe rose. Her arm brushed Grant's chest when she moved past him and sat again on the end of the bed, now closer to Stone, who smirked. Grant hadn't done anything overt or with intent, but he felt like a teenager, anyway. He leaned against the wall again and folded his arms.

"Which brings me to you." Henricksen motioned to Zoe. "Why did you call me now?"

She stuck her hands under her thighs and stared at her knees. "We're getting close. It was possible Carling no longer had the totems, but if he does, I won't be able to keep Pat at bay anymore. I wanted to make sure you were fully informed of what was happening so…so you wouldn't think I was cooperating unlawfully with him," she rushed, still not looking at anyone.

"Without telling us," Grant pointed out. Stone shot him a look, but Grant ignored it. "We'd have appreciated a heads up, Zoe." His tone came out harsher than he meant. It was less about not telling them than it was about her lack of trust. Now he had an inkling how Stone must have felt.

"I didn't get a chance to tell you." She stood again and faced him. "I was going to when we met up in the ballroom."

"But you're not alone in this. You had to know we wouldn't let—"

"Let what?" She held out her arms, less cowed now, more intense. "If I got in trouble, so would you. Accomplices. It's better to at least keep the FBI in the loop. Which was what I intended." She spun on her heel. "I really didn't know you'd come out here."

Henricksen shrugged. "Like you said. You're close."

His caginess told Grant more than words would have. The agent was also concerned about what Zoe would do. Or maybe about what would be done to Zoe. He had some investment here, but Grant wasn't sure what it was. Coming out here on his own time, without agency resources? He was going to keep an eye on this guy.

"So what's the plan now?" Stone asked her. "Are you sure Carling still has them?"

"Yes, he described some things he has that he thought I'd like. One of them was definitely the totems."

"What did he say about them?" Henricksen asked.

"Not much. He hinted at the legend but said he'd tell me the story when he showed them to me." She frowned. "He described them as not worth much themselves, but that the legend elevated their value. Even so, why are so many people willing to come after them?"

"Near as we can tell," Henricksen answered, "it's a treasure thing. Hunters aren't looking for the score so much. They want enough money to keep them hunting, but it's more about the cachet of the find. Being famous in that world. One of the people we talked to said their family had kept an eye out for them for decades, which of course would predate your kidnapping and Rhomney and Thomashunis's first involvement."

"They'd been looking for a while, too," Zoe said. "But they don't want them for the same reasons."

"No."

Since they all knew or at least suspected why that was, no one said more.

"When are you supposed to go over there?" Grant asked her.

"Tomorrow for brunch. He's sending a car at ten-thirty."

"You're not going alone." Stone straightened and looked down at Zoe, his resolve clear. "I'll go with you."

"Hold on." Grant stepped forward. "I can protect her better. You know that."

"I don't know that." His blue eyes latched on to Grant's, and he understood what made him an effective attorney. "But it's beside the point. I fit in better. We've been a couple for years, and Carling's world is my world."

"Not quite," Henricksen broke in. "He's new money, still struggles to feel like he's a part of the elite. He's as likely to resent you as feel comfortable with you."

"I still fit there better than he does."

"I fit in just fine tonight," Grant argued. "What are you going to do if he has ulterior motives? If Pat and Freddie have him on the hook? You're not equipped to handle that."

"That's an important point," Henricksen conceded. "More importantly, if Carling tries anything with these two, they'll need *you* on the outside." He met Grant's eyes, and he understood. The agent's resources were limited. Even if he wanted to, he couldn't get authorization for surveillance on Carling. Which meant the three of them were still on their own.

"All right." Grant tensed his jaw at the look of

gratification on Stone's face. "Zoe, what are you thinking?"

"I'm thinking we get in the car, and when we show up and Carling asks who he is, I tell him it's my fiancé and he doesn't mind that I brought him, does he? He's too polite to say anything but no. We go in, eat—"

"No," Grant and Henricksen said together.

"You make sure you see the artwork first. Eating is dangerous," Grant added. "He could drug or poison you. It's better to convince him you're eager to see his collection, then, before the meal is served, you fall ill and get out of there."

Zoe looked skeptical, but Stone nodded. "What else?"

Grant relaxed. Stone could take direction. He wasn't going to be macho and act like he could lead this thing, and that made Grant feel a lot better.

They hashed out details and addressed what-ifs until midnight. Henricksen promised a communications system for their use, even if he couldn't officially be involved at this point, only authorized to gather information and assess. He'd have it by nine the next morning.

As they planned, Stone got cozier and cozier with Zoe, ending up on the bed with her braced against his shoulder, yawning. When Grant and Henricksen left, Stone stayed. Grant suspected he had more than planning for tomorrow in mind.

The hell of it was, Grant couldn't blame him. He couldn't use it to spur his own plan to woo Zoe—not that he really had one. It was truly a case of letting the better man win.

And Grant suspected the better man wasn't going to be him.

* * *

Kell knew he should go to his own room now. His right arm, the one Zoe leaned against, had stopped tingling about ten minutes ago, but he didn't want to move. It felt like months since he'd held her like this. She was lost in thought, probably working out how they'd handle tomorrow, maybe thinking about what Henricksen had said and leaned on Kell out of fatigue and maybe habit. But he didn't care. He let her, quietly inhaling her scent, soaking in her warmth, thinking about the smooth skin of her shoulder inches away from his mouth.

He should be conflicted. The secrets, outright lies, and destruction of trust—all of that had been a dragging weight since he got here. But right now, he couldn't feel any of it. Jealousy had rooted deep, making him think of all the reasons he'd been with her in the first place. How much he still loved her, despite everything.

After a few moments when Zoe didn't move or speak, he lowered his head and drifted his lips across that skin. Goose bumps erupted and she gave a tiny shiver. He pressed his mouth harder, against her neck, and touched her with his tongue. Her head tilted a fraction and she eased into his body. Relief and need flooded him. He twisted her in his arms, his mouth sliding over her neck and up. When he captured her mouth it parted immediately, letting him in, and he pressed deep but kept it slow. If he pushed too hard, too fast, she'd remember her guilt and shut him down.

But God, it had been so long, and she smelled so good, and his hands tightened on her back and pulled her against him as best he could while they were both sitting. She made a little noise in the back of her throat and he grunted, gripping the back of her neck, stroking his fingers down below the edge of her dress. His tux trousers drew tight and he stood, drawing Zoe up without breaking the kiss, and she let him.

His brain started to fuzz out. Zoe's tongue stroked into his mouth. She went up on her tiptoes, pressing closer. Kell thrust a hand up into her hair, tugging until the pins loosened and it tumbled down over his arm. The zipper tab of her dress tickled his other hand. He twisted his fingers to grasp, started to pull…

And he stopped. Zoe dropped to her heels and slowly broke the kiss, staring up at him with those gorgeous eyes that churned with a dozen emotions. He suddenly felt like a cad for even considering making love with her right now.

"Kell," she murmured, regret dominant in her voice.

"I know." He forced a smile and rubbed her shoulders, wishing her skin wasn't so damned silky. "Get some sleep, Zo. We need to be at full speed tomorrow."

She made a face. "You should talk. You and Grant haven't slept in two days."

He felt his face go blank when she mentioned Grant. He wanted to hate the guy who was pulling his fiancée from him, but so far, the only reason he'd given to hate him was how much he cared about Zoe.

He said goodnight and waited outside her door, listening to her engaging all the locks before he walked to his own room. Not that all the locks had helped last night. With Zoe on the other side of the wall, he wasn't sure sleeping would be any easier tonight.

He lay in his soft bed, listening to the silence occasionally broken by voices in the hall or doors opening and closing. He doubted he'd be able to detect anyone suspicious just by ear. Maybe Grant could. He was on the other side of Zoe, closer to the elevator. And he obviously had training in stuff like that. Kell didn't care if the other guy's ability to save Zoe gave him an edge, as long as he saved her. He had a fight ahead of him, to rebuild their relationship, but he could be civilized about it. That was *his* edge.

Kell sighed and rolled over, forcing his eyes closed. Sometimes being civilized sucked.

Natalie J. Damschroder

Chapter Twelve

Zoe leaned against her locked door like a primetime drama heroine, her chest heaving and her insides trembling. She held up a hand, expecting it to shake just as hard, but it looked steady. Such a liar.

Why had she been remembering Kell's kisses as *tender?* That one was anything but. His hunger had only been half of what rattled her. He'd been so in control, as if afraid to spook her. Or maybe afraid to encourage her. So much held under the surface…if he'd unleashed it, she'd have drowned in him.

She got ready for bed in a daze, unable to stop thinking about both kisses and wishing neither had happened. After managing to fall sleep with the help of a tiny bottle of vodka from the minibar, she woke determined to stop giving Grant-the-man and Kell-the-man so much attention. It distracted from the mission. Nothing could be resolved until the totems were retrieved, so she'd put all her focus on that and make them do the same.

Her plan went to hell as soon as they gathered in Grant's room to mike up and she remembered that Kell was going in as her fiancé. It was going to be weird to act the way they'd naturally been, for it to be pretend, and…oh, no. She looked down at her left hand. Will Carling hadn't seen a ring on it last night. She was sure he'd noticed and probably wouldn't have been as open and flirtatious if she'd been wearing it.

But Kell stopped her in the small foyer and lifted her hand. "I thought you should put this back on." He slid the engagement ring over her finger. It winked up at her, and her hand suddenly felt more normal. Odd, since she'd been without it almost as long as she'd worn it. The glitter blurred and prismed, and she blinked back moisture. "Thanks," she murmured, her voice husky. She ran a finger over the gem. She'd been so wrong, thinking Grant knew her better than Kell did, just because she hadn't told him everything.

She looked up to find both men watching her. A flush surged up from her feet and made her scalp tingle. She had to stop doing this.

"All right, we need to hurry now." Henricksen held up a tiny button-like device attached to a strip of paper. "These are the comms. It sticks just inside your ear. You don't want to touch it after it's placed. Dislodging it can drop it into your ear, and I don't want to have to go digging." He set down the strip on a black cloth laid out on the table and indicated four slightly larger circles. "These are the mikes. They attach on your chest, below the collarbone, so you'll have to wear shirts that cover them."

Grant would be staying outside Carling's property, and Kell already had on a button-down dress shirt under a sport coat. Zoe's dress was a soft, light-green wraparound that she'd shoved into the bottom of her bag before she flew to the Keys. She'd wanted to cover every wardrobe contingency. And, luckily, it had a boat neck that covered where the mike would be.

But… "What about heartbeat? Won't that interfere?"

"They're directional, so no, the heartbeat won't be picked up."

"Do we have to do anything to activate them?" she asked.

Henricksen shook his head. "They'll be on continuously. And there's a strong filter, so covering it with your hand won't block your voice. We'll hear everything."

"Thanks for the warning." Not that she expected to have private conversations while she was in Carling's house, but it was good information to have.

Grant stood to the side, his expression wry, his arms folded. "This is pretty advanced equipment for the FBI."

Henricksen flicked him a glance. "I know a guy."

"Wait." Zoe held up a hand. Her knowledge of this stuff all came from fiction. She'd never have known this wasn't standard issue. "Why do we get the good stuff?" To her and to Kell, the situation was life-altering. But in the big picture it meant very little. Pat and Freddie weren't terrorists, they didn't threaten huge numbers of people or economic stability. She didn't want Henricksen getting in trouble because she'd dragged him into this.

"Relax," he said. "They're prototypes, and my friend wanted a real-world test. I can't use them on sanctioned events because the risk of failure is deemed too high."

Well, that wasn't very reassuring. "So they could fail? We could need help, and you wouldn't know it?"

Grant picked up one of the strips and studied it. "It's not likely. I know the designer's work. He knows what he's doing."

"Okay." Zoe took a deep breath. "Anything else we need to go over?"

They spent a few minutes attaching the devices. Zoe insisted on doing her own, though both Kell and Grant offered. Henricksen wisely gave her instructions and sent her to the bathroom to stick them on. She did the mike first, placing it where her cleavage started so the outline wouldn't show against her dress. The earpiece made her more nervous. She pictured Henricksen aiming a pair of tweezers at her ear and shuddered. She tipped her head to the side, placed the strip inside the curve of her ear, and pressed the button hard against her skin. When she lifted the paper strip the button stayed, feeling heavy and well stuck. She let out her breath slowly and returned to the main room.

"Ready?" Henricksen glanced around at them all, and when they nodded he flipped a switch on a box that looked an awful lot like a remote control for a model truck. Zoe expected to hear static or hissing or even just the faint electronic hum you don't notice until it turns off, but nothing happened. Then Grant said, "Cool," and she jumped at the echo in her ear.

"Fine here," Kell said, and she heard that in stereo, too.

"Weird," she contributed, and everyone nodded again.

Henricksen turned off the switch. "Neely and I will be outside," he said. "As close as we can get."

"Which isn't very close," Grant offered. "There's no on-street parking, so we'll be a few blocks away. What's the range on these?" He tapped his chest.

"A mile," Henricksen said. "Supposedly."

"All right, so we'll be at least that close." Grant's mouth quirked. "Best if you don't get into trouble."

Zoe kept silent. She didn't feel that Carling himself was a threat, but saying so would be foolish. Not that she believed in jinxes, but still. And even if he was okay, maybe someone close to him wasn't.

Kell's watch beeped. "It's time."

Zoe pressed a hand to her fluttering stomach. "Okay. Let's go."

Grant took the elevator down first so he could watch them outside. Zoe and Kell stood awkwardly outside the elevator, waiting for the next car.

"Are you okay?" he asked.

"Of course." But she found herself unable to look at him and not sure why.

"Zoe." He waited, and she pressed her lips together and turned to face him.

"What?"

"It's not going to work like this."

"I know."

"What's wrong?"

She tossed her hands. "I have no idea." As soon as she said it, though, she did. Grant was listening to them right now. He would hear everything they said and did. And they would be acting like an engaged couple, something that should come naturally, and probably would…if Grant wasn't listening.

She couldn't admit that to Kell. Last night's honesty had been painful enough. Plus—Grant was listening.

Which meant she'd better get over herself.

She drew in a deep breath. "I'm okay." Reaching out, she threaded her fingers through his and stepped closer to his side. He smiled down at her, and everything slipped into place.

The elevator dinged and opened, and they stepped into the empty car. "We're on," Kell announced.

"The limo's coming down the street," Grant replied. "I'm at the valet. Gave the attendant an old ticket, so he won't find my car. I'll be right here, ready."

"I'm in the garage," Henricksen added. "I'll pick up Neely as soon as the limo pulls away."

"Tip the valet well," Zoe advised, smiling. "Never know when you need them on your side."

Grant chuckled and Kell squeezed her hand. They stopped on a lower floor, where a group of women wearing conference badges stepped on, talking animatedly. She and Kell stood in the corner, silent, until they reached the lobby.

The bright sun made her blink hard when they stepped through the automatic doors, but Will Carling was immediately at her side, kissing her cheek. Then he caught sight of hers and Kell's linked fingers and frowned.

"I'm sorry, I don't think we've had the pleasure?" He straightened and reached to shake hands with Kell.

"Will, this is my fiancé, Kellen Stone. He's very interested in seeing your collection. I hope you don't mind if he joins us?" She held her breath and her smile. Carling looked a little like he'd bitten into a lemon while expecting candy. She knew what he had to be thinking. She hadn't mentioned Kell the night before. She was a tease, or he'd misinterpreted.

Suddenly, their plan made no sense. Will's eyes cut to her, and in a split second she made a decision. She looked steadily at him, trying to convey a whole history. *I don't love him. I'm interested in you. Last night wasn't a lie, and I don't want him here, but what can you do? Political expectations.* She lifted her shoulders in a tiny shrug and Will smiled, a knowing look coming into his eyes.

"Of course it's all right. I love sharing my art with knowledgeable people." He tucked Zoe's hand into the crook of his arm and turned his back on Kell, leaving him to follow. Zoe let her body relax slowly, so he wouldn't sense it, but thought, *Man, guys are so easy*.

Will handed her into the limo and slid in beside her. Kell sat on the other side, facing them. Apparently Will had insulted him enough, however, because he began making small talk with him.

After a moment, Will asked, "What's your interest in art?"

"Purely creative."

"You create?"

Kell shook his head. "God, no. I'm fascinated by how a hunk of unformed material can be shaped into something amazing. By the act of transferring a vision from brain to hand to sculpture or canvas."

Will nodded. "It's the most unquantifiable discipline in the world. That's why I love it. When you work in an industry that's all about measurement and statistics and defined characteristics, you need to balance it with the opposite."

They passed the rest of the drive exchanging opinions along the same lines, and Zoe marveled at how easily Kell donned his role. Of course, he'd been bred to be able to communicate with anyone about anything, but this was a different situation. And in the years they'd been together, she'd never heard Kell talk about paintings and sculpture the way he did now.

She raised her eyebrows at him once, and his eyes crinkled, but he didn't take his attention off Will.

The limo slowed and pulled into a long driveway. At the end of the drive was a magnificent stone mansion with exquisite landscaping. It reminded Zoe of Kell's parents' home, though much larger. When they got inside, though, right away she changed her mind. Where the Stones' home welcomed you in and made you comfortable even as it showcased their wealth, this house was no home. It was showcase only.

The foyer walls were lined with paintings, old portraits she was sure were worth a fortune but that looked down on them with stern disapproval.

"Are these ancestors?" she asked, and Will laughed.

"No, they're just acquisitions."

"Degas?" Kell asked from where he stood examining a small bronze statue of a ballet dancer.

"Good eye. She was a young girl…" He rattled on for a couple of minutes about the supposed inspiration for the piece, and Degas' working conditions, and the provenance of the original. "Of course, this is a reproduction, so I don't count it among my actual collection."

Zoe forced back a groan. If he was going to rattle on like this about every single thing… "I can't wait to see," she said brightly, thinking it was almost as big a lie as the one she'd told Kell when she left him.

"Brunch should be ready in just a mo—"

"Oh, no," she interrupted, "I'm too eager. Can we see your pieces first?"

Will seemed taken aback, but agreed.

Let the boredom begin.

* * *

"Oh, my *God*!" Grant pushed back against the car seat, stretching as much as he could. "I thought this was going to be dangerous."

"It is," Henricksen growled. "To our sanity."

"If he goes on about one more fucking glass tile—"

"At least we're out here," the agent reminded him. "Imagine being in there and having to pretend you're interested."

"Good point." Grant reached for his soda and sucked it down, listening to Stone excuse himself from whatever room they were in. "What the hell is he doing, leaving her alone with Carling?"

"At this point, I don't think—"

"Hey!" The word was hissed from the back of Stone's throat. There was the sound of a door closing, and Stone whispered, "We can hear everything you say. It's damned distracting, and this is hard enough without listening to you complain!"

Fuck. Grant hadn't exactly forgotten they could hear him as clearly as he could hear them, but he wasn't used to working with people who hadn't learned to block it out. "Sorry, man."

"Yeah, well, just shut it, all right?"

"Any sign of the totems yet?"

"No, but we've progressed from the classics to the more esoteric and legend-based stuff. We should get to them soon."

"Good. I'm—"

"Don't say it."

Grant fell silent and sat still while he listened to the conversation Kell rejoined. Zoe was apparently asking Carling about a…decoupage frog? Had he heard that correctly?

It had been well over an hour since they started. Grant hoped to hell they were almost at the—

"Okay, here we are at my prized pieces." Carling's voice had taken on a note of greater pride and even a hint of excitement. After a few metallic clinks and a whir, he heard Zoe gasp softly. He straightened a little in his seat, and Henricksen stopped leaning on his hand, elbow braced on the edge of the car door. Was this it?

"Those are…unique." Her voice shook. A moment later, a double-tap on the mike just about shattered Grant's eardrum. He bit back a shout and glared at Henricksen. He couldn't even yank out headphones or cover the button. Henricksen shrugged, but smirked. It had been his idea for Stone to tap the mike when Zoe confirmed the totems were the ones she'd dumped sixteen years ago. Carling droned on about how he'd found them, how much he'd paid for them, and why. It was dry stuff, no better than the rest of his stories, and barely touched on the Jacob Farmer legends. But Zoe's breathing rasped a little in the earpiece, and Grant knew they were the right ones.

"That's good enough for me," Henricksen said.

"Get out of there," Grant ordered. "But subtly." Boredom had turned to urgency. Now that they knew where the totems were, he wanted Zoe as far away from them as possible. The FBI could take it from here.

"Are you all right, honey?" Kell asked, initiating their exit strategy.

But Grant knew better than any of them that it was too early to relax.

* * *

Illness was difficult to fake when your primary emotion was elation. Zoe knew the polite interest she'd held on her face all morning had changed the instant Will removed the bear totem from its case. She let Kell take over and faded back a little, willing her flushed face and quick breathing to appear flu-ish.

"Are you okay, hon?" Kell asked. She glanced up to

see him and Will watching her with concern.

She almost said, "Of course!" but, duh, that wasn't the right response. "I'm sure it's nothing," she assured them as you do when you know it's not nothing but you don't want someone to worry.

"You probably need food," Will decided. He started to replace the totem in the case, but Zoe stepped forward.

"You might be right, but I don't want to cut this short. These are so unusual." She held out her hands as if to cradle the totem. "May I examine it?" She and Kell had both examined a couple of other things more closely, so asking to look at these wouldn't be as suspicious.

Will smiled. "Certainly." He settled it into her hands, and a shiver went up her spine.

"Heavy," she marveled.

"Iron," he agreed. "An unusual manufacture, of course. Weight—perhaps stability—must have been important."

"Why would someone make something like this?" she asked.

"Well, Jacob Farmer had mixed ancestry, with multiple influences, and probably a difficult life because of it." Will eased closer to her side and pointed to the markings near the bottom. "You can see where he tapped into his African culture here, where symbols are reminiscent of tribal storytelling. And, of course, the animals at the top are Native American. The prevailing belief is that he was attempting to transcend his failure to belong to any of these cultures by belonging to them all."

"Just by making some sculptures?" Kell looked skeptical. Will chuckled.

"Probably not. Farmer never documented his intent, as far as anyone has been able to find, but there is a key that supposedly goes with these. Like a map, to unlock the connection." He described the piece of leather Zoe had found a picture of.

Kell shifted his weight, his elbow nudging hers. It was time.

"Oh, Kell, this is perfect!" She hugged the totem to her chest, then gazed reverently at it.

"Are you sure? You didn't look at all of them."

She shook her head. "I don't need to. They're exactly what I was looking for."

"All right, then." Kell's posture tightened, and he turned to Will. "I'd like to make an offer for the set."

But Will laughed. "I'm sorry, I don't sell anything from my collection."

"Well, I'm sure we can come to an agreement, given the circumstances. Every—"

"I don't sell." Will's tone was still pleasant, but brooked no argument. "Ever."

Kell kept negotiating. Zoe knew she should help. They had to convince him. But she'd become absorbed in the totem in her hand, thinking how different it looked. Smaller than she remembered, but of course she'd still been a kid then. Far more inert, absent the power she'd subconsciously attributed to it. She'd associated her entire captivity with these things by the time she escaped, and she thought they had to show some signs of what they'd wrought. Scratches and dents, at least. She ran a finger over the lines carved into the gold, peering hard, looking…

She swallowed audibly. Looking for blood. Jordie had died for these.

Suddenly, illness wasn't so difficult to fake. She went lightheaded and queasy at the same time, faint screams echoing in the back of her mind. For an instant, the distinctive blend of the tang of blood, mildewed wood, and dirty clothes hovered on the air.

Zoe started to fight it, to force herself back into the carefully lit and expensively carpeted display room she stood in, but she heard Grant in her earpiece, urging them to hurry and get out of there.

"Oh." She opened stiff fingers and let the totem fall to the ground, swaying a little. The men swung toward her, alarm apparent on Will's face. She closed her eyes and tilted as the walls of the cabin closed around her and she could have sworn a big, dumb man sat in the corner to her left. Freddie's high-pitched laughter pierced her eardrums, and panic swept through her, convinced the woman had either appeared in Will's mansion or that she was somehow going back there, like the totem had opened a time portal.

"Kell!" she cried out, reaching, and his arm came around her back as her knees gave out. He swept her up in his arms and the cabin disappeared, the smell returning to "rich guy's house" and the laughter and screams blinking out like someone had turned off the TV. But her vision didn't clear. She squeezed her eyes closed, but when she opened them could only see hazy light. The panic increased, this time more rational. "Kell," she said again, clutching the front of his shirt in her free hand.

"This way," Will said from somewhere in front of them. Kell started walking, and Zoe closed her eyes and pressed her face to his shoulder, wishing he wasn't wearing the jacket so she could feel his warmth and strength. His arms under her were tense, and she knew he was aware she wasn't faking.

"It's okay," he whispered against her hair. "I'll get you out of here." A few steps later he bent and settled her on some kind of settee, stiff fabric over stiffer cushions. A pillow was stuffed under her head as he laid her back, and she heard Will calling for water and a compress.

She'd be embarrassed if this was real. Swooning in the twenty-first century, for cripes sake.

The thought seemed to reboot her brain. Tingles ran up and down her body, her nerves testing themselves, and faded. The queasiness disappeared, and her head felt more stable. She was afraid to open her eyes, though, and find herself still blind.

A cool cloth draped over her forehead. "Take it easy," Kell murmured, and she sensed that he was kneeling on the floor next to her. "Do you want an ambulance? A doctor?"

"No. I'm okay." She cracked her eyelids and was relieved to see olive green silk fabric covering the roll of the settee's arm at her feet, and pale walls, crown molding, a uniformed maid or housekeeper hovering in the doorway, twisting her fingers. She breathed deep and let it out in a long sigh. "I don't know what came over me."

Kell wrapped his hand around hers and pressed it to his lips. "Could it be…?" He looked exactly like a half-hopeful, half-worried fiancé asking if she was pregnant.

She smiled sadly and stroked her hand down his cheek. "Maybe." She was acting now, of course, but couldn't help wondering if Kell wasn't. They hadn't talked much about children, certainly not since he'd proposed. They both wanted them eventually, was all they knew.

But if she *was* pregnant, it would be Kell's, and he'd win.

"What can I get you?" Will broke into their moment. "Brandy? No, of course not. Here's some water." He handed Zoe a glass, and she thanked him and sipped at it.

"I'm okay, I think, Will, thank you. But I'm afraid we'll have to skip brunch. I should go back to the hotel and lie down." She tilted her head to look at him. "I'm so sorry."

"Don't be ridiculous, of course you do. Perhaps we can try again next time you're in town."

"That would be lovely." She let Kell help her to her feet and was grateful her head didn't swim or her legs wobble. She smiled at both men and glanced around. "I'm afraid I don't know—"

"This way." Will jumped to lead them to the door. "Selma, please let Edward know we're ready for the car."

They made small talk on the front steps while they waited for the limo to glide up, mostly about how San Francisco weather was so different from the rest of the country, being so warm in October and chilly in the middle of summer.

Finally, the car was there, and she and Kell slid into its dim comfort. Moments later, they were rolling down the drive and gliding out the gate.

"We're clear," Kell said in a voice low enough that Edward couldn't hear it.

"Roger that," Grant came back. "You should pass us in thirty seconds, and we'll be right behind you. Hotel in twenty minutes, barring traffic."

Zoe automatically looked out the window at the empty street. The limo eased to a stop sign and waited for another car to turn from their right and pass on the left. Zoe followed the car's path, barely noting that it was at least a decade old and didn't belong in this neighborhood. Then it passed her window and she looked at the driver. Her gasp was almost a scream.

The man in the beater was Patron Rhomney.

Natalie J. Damschroder

Chapter Thirteen

"Are you absolutely sure?" Grant demanded for the third time. Henricksen barked orders into his cell phone, trying to organize a way to get the totems from Carling, now that he'd refused to make it easy and sell them.

"Of course she is." Kell glowered at Grant. "Stop badgering her."

"She just had a regressive episode, she said it herself." Grant leaned aggressively toward Kell, who stood with his hand on Zoe's arm as if expecting her to faint again. She'd kicked off her shoes as soon as they entered the hotel room, just in case, but she felt physically fine. The "episode" in Carling's house seemed long ago, residual effects banished by the shock of seeing Pat in that car.

"So?" Kell shot back at Grant. "What's that got to do with anything?"

"It's been years since she saw him, and that car went by too fast to make a positive identification."

"He's right." Zoe pulled away from Kell and sat on the bed, tiring as adrenaline seeped away. "It looked like him, but not exactly. He was older, and his hair wasn't as long. It was nicely trimmed. His face wasn't clean-shaven, but it was trendy scruff, not the bushy beard he used to keep." She rubbed her forehead and leaned forward over her knees. "I can't believe I would ever not recognize him. But it's easy to see someone you know in a stranger."

Kell didn't look convinced, but Grant settled back on his heels. "Exactly. We can't react haphazardly. Rhomney shouldn't be out of Ohio."

"He'd come for the totems," she argued. "Nothing would stop him if he knew where they were. Maybe he wouldn't let a minion handle it, not after all this time, not after losing them before."

"I get that." Grant pulled the desk chair over and straddled it backwards. "I'm not saying you have him pegged wrong. But how would he know they were here, not to mention get here so fast?"

"We know they're tracking us," Kell offered.

Grant looked up at him. "Yeah, but they've been tracking us since Florida. How would they know we found them now, as opposed to in Utah? Rhomney's not going to skip on parole without proof. He's not stupid."

"Whacked, but not stupid," Zoe confirmed. Still, when she'd seen that driver, something sharp had stabbed into the base of her neck, and it stung there. She was absolutely certain that man was Rhomney, and equally certain she didn't ever want to be that close to him again.

Henricksen snapped his phone shut and crossed to

them, looking grim. A wave of foreboding raised the hair on Zoe's back and arms. "What is it?"

The guys turned to face the agent.

"They got to Cocalico."

Zoe gasped. "Is he dead?"

"No, but he's in the hospital, unconscious, possible brain injury."

Oh, no. "What about Rudy?" Her voice shook. It was her fault. She'd led them to those innocent men.

"I have them checking. There's been no police report."

"Shit." She stood to pace, but Grant was in front of her before she took a step.

"It's not your fault," he growled so fiercely it derailed her guilt with surprise.

"But—"

"No buts. Whether or not you tracked them down, somehow whoever did this would have connected him to the totems."

But he was wrong. "No one knew I put them on a train. If I'd just stayed away from everyone and left all this alone—"

"They'd have you by now." He stepped even closer, wrapping his hands around her upper arms. His intense blue eyes trapped hers; she couldn't look away. "You are just as important and innocent as Ozzie Cocalico and anyone else that gets in Rhomney's way. I will *not*"—he shook her a little—"let you take responsibility for this."

It was as if he poured his will into her. Heat welled up inside her body, like hot water in a bath, soothing and healing. It left no room for guilt or regret, and after a moment, she felt nothing but determination and slight anger. The kind that compelled.

"How do you do that?" she murmured, and his eyes blazed in an entirely different way. His fingers loosened to a near-caress on her bare skin, and his mouth parted slightly.

"Unbelievable."

Kell's exclamation broke Grant's spell. Zoe jerked back, but she was standing too close to the bed. Grant tightened his hold to keep her from falling. She had to brace her hands on his chest to keep from falling against *him*. In the brief moment she touched him, she could feel his heartbeat, hard and fast under his T-shirt.

"Look, Neely, I've been cool about this, but you can't think I'm gonna stand here and watch you seduce her in front of me." Kell pulled her away from him by the hand and wrapped an arm around her shoulders.

Grant looked angry for a moment, his arm actually lifting like he was going to pull her back, but then amusement took over. "I wasn't seducing her."

Yeah, right. Zoe couldn't look at any of them. If she and Grant had been alone, they'd probably be in bed right now. No one should underestimate the power of guilt alleviation. She'd needed that, and somehow he'd known not only that she did, but how to do it.

Henricksen cleared his throat. "Can we get back to this, please?" He waggled his phone in the air, and they gave him their attention again. As he began to speak, Zoe eased away from Kell and sat back on the bed. He followed, staring pointedly at Grant, but didn't touch her when he sat.

"I've confirmed to the Bureau that we've got positive ID on the totems and that Rhomney may be here. But the agent charged with keeping tabs on him and Thomashunis talked to the parole officer today, and she insists Rhomney's in town."

"It's Sunday. Your agent talked to a parole officer on Sunday?" Grant looked disbelieving.

"I've kept my team alerted to what we're doing here, and to the actions against Ms. Ardmore and Mr. Stone."

"How does the parole officer know Pat's still in town?" Zoe asked. "Did she see him?"

"I don't know."

"Great. So that *could* have been him." The queasiness returned. "Will. Someone has to contact Will Carling. Pat was on his way to his house." She pulled out her phone and pulled up the contacts, swallowing over and over to keep the nausea at bay. She already felt bad for playing Will, lying and pretending, and now he was in the line of fire, too.

She hit the dial button and pierced Henricksen with a glare. "You're getting the totems, right? Now? They're going in today?" The call went directly to voice mail. She hung up without leaving a message, because what the hell could she say?

He shook his head. "We can't just go in and take them. We need Carling to agree to sign them over or a compelling reason to seize them, which takes a warrant. Which is impossible to get on a Sunday when there's no confirmation of physical threat. I had to do a lot of fast talking to even get that far."

"So, tomorrow?"

"With luck."

Zoe stood again, her eyes burning. "We can't let Will just swing in the wind. He didn't answer his phone."

"You saw his security setup." Kell stood, too, his brow furrowed with worry, but logic still dominant. "He's going to be fine."

"I've asked the local office to send a patrol car by," Henricksen assured her. "But we don't even know for sure Rhomney's here."

He's here. But she nodded. For a moment, they all stood, unmoving. She could almost hear engines revving, waiting for the green flag. But it wasn't going to come for a while, and she couldn't handle the collective tension. "I'm going to change and take a nap."

"Good idea." Kell stood and made to follow her. She stopped.

"What are you doing?"

He grinned. "I'm walking you to your room. Don't worry, I'll go on to my own."

Zoe would have said she was fine walking the twenty feet to her door, but the possibility of Pat being nearby made her jumpy. They walked in silence down the hall, and she paused at her door to thank Kell. He seemed strangely taller than usual, and she remembered she'd left her shoes in the other room. Oh, who cared? She wasn't going to be wearing them again soon.

"You'll be okay alone? I don't mind coming in and just being here. I can rest in the other bed."

She smiled. "Tempting." He'd taken off his jacket and rolled the sleeves of his shirt. He'd gotten warm, because he smelled good. Not the intentional scent of cologne, but the real, deep scent of his skin and need.

"Yeah?" His lips curved and he braced a hand on the door to lean over her. "How tempting?"

"Too." The memory of her panic at Will's was strong, and Kell could take her away from that. He was the "after" part of her life, the part she'd kept distant from the horrors, and she knew if she let him in, if she made love with him, it would banish the fear and pain, at least temporarily.

But she didn't move. Didn't open her door to escape him or let him in. Didn't stop looking into those gorgeous blue eyes, so deep and oh, God, so wanting. She whispered his name, and it came out a plea rather than a warning.

Kell dipped down and touched his mouth to hers, his eyes closing before they met. Zoe kept hers open. She wasn't sure why. His lips were gentle and undemanding, just offering her a taste, a promise. But his face was taut, his eyes scrunched a little, so that she knew he was closing off something else—pain, regret, betrayal, anger?

The last thing she wanted to do was lead him on and hurt him again later, but his mouth parted and coaxed hers open, his tongue smoothly invaded her, and something cracked. Her eyes closed, her hand came up to the back of his head, and she kissed him back. Just a little. Enough to keep from crushing him, or so she told herself. But a whimper escaped, and her body arched toward him.

Down the hall, a door opened. Zoe jerked back and thumped her head against the door. "Ow."

Henricksen stepped out and spotted them. "Hey." He waggled his phone and walked halfway down the hall toward them. "Grant's talking to his guy in Boston. They've got eyes on Olivia, and she's fine."

Zoe shivered. She stopped rubbing the back of her head and kept her gaze fixed on Henricksen. "Thanks."

Kell had shifted away from her. He waited until the agent had gone back into the other room before turning to her. All soft feelings were completely gone. His expression could have given Grant's stone face a run for its money.

"I asked Grant to check," she said, her voice barely above a whisper. "If Pat knows the totems are close and thinks he can't get to me—"

"Yeah. I get it. I know what's at stake." He thrust his hands into his pockets and his chin at her door handle. "Go inside. I'm going to go check in with my parents' people, too. Let them know what's changed."

"Kell—"

"You don't want to talk about this," he warned. "You don't want me to start thinking about whether I should go be with my sister."

"You should," she squeezed through her tight throat. Her eyes burned with dryness, and she fiercely shoved down the misery his words brought. She deserved them, after all. And far more. "Olivia is the vulnerable one, and she did nothing to become a target." She would die before she'd let anything happen to Olivia, but didn't think Kell would react well to hearing it.

To her surprise, he blew out a loud breath and dropped his head. "You didn't, either."

"What?"

"Look, you did plenty wrong here. Made some questionable decisions. But we're all in this because you became a target through no fault or will of your own sixteen years ago." He pulled one hand out and nudged her. "Go ahead. Go inside. We'll talk about this later."

She pulled her keycard out of her purse but otherwise didn't move. "Are you going to Boston?"

"I don't know. Let me talk to people. We'll see."

He went inside with her and checked the room, amusing her when he peered behind the shower curtain and in the closet, even pulling the safe door wide to check inside. Then he left without saying anything else, and Zoe collapsed onto her bed, even more conflicted than before.

Because she didn't know which she wanted more—for him to leave or for him to stay.

* * *

"Almost over" was usually when everything turned to shit. So even though Grant agreed they should sleep during forced down time, he found it more difficult than it should have been.

Normally, power naps were a piece of cake. But

normally, he had nothing personal at stake in a job. So instead of falling asleep as soon as he fell onto the bed he stared at the ceiling, wondering if Stone had really left Zoe at the door to her room. If he himself had a chance with her at all. The idea that he didn't made him want to go roaring out of the room to demonstrate his beat-down skills to Stone. So he didn't have to wonder if he really wanted her or just wanted what she represented.

Okay, that was too psychobabbly. Think about the op. Ideal progression: Henricksen would get the warrant tomorrow morning, they'd go in, confiscate the totems, placate Carling with false assurance that it was temporary, and destroy the damned things, somehow letting Rhomney know that it was all over.

But that would leave Rhomney and Thomashunis at large, and who knew what they'd do in retaliation? They hadn't done anything the government could prosecute them for, unless it could be proven they were responsible for Cocalico's assault. That wouldn't be easy. Rhomney wouldn't have allowed any trail back to him, not anything that was solid enough for charges to be levied.

So to Grant's mind, that meant Zoe would still be vulnerable. She seemed to think Pat would let it drop if he had nothing to gain, but Grant knew that was wishful thinking.

The second possibility was that the FBI would secure the totems, then put people on Carling to see if Rhomney went after him. They could arrest him for parole violation, at the least, and assault or attempted whatever, depending on what he did when cornered. That *could* have the potential of tying Freddie to it, adding conspiracy, and getting them both back off the street, but it wouldn't be for very long. Pat and Freddie on the street put a lot of people at risk. The profile that had been written up on them put murder low on the probability scale. But Grant knew better.

He hadn't allowed himself to think about his brother all week. He'd blocked off that part of him long ago, and was good enough at partitioning to look at it distantly, like something that had happened to someone else, even when Zoe dragged up the past.

But, hey, might as well add to tonight's torture. The word immediately drew up his prevailing memory: The house Rhomney's thugs had dragged him to. Grant had been thirteen and full of mixed feelings toward his brother. He'd worshiped him as a little kid, but that had faded as they got older and grew further apart. Jordie was smart but had no common sense. He liked people, and people liked him, and all it took was doing one favor for a friend who dealt drugs to drag him onto a dangerous career path. People gave him things, or did as he requested, a lot more easily than they did under threat. He got stuff done.

But he was never a bad kid. Rhomney had somehow found out about his "talent" and recruited him into his…cult, he supposed he could call it. Grant didn't like giving them that much credit.

When Rhomney tracked down the totems, he tried to send Jordie to take possession of them. Jordie had come home one night agitated and snapping at everyone. Grant, mad when his brother yelled at their mother, chased him down to his room in the basement and pushed him to tell what was going on. His brother hadn't had anyone to confide in, so he caved.

Jordie hadn't known at the beginning, but after a few weeks he'd figured out that Freddie's "daughter" wasn't her daughter, but a girl being held against her will. He'd gone outside to take a leak one night and heard a couple of the "lieutenants" talking about the totems and how after they got them they'd have it made, and they couldn't wait to do the ritual with the girl. He hadn't wanted any part of that, but Pat had told him that night to get the totems or pay the consequences.

Grant tried to convince his brother to go to the police, but Jordie refused. He didn't trust them to believe him, and his history meant he wanted to stay far away. But he'd been more cheerful the next morning and apparently went to tell Rhomney he wasn't doing it. When Grant left school that afternoon someone hit him on the head and shoved him into a van, where they knelt on his arms until they got to the house.

Jordie was standing in the middle of the living room, talking to a ratty-haired redhead with big boobs sagging out of a tank top, when they shoved Grant to the floor in front of him. He'd never forget the way Jordie's expression changed. The glazed look in his eyes gave way to horror, then fury, and he'd launched himself at the goon standing over Grant. But instead of fighting Jordie, the man held a knife to Grant's throat, which of course stopped Jordie in his tracks.

There'd been arguing. Pat came in and calmly told Jordie to go get the totems. Jordie told them to let Grant go first, but instead the guy had sliced off Grant's earlobe, tossed it at Jordie, and told him to do the job or he'd slice more pieces off his little brother.

Grant had spent much of the rest of the day in a haze of red pain and terror. They'd put him in a bedroom with Zoe, who bandaged his ear with a dirty cloth and held him, wiping away sweat and tears and giving him reassurances she shouldn't have had the strength to even consider. Sometime after dark, Jordie snuck in. He came into the bedroom, apologized to Zoe, and carried Grant out to the van.

He hadn't known it at the time, but Jordie's goodbye had probably been intentionally final. He'd decided to let them do whatever they'd do to him to save his little brother. Grant had called Jordie when he got dumped in front of their house, told him he was home okay, and never spoke to his brother again.

Of course, the police had gotten involved when his mother took Grant to the hospital, but with the very little information Grant could give them, no trace of Jordie, and his history of screw-ups, the investigation had gone nowhere.

He threw himself off the bed and into the bathroom to twist on the tap. Cold water splattered the countertop and numbed his fingers. He filled his palms and tossed the liquid onto his face. Then again. It did nothing to chill the burning pain or relieve the clawing in his throat. Water continued to gush as the edge of the marble dug into the heels of his hands. He stared through reddened eyes at a face he barely recognized, twisted with grief.

He'd opened the door. Now he had to walk through it: No outcome the government achieved would be enough for him. He'd started this because Zoe, the only woman he'd ever loved, had needed his help. He'd been able to keep his attention on that need, plus his desire to be back with her. But this could never be just about that. If Grant had been the one to spot Rhomney today, Zoe—or worse, Stone—would be bailing Grant out of jail right now.

Hell.

He slammed the faucet handle down and swiped a towel across his face, dropping it onto the floor. He returned to the bed, stretching on his stomach this time, and shoved his arms under the pillow. Would his brain shut the hell up and let him sleep already? Because if he had a hidden need for revenge, there was no way he could ever be with Zoe. She deserved a man without the ability to wreak vengeance at any cost.

A man like Stone. Fuck.

A door opened down the hall, then closed. A moment later, the sound repeated further along. Fuck again. Had Stone been with her all that time, taking the advantage back?

Grant should let him have it. Zoe had chosen Kell in a way she'd never chosen him. They'd been pushed together by crime, then by their mothers, who'd clung to each other in the aftermath of their tragedies, throwing Grant and Zoe together. For their part, they'd each latched on to the one person who understood what they'd endured. It had grown, and Grant believed the love they'd felt had been real, but it had never been choice.

He didn't have much longer to decide if that mattered.

* * *

"You're staying here."

Zoe didn't know why Henricksen didn't trust her. They stood near the FBI trucks across the street from Carling's mansion. No one had been able to reach Carling since yesterday, and Henricksen had worked all night to finalize a seizure warrant for the totems. He'd apparently been building his case for that all along, and was hoping to get it fast by showing a convincing connection between Cocalico's assault, the totems, and her sighting of Pat.

He'd tried to get the three of them to stay at the hotel this morning, but gave up after two hours of arguing, knowing damned well they'd just show up anyway. They were waiting for the warrant now. She didn't know what he planned to do with the totems, if he thought federal custody would be sufficient to stop Pat from doing anything else. She didn't want to ask, because he had no idea her intention was to destroy them. Assuming, of course, she could find a way to get her hands on them long enough to do so without going to jail herself.

She folded her arms and paced along the side of the truck, wishing again that she'd never called him. That had backfired painfully. If the FBI took the totems out of her reach, that would put everyone in even greater danger.

Why hadn't she just snatched them and run yesterday, when they were right there *in her hands?*

Because you couldn't, moron. Will had only taken one out of the case, locking it back up as if it was an ingrained habit. Now, she realized if she could have destroyed even that one, it might have been enough to stop Pat's plans. Maybe he'd have left them all alone after that. Or maybe he'd have just killed them all in retaliation.

She wished she hadn't thought of that.

Refocusing on what was happening around them—which was nothing—she said to Henricksen, "What in our brief history has given you any indication I'm more than a coward? I'm not getting anywhere near you guys while you're working."

"Good." But he eyed her mistrustfully, then gave a harder glare to Grant and Kell. "Keep her here."

"No problem."

She rolled her eyes. She wanted to bitch at Grant for dismissing her, but that was just impatience and frustration. She leaned against the truck, staring up the driveway the three agents would soon be ascending. As soon as the junior agent who'd been waiting to receive the paper warrant showed up with it. He was late.

Hopefully that was due to traffic or a printer out of ink. She'd give him a few minutes before turning the fret machine to that channel. Right now it had its hands full with the men flanking her.

She'd seen Grant first this morning, and he'd looked at her with such sad eyes she was sure he knew about her kiss with Kell the night before. Then Kell had left his room and hadn't given any hint that anything had happened. He treated both her and Grant the same way he had all along.

The kiss and the report on Olivia had apparently canceled each other out.

When the junior agent's few minutes had passed and he still hadn't arrived, she pushed away from the truck, determined to go find out what was happening. She'd only taken a step when her phone buzzed in her jeans pocket. "Oh, no."

Grant glanced down at her. "What?"

Kell didn't move. "Her mother's calling."

Grant frowned. "How do you know?"

"She always calls Zoe at work on Monday mornings." He leaned to look at her past Grant. "Did you talk to her last week?"

"Yes." The phone buzzed again.

"Did you tell her not to call work this week?"

"No." She hadn't thought that far ahead, dammit.

Kell resumed his position. "They'll have told her she sold the company."

"No, they won't." She sighed and pulled the phone from her pocket. "Sherry knows better." Kell didn't respond. She sighed again and answered the call. "Hi, Mom."

"Zoebaby, where are you? What's happened? I called the office, and they said…they said…" She began to hyperventilate.

Natalie J. Damschroder

"Mom, I'm fine." She had to work to keep the anger from her voice. She'd *thought* Sherry knew better than to tell her mother about the sale. "Honest. I'm in California with Kell, on a trip. What's going on?"

"They told me you don't work there anymore!" The wail was so loud, Grant flinched.

"I don't, Mom." She sighed yet again. She couldn't lie to her mother outright, but God, she hadn't worked out what to say to her. Her focus had been too narrow once she started down this road. "I sold the company. I'm ready to move on to something else."

"What? You…oh, nooooo, Zoe!" She started to cry. "You love that business! You've built something so wonderful! Why, just last week I was shopping for new draperies for the dining room online and the one store said 'Designed by Zoe Enterprises' and I was so proud! Now what will you do?"

She didn't want to have this conversation. Ever. But certainly not now. The only way to cut off her mother's histrionics was to be sharp and swift. "I don't know. Listen, Kell and I are kind of busy. Can I call you next week?" She should have some idea of what her life would be by then.

"Oh, just a moment longer, dear." She drew a deep, shuddering breath. "I need to hear your voice. I thought you'd been killed and no one had told me."

The sentence was too ridiculous to respond to, but it was the kind of thing Zoe had heard regularly since she went to college. "That would never happen, Mom." Her attention was caught by everyone's heads turning to the right, and she leaned forward to see what they were looking at. A black sedan sped down the street toward them. "Mom, I'm sorry, I gotta go. Love you." She shoved the phone in her pocket as the car screeched to a stop and a very young, very lanky man stumbled out and jogged up to Agent Henricksen.

"Where's the warrant?" The older agent gazed at the young man's empty hands. "Didn't you get it?"

"You won't believe it, sir. The warrant's in the car, but we can't use it."

"Why?"

Zoe, Grant, and Kell had all moved in unison, closing around the two men. She couldn't seem to catch a breath.

"Carling had a break-in last night. The totems are gone."

Natalie J. Damschroder

Chapter Fourteen

Grant and Kell grabbed Zoe's arms with barely enough time to keep her knees from cracking on the pavement. They hit hard enough as it was, but the pain was incidental.

"Are you fucking kidding me?" Henricksen roared. "How were we not informed about this?"

"It just came into the office half an hour ago," the other agent explained. "I tried to call you, but...um...my phone went dead."

"Son of a bitch!" Henricksen whirled and slammed a flat hand on the hood of the truck. The other agents fell in, and he started giving new orders.

Zoe knelt, numb, on the pavement. Gone. They were gone. It had been a miracle that they'd tracked them down in the first place, and now they had to start over. With only five days until the blood moon, Pat's target for the ritual.

"Pat," she managed to say. Grant and Kell both bent over her, and she felt a spark of annoyance at their hovering. "It had to be Pat."

"No, it didn't." Grant moved to help her up, and

Kell joined in, and Zoe gritted her teeth that she needed them to. But as soon as she was on her feet, she yanked her arms away and stepped back.

"What do you mean, it didn't?"

"It didn't have to be Pat. Remember, there are—"

"It was him!" She didn't care what cold logic Grant had to offer. She wasn't operating on logic right now. "It was Pat in the car yesterday, in this neighborhood. I *led* him to the totems, and now he's got them, and now what do we do?" She struggled not to imagine what was coming next. *Olivia is protected*. *He can't get to her.* "Don't you *want* it to be him?" she demanded, only partially aware of everyone staring at her, including Kell. She just wanted Grant, the one person who could know what this meant, to *crack* a little, goddammit. "After what he did to your brother? Don't you want an excuse to—"

Grant's hand slapped over her mouth, and he yanked her against him with his other arm tight across her back. She struggled to breathe through her nose, but it was agitation, not because he was cutting off her air. One of the standby agents stepped forward, but Kell stopped him.

"That's exactly why I *don't* want it to be him," Grant growled low in her face. "I've been fighting bloodlust since I found out he was free. I'm not that man, Zoe. I won't become that man." He eased off a little, resting his hand lightly on her mouth now, holding her a little more loosely. But she could still see desperation in his eyes, something he'd never let her see before, not since that night in Ohio.

"If someone else has them," he continued with less vehemence, "one of the treasure hunters they hired, maybe double-crossing Pat and Freddie, then those two are no closer than we are, no closer than they were yesterday."

Blinking back tears, Zoe nodded. Grant removed his hand, and she said, "I'm sorry. I shouldn't have said what I did."

"It's all right."

But she shook her head. "It's not. Because you're right, if someone else took them, that might mean Olivia is safe. But it won't stop them. Time is getting short. We can't split our focus when the likelihood is that Pat has them now." Her mind raced. "The key. He can't use them without the key."

"He might have it," Grant said reluctantly. "We found no trace of it. If he has it already—"

Kell cursed and whipped out his phone. "I need to go back to Boston. I can't be this far away when my sister—"

Henricksen interrupted, ending his own call. "Delmarry just talked to Carling's housekeeper. She reported the break-in and the missing totems, which she said was an odd coincidence since they were the last thing you looked at yesterday." He held up a hand when Zoe opened her mouth to protest. "Obviously, you're not suspects. You were with me. But she doesn't know where Carling is."

"He's not here?" Zoe's blood had gone cold so often in the last few days, it should be slush by now.

"She claims he had a date last night and didn't

come home, which isn't unusual, but he doesn't answer his phone, either."

Zoe didn't know Will very well, but even after one meeting, she knew that wasn't right. The foreboding she'd had all night grew. "Shaun…"

"We're on it. We'll track him down, don't worry. The cops already have his outdoor surveillance tapes, so we're getting those. A team is coming to print the house, determine how they got in, etcetera."

"Then what?" Kell asked.

"Then we investigate." He opened the driver's door of his vehicle and motioned to the back seat. "Get in. We'll drop you at the hotel."

"Wait here," Grant ordered Zoe and Kell and walked over to confer with the agent. Zoe would have followed if Kell hadn't been holding onto her. She was steady, but didn't tell him so. She had a feeling he was stabilizing himself by helping her.

Grant came back and nudged them to the side as the junior agent backed up his car and the other agency vehicle headed down the street.

"We're not going back to the hotel," he said. "Another agent will drop me there to get our stuff while Henricksen takes you two to the airport to buy tickets. I'll get a cab over and meet you there."

Zoe stared at him. "Where are we going?"

He shrugged one shoulder. "Stone wants to go to Boston. I want to take you back to the Keys, but that's up to you. I don't think we should hang around here."

"But the totems—"

"Whoever took them, they're not staying in San

Francisco. And if you're right, and it's Pat and Freddy, you may still be part of their plan. I want you away from them."

Kell gripped her elbow as if Grant was trying to take her away. "We can protect her better if there are two of us."

Grant nodded, but without agreement. "We could. But your sister is the more vulnerable party, and I don't think Zoe should go near her."

They all stood stock still for several seconds, indecision flavoring the air around them.

"Okay, then." Zoe broke away and headed for the car. "We'll decide on the way." She didn't like Grant being on his own, but he was the one who could most take care of himself, and she supposed speed was priority. The sooner they got away from here, the safer they'd all be, not just her.

She sat silently in the back of the car, staring out the window, debating what to do next. Barely a month ago she'd been brave enough to break her engagement, sell her company, and try to draw the bull's-eye away from those she loved. A few days ago—though it felt like far longer—she'd had the courage to charge toward the danger. But right now, she was weak. She couldn't think clearly, couldn't decide the most logical, safest move. And it made her sick to admit it, but it was because of fear. Not just fear for Olivia, but fear for herself. Seeing Pat had changed everything. Even if it wasn't him in that car, the moment had rendered any ounce of bravery inert. She *hated* it—and she couldn't let it stand.

They were halfway to the airport when Zoe's phone buzzed a text message. Assuming it was her mother again, she absently pulled it out to check. Her gasp at the image on the screen had Kell sliding across the seat to her side.

"What is it?" He craned to see the phone, which she kept tilted away.

"It's…" She scrolled down, read the words there, and scrolled back up so the picture filled the little screen. "It's Carling." She turned the phone so Kell could see the picture. The man was tied to a bed, a rag tied across his mouth, something red on his forehead that she assumed was blood. Even on the small screen, his terror was obvious.

"Pull over," Kell told Henricksen, and he immediately swerved to the shoulder. Once he'd thrown the car into park, he twisted to look into the back and Zoe showed him the picture. He cursed.

"When did you get that?"

"Just now. The number's blocked."

"We can trace it. But it will take time." He cursed again and dialed his own phone, taking Zoe's from her and relaying information, presumably to an agent on his team. He thumbed the screen and she knew he had to have spotted the message. For a moment his eyes met hers in the rearview mirror. She silently begged him not to tell Kell what it said, and for some reason, he just cleared his throat and dialed his own phone once again. When he was done giving more orders, he pulled back onto the road and drove quite a bit faster than the speed limit.

"What are you going to do?" Kell asked him, his arm firmly around Zoe. She could feel fine trembles in his torso and knew his own fear was growing.

"Keep investigating," Henricksen growled in a way that invited no more questions. "I have to keep your phone, Zoe. I can give you another one temporarily."

"Okay." Her throat burned with everything she wanted to ask, but in actuality, what the FBI did no longer mattered. She didn't need her phone back for the message on it—*Which of your boy toys is next?*—to burn itself into her brain. That had taken all of three seconds, and it made her decision so much easier. There was only one thing left to do. The problem was that she'd never convince any of them to let her do it.

She huddled in Kell's arms the rest of the way to the airport, planning, scheming, visualizing tricks that were going to annihilate her stupid love triangle if done right.

Henricksen parked in the drop-off zone and got out, scoping the area before opening Zoe's door. "Here." He handed her a small, cheap-looking smartphone. "From my equipment bag. Not a lot of bells and whistles, but there is GPS," he joked, winking.

Zoe nodded, not sure if she was picking up on a message or if it was wishful thinking. "Thank you for everything," she told him, holding out a hand that he ignored in favor of a hug.

"We're here for you. Don't worry." It was inadequate reassurance, and an odd thing to say, but when she pulled back and caught his eye, she thought maybe he understood her best of all.

"Keep me posted." As if he'd need to. The glint in his eye confirmed it. But he promised and walked them inside to the departure counters before he left them. Kell grumbled about FBI protection being more important now, but Zoe didn't respond, and he went silent as they paused to check the departure TVs. She let him hold her hand, struggling not to distance herself and make him suspicious. But every touch about killed her.

"There's one that goes to Cleveland in an hour," Kell said. "We can connect to Boston from there." He let go of her to pull up an app on his phone, tapping in the codes to pull up flight information. Then he scrolled, his features pulling tighter the longer he did. "That's the only one that will get me there fast. The others all have multiple connections."

Grant probably wouldn't get here by then. She could make this work.

She turned and braced for the best acting job of her life. She'd completely blown it last month when she left. Now, everything hinged on convincing him. "I think Grant's right."

Kell's jaw flexed, and a sharp pain went through her knuckles when he grabbed her hand. "I would rather keep you close. I can protect you. Grant can come with us, then someone's always—"

"No." She shook her head and cupped her free hand over his. "I won't put Olivia at greater risk. Pat might not have the resources to go after both of us. You need to be with her."

"We can hire additional protection."

She raced through possible arguments against it, urgency buzzing in the back of her brain. "There's no time to do it right. You have to make sure it's not someone Pat could have planted. I know it sounds farfetched," she said before he could, "but you don't know him or his followers."

Kell blew out a breath and looked around the bustling airport. "I don't know what to do. I can't leave you."

"Yes, you can."

"No, I mean— I know Neely can handle your protection. But I'm going to have to get a ticket now if I'm going to make that flight. Look at the security line."

"I'll get tickets to Miami for me and Grant. Then I can go through with you."

"Except how will you get the ticket to Neely?" She watched him examine the way security was laid out. There wasn't any way she could pass it directly through from one side to the other, another thing Zoe was counting on. "You can come through to the gates, then come back when he gets here. They'll let you back through security as long as you have your boarding pass and ID."

It wasn't ideal, but Zoe nodded. She'd find a way. As long as she was moving forward.

They went to the kiosk to purchase tickets. "Let Neely know what's happening," Kell told her once they were standing in the long, slow-but-steady line. "Did you tell him about Carling's photo?"

She shook her head, ducking it to look at her phone so Kell wouldn't see the tears stinging her eyelids. Too many people had gotten hurt in all this, despite her best intentions. "Dammit." She sniffed as quietly as she could, blinked hard, and waved her blank phone. "I forgot this isn't my phone. I don't have Grant's number. I'm sure Henricksen notified him, so—"

"Here." Kell pulled up his contacts. "I have it. We need to exchange numbers, too, while we're at it."

"Of course." She added the numbers to her contacts list, then slowly typed out a text. She didn't want Kell to see what she said. When he shifted his attention to the TSA agent, she sped up to finish. *I decided to go back to Boston with Kell. Flight leaves in 30 min.* Rounding down, but that part was the least of the lies. *Need to get the totems, and that's most likely direction Pat will go.* She didn't think that was true. He was most comfortable in his own space. He'd go back to Ohio and keep incentivizing Zoe to go to him. Grant would realize that, but hopefully he wouldn't think Zoe would be as stupid as she was about to be. *Call you when I get there.*

Then she shut down the phone and followed Kell through the scanners.

"Our gate's down that way." He pointed.

"Okay." She looked around for the restrooms. "I need to use the bathroom first."

He walked her over and said he'd wait outside. Like there was an alternative. She followed the maze of the giant room of stalls until she reached the point farthest from the door he stood outside. The room was crowded overall, but few people made it back this far.

She checked the cell signal. Four bars.

She had to time this right. Her plan was to text Kell that she had an upset stomach and he should go, not miss his plane waiting for her. It had to be so close he wouldn't have time to argue, but early enough that he could make it to his plane. She watched the seconds hand on her watch sweep around, and around. Five words into the text message, her phone buzzed. She jumped, bobbled it, and almost dropped it on the tile floor. With a curse, she called up the text that had just come in.

Neely's here. He didn't get your text, but I updated him on the plan. He's waiting outside security.

Crap. He'd gotten here far faster than she'd expected him to. But that was okay. He couldn't get through without the ticket. *I'll be out soon. Upset stomach. Go ahead and get on your plane so you don't miss it.* She hit send and bit her lip, bouncing her knee as she watched the screen. It darkened, and she thumbed it back on. A woman stepped out of a stall and went to the sink to wash her hands, frowning at Zoe's legs. Her anxiety was making her look suspicious. She gave a wan smile. The woman moved her lips and quickly left out the other door.

Finally, the phone buzzed again. *I don't like this. Let me know once Neely's with you.*

Okay. Stay safe. It felt weird not to sign off with "love you," but she had no right to that already, and what she was doing now was just piling on to the death of their relationship.

The minutes dragged, slower and slower, while the

conversations in her head rambled faster and faster, as if she had to convince them—or herself—that she wasn't being too stupid to live. Their plan was falling apart, and they didn't have time to wait for Pat to make another move. With the photo of Carling, the FBI finally had something to act on, but she couldn't sit on her ass and wait when there was something she could do.

Ten minutes after Kell's text, she finally left the bathroom. And ran right into Grant, standing outside the door with her luggage.

"What— You— How'd you get through security?"

He shouldered his bag and hefted hers, heading toward their gate and forcing her to walk with them.

"Bought a ticket." He fluttered the paper he held between two fingers.

"But I have a ticket for you."

"I know, but I wanted to get Stone his suitcase, and I knew he was about to take off. He told me you were stuck in the bathroom." He studied her, as if he could see her twisted intestines through her T-shirt. "I caught up to him at his gate and came back to meet you. You okay?"

"Fine." That probably wasn't the best response, but she was already trying to figure out plan B, now that sneaking away before Grant got here was off the table.

"You wasted money," she said after they'd walked swiftly for a good half a minute and she realized she wasn't acting normally. It was the logical thing to say. Would her delay make him suspicious?

But he just shrugged and adjusted his duffel. "It's a

refundable ticket. I can turn it in at the gate if there's time."

It didn't matter whether there was or not. She nodded and they kept walking while she ran through a few scenarios, most of which ended with Grant handcuffing her to him, before she hit on one that might work. Less lying, more timing. She'd already set it up, in fact.

When they got to the gate, the attendant was calling to board first class. Her heart started to pound. This was going to be much harder. She stood at the end of the aisle to the check-in desk, waiting for Grant to get his ticket taken care of while they called for passengers to board, row by row. Her muscles tightened with tension as they got in line and moved slowly toward the attendant. Their boarding passes scanned, they strode down the jetway. Her head throbbed in time with her heartbeat. Any second she expected Grant to call her on her plan, and when he stopped her halfway to the plane, her heart leaped into her throat.

"Don't worry, Zoe. Kell and Olivia will be fine, and I *promise* you, I'll keep you safe."

She had to swallow so she wouldn't choke on her response. "I know you will. I trust you."

"I hope so." He slid his hand through her hair and braced the back of her skull. "We're not helpless kids anymore. We *will* beat them at this."

She would. Somehow.

The line inched onto the plane and down the aisle. People clogged the narrow space, stowing their bags and collecting reading material before cramming themselves into their seats. Zoe shifted her weight, put her hand on her stomach, and hunched a little as they moved into the first class section.

"You okay?" Grant, behind her, asked.

"Yeah." She craned her neck to look past the crowd, then back over her shoulder, as if gauging distance. The bathroom behind her was closer. "I can't wait. You go ahead, I'll be right there." She squeezed past him, her head down because she knew there was no way she could hide her intentions from him, not this close up. She grabbed the handle of the restroom door just as he caught her arm, and he released it immediately, looking sympathetic. She heaved a sigh as soon as the bolt was shot home. *Please, Grant, go sit down. Pleasepleaseplease*. She could hear the line of people shuffling past, random coughs and murmurs, a couple of grumbles and exasperated breaths before things seemed to flow better. She imagined Grant had given in and moved on down the narrow aisle.

The seconds hand on her watch swept slowly around again, then again. They were due to leave the gate soon, but the weight of people outside the bathroom door made her wonder how far behind they were going to be. She had to time this right. Grant had to be unable to get off the plane. Another minute went by. Another. People moved faster past the restroom door, the walkway clearer.

Finally, one of the attendants said, "That it?"

"I'll check." A moment later she confirmed, "Yep, that's all of them."

Zoe burst out of the bathroom and darted past the startled attendants, swinging out through the door and onto the jetway. She ran full out back toward the gate, moving so fast she thought no one even called after her, and God, she hoped they didn't think she was a terrorist. She slowed as she neared the main door, which was closing. "Wait!" she called, and a round, rumpled face topped with dark gray curly hair peered around the edge of the door. The woman saw her and quickly pulled the door open.

"Just can't do it, sweetie?"

Panting, Zoe shook her head. "No. I thought I could, it's important enough to, but…"

"I understand. See it all the time!" She patted Zoe's hand and closed the door behind her. "You're not alone, dear."

"Thank you. That helps." Zoe chanced a glance through the narrow glass pane, but the jetway was empty. She forced a smile for the helpful lady. "I guess I'd better go get a train ticket."

The woman laughed and waddled back to the gate desk, and Zoe hurried toward security. She'd memorized where she needed to go and what she needed to buy, and luckily the line at that particular counter was short and, even more shocking, the clerk efficient.

There was one moment of heart-stopping fear, however, when the clerk frowned at the screen and said, "Did you just buy a ticket to Florida?"

"Yes." Her throat rasped, and she swallowed. "My…" *Keep it simple.* "My plans changed. Family emergency."

"Okay." Her careful wariness eased into concern, and she tapped away on the keyboard again. "Let's get you moving, then, shall we?"

"Thank you." If this was real, she'd be grateful for this woman's compassion. She *was* grateful, and it made her feel guilty. Guiltier than she already was, lying to Kell and ditching Grant after all they'd done for her.

She couldn't think about that. She had to focus on what to do next, and fast, before…

A shout sounded somewhere off to her left, and her heart bounced into her throat. She looked with everyone else and saw a man chasing a toddler down the walkway. The child's giggle echoed to them, and Zoe fought to react normally, not sagging against the counter or closing her eyes against the well of nausea.

Jesus, she couldn't even handle this little bit of subterfuge. How was she going to carry off anything else?

Planning would help. But that could wait. She wasn't out of the danger zone yet.

Grant didn't show up as she went through security again with her new ticket. Nor did he appear on her concourse, or at her gate, or racing down the jetway onto her plane. She kept a wary eye on every body that turned into the plane, going through a mini tense-release rhythm for each passenger. But she didn't know any of them. Finally, the door closed, the plane backed away from the gate, and she eased into her seat, forcing herself to relax before she fell to pieces. A faint hiss preceded the captain's announcement, and she half listened until his final words made her stomach cramp harder than ever.

"And we hope you enjoy your flight to Columbus."

* * *

"You *what?!*"

Kell couldn't process what his mother had just said to him. "With who?"

"With…" Her mouth formed the word whom but she didn't seem to be able to bring herself to correct his grammar. "With my sister and her family. They're traveling on a random itinerary."

He didn't get it. It was the middle of the school year. Why a random itinerary, and why was that the first bit of information she shared? Had there been a threat? Had someone updated his parents about the Rhomney situation?

"For how long?"

"As long as necessary. Please, Kellen, come into the house." She held out a hand, the giant anniversary emerald on her hand winking in the light through the glass panels next to the door. "I'll have Genovese get us some drinks."

Her hand shook right before he took it, and he realized she was pale. He should have noticed sooner, but he was exhausted after several sleepless nights and overwhelmed with worry about Zoe—whom he couldn't reach—and even Grant—whom he also couldn't reach. There'd been so many ugly scenarios running through his head, he hadn't been paying attention to anything else.

"Where's Dad?"

"Dealing."

That was not how his mother typically described things. What the hell was going on? But as soon as she settled him on a settee she swept out of the room, no doubt to ask Genovese, the household manager, to get the drink Kell didn't want.

The antique mantle clock ticked loudly in the silent parlor. A few dust motes floated lazily in the sunbeam angled at the floor in front of Kell. His nose twitched against the scent of lavender, his mother's favorite. He sat back, then immediately lunged forward again, checked his watch, and tried not to bounce his knee, because his mother hated that.

Waiting was intolerable. He pulled out his phone and dialed Zoe's number again. Voice mail, of course. For the sixth time. He disconnected and dialed Grant's cell. This time, the man answered, sounding every bit as frustrated as Kell felt.

"What the hell is going on?" Kell asked without greeting. "Where's Zoe? She's not answering her phone."

Grant hesitated only a moment. "She played us. Jumped our plane too late for me to get off. Your sister okay? My guys told me she flew somewhere with your aunt and uncle, but they weren't able to determine where."

"I have no fucking idea." Alarm jumped through the phone connection, and he hurriedly corrected himself. "Yes. I think so. My mother sent her to Europe. Something's wrong here, but she hasn't told me what yet. I think she went to collect herself or something." God forbid she show any emotion to her son. "Where's Zoe?" Because for damned sure by now Grant would have tracked her. "And why didn't you call me?"

"I didn't call you because your sister is your priority." There was no judgment in his tone, but Kell felt his face redden with shame nonetheless. "She's in Ohio."

"Fuck!" He'd never said that word so often in so short a time. "What the—" He didn't need to finish the question. After seeing Carling's photo, there was only one thing she could be doing. "She's offering herself up for us."

"I talked to Henricksen. He told me about Carling." Grant's voice was measured, unaccusing, but Kell knew the guy had to be as much a roiling mess inside as he was. He was just more practiced at hiding it.

"Zoe didn't tell you? She was supposed to be texting you from security."

"She did, to tell me she was going back to Boston with you. Didn't mention Carling."

Kell cursed again. How had she played them both so smoothly?

Grant went on. "Henricksen said there was a note with the picture. Did you see it?"

"I saw the picture. Carling, injured, trussed. No words. I assumed it was meant as a message."

"It was a message, all right. But he spelled it out for her. It said 'Which of your boy toys is next?' "

The roiling mess in his gut hardened and sank

heavily. "And she took it to mean us."

"Who else?"

Kell paced, fuming, holding up a finger to his mother, who'd come back into the room with a tea tray. "So she's trying to protect us. But how? She doesn't have the totems." The realization hit him before Grant said it. Pat and Freddie had the totems already. The message they sent hadn't been about the damned gold statues.

It had been about her.

Chapter Fifteen

Zoe hadn't expected it to be so easy.

As soon as she crossed through security, there he was. She didn't remember his name, couldn't recall the names of any of Pat and Freddie's followers, but he'd guarded her enough that the years and hard living didn't make him unrecognizable. She had a brief flashback to a smelly, stuffy room, the rasp of a rope around her ankle, and a stoic, unmoving presence in the corner.

He spotted her as she walked past the scanners and strode over to her, twitching and fidgeting as if he didn't know what to do without a cigarette in his hand. His jeans bagged between his knees, and he hitched them up over his butt as he stopped in front of her, a grin showing two missing teeth among the yellow ones that remained.

"He was right." He giggled. "He's always right."

Zoe clenched her teeth, not trusting herself not to say something stupid. Stupider than what she was doing.

"Well, come on then. You don't have any checked

baggage, I'm thinkin'. Too bad if you do." He giggled again and turned to walk beside her, grabbing her left arm above the elbow hard enough to create another flashback. She flinched, startled at both the memory of violence she didn't think had happened and her brain's automatic suppression of it. Had she forced so much of her experience into a locked box that there were things she actually didn't remember? A cold, hard rock rolled in her stomach, and for a moment she thought she'd be sick.

The moment passed when Kell's face popped into her head, reminding her why she was doing this. She swallowed back the bile rising in her throat and asked, "Where are we going?"

He glanced askance at her and shook his head. "You better not be dumb enough to be wearin' a wire. Pat said you weren't that dumb."

"I'm not." Not exactly. She faced forward so he couldn't read anything in her expression and didn't press the subject. "What's your name?"

He worked his mouth around a little as he maneuvered her through the door to the outside, then finally said, "Stew," as if he wasn't sure he could trust her with it.

"I'm Zoe," she told him, thinking that trying to humanize herself to him, make him think twice about whatever they were going to do to her, wouldn't work. It was pointless, since she'd willingly gone to them, was about to walk right into their lair. She shuddered and clenched her hand around the strap of her bag to keep from touching the inner jacket pocket her phone was in.

"I know who you are." He chuckled. "We're gonna be *good* friends. Not like last time." He leered. Unable to help herself, Zoe shot him a glare. He cleared his throat and looked away to check traffic, then hustled her across the street to the parking area.

Her mind raced with ways she could get away, a fruitless exercise since that would defeat her purpose. *Just hold on. Shaun will come through.* She repeated it, imagining the FBI swooping in shortly after she arrived in…wherever they took her. God, she hoped this worked.

Pat had made a big mistake when he took Will Carling. Before that, he hadn't done anything the FBI or anyone else could do anything about. Maybe parole violation, but they couldn't prove that, especially if he was already back here. They couldn't officially trace the threats, or the assault on Ozzie, or the theft of the totems to Pat or Freddy.

But if she got to the shack—she knew they weren't going to the original shack, it didn't even exist anymore, but she couldn't get that image out of her head—and could stall Pat long enough for Henricksen to track the location and connect him to Will's abduction…then it could all be over.

That was all that kept her feet moving forward.

Stew stopped next to a squatting, rusting hulk of a car, something she guessed was from the seventies or maybe early eighties. The back door opened and he shoved her toward it. She slid in, squinting in the dim light at the person next to her. This one, she didn't recognize. He was younger, probably even younger than her, and cleaner than Stew. He had all his teeth, and they'd definitely had orthodontics at some point. His clothes were good quality, his haircut a deliberately shaggy style, and his smile reminded her of some of the young people at the Stones' country club. She wondered what the hell made people like this kid follow someone like Patron Rhomney.

"Well hell-o, Miss Ardmore." He eyed her up and down and even stroked his hand down her arm. "Pat didn't tell us how lovely you are. This is going to be much more fun than I expected."

Zoe couldn't hide her disgust. "Can't get it up for a willing woman, huh?"

The cocky grin snapped off his face like it had been snatched away. "Drive, Stew. They're waiting for her."

Stew didn't move. "Fergettin' somethin'."

Pretty-Boy grimaced and lifted his hip to pull a bandanna out of his back pocket. He wrapped it around Zoe's eyes, tightening it just a bit more than necessary. She put her hand up to touch it, and he slapped it away.

"Don't make me tie you up."

Relieved, she let her hands settle into her lap. They wouldn't bother blindfolding her if they were going to kill her. Of course, she didn't think they planned to kill her, at least not yet. And there were worse things than death. But their attempt to keep their location secret from her meant they expected her to somehow have a way to relay that information to someone, and that made her feel better.

They drove for a long time, and being blind made her unable to gauge distance. Everything felt longer than it probably was. The men didn't talk, so she didn't get Pretty-Boy's name, and she decided silence, at least for now, was best.

Finally the car bumped—a lot—down what was probably a rutted dirt road or trail. Zoe was glad they hadn't bound her, because she needed her hands to brace herself on the door and seats to avoid injury. PB dragged her out of the car and across several yards to a few wooden steps, where she stumbled and had to catch herself. The planks felt dry and both flaky and splintery against her palms, like weathered painted wood. Just like the shack she'd been in sixteen years ago. Her heart thundered and she lay sprawled against the steps, frozen, unable to make herself rise and go inside.

The door opened and mingled scents of unwashed bodies, pot, dirty dishes, and stale beer wafted out. Zoe squeezed her eyes shut and breathed through her mouth, focusing, thinking of Olivia and Kell and Grant and Jordie and her parents.

You can do this. Her breathing echoed harshly in her ears, and she realized Pat would hear it and know she was afraid. She snapped her mouth closed and pushed to her feet. She was *not* a child anymore. She was a strong, brave adult, and she would *not* allow Pat to control her. Not like that.

"Atta girl." PB sounded strangely pleased, considering how eager he'd been to provoke her with innuendo in the car. His hand closed around her arm again, and this time he guided her, murmuring how many steps she had, and then "door" and even bending to help her lift her foot to step inside.

Once the door closed behind them he whisked the blindfold away. His grin was the first thing Zoe saw. She latched on to it, comforted, but she'd been through enough therapy and read enough clinical articles to know what she was doing. He was not her friend. None of these people were. She could only count on herself to get through this.

When she looked away, she saw a cluttered, ramshackle room very much like the old one, but empty of people. Weak sunlight filtered through boarded-up windows, and straw and droppings in the corners were evidence of tiny inhabitants. They'd taken over an abandoned house, their usual MO. She curled her lip. They didn't have to live in squalor. They were just lazy and dramatic.

Footsteps sounded from an adjacent room and Patron Rhomney appeared in the doorway. He looked exactly as he had in the car that had passed them, and he smiled when he saw her recognition.

"Zoe, my dear, so good to have you back!" He held out his arms and stepped forward, as if he'd embrace her. She managed not to cringe. He'd never harmed her physically, not personally, so as detestable as he was, she could hide her response. As long as he was quick about it.

But he never reached her. A screech came from behind him, and then billows of thin, fluffy red hair appeared under his arm, followed by Freddie, who looked so much like a Hollywood-style witch Zoe stepped back, bumping into PB behind her. His chuckle reached her ear under Freddie's gleeful squeals, but his steadying hands only held her in place for Freddie to fall on her.

"My child my child my child! You're home you're home you're home!" Freddie crowded up against Zoe, long nails snagging her hair when she tried to stroke it, her body bony and insect-like with her long arms and legs. She wore a flowered dress that gaped across the chest and hung off her hips. One of her "mother dresses." Zoe turned away from her fetid breath, coming, no doubt, from the rotted teeth. She'd have thought they got better dental care in prison.

"I'll leave you two alone." Pat stepped back out of the room, his expression satisfied, as if knowing how freaked out Zoe was right then. Stew moved to stand in front of the front door, and PB, with a huff of disgust, dropped lazily onto the sofa, examining his nails and for all appearances ignoring the spectacle before him.

Zoe couldn't move, as paralyzed as if a big, mean-looking dog sniffed at her feet. Freddie circled her, muttering in a sing-song that Zoe couldn't understand. Her nails were jagged and sharp and scratched Zoe's neck and arms. Freddie plucked at Zoe's clothing, shaking her head loosely but fiercely, with a grumble about shopping for proper clothes.

"Comecome!" Freddie caught Zoe's hand and tugged her to a scratchy plaid armchair. "Sitsit! I'll make you pretty. Preeetttty." She snatched a brush out of a box next to the chair, as if she'd placed it there for just this purpose. And maybe she had. She'd been odd when she had Zoe before, her eyes lit with an eerie type of glow that made her look crazy. The glow was gone, but the crazy remained. Worse.

Zoe fought. She tried, mentally, not to slide back, but as soon as the brush touched the top of her head she filled with despair. Hatred. Sorrow. Guilt. Longing. Freddie crooned as she stroked the brush through Zoe's hair, over and over and over. Hot tears singed her face and she thought of her mother, and wished she'd been more understanding, less dismissive and frustrated. She used to picture her mother when Freddie did this. Remembered warm bread baking, her mother's smile and reassuring hugs. It hadn't made her skin stop crawling, or her stomach stop hurting, or eased the scream building inside her.

Nor did it help now. All of those things returned as if they'd never gone. She couldn't remember her life before she got here. She'd had a job, and a fiancé, and friends, and family, and *herself*, but it was all gone, vanished in a void that squeezed those sixteen years to nothing, until all she knew was then and now.

Freddie set the brush down and separated Zoe's hair to braid it. Zoe squeezed her eyes so tightly that golden suns exploded on a red background, spreading and fading and reforming. She concentrated on them. Focused hard on the shapes, the patterns, until she was immersed in them and could no longer feel the scrabble of Freddie's fingers at the nape of her neck.

Pull yourself out of this. It was a command. Weak,

but her own voice. Her own power. *You're not twelve.*
You're not helpless. You're stronger than her. Overpower
her. NOW! Zoe shot to her feet, surprising herself.

Freddie screeched and grabbed at the end of the
braid, a rubber band stretched around her fingers. "No
no no! Fix it! Fix it!"

"I don't want you to braid my hair." Zoe stepped
away and turned, bracing her feet and holding out a
hand—as if that would stop Freddie. The woman was
totally around the bend.

"Excellent!" Pat's pleased voice sounded from over
her shoulder, but Zoe didn't want to take her eyes off
Freddie, who was trying to get around her to secure
the braid. Zoe defiantly shook out her hair.

"I have to say, I'm very pleased." Pat circled in
front of her and touched Freddie gently, almost
lovingly, on the shoulder. Freddie pouted but settled to
the floor next to the chair.

"Pleased about what? I'll make sure not to do it
again." Zoe was amazed at her cheek. A moment ago,
she'd have thought she'd never have the strength to go
up against either of them, ever.

"I'm pleased at what you've grown to be. I wasn't
sure you would be able to do the job, but you've given
me confidence." He nudged her toward the plaid chair,
settling onto the recliner next to it. "Please, sit. It's a
request, not an order. For comfort purposes," he added
when she didn't move.

Ignoring the request felt like childish stubbornness
now, not strength, so Zoe did as he asked.

"Thank you. Would you like a drink or something

to eat?"

"No." Instantly, she craved water. But she would never ingest anything these people would give her.

"Your choice." He settled onto the recliner next to her.

"What now?" She swallowed hard and forced herself to ask a question that had plagued her since she decided to come here, putting as much of a sneer into her voice as she could. "Are you going to punish me for getting you arrested?"

He shook his head, still smiling. "Oh, no, don't worry about that. I know it's not the best incentive for you." Before she could ask what he meant, he held out his hand. "Before we get started, please give me your cell phone."

She stared at his wide, roughed-up palm. He shook it impatiently. "Don't play games, Zoe. Give me your cell phone."

"Wait!" Freddie jumped up from where she'd settled on the floor at Zoe's feet and dashed out of the room, back in seconds with a battered cardboard box. "Here! I saved your toys!" She sank down again and pawed through the box, holding up a yo-yo. "See? We'll play." The yo-yo fell out of her hand and rolled across the floor. "Oooh, blocks! You love blocks, baby." She started stacking them.

Zoe stared. She'd never played with toys with Zoe, who'd been far too old for the kinds of things she was pulling from the box. She turned back to Pat, who nodded sadly.

"Prison wasn't very good to Freddie, I'm afraid.

But that will be rectified. The phone?"

Zoe didn't know how he expected to fix Freddie. The woman was clearly off her nut, irreversibly damaged mentally. A whisper reminded her of the things she'd read about the totems, and their powers. She'd suspected Pat believed those stories, and this was evidence. It increased the sick feeling in the pit of her stomach.

But she had more immediate concerns first. She sighed and pulled her phone from her pocket, setting it in his hand. "It's off," she told him. "I'm not trying to record you or anything. And it can't transmit my location while it's off," she added, hoping that wasn't overkill. This was the phone Henricksen gave her, and if she'd read him right, it *could* be tracked without being on.

The phone chimed as Pat thumbed the power button. They all waited in silence as it booted up. He pressed a few buttons, scrolled around, and pierced her with a sharp but smug gaze. "This isn't your phone."

"But—"

"Where's the picture of our friend Mr. Carling?"

Her heart sank. "I deleted it."

"Hmm. I don't think so." He stood, dropped the phone onto the floor, and ground it under his boot heel. Plastic and tiny pieces of the innards skittered across the floor, along with most of Zoe's hopes. It was possible they'd tracked her location already and the FBI could be entering any minute.

Yeah, right. Things didn't work that way in real

life.

"I wondered why they didn't check me for weapons," she said, struggling to sound as strong as she had a moment ago. "Now I know you just wanted to be dramatic."

He laughed. "Okay, you got me. A little." He held up his finger and thumb to indicate how little. "But I knew you wouldn't have weapons. That's not you."

She ground her teeth, wishing she could whip out a forty-four and prove he didn't know her at all. Not that she knew how to use a forty-four. Or could have taken a weapon of any kind on the plane. She stared at the pieces of the phone, shattered like her stupid, last-ditch plan. Now what?

"We won't be here long enough for the FBI to arrive." Pat roamed the room, almost pacing but with a more leisurely intent. He paused by an old fireplace with a stone mantle, and Zoe realized the totems were on display there. They looked smaller for some reason, but gleamed among the room's dinginess, and she was surprised she hadn't spotted them. Fear trickled through her and she allowed a piece of her brain to pray and beg for the FBI to show up *now*. She really didn't want to be part of whatever Pat thought they could do.

But then she remembered the key. He couldn't do anything without the key. If he didn't already have it. He could have found it since he got out of prison. Or even had someone find it for him while he was still there. She sat, watching, unable to swallow or even breathe very well through the lump of anxiety in her throat, as he stroked a finger over the shapes traced in the gold.

"You recall Jordan Neely." He wrapped his hand around the center of the totem and squeezed. Zoe's eyes stung and she blinked hard. Is that how he'd killed him? How he'd kill her?

"Yes," she said softly.

"You recall the circumstances of his failure?"

Heat flooded her face and burned away the tears. She found herself on her feet, hands clenched. "He *didn't* fail. He found the totems. And you killed him anyway."

Pat shrugged a shoulder, but his mouth twitched in a smile that made Zoe want to throw up. "You're quite correct. But he didn't obtain the key."

"You knew where the key was. You were on your way to get it when—" She broke off.

"Yes, when you escaped with my treasure." He let his hand drop and swung to look at her. "You're in a similar situation. Jordie needed to obtain the totems to save his brother. He did that, but since he didn't get the key, he forfeited his life. I knew where the key was then, and I know where it is now. You'll obtain it for me, bring it back to me."

Oh, God. "Or?"

"Or." He smiled that smug twitch of a smile again and motioned to a room behind Zoe, nodding for her to look around the blanket hanging in the doorway. Slowly, and without an ounce of needing to know what was on the other side, she crossed the creaky wood floor. Slipped her hand between the crooked doorjamb and the ragged cotton blanket that smelled of cigarettes. Nudged the cloth aside just enough to see past it. And retched.

Carling was there. She hadn't expected it. Pat couldn't have flown with him, so she'd assumed someone else was driving him cross-country. He looked much the same as he had in the photo, with dried blood on his forehead partially obscuring a deep purple, raised bruise. His hands were tied with narrow rope, then attached to one of the bed's feet, as were his legs. He had enough slack to change position a little, but not much. He was awake, his eyes dull and hopeless until they landed on her. Then they lit with hatred that sparked an answering guilt in Zoe.

But it wasn't Carling that made her back out of the room, turn, and gack on PB's shoes. On the king-sized bed next to Carling, curled in a ball against his back but tethered by one ankle, was a girl about twelve years old.

Olivia. She could barely hear the noises of disgust around her over her great, gasping heaves. She hadn't eaten anything for hours so not much came up, but that didn't stop her stomach from trying to turn itself inside out. It cramped hard, and her head swam, her pulse slamming in her ears. All she could see was Carling, beaten, bloody, and the delicate, vulnerable body huddled next to him.

It's not her. It's not her. It's not her.

The words kept echoing, louder and louder over her desperation until she realized it wasn't denial, but assertion. The girl's hair might not be dark enough. She was curled up, but seemed too small, too short, to be Olivia. She braced her hands on her knees and forced herself to concentrate on the brief tableau seared into her brain. It had been too quick. She couldn't be sure. And did it matter? She couldn't let Pat harm any young girl, whether or not she was Kell's sister.

PB pulled her to her feet to face Pat. She wanted to cover his mouth with her hands, drag him outside so that poor girl couldn't hear what he said, but she couldn't move. Her limbs were limp and weak, and she could barely speak past the burn in her throat.

"*How?*" she rasped.

"Efficient travel. Don't make the mistake of underestimating me," he said softly. "Zoe Ardmore."

He said her name deliberately, reminding her of the resources he must have at his disposal. She'd changed her name. Moved. Lived a decade and more since she put him in jail. And still he'd found her. He'd used her, and when his objective was reached, he'd orchestrated this scene in a very short time. He was more powerful than she'd ever imagined.

But she'd put him away. She straightened and slowly swiped the back of her hand over her mouth, watching him. He was different now, no matter how *the same* everything had seemed when they pulled that blindfold off her. He was harder, smarter, and had probably spent all these years planning what to do. He certainly had control now. And yet, at barely thirteen she had escaped on her own, gotten to the authorities, and had him sent to prison. She could damn well do it again.

"What do you want?"

"You will retrieve the key and return it to me within seventy-two hours. If you don't, Mr. Carling will be dead and we'll rehearse on your replacement." He swept a hand toward the other room. "Then we'll obtain another. Should it be necessary, we'll repeat the process many times until you fulfill your obligation to us. The final ritual, of course, will be performed with someone quite close to you. I don't think I need to say her name, do I?"

Panic filled Zoe. "Where is she?"

He smiled. "Don't be stupid. I'm not telling you. Do we have an agreement?"

No way. She couldn't agree to any of this. She wouldn't have to. The FBI had to find her. They'd rescue these people. Even if they left this place, the FBI *had* to be able to track them. She'd tell them what she'd seen. It would be enough for them to act on. They weren't hampered anymore.

But Pat wasn't done.

"I'm sure you think the corrupt government agencies can intervene for you. I assure you, they won't find us." He lifted one shoulder. "Perhaps they'll get lucky and rescue the girl. I won't be around, and it won't stop me from fulfilling my promise." He stepped closer, and PB pulled Zoe higher, onto her toes, so she was face to face with the man she hated more than anyone or anything in the world. "Do you understand me, Zoe?"

She almost spat in his face. "How do I know you won't just kill them both as soon as I'm gone?"

"Well, that wouldn't be logical, would it? You have my word the girl will be safe until your time is up."

"And Will?"

"He won't be harmed until necessary."

Zoe didn't know why she believed him, but he *was* smart. And he was right. If she was going to believe he'd follow through on the killing and torturing, she had to believe he'd follow through on his promise to keep them unharmed.

But three days wasn't nearly enough time. "I don't know where the key is."

"I do." This time his smile was pure, malicious glee. "It's with Grant Neely."

Natalie J. Damschroder

Chapter Sixteen

Kell watched his mother prepare the tea, following the rituals she'd learned in London, knowing the familiar movements steadied her. But why did she need steadying in the first place? She couldn't know about Pat and Freddie and what he'd been doing with Zoe. Every individual step of the process chafed at him. Zoe was in danger, possibly already in the lion's den, maybe already hurt or confined, and he was having *tea*.

"Mom, why is Olivia in Europe? During school? Without you and Dad?"

She carefully dropped a cube of sugar into each cup and stirred with a tiny spoon so delicately that it didn't clink once. "Your father hasn't officially declared, but he intends to run for state senate," she said.

"Yeah, I know. What—"

She shot him a warning look that was much more normal than her fragile demeanor.

"Sorry. Go on."

"Today photos surfaced that showed him in a compromising position with a girl who is certainly not of age."

Kell shot to his feet. "What? No way." He shook his head and crossed the Aubusson rug in one stride. She didn't move, so he dropped to a knee and took her hand. "He wouldn't. You know you wouldn't."

She smiled wanly. "I can believe that deep in my soul, Kellen, and it wouldn't make it less true."

His heart thumped, paused, thumped. "No. What happened? Where did these photos surface?"

"Everywhere." She withdrew her hand. "All the media has them, and they were e-mailed to us and every member of your father's firm."

He rubbed a hand over his face. "Where's Dad?"

"At the office. He's meeting with the other partners and a crisis manager to discuss how to handle this." She handed him a cup and saucer, and he got the message. He was to move back to his seat on the sofa.

He took the tea and obeyed. "You sent Olivia to Europe so she wouldn't see or hear about this."

She nodded. "And they're on a random itinerary to keep the media from finding her. You know how relentless the sharks are." She drew a deep breath that shook halfway through. "A side benefit is the additional safety. Unless you coming home means that's no longer a concern."

Kell closed his eyes for a second, sick with relief. Olivia was out of Thomashunis's reach. The rest of this was meaningless crap in comparison, but he knew it didn't feel that way to his mother. He should be out of here *now*, working on a plan with Grant, finding out what the FBI was doing. But he couldn't just abandon his mother.

"No. Not yet. I'm glad she's safer." She didn't need to know what was happening with Zoe, not with this on her shoulders now. "I want to see the pictures," he told her.

She sipped her tea. "That's not a good idea."

"They're not real," he argued. "We'll hire an expert to prove it."

"The firm has someone. They're working on it." But she didn't sound hopeful, and he didn't understand why.

"Where are they?"

She shrugged and patted her lips with a napkin, so Kell got up and went looking for Genovese. He found her in her office, scanning receipts into her computer.

"Where are they?"

She nodded once at a manila envelope in her in-tray. He snatched it up and dug inside. There were only three photos. Whoever had sent them had printed them eight by ten. The first was poor quality, grainy and pixelated at that size. A guy was kissing the neck of a girl who looked like she was still a teenager, her head thrown back, hand curled around the man's head. All he could see of the man was a dark suit. His hands and face weren't visible.

"Bullshit," he muttered, tossing the picture onto the desk. Genovese sat watching him, her hands motionless on her lap. She didn't react to his grumble.

The second photo showed the same girl, wearing the same maroon-colored dress or top, standing in front of the window the photographer had shot through. They hadn't zoomed as much, so the photo was marginally clearer. This time, the man's face was visible, though in shadow, his hands wrapped around the girl's waist. He did look like Kell's father, but it wasn't definitive.

The last one was the punch to the gut. It was taken outside a bed and breakfast, next to a sleek car of the same make and model as his father's. The girl now wore a black sweater or something over her dress. She was arching her body toward the man, who was bending as if about to kiss her. This one was clear enough to see his face, and it was definitely Robert Stone.

"This is ridiculous," he told Genovese. "You can't identify anyone in that picture." He jabbed a finger at the one he'd tossed. "This one isn't clear." He dropped that one, too. "And this is meaningless. He could be about to kiss her cheek. It's not even evidence of an affair, never mind proof."

Genovese nodded but didn't speak. Kell peered more closely at the details in the photo. "Can you pull up this bed and breakfast? The Gloria Rose." He leaned over her shoulder to see what came up. She clicked on the business website, and the screen filled with a photo of the front of the white building.

"It's the same." He held up the photo next to the monitor. The angle, distance, and frame were exact.

"Well, it makes sense that the photographer—"

"No. It's *exactly* the same. Pixel for pixel." He pointed to a rosebush next to the sign. "Four blossoms." He pointed to the photo in his hand. "Four blossoms. Same size. The lighting is the same. Look at the patch on the roof." Sunlight filtering through a tree left the exact same pattern in both shots. "What's the only thing that's different on here?"

She shifted closer and looked back and forth. "There's no driveway in the website shot."

"Exactly." He flicked the edge of the photo. "This was faked."

She swiveled to face him. "The part with your father and the girl appears to be one image, though."

Kell shook his head. "So what? She could be anyone. It could have been taken anywhere, and 'anywhere' is obviously not as incriminating as Gloria Rose B&B. Can you please print that?"

She did, with a few taps on the keyboard. He grabbed the page off the printer and kissed the top of her head. "Thanks, Gen."

"Of course."

His mother was sitting just as he'd left her, the barely touched tea cradled in her hand as she stared out the window into the empty side yard.

"Mom." He showed her the two photos and explained what they revealed. To his surprise, she waved them off.

"Oh, we know all that already. The inn has no record of your father staying there, and the girl is the daughter of a paralegal who used to work for him. She brought her to work when she was a baby for a couple of years. They were in town a few weeks ago and had lunch with Robert. It's all ridiculous."

He let his arms drop. "Then why are you—"

When she looked up, the sorrow drowning her

eyes laid him low. "Oh. Oh, Mom." These photos weren't the issue. They were just the catalyst for something worse.

She nodded and sniffed. "I never wanted you to know."

He sat on the edge of the sofa and laid the photos next to him, face down. "When? You make it sound like it wasn't recent."

"It was two years ago." She looked at her left hand and adjusted her wedding band with her thumb. "Long over. We had an in-house separation while we went through counseling. It was actually good for us, in the long run. But you'll never convince anyone else of that, and this fraudulent scandal will send everyone digging for more."

Kell wanted to tell his mother not to care what anyone thought, but he knew it was pointless. "Who was she?"

She shrugged. "An interior designer who bid on the office reconstruction."

Well, at least the real one wasn't underage.

"She didn't even get the job. It was, apparently, 'a chemistry thing.' " She seemed to remember her tea and drank before setting it back on the table. "We'll get through it, of course. I just didn't want your sister suffering through this part. She's continuing her studies as she travels, and as long as she keeps up her work, the school approved a two-week educational absence. By the time she returns, the news cycle will have moved on, and we'll be prepared to help her handle any fallout at school."

Olivia would probably be more upset that they'd tried to shelter her, sent her away so they didn't have to deal with her, more than she'd care about what her classmates said. A month ago, he would have argued with his parents about that. Now, though, it made everything simpler here. He doubted Pat's resources would allow him to track Olivia on a random itinerary in other countries.

He reached for his mother's hand, expecting it to feel frail in his, but she gripped with familiar strength. "I'm sorry, Mom. Sorry you're going through all this. Sorry Dad's an ass."

She actually laughed. "Oh, Kellen, he was an ass when I married him. But I loved him anyway, and I still do. We'll get through this. It's the resurfacing after you get plunged in it that's hard."

It seemed she was already above water. She patted his hand then withdrew both of hers with a sigh.

"I can't believe he left you alone like this."

But she waved that off and refilled her teacup. "You know he had to go do damage control. I'm fine. All right," she admitted when he raised his eyebrows, "I will be. You don't need to worry about me."

His phone buzzed in his pocket, reminding him of the mess he'd left. He wanted to be here for his mother, but she'd laid out the reasons she didn't need him, and Zoe did.

He stood again. "Mom, I'm really sorry, but I can't stay."

She rose, also, her chin raised. "Oh, darling, I don't expect you to. I don't even know why you came, since you obviously didn't know about all this."

He didn't know what to say. Not without explaining everything, and there just wasn't time for that. "I wanted to check on Olivia."

She raised an eyebrow. "You've called her every day, which is about four times as much as usual. What happened?" Fear flashed in her eyes. "Has something changed? Is she in further danger?"

"No. I don't think so. Especially now that she's in Europe." He shoved a hand through his hair and tried to decide what to tell her that wouldn't hold him here too long. "It's a long story."

"I know."

Now his eyebrows went up. "What do you mean, you know?"

She shrugged. "You've missed work. James is running interference for you. Tanicia called Genovese to confirm your tux size and preferences, but was cagey about where you were and the event you needed it for. And you showed up in the middle of the day on a Tuesday, which didn't ring a bell until it was clear you didn't know what had happened. The fear in your expression hasn't left since you arrived." She laid a hand on his forearm. "Is Zoe okay?"

An awful burn hit his eyes. He blinked. "I don't know. Maybe not. Maybe *really* not."

"Then you'd better go." She took him by the elbow and started ushering him toward the door. Her posture was stiffer, her color better. Stronger when focusing on others than on herself. "I'm sure you'll tell us everything when it's over. Olivia doesn't have her phone with her. We bought her a temporary phone, something basic, and told her it was so hers wouldn't get lost. I'll have Genovese send you the number, but you should be careful about when you use it. You probably didn't need me to say that. Be careful, Kell." She angled her head for a kiss on the cheek, so he obliged.

But guilt wasn't absolved so easily. "Mom, I'm sorry. I'd stay if this wasn't—life-or-death important."

She seemed to understand that he wasn't exaggerating. "It's all right, sweetheart. Just please be careful. Don't put yourself in harm's way if you can avoid it. I love you."

"I love you, too. Tell Dad—"

"I will."

Her words stuck with him as he headed back to the airport. He'd been furious with Zoe for making decisions that could put his sister at risk, for not trusting him with her secrets, and that had made it a struggle to know if their relationship could be salvaged. Not their love, because that wasn't going away. But he'd seen her actions as a reflection of her lack of respect for him instead of what it really was. She valued him more than she valued herself.

What she'd done today proved it, and he hated how that made him feel. Despondent and weak when he should be strong.

He needed his rage back.

* * *

Grant was ready for the fist that plowed into his face. He allowed it. Welcomed the pain that blasted through his cheekbone and rattled through his skull. After all, he was the professional. He should never have let Zoe trick him.

But he'd be damned if he'd take more than that from Kellen Stone.

He dodged the second swing, but Stone surprised him. Instead of being thrown off balance, he anticipated Grant's move and followed him, plowing his shoulder into Grant's midsection and knocking him against the wall of the FBI conference room. Grant's breath whooshed out, leaving room for anger to blow in. He shoved Stone away by the shoulders and positioned himself to block the next blow, to throw a solid punch of his own.

But Kell was clearly beyond simple anger. He didn't charge or swing at Grant again. He grabbed a chair and threw it at him.

"Fuck!" Grant ducked, but the chair bounced off the cement wall and landed on him. He staggered, pain lancing across his lower back. Damn this guy. He wasn't taking this. All his frustration and impotence since he realized the plane was leaving the gate without Zoe built like a pressure bomb in his chest. When Stone came at him, Grant released it with a punch straight in the face, a blow calculated to flatten his opponent. Satisfaction was a cooling balm as Stone hit the floor. Grant knew from experience that Stone wouldn't be able to see past the exploding lights and shocking pain. He bounced on the balls of his feet, waiting for the lawyer to recover, itching to knock him back again.

And the bastard surprised him. *Again*. He didn't roll and moan, though he did hold his hands to his face. After a scant couple of seconds, he swept his legs around Grant's—one in front, one in back—and sent Grant slamming to the ground beside him.

The impact left him stunned, giving Stone time to get on top of him. He got in a couple of lightweight blows, one off his ear, before Grant flipped him.

"I didn't do this!" he growled, trying to hold Kell down. "It's not me you want!"

"The hell it's not!" Kell stopped attempting to get free. He glared up at Grant. "You're trying to take her from me, you asshole, and I still trusted you to keep her safe!"

"I tried!" Grant shifted to let Kell up, braced to be attacked again. "She's a grown woman who makes her own decisions. She tricked us *both*, and don't think I don't blame myself!" The reality of what she'd done hit him, and he doubled over, bracing his hands on his knees, nausea coming in ever-increasing waves. What Pat and Freddy could be doing to her…carving her up, raping her, torturing her—every horrible thing he'd seen in his career, everything they'd done to Jordie, flashed into his brain. He'd kept it at bay as long as he could work, plan, prepare, but that just made it worse when he broke. His breath sobbed out of him and he swallowed hard, trying not to throw up. Embarrassing himself in front of the competition was a good deterrent.

A hand patted his shoulder, hesitantly, then squeezed. "It's all right," Kell said heavily. "She'll be okay." He actually sounded like he believed it, and Grant snorted and straightened, shaking his head at the other man's abrupt shift.

"Sure. We'll get to her. They won't have time to do anything." He sounded less convincing.

Kell slowly bent to right the chair he'd thrown, then lowered himself into it, his head dropping back. "What are we doing here, man? Why aren't we in on this?"

"FBI regulations. This is much bigger now, and official, finally. Henricksen can't let us near them."

"So?" Kell slammed a hand on the table next to him. "Since when do you defer to the FBI?"

Grant's mouth twitched but didn't make it to full-blown smile. "I work with them all the time." He'd made his own plans, but he couldn't say that here at the FBI field office, where they were being monitored.

Now Kell snorted, and it sounded a lot more elegant than Grant's had. "Not like this."

"Henricksen—"

"I know. He's competent."

"And he cares." Something Grant saw less and less of…and felt less of, himself, until it had become personal. "He'll get her back."

On cue, the door opened. Henricksen scanned them with an unreadable look. "You guys done?"

"For now." Kell prodded at his swelling nose. "Where is she?"

"We lost transmission."

Grant and Kell swore together.

"I know. We're closing in on her last known

location, but we don't know what caused the signal loss. It could be simple malfunction."

Grant didn't believe that and doubted anyone else did. "How long?"

"A couple more hours." He shook his head when they cursed again. "They're not where we expected them to be. We have limited resources here and no second team we can mobilize. We're doing the best we can."

It's not good enough echoed around the room, though it went unspoken.

After a moment, Henricksen said, "I'll keep you guys posted," and left. Grant paced, his mind racing with plans and no way to execute them. He had people who could help, who owed him favors or would let him owe them later. He'd called a few of them, and they were on their way to Columbus. He could also make some guesses about what they'd be going into and plan the extractions of both Zoe and Carling. But none of that did him any good if he couldn't find out where they were. Right now, the best way to do that was through the FBI.

Except Henricksen wouldn't give it to him, the bastard. He was too smart, and too cautious to risk Grant and his team interfering. Grant could be standing here, filling the room with resentment and fighting with his prime rival for the woman he loved, when they told him she was dead.

It was an unacceptable possibility, and one he had no way of preventing.

* * *

Kell watched Grant pace for a while, but the echo of his footsteps grated and his circular pattern made him dizzy. He'd been popping antacids since he left the airport in San Francisco and hadn't had anything but coffee since. Dizziness didn't improve the mix.

God, this sucked. At least before, they were doing something. Tracking leads, following a plan. Grant probably had one up in his head, just biding his time until he could implement it. Kell knew he he had the resources and experience to get it done. And the guts. All Kell had was hours of crime-drama-watching experience, in which the fretful fiancé fell apart when they delivered the bad news.

He couldn't be that guy. He'd have to find a way to go along when Grant mobilized. Geez, listen to him. He shoved his hands into his hair and rested his elbows on the table, staring without seeing the reflection of the overhead light in the metal. Listening to anyone else who sounded like this would make him laugh. *Mobilized*, for God's sake. He'd be a liability in a mission like that, even an unsanctioned one. Sure, he'd held his own so far, but that was when it was just the three of them. He'd shown Zoe he could be just as strong, just as protective, without taking over. But put him in a real situation? With bigger stakes? He could fuck it up, and Zoe would be the casualty.

Kell launched to his feet and went two steps before halting. No way could he pace in this small space with Grant already prowling. He leaned against the wall furthest from Grant and checked e-mail on his phone with faint hope for some kind of lead, something new to concentrate on. Nothing from Rhomney or from Zoe. A few messages from work, fires Tanicia could put out on her own—and had, he saw as he scrolled on. Nothing to distract him from the numbing nothingness in this room.

Grant's footsteps stopped and Kell glanced up to find him staring off into space. Or maybe at the video camera in the corner. He scrolled again. James had e-mailed. He opened it, and found only CALL ME with six exclamation points. With a sense of dread, he hit the speed dial for James' office number and lifted the phone to his ear. Grant's phone rang at the same time.

"Hey, man," James answered. "Hold on."

Kell's heart raced as he listened to his friend instruct his paralegal to hold calls. He'd asked him to monitor things and let him know if they got worse. The sound of the office door closing didn't help.

"Sorry about that. I have an update on your father's situation."

"What happened?"

"Well, as your mother expected, they found out about the affair. One of the bigger media outlets already tracked down the woman. She refused to talk to anyone, but they're dragging up her history, and it isn't pretty."

Kell pinched the bridge of his nose, eyes closed. The timing of this couldn't be worse. Then his head came up. Of course it couldn't. He'd bet anything Rhomney had something to do with this. The other threats hadn't stopped them, so they were trying to break up Zoe's support system this way. Probably figured Kell would run back to Mommy and Daddy and far away from Zoe.

They'd underestimated him.

"There've been reporters here," James told him, "but since you weren't, they drifted away. Still, you being on a leave of absence isn't helping."

"Thanks for letting me know."

"When are you coming back? We can only do damage control for so long."

"I know, and I can't ask you to do more. But I've got bigger things going on."

James whistled. "Bigger than family scandal? What is it?"

"It's Zoe." He hesitated. James' anticipation rose on the other end of the line. What the hell. It wasn't like anything was happening here. "She's been abducted. Kind of." After James got the what-the-fucks out of the way, he encapsulated her past and what had been happening since she broke up with him. He left Grant out of the story.

"Holy shit, man. What can I do?"

"Just hold down the fort as best as you can. I don't know how much longer this is going to play out. I'll need my job when it's all over."

"Yeah, sure. I'll run interference for you. But jeez, man."

"I know."

The door opened and Henricksen walked in, without a remnant of his usual implacability. He looked mournful, and Kell's heart not only sank, it left his body, ripping hard as it did. No. Please, no. On the other side of the room, Grant said goodbye to whomever was on the phone. Kell didn't bother, just shoved his phone into his pocket.

"What happened?"

Henricksen braced his hands on the back of a chair and shook his head. "We were too late. They got to the location they'd tracked and found her phone, smashed, but no one was there. Plenty of evidence it was Rhomney and Thomashunis, plus a bunch of other people."

Kell's heart started beating again, but his lungs constricted now. They hadn't found Zoe dead, but *not* finding her wouldn't have put that look on Henricksen's face. "They found something else."

Henricksen nodded slowly.

"What?"

He looked up, his eyes haunted. "Lots of blood."

* * *

Grant approached his shack with a combination of exhaustion and jittery urgency. No matter how much he worked, he didn't travel in a month as much as he'd traveled in the last week. His body kept sending him signals that he needed to crash for about twenty-four hours. Like now, when he lifted his right foot to go up the steps, and it didn't go high enough, and he came close to smashing his face into the deck.

On the other hand, his brain sent opposing signals, telling him to run-not-walk to Zoe, calling him a moron for coming back here when she was in Ohio. It kept trying to send him back to the docks for the next boat out.

But right before Henricksen told them they'd lost Zoe's signal, Grant had been on the phone with his mother. She wanted to see how things were going, if Zoe had contacted him, how they were getting along, wink-wink-nudge-nudge. She'd asked about the package she sent, and at first he just thought she meant the articles she'd faxed and e-mailed before all this started. But after Henricksen dropped his bomb, after Stone fell completely apart and Henricksen led him off to find someplace to pull himself together, her words had come back to him. She'd specifically said *package*. And he hadn't gotten one. When he called her back to ask about it, she confessed she'd sent him some of Jordie's old things. Nothing exciting, just some stuff she'd packed away when she cleaned out his room years ago. She'd found it in the attic and thought he might like to have some of it, since she was pretty sure he didn't have much.

Grant should have dismissed it. It should have had nothing to do with what was going on with Zoe. But instinct screamed at him to get home and find it. He rarely ignored his instincts, and he was tired of being impotent and scared. So he'd flown home.

He managed to get inside the shack and flipped on the light switch, which lit a small table lamp next to his one comfortable chair. A figure moved and he jerked, reaching for a gun he wasn't wearing. But it wasn't a threat.

It was Zoe.

"Where is it, Grant?"

Her voice rasped, the sound of someone who had

screamed over and over. Like at a concert. Or during torture. It shook with fear but held a core of steel that told him she was on a mission he would not deter her from.

But she was alive.

He dropped his duffel in the corner and tensed his jaw so he wouldn't yell at her for tricking him. "I thought you were in Ohio."

"I left."

"You should call Stone. He's pretty—"

"Where is it?" She shot out of the chair, eyes blazing, hands fisted. But then she swayed and did a vague eye-blink-head-shake thing, and he knew she was as dead on her feet as he was.

"Where is what? What happened? How did you get here? Your funds were almost depleted."

"Flew. Boat. Credit card. None of that matters." She drew a deep breath, her spine lengthening as she visibly drew strength from nothing. Her jaw barely moved as she gritted out, "Pat has Will and a girl. Not Olivia, I don't think." She inhaled a quick half-sob.

"Olivia's in Europe."

Her eyes widened. "What?"

"There was some kind of— Never mind. She's safe in Europe with her aunt and uncle. Pat can't get to her."

She sagged, and he lurched to grab her and help her back into the chair she'd been sitting in.

"It doesn't matter," she said. "I mean, it does, but he's got someone else. And he threatened if I don't bring it. Two days. Fast—I have to move fast. God, I'm so tired." She slumped over, her head dropping onto her arms in her lap. But she kept talking. "I took the FBI phone with me to meet with Pat. I thought Henricksen understood what I was going to do and would follow the signal."

"He did. They were too late."

She shifted her head in a kind of nod. "I know. Pat smashed the phone. He said you have the key and I have to get it back to him in seventy-two hours—a lot less, now—or he'll start killing." She lifted her head. "Please tell me you have it. Even though I might kill you if you do."

"I don't. I've never even seen it." But as worn out as his brain was, he was putting three and five together and coming up with eight. Almost. "Did he say how I got it?"

"No." She sat up and pushed her hair off her face. It was a limp, tangled mess. "But I was thinking about that on my way down here. He thought he was supposed to get it the night I escaped. But what if Jordie got it first? What if he got the totems but hid the key, and Pat never knew until now? The person he was supposed to meet with might have told him he gave it to Jordie."

Grant stiffened. "And he told you *I* have it."

She nodded, but then flattened out her hands, palms up. "But why?"

"I don't know. I mean, I think I know. But I'm not sure how." They might have been watching his mother, or maybe somehow listening to her phone conversations or hacking her e-mail. Somehow, they'd determined that she'd sent a package here and assumed the key was in the package.

The problem was, he didn't have one. Of course, he'd been gone for five days. When he traveled, the mail carrier shoved his regular mail through a slot next to the door. He went over and crouched to dig through the bin that caught it all.

"What are you doing?" Zoe got up and trudged over, pressing a hand on his shoulder as she leaned to watch him.

"Looking…" He pawed through the junk and bills and coupon flyers. Nothing. Starting again at the top, he methodically pulled out each piece of mail until he found what he was looking for. A pinkish slip with his name and address scrawled in one box…and his mother's in another.

"What? What is that?" Zoe plucked it out of his hand and backed up so he could rise. Her eyes flew over the paper once, twice, three times before she looked up, her mouth falling open. "She had it. She sent it to you."

"Maybe."

"We have to make sure she's okay! What if they tried—"

He held up a hand. "She's fine. I just talked to her a few hours ago. She mentioned the package, which I obviously hadn't gotten yet. That's why I came down here instead of staying at the FBI office in Ohio."

"Where's the post office? How do we get this?"

He rasped out a humorless laugh. "Zoe, it's nearly midnight. We can't get it until morning. And we both need to sleep."

"I can't. I only have hours—"

"Neither of us can do anything if we keel over." He'd have included himself regardless, just to convince her, but he was almost as desperate as she was. "Sleep, Zoe. We'll go to the post office first thing in the morning and then take it from there."

"We should talk about—"

"No." He nudged her toward the bed. "Sleep. Non-negotiable. We'll figure out what comes next after what comes next."

She managed a chuckle and sank onto her side, adjusting the pillow, her eyes already closed. "I hate that I understood that."

"You probably hate more that you could have said it." He settled next to her, back to back, and matched his breathing rhythm to hers. "It'll be okay. I promise."

A little murmur was all he got back. She'd already fallen asleep, which was good, because it was a promise he didn't know how the hell to keep.

Chapter Seventeen

Zoe burst from deep sleep into bright sunlight, her sharp intake of breath lingering on the air. She blinked, frowning up at the tin roof until her brain caught up. Morning. Grant's. Alone. She sniffed. Coffee?

A rustle of paper and scrape of a box on wood made her sit up. Her shirt and jeans were twisted on her body and her face felt stiff, as if she'd been crying in her sleep. She threw off the blanket and eased her aching muscles out of bed. Grant didn't look up from where he stood at the table, lifting packing paper out of a box.

"You went without me," she accused. Her throat rattled, making the words husky. She rubbed sleepy sand out of her eyes.

"I didn't want to wake you. It didn't take long, and there was no point in both of us going." He crumpled the paper and tossed it toward the trash can, missing by several feet.

"Well, hold on. Don't start digging yet. I have to…" She rushed into the bathroom and straightened herself out, taking care of urgent business before washing her face and pulling her hair back into a rubber band. "Okay," she called, opening the door. "I just have to get some—" She stopped short. Grant held out a mug of coffee. "Get some of that. Thank you." She wrapped her hands around the mug and inhaled, easing closer to the table as the world perked up around her.

He removed a few battered books from the box and set them on the table. Zoe tilted her head to read the spines. Hardy Boys hardcovers and a copy of *The Five Little Peppers and How They Grew*. One of her favorites as a kid.

She watched him remove a soft old baseball shirt, a trophy, and a glove from the box, and bit her tongue to stop herself from urging him to hurry. A tingle went up her spine, and when Grant drew out a roll of leather, she almost cried again. The key.

"Oh, thank God," she breathed, reaching a tentative hand toward it. She didn't really want to touch it, but couldn't help herself. Was it real?

"Hold your horses. We're not sure yet." He cleared some space, letting the rest of the twisted packing paper fall to the floor. She stepped closer as he untied the leather thong holding the roll in place, then gently laid it out on the table. The leather had darkened over time, the markings harder to see than in the picture Zoe'd found, but they were the same. Four squares connected in a diamond pattern by filigree chains, with a few symbols in the center. After seeing the totems at Will's house and again at Pat's shack, she recognized the symbols. They were small images that were carved on the totems. The ones on the key were angled, as if pointing to each of the squares the totems needed to be placed on.

The drawing she'd found had been incomplete, though. There was writing across the top and bottom, a language she didn't know, and she wondered if that was what was supposed to unlock the supposed powers of the totems. Like a chant. But then she remembered the girl, and that Pat thought there was a ritual involved. And the burden of what she had to do descended on her. She sat with a sigh.

"I don't know how to do this," she told Grant.

"Do what, exactly?"

She flicked a corner of the leather. "This. Do I take it to Pat so he doesn't kill Will, then convince him to let him and the girl go? He won't do that. Will, maybe, if he doesn't think he needs him anymore. But he needs the girl. Or *a* girl."

Grant crouched in front of her. "You don't need to do any of it. I have a team gathering. You just tell us where you're supposed to go and we'll do the rest."

It was tempting to simply let him take over. But the risk was too high. "I can't stay here, and I have to travel alone. He had people follow me down here. I couldn't get away to call Henricksen to tell him anything. PB even went into the bathroom with me so I couldn't borrow a cell phone from a stranger."

"I called Henricksen this morning," Grant told her. "So they know what's happening. And Kell, who was devastated when they found the house where you were was empty."

"God, Kell." She rubbed her face with her hands.

"He's got to hate me."

"No, he doesn't. He's crazy in love with you." He stood and rolled up the key, replacing all his brother's other things carefully in the box. "So here's the plan. You and I are going to meet up with Kell, who will take you to an FBI safe house while I go connect with my colleagues, who are all eager to kick ass and take names and under fewer restrictions than the FBI. We'll go to your meeting spot and extract Carling and the girl, then hand them off to the FBI, who can clean up whatever mess we leave behind while we melt into the wind. 'Kay?"

He made it sound so easy. "What about Pat's tails?"

"Where are they?"

"I don't know." She waved a hand at the beach. "Watching."

"They'll expect me to go with you. Rhomney won't care. He'd be glad to have another person to use as leverage. Don't worry, Zo, the plan will work."

She finally nodded, reluctantly. She should see this through to the end, but didn't know how without getting in the way. The idea of going into hiding with Kell was almost more frightening than going back to Pat and Freddie. She'd lied to him, *again*. And how were they going to handle being alone together with nothing to do? All the questing and running and adventure stuff had been sufficient distraction from their main problem, but if they had hours to kill, she'd have to face the reality of what came next.

It wasn't just that Kell didn't know her past. She'd

changed over the last week. Grant fed a fierceness in her that she'd packed away when she went to college, like everything her abduction had touched. That part of her wouldn't be buried again. She wanted to be whole, to embrace everything she was, whether the influences that carved her were good or bad.

So which man would accept her that way? Grant had at least witnessed some of the carving and hadn't expressed any doubt in his belief that they belonged together. But how could she assume Kell couldn't love her without giving him a chance to try?

She glanced up to find Grant watching her with equal amusement and longing. When she met his gaze, he smiled and hid the latter.

"Don't worry," he said. "You'll get there. And it will be right, whichever way you choose."

Zoe wasn't sure choice had anything to do with it.

* * *

A few hours later, Zoe walked into a pleasant suburban home on a cul-de-sac near Miami, accompanied by two FBI agents. She didn't take note of the neighborhood or the décor. She was still exhausted and scared of what would happen when Kell saw her. He'd insisted on flying down here as soon as he found out she was okay, and the FBI was meeting him at the airport to bring him here. If Grant found out that meant leaving only one agent at the house with her, he'd freak. But Zoe didn't think she was in much danger. Grant had arranged for a female mercenary he knew to impersonate Zoe and travel with him back to Ohio. That should keep Pat and his people on hold unless and until they caught wind of something hinky.

Unable to eat the soup the agent offered her or to sleep in the bedroom, Zoe curled into a corner of the couch and propped her head on a toss pillow. Kell's flight should be landing in a few minutes, so it wouldn't be too long before he got here. Grant would already be in Ohio, because he wasn't using a commercial flight this time. How long before he got to the meeting place? How long before they heard if the girl was okay? If Will was alive?

She didn't realize she'd dozed until she woke to a hand on her face and her name murmured close by. She cranked open her eyes and rested her hand on the one cupping her cheek. "Kell?"

"Zoe. You're safe." He closed his eyes and kissed her, a tender, trembly kiss that brought tears to her eyes. "I was—" He sighed and rested his forehead on hers. Zoe absorbed his closeness for a moment, then struggled to sit up.

"You're okay? I'm so sorry." She didn't know what she wanted, didn't believe he could ever forgive her, but she had to apologize, to make him understand, at least. "I'm sorry I tricked you and—everything. But I can't say I shouldn't have done it. And the situation with your father…I'm sorry," she said again, lamely. "How are they? Your family?" She wasn't sure if anyone had told him about the girl Pat had taken, about her fear that it had been Olivia—and that she'd left her there without knowing for sure it wasn't his sister.

Kell dragged himself up onto the sofa next to her.

He rubbed his hands over his face, and when he dropped them to dangle them over his knees, she saw how haggard he looked. His eyes were red-rimmed and heavy, his face puffy and gray. "They're enduring. Mom's a mess. I mean, you know." He smirked. "Her hand trembles sometimes. She knows the initial accusations are fake, but he did have an affair, and that's all coming out now. She's standing by him because they repaired things and she says they're stronger now. I didn't get a chance to see Dad before I left again."

"I'm—"

He held up a hand. "Stop apologizing. It could go on forever."

She wrapped her arms around herself. "Do you know what's been happening?" she asked.

"Some, but not all. Tell me what happened when you were in the house. Where did all the blood come from?"

Since she'd given the details to Grant and then to the FBI, they flowed easily now. But Kell turned even paler when she told him about the girl, and he reached out to grasp her hand tightly in his.

"The FBI said they think they know who she is. She's been missing only a few days. And she didn't really seem hurt. At least, as far as I could tell." She trembled, and Kell's hand tightened around hers. "The blood was all Will's, I think." She swallowed hard. "Scalp wounds bleed a lot, but it could have been from something else."

"It's okay." Kell tugged her toward him and

hugged her. "They'll get them."

She nodded. She meant a different "they" than he did, but the goal was the same.

A jaw-cracking yawn took her by surprise. Kell steered her toward the bedroom. "Come on. You need to sleep."

"You do, too," she murmured, crawling onto the bed and collapsing on a pillow. The case scratched her cheek, and she rolled toward the dip in the center of the bed. "This is the only bed." She patted the old polyester comforter. "Here." She was too tired to say more than that. Kell lay down and tilted her way, influenced by the mattress's crater. He tucked her head under his chin, rubbed her back, and sighed, and Zoe faded to oblivion.

When she jerked awake some time later, it was dark in the room. Kell snored softly over her head, his arm still curved protectively around her. No light filtered down the hall from the living room, and she couldn't hear the agents moving around. Maybe they'd fallen asleep, too, though that shouldn't have happened. At least one should be awake.

Thinking she'd go see if there was coffee and any news, she slowly slid out from under Kell's arm and off the bed. He rolled into the center and snuffled into the pillow just like he had hundreds of times throughout their relationship. She smiled bittersweetly and started down the hall.

Her stocking feet were quiet on the ugly sculpted carpet, and she didn't brush the walls or clear her throat or anything. Not quite intentionally—it just seemed like a good idea to be quiet. And it probably saved her, because she saw the body on the floor and the figure standing over it before it saw her. She swallowed her instinctive yelp and jerked back into the hall, mind racing, adrenaline pumping once again into her system.

Pat had found her. His guy was disabling her protection before he came for her. Was he alone? She craned to listen. Soft footsteps tapped on the linoleum in the kitchen, moving away from her, and all she could hear in the bedroom was Kell's mild snore.

But then another noise overlaid that. A scraping glide. Like a window going up. She whirled and dashed as quietly as she could down the hall toward the bedroom, diving at the last second into the bathroom. She needed some kind of weapon, but dammit, what would she find in here? She spun in place, afraid to open the drawers and make noise, and Holy God of Luck, there was a pair of scissors in a cup at the back of the sink. She snatched them out, and they were short but very pointed. Haircutting scissors.

Praying they'd be enough, she stuck her middle and ring fingers through the holes and made a fist. Then she crept back out into the hall, peering both ways before moving toward the bedroom again. Her eyes had adjusted to the low light. Kell was a lump on the bed. A silhouette straightened in front of the open window. Before it could register her presence, she lunged ahead and sped into the bedroom, across the empty floor, leading with the scissors and barely missing the end of the bed. She landed on the figure hard enough to send it crashing into the desk next to the window, then to the floor, the rolling chair falling over on top of them.

Zoe was yelling now, no sense staying quiet anymore after the noisy crash, but the man under her caught her arm before she connected with the scissors. She should have the leverage, but he was strong and easily held her at bay. Good thing she had two hands. She stiffened the fingers of her left hand and jabbed down at his throat. Her aim was off the soft spot, but he still gagged and let go of her to clutch at his neck. She shifted back on his body and punched toward his solar plexus. Again left-handed, because now that she was in it, she found herself too squeamish to stab him.

"Zoe!" The commotion had awakened Kell. Zoe heard the click of the lamp next to the bed, but the light didn't come on. They must have cut the power.

"We've got to get out of here!" she cried, lurching to her feet. The guy on the floor grabbed at her legs. She kicked him in the side of the head, not too hard, but enough to make him flop back, possibly unconscious. But there'd be another any—

She screeched as arms came around her from behind. Then Kell was there, punching, trying to separate them. The arms tightened, higher on her body, so she just dropped her full weight to the floor. He couldn't hold her, but the smack of flesh on flesh told her he was fighting Kell. She couldn't tell who was doing what, couldn't even tell which one was Kell, so she couldn't help.

Nine-one-one. She could do that. The FBI had given

her another temporary phone and she'd kept it in her back pocket. It lit up when she hit the home button, which wasn't the best idea because it turned out there were more than two invaders. More arms grabbed her, knocking the phone out of her hand. She screamed, but whoever had her swung her up into a fireman's carry, heading immediately out the door.

"Kell!" she screamed again. He was fighting, he couldn't help her, but she had to let him know what was happening. She tried to kick, but had no target. Tried to punch or pinch or tear or gouge, but he had both hands wrapped in one, a vice-like grip. She bucked her body, but he just pulled down harder on her legs and arms, straining her joints and shoving his shoulder into her gut so that she retched and wheezed.

"Zoe!" Kell shouted from way back in the bedroom. She craned her head around and could see him in the doorway, struggling, two people holding his arms back while he twisted and jerked to get away. "No!"

"Don't you hurt him!" She bucked again, stretching her legs out so her feet knocked over something on a table. There was the clatter of broken ceramic, but it didn't even slow her captor down. Her only chance was at the door. He'd have to angle her through and even let go to open it. Maybe she could use the wall to break his hold.

The fighting behind her came closer and she went limp, as if giving up, just as her captor reached the front door. He let go of her legs instead of her hands, probably figuring the hands would give her more leverage, but it gave *him* a more awkward angle. He dipped to reach the handle, and Zoe swung her body up and off his shoulder, dropping down his back and onto her feet. It broke his grip on her wrists, and she shoved him into the door. Then she ran.

Blindly, badly, but she couldn't help Kell like this, and she needed…something. Unfortunately, she forgot the agent lying on the floor and tripped over him, flying through the air and landing with a *whoomp* on her stomach a few feet away.

"Stupid, fucking, cracking whore!"

The curse wasn't very imaginative, but Zoe figured he was under pressure. She GI Joe-crawled across the kitchen toward the back door, knowing she wasn't going to make it. She struggled to draw breath, the panic when she couldn't making her weak and slow. Then her lungs magically expanded, and she sucked air in so gratefully that for a moment she lost awareness of anything around her.

Then hands grabbed her again, dragged her upward, but they were different and she didn't fight them. Her subconscious knew first that it was Kell. He urged her to the door and reached past her to yank it open.

"How—"

"Scissors." He pushed her out onto the small back porch and down the steps. "Hurry."

She hurried.

Terror put wings on her feet, and they raced down the dark, quiet street, her mind keeping pace. They needed a phone. Call the police. Henricksen. *Grant*. If

Pat knew Zoe was with the FBI, his people would be prepared when Grant and his friends showed up. Will and the girl flashed into her head. No! Grant was a professional. Pat's people were just followers. They were no match for Grant.

It was the last thought she had before something slammed into her and everything went black.

Natalie J. Damschroder

Chapter Eighteen

Grant had underestimated Rhomney. And that really pissed him off.

He'd met the four men willing to go in with him at a bar a mile away from the address Zoe had provided. Others were standing guard on their perimeter. Gut told him not to let the FBI go in first, and with no red tape to deal with, he and his team could mobilize faster. He knew Rhomney, or thought he did. Knew enough of his goals and plans to anticipate and intercept.

But when they got to the barn on deserted farmland out in the middle of Nowhere, Ohio, he realized how smart Rhomney really was. Maybe he'd learned from the men who shared his prison cells. Or spent his entire incarceration planning for every possibility. Maybe Grant was hampered by his teenager memories. It didn't matter. What mattered was that Rhomney had picked a location that couldn't be infiltrated. The land around it was barren, with absolutely no cover for fifty yards all the way around. Windows from the loft, empty of glass and revealing nothing but darkness inside, were perfect locations for anyone with a gun. They wouldn't even need sniper training.

The original plan had been to send in Vazquez, who was roughly Zoe's build and had similar coloring. She'd relay the status of the people inside, and Grant and the others would move in and secure the scene, then call the FBI, who was probably not that far behind them.

But now that plan was fucked. The open space around the barn meant Rhomney and his people had plenty of time to determine that Vazquez wasn't Zoe, and she'd probably be shot before she made the doorway.

Grant's cell phone buzzed against his thigh. He cursed, then gave the order to fall back. The others melted into the narrow strip of woods between the barn and the tractor road where they'd left the SUV. He waited until he was back at the truck to pull the phone from the pocket of his cargo pants. The light would have made an excellent target for a sniper, and he wasn't assuming Pat didn't have one.

The number on the screen froze his intestines, even though he didn't recognize it.

He thumbed the phone on and didn't bother playing dumb. "Pat."

"Grant Neely." His tone was fondness over sanctimonious amusement. "How excellent to have the old gang together again."

Fuck. Fuckfuckfuckfuck. Did that mean he'd somehow found Zoe? Grant signaled to the others so they'd know what was going on. The three who were watching him passed the message on to the others.

He couldn't let Pat know he'd gotten to him. "Last I checked, the 'old gang' was scattered all over the country."

"Perhaps your 'checking' isn't as thorough as you'd like. Or you trust in the wrong people."

"What do you want, Rhomney?" Grant wished he had the ability to trace the damned call.

"I want the key." The false-pleasant tone didn't change, but a new hardness came into the man's voice. "I'm tired of these games. Come to the coordinates I'll text you. Alone. Or Zoe will be the new Jordie."

Rage and fear turned to acid in Grant's gut. "You don't have Zoe."

"Of course I do. And her little dog, too."

The line went dead. A moment later, the phone beeped. Grant opened the message and noted the coordinates at the top. They weren't very far away. But Rhomney had attached pictures. Grant's jaw tightened when he saw Kell's and Zoe's pale faces, eyes closed, bodies sprawled. The images could have been faked, but Carling's hadn't been, so he had to operate on the assumption that these were real.

"What's the plan?" Vazquez asked quietly.

"He's got them all." Grant gave her the coordinates and instructions, then had the team drive him back to the hotel to get his car. They'd follow him to the rendezvous, slightly behind. Vazquez would have to operate on the fly after they got there, because Grant couldn't ensure he'd be able to keep his com. But he'd relay as much information as he could. Rhomney would expect Grant's people to be behind him, though, and Grant didn't want them hurt. Not on an unpaid job. Which meant they couldn't go in blind.

The drive to get his car took way too long, and the drive back to the coordinates was way too short. He cursed himself for only taking one vehicle to the barn. More would have drawn more attention, but the delay was killing him.

He'd never felt so vulnerable as he did on the lone drive to where Rhomney had Zoe. No intelligence, no team, and the person he cared most about in this world, besides his mother, enduring God-knew-what in the hands of a madman. Even if it was just the fears of the past, she didn't deserve it.

Neither did Stone. Grant cursed under his breath. Kell was just as in love with Zoe as Grant was, and he could have blown her off when he found out she'd hidden stuff from him. Could have let her go off on her quest, or even tried to talk her out of it. Instead, he'd joined her. And done a pretty damned good job up to now.

Fucking FBI. He hoped the agents who'd been guarding Zoe and Kell weren't dead, but how the hell had they let Rhomney's amateurs get the drop on them?

Maybe they're not amateurs. The idea chilled him. There was no rule that said Pat couldn't have recruited or hired people with skills. He needed to be prepared for anything.

"We're on our way," Vazquez told him over the com.

"Roger. I'm almost there."

"Good luck, Neeley. Be careful."

"You, too." His hands tightened on the wheel, and he juiced the accelerator. *I'm on my way, Zoe. Hang on.*

* * *

Instead of an old farmhouse, Rhomney had gathered his people in a clearing in the woods. But they'd draped the trees around them in sheets and blankets and strewn large cushions in a circle, interspersed with an old sofa and the chair that had been Pat's the last time Zoe saw him. Freddie sat there now, languid and unfocused, crooning softly to herself. Drugged?

A scarred kitchen table held the place of honor in the center of the circle, the totems standing at the corners, leaving room for the key between them. Kerosene lanterns dotted the clearing, making the shadows long and ominous and giving the impression of twice as many people present as there really were. The sky had begun to lighten on the horizon, that clear blue color that graduates to midnight on the other side of the sky. In between hung the blood moon, a hazy, dark red shadow that almost seemed anticlimactic considering the importance Pat had placed on it.

The clearing crackled with energy. Pat's charisma had been on full display, his fervor shining in the eyes of his acolytes. Zoe was tied, just as she'd been as a kid, only this time Pat had gotten tired of listening to her yelling at him and had her gagged. Showing surprising lack of insight, he'd had PB do it. Even though she'd barfed on his shoes, he seemed to have a soft spot for her. Or maybe he just wanted her to owe him. He'd tied the bandanna loosely enough that she could swallow and breathe, and it didn't hurt.

Last time she'd been at Pat's mercy, she'd struggled to overcome the terror inspired by her past. But her fury that he'd dragged Kell into this had burned that away completely. Kell's presence behind her, solid and reassuring, drove her to find a way out, a way to stop Pat before he sacrificed anyone. She watched the man direct his people, watched them mill around, and tried not to be overwhelmed by the task ahead of her. There were too many people this time, not just herself to get out of there.

Will Carling lay across the circle, leaning against a pile of cushions. He was a sickly green, his eyes no longer glaring at her, but dull, defeated. The girl was still bound to him. She sat close, their shoulders touching, and Zoe hadn't figured out if the girl was getting comfort or trying to give it. She had learned her name was Amelia, and her name wasn't the only similarity to Olivia. She'd clearly been chosen for her hair color and gamine features, and Zoe's stomach rolled over every time she looked at the poor kid. She held down a sour mash of relief that it wasn't Kell's sister and guilt that she was relieved.

Behind her, Kell was awake. He hadn't stopped trying to get their ropes untied. Whenever no one was close to them, he'd murmured reassurances that he'd get them out of there. But Zoe knew she was going to be his priority, and that would make it harder to get Will and Amelia out.

Pat needed only one thing to begin his ritual—the key. After a phone call half an hour ago, he'd rested smugly in his chair. She had no doubt Grant was on his way.

The idiot.

Sure enough, there was a commotion outside the circle, and three men pushed through one of the blankets. Grant, whole and strong and powerful in his fatigues and combat vest, eyes blazing. He could have snapped in half the two tall, thin followers holding him.

Zoe should have been in full despair, but as soon as she saw him, relief and strength flooded her. Almost everyone she cared about was now in danger. But they were stronger, too, a team. Their chances of surviving this had increased.

"Nice crowd," Grant observed. He'd spotted Zoe and Kell, his gaze sweeping around the clearing to note Carling's and Amelia's positions, then count the other people. Half the followers lazed around, but the armed half had gone to alert when Grant was dragged into the circle. "About double what you had last time you grabbed me off the street," he told Pat, then made a face. "Not impressed with the décor, though. Sheets hanging off trees? So Woodstock."

He was communicating with his team somehow. But Zoe wasn't the only one paying attention, and she watched with dismay as Pat flicked a hand and the guy on Grant's right dug in his ear. He handed whatever he found to Pat, who smiled a little and dropped the communicator into a takeout coffee cup with a barely heard splash.

"So glad you could all make it." Pat stretched languidly out of his chair and strolled over to Grant. "The key, please. Don't make me ask twice."

Grant narrowed his eyes at Pat and yanked one arm free. He pulled the rolled leather out of a side pocket of his cargo pants and slapped it into Pat's hand. Zoe wanted to yell at him not to, but she knew Grant well enough, was looking closely enough, that she saw him tense. She braced, ready to react to whatever he was going to do.

But he didn't move. Pat turned away from him, cold dismissal that iced Zoe's insides. "Bring the girl here," he ordered someone. "North side." He unrolled the key onto the table, his eyes firing with unholy glee. "Mr. Carling here." He tapped the long side on his right. East. "Zoe and her true love west and south." He began circling the table, studying the key, as the milling followers gained purpose and moved to obey his orders.

A couple of the bigger guys came over and hauled Zoe and Kell to their feet.

"How are we gonna do this?" one muttered to the other, eyeing the rope binding both of their wrists. He glanced up at Kell and actually took a step back. Zoe could only imagine the look on Kell's face. The guy holding her arm got up close to Kell and murmured something in his ear. Even as close as they were, Zoe couldn't hear it. Before the guy even finished speaking, Kell exploded into motion, yanking at the bonds and yelling, "Over my dead body!"

"Yeah. Exactly." The murmuring guy flashed a switchblade, out of Pat's line of sight, and Zoe's heart surged into her throat. Thankfully, Kell settled. A quick slice separated their ropes. Zoe felt hers give and wrapped her fingers around what she could reach. The knot must have been on Kell's side, and she didn't want anyone to know she might be able to get free.

Now that they were separated, the followers dragged her and Kell to the table, where others already had Carling and Amelia. Carling drooped between two of them, his eyes glassy, but the girl stood straight, defiant.

Oh, honey, don't do something to make him angry. Zoe tried to catch the girl's attention, but she could feel resentment coming off her as Zoe pulled away from her captor. What had they been telling her while Zoe was gone?

Grant hadn't moved. What was he waiting for? She didn't want Pat to start anything. She knew what "ritual" meant to him. But Grant just stood, watching them. He caught her eye, and she frowned. He gave a tiny shake of his head, then moved his hands. Held up four fingers. Made a shoving motion, ended in a wave. Zoe had no idea what that meant. His eyes darkened with frustration. He signaled four again, then pointed toward himself. Four of him? Ah! His team! She tried to keep her expression blank so no one would know they were communicating, but somehow Grant knew she understood. He made the shooing motion again. Had he sent the team away? Away. No, they were too far away! He shook his wrist, the one wearing a military-style watch, then quickly flashed ten fingers. Ten minutes. She hoped. Ten minutes wasn't that long.

Yeah, no. It was *eternity*.

The followers spread out in a circle around the table so they could see. A buzz of excitement filled the clearing. Grant shifted behind the group, but Zoe didn't know what he could do. They'd have disarmed him, and he was one man against a dozen. Even though his training could triumph over every other person here, he was vastly outnumbered. Zoe and Kell might be able to do some damage, but not much. And PB—who looked up, noticed Grant was unguarded, and moved to cover him—looked like he knew his way around a gun.

"Tell us—" she tried to say, and Pat looked up from the corner of the table where he stood between Amelia on her left and Carling across from her. He nodded to someone behind her, and they slipped the gag off. She tried to lick her lips, but everything was so dry it all just stuck together. "Tell us," she croaked, "what you're going to do."

Pat's eyes lit with glee, and she was sorry she'd asked.

"Are you sure you want to know?" he teased, his voice smooth and eager, and he didn't wait for an answer.

"We're in this clearing"—he motioned toward the dark sky above, pausing to stare at the moon, almost in full eclipse. "Almost time," he whispered. Everyone stood frozen, looking up. Even Zoe couldn't avoid following his gaze at first. When she realized it, she looked down just in time to see Pat bump his knee under the edge of the table. She frowned. What was he doing?

He lowered his head and continued. "The totems need access to the sky. The energy they will draw is very powerful, and fed by this special blood moon, will be even more so." He chose one of the totems and cradled it lovingly, running one finger down the images shaped into it.

"What energy? To do what?" Hey, if he was willing to talk, she was willing to make him. Grant shifted behind the crowd, but PB tracked him. Grant circled his fingers, out of PB's sight. He wanted Zoe to keep talking. Keep Pat talking.

But Pat just lifted his lips in a smug curl and set the totem on its square. Zoe held her breath.

Nothing happened.

She let it out slowly. What had she expected? Fireworks? A loud bang? She didn't really believe these things had any inherent power. Her heart began to lighten. Maybe they'd all get through this okay. Pat was so sure his plan would work. He'd be shocked when nothing happened. Maybe then Grant's team could take him by surprise.

His hand lingered on top of the totem. "Poetry. Each totem represents a desirable trait. Each of you also represents that trait. Youth." He shifted his hand to caress Amelia's arm. Bile rose in Zoe's throat and she wrenched at the ropes around her wrists. They gave way easily, but she maintained enough control over her anger to realize that lunging across the table at Pat would be stupid.

Pat, though, wasn't paying attention to her. He'd become wrapped up in his tale, in his ritual.

"Ambition. Wealth. Beauty." He placed a totem on each of the squares closest to Kell, Carling, and Zoe as he said each word. Still, nothing happened. But Pat seemed unfazed, and Zoe realized why when he circled the table and reached underneath to retrieve a wickedly curved knife.

"Four energies. Four sacrifices. Tapping unmatched power. All that remains is the connection." His clear-eyed gaze met Zoe's, and awareness of his absolute sanity made her blood run cold. She let the ropes drop to the ground. No one noticed, apparently mesmerized by the promise in Pat's words.

"The other one is unnecessary," Pat said conversationally, slightly over his shoulder.

His meaning didn't register with Zoe right away. It didn't register with anyone, apparently, as no one moved. But then PB flinched, aimed the rifle, and fired.

Right into Grant's chest.

Chapter Nineteen

Zoe screamed and moved to jump to Grant's aid, but all her muscles locked when Pat lazily lifted the knife to Kell's throat. Kell had stepped back from the table, too, but that only gave Pat a better angle.

"Leave him," Pat ordered, his voice hard. People who'd been craning to look at Grant on the ground started guiltily. Zoe could only glimpse him lying on the other side of the table—part of a boot, one hand, his camo-covered thigh. Every nerve vibrated with the need to help him, put pressure on the bleeding, get him an ambulance or, even better, an airlift. But vying with the list of actions was the absolute terror that Pat would slit Kell's throat if she moved. Intellect said he wouldn't, that he needed Kell for this ritual, but PB seemed plenty ambitious. Kell could be replaced.

Never. It whispered in a shout across her heart, but there was no time to catch it. Chaos seemed to rage through the clearing, but everyone stood still, outside the circle, watching those around the table as if at dinner theater. No, the turmoil was only in her head. *If Pat moves the knife, you can take him by surprise. You didn't see where Grant was hit. The shot might not have been fatal. There's still a chance you can help him. If you get Kell free first. And protect Amelia. And Carling. Grab the knife, push Pat away, cut Amelia's ropes, Kell will check Grant, you get Carling, avoid the guns, get away—it'll never work, there are too many, he'll kill Kell if you even flinch and oh God I'll lose them both at once.* It went around and around until it all merged into one frantic, high-pitched scream.

Useless. Concentrate. Force it all into a bottle and seal it. She squeezed her eyes tightly, pushing back at the panic, leaving it to rattle fiercely in the background.

"All attention on the totems. Unless you prefer to be part of the sacrifice rather than part of the reward." Pat blinked in satisfaction when his followers fell in around them again. He released Kell and took the three steps to Zoe's side. "Since you've freed yourself, we'll begin with you." When he waved the knife, someone stepped to his side with a jar of what looked like metallic paint. After dipping the blade into the jar, Pat lifted Zoe's right hand. The rope around her wrists fell away. His skin was smooth, almost oily, but when she twisted and pulled, he tightened hard enough to make her bones rasp together. The knife slashed once across her palm, so sharp there was no immediate pain, and he slammed her hand down on the top of the nearest totem.

Then he let go and moved to do the same to Carling. Zoe tried to back up, to run, but her hand was seared to the totem, which stood as solidly as if Pat had magnetized it to the table. She yanked, and pain finally shot through her palm. But she couldn't break away. A sob escaped her throat, her vision hazing, her breath harsher and faster. She twisted and pried and jerked her whole body against the pull, all to no avail.

In quick succession Pat dipped the knife, slashed their hands, and fused each of their right palms to a totem. Will let him, limp and unprotesting. Amelia tried to bite Pat, who laughed. Kell had to be unbound first, which was probably why Pat saved him for last. He fought, roaring, but four men held on to him and Pat eventually succeeded in making the connection.

How was he doing this? Zoe curved her fingers over the top of the totem and pulled. It didn't budge, but she felt a faint hum into her fingertips. She leaned into the table and sensed the same faint vibration against her hipbone. Holy shit, he *had* magnetized it. What the hell did that mean? He didn't believe the legend after all?

The buzz of noise escalated and the circle shrank, bodies pressing closer and closer. The air warmed and reeked of excitement, body odors Zoe tried not to breathe in. Her vision tunneled to the table and the few people closest to it. Amelia sobbed and jerked, trying to get away, while Carling hung against the table, his arm dangling from the totem. Zoe reached for hers with her left hand, thinking maybe she could pry at the base, but the angle was bad and she couldn't get near it. The four guys who'd held Kell let go of him. He strained against the totem, lips curled, teeth bared, looking more feral than she'd have ever thought possible.

This was all wrong. A big show. She didn't understand what Pat was trying to do now. And where the hell were Grant's people? The FBI? Surely Grant hadn't come here without giving them the location. Surely someone would come, stop this, now.

"Calm," Pat said, and she could have sworn the totems responded, a surge of energy sweeping out of them into their attached victims. Amelia stopped jerking and her sobs faded, the tracks on her cheeks suddenly unfed by new tears. Kell, too, ceased fighting. For Zoe, it was like becoming possessed. The totem layered a soothing balm over her that relaxed her muscles and the sharpness of her emotions, but inside, where she could feel but not touch, the terror and anger churned, banging against the barrier Pat's one word had created.

This is ridiculous. It's not happening. Drugs. He put drugs in the paint, not just metal. It's got to be something real. Something we can escape. We have to escape!

Pat tossed his head back and laughed. Zoe's legs went weak and she sagged to her knees. Her shoulder screamed, pulled by the anchor of the totem, but she couldn't seem to get the strength back to stand.

Pat grabbed Amelia by the hair and pulled to expose her throat. But he applied the knife to her chest instead, the point scraping a long line of welling blood across the skin exposed by her scoop-neck top.

No! But the word only echoed in her head. She couldn't speak. Amelia's eyes swam with pain and terror, even though she didn't cry out or struggle. Zoe sobbed inside, guilt and fear and anger boiling ineffectively.

Out of the corner of her eye she saw PB step closer to Amelia. Grant's legs whipped into PB's. The man fell onto his back, but he hadn't hit the dirt before Grant scissored his legs around Pat's to knock him to the ground, too.

The air *whoofshed* out of Pat with a loud, gusty grunt. Shouts exploded into the clearing. Screams of outrage tore out of Zoe's throat. Roars from Kell battered against Amelia's bloodcurdling shrieks. Even Will moaned, while followers shouted and scrambled and wailed and wrung their hands.

Zoe strained to see Grant, to look for blood, but he was moving too fast, on his feet, slugging his way around the table. He'd confiscated PB's rifle and used the butt to knock people away from Kell and clear his way to Zoe. Before he got to her, several people dressed just like him burst into the clearing, tearing down blankets and sheets from the trees, shouting at everyone to get on the ground and other things Zoe couldn't hear. Pat had disappeared. Scrambled behind the sheets? She spun, watching the melee, struggling to see if one of the commandos had him.

Another wave of people flooded the now-crowded space. Behind Zoe, some of Pat's followers tried to run into the woods. A woman with "FBI" in big white letters across her jacket caught two of them, flung them to the ground, and cuffed them—one-handed, the other wielding a pistol. A handful of cops joined in the attempt to corral the freaked-out followers, adding to the chaos.

Zoe absorbed all this with half her attention. The rest was on the table, the totems, and their complete inability to get free of them. She glimpsed Pat crawling across the ground, using the stomping, dashing feet of dozens of people as cover.

"Are you all right?" Grant had reached her side. He wrapped an arm around her waist and made like he was going to carry her off. "We've got to get you out of here."

"Not happening." She demonstrated, yanking at the unseen restraint. "Someone's got to get Pat." But not Grant. He'd been shot. She put her free hand on his chest and felt, instead of sticky, oozing blood, a hard plate under his jacket. "You're wearing Kevlar."

He gave her a scathing look. "Of course. I'm not stupid." The scathing became a scowl when he realized her hand was stuck. "What the hell?"

She didn't care about that for the moment. "You were on the ground. He shot you. You weren't moving."

Grant ran his hand down the totem and under the edge of the leather key. "It stops the bullet from entering my body, but the impact still hurts like hell. Knocks the breath out of you. Plus, that guy still had his gun on me. The vest doesn't stop a head shot." He shook his head. "I can't undo this, and the table is too sturdy to break." One of his team stopped next to him. "Find Thomashunis," Grant ordered him. "I don't see him in custody. He was over there." He motioned to where he'd knocked Pat down and went back to examining the totem under her hand. Silvered blood ran down over the carvings and pooled on the leather. Grant stared at a blotch of it on his finger. "What the hell?"

"I think you need to slice the key. Or cut off one of our hands." She could joke now that most of Pat's gang had been subdued. "You know, break the connection." When Grant looked at her as if she'd gone insane, she shook her head. Maybe she had. "Forget it. I'm fine. Go get Pat! I think he went behind the sheets."

But Grant ignored her. He ducked to examine the underside of the table.

"At the end," she told him, leaning over. "Near Will. Pat kneed it earlier. I think there's a—"

"Magnet, yeah. I see it. Hold on."

Like she was going anywhere. She checked on Will and Amelia, who both had one of the good guys puzzling over their totems. Will seemed to be coming back to himself, maybe recognizing that he was going to be okay. Amelia cried again, but silently, almost motionlessly. Zoe's heart ached for her—she knew what the girl would go through, trying to overcome this experience. Hopefully, it would be easier than it had been for Zoe. That she would have the right kind of support from her family, and that the short duration of her captivity would fade faster and more completely than Zoe's memories had.

Satisfied that the others would be okay she turned to Kell, who stood watching her, his hand flexing and curling over the top of his totem. He looked tormented, and God knew he had too many reasons to be.

"I'm sorry," she said, but he shook his head.

"You don't have anything to be sorry for." He sounded lost, resigned, and her throat closed. She had so much to say, so much to figure out—

The table shook. At the other end, Grant bent and hit something again. The faint hum clicked off, and Zoe's hand slid off the totem just as long fingers closed around her throat and dragged her away from the table. Pat's knife flashed past her face and pressed against her chest, digging in when Kell lunged toward them. He froze the same way she had when Pat had put the blade to his throat.

Kell's "Son of a *bitch*!" echoed in her ears as she backpedaled, pulled by Pat into the woods. She choked trying to call to him, and heard him shout again as leaves and branches closed behind them, blocking her view of the clearing. Pat dragged her by the throat deeper into the dark woods before he stopped and pulled her flush against him, her back to his front, and dug the point of his weapon into her ribcage.

She stilled, not knowing what she should do.

"Good girl," he murmured into her ear. "Let's go." He maneuvered her easily through the woods as if he knew exactly where he was going. Dawn broke enough to cast a faint light over the woods, but they were still in deep shadow. Their slow pace was quiet, but Zoe couldn't hear anyone following them. She didn't know how that could be. Kell had seen it happen. He wouldn't let Pat just take her.

Soon, though, they were deep into the trees, darkness prevailing, the only sound the soft rustle of their feet over the ground. She strained but couldn't hear anything else, not even insects or animals. After a while she lost track of time, and it was like she and Pat were alone in the world.

The surreality of what had happened faded, and new fears swelled to fill the space. What was he going to do to her? It was down to revenge now. No rituals, no power play. He could move faster without her, so she wasn't just a hostage. And once he was done with her, what would he try to do to everyone else?

Abruptly, he released her. She staggered, but he yanked her by the wrist into an old hunter's shack. She stumbled and almost let herself fall. What was the point? No one was going to find her. Not until it was too late. Was she going to lie here and let him cut her up? Leave him to harm the people she loved?

Fuck, no.

"There's no point in doing this." Her voice rasped, throat tight and tense. "The totems are gone. I can't help you anymore."

"You are the point, Zoe Ardmore. You stole my power from me. All those years of hard work and preparation, the long wait. All gone. For good this time." He stood between her and the door, picking at the end of the knife with a fingernail. He projected an air of indifference that she knew was fake. Somehow, he'd learned to bury his emotions deep, hide them from anyone around him. Given what he'd said, he should be furious—but that fury wasn't going to make him lose control.

Too bad for her.

She shuddered, then pulled herself together to

study the empty shack. It had almost no roof and let in plenty of light now that dawn had broken completely. The walls were solid with small, high windows that she'd never have time to get out of. But the wood underneath them was weathered and splintered. She might be able to pry off a big enough piece to use as a weapon.

Apparently her thoughts showed on her face, because Pat grinned at her.

She wasn't going to live through this.

Stop it. All you have to do is hold on until they come for you. Except she knew it wasn't that easy. Kell was no woodsman, and Grant wouldn't dash in after her with no recon. It might have taken them time to find the trail, and they'd have followed carefully so they didn't spook Pat. So no, all she had to do wasn't hold on until they came for her. All she had to do was rescue herself.

Impossible.

Shut up. You didn't give up then, and you won't let him win now. Just bide your time. There's always an opening.

She drew a fortifying breath and swallowed to loosen her voice. He had buttons. She just had to find them. "You've got to be crazy if you think those totems had any power to give you." She watched his reaction. His grin became more of a smirk, but he didn't move, and his eyes stayed as intently unemotional as they had been since they entered the shack.

"You felt it," he reminded her dispassionately, lifting his knife to study the blade, or his reflection in it. Her blood stained a couple of inches of metal, and she shuddered. "Crazy is an ill-chosen word, Zoe, and not just because the power was there for the taking."

"If by power you mean electromagnetism," she sneered. "I know how you did all that." Well, not all of it, but it didn't matter anymore.

His gaze flicked up to meet hers. "Haven't you wondered why I am the way I am? Why I've made the choices I've made?"

She really hadn't. "I'm not a psychologist. Empathic justification isn't in my repertoire." He opened his mouth, but she cut him off, not caring if it made him mad. *She* was mad, dammit. "I don't care, either. I'm sure you have a tale of poverty and abuse or something, but you know what?" She drew herself up, ignoring the stinging pull where he'd cut her across the chest, the throb in the palm of her right hand. "When I was twelve, some psycho abducted me!" She advanced on him, so incensed he actually backed away a couple of steps. "He and his common-law wife kept me for a year, while she acted out some sick Mommy fantasies and he prepared to sacrifice me in an insane quest for power. But hey, you don't see me dragging people into the woods and threatening them with sharp knives, do you?" She thumped him on the chest. "*Do you?* Well, maybe I *should!*" She swept her arm across her body, her hand closing over the hilt of the knife, and before Pat could even blink, she'd snatched it from him. Hate tried to make her backhand it across his throat, but that wasn't in her. That was the whole point of her rant, after all.

Instead, she shoved past him and ran out into the dawn.

A moment ago, she had been grateful for the light that allowed her to see her surroundings and her abductor. But now, that same light dappling through the trees would reveal her location to him. The long shadows cast by the sun's low angle would help, but her movement would be obvious.

So would her path. She had a general idea of the direction of the clearing, but that was exactly where Pat would expect her to go. And he was already chasing her—unlike his stealthy, slow progress to get here. He yelled her name, emotion finally clear in his tone. Footsteps crashed through the underbrush. He had longer legs, a better knowledge of these woods.

Amazingly, all the terror that had paralyzed her while he dragged her out here was gone. She could think clearly, breathe easily. The clearing was somewhere to the right, probably not as far away as it seemed. To her left, the ground rose at an angle to a slight ridge. She dug in her toes and scrambled up the slope, elated when she saw the steep drop on the other side. She slid down and hunkered behind a rock outcrop. Her heart pounded and sweat gathered along her hairline and the back of her neck. Something felt so familiar about this, but it was nothing like her last escape. She swallowed the saliva pooling in her mouth, and her dry throat protested like sandpaper on rubber.

Then it hit her. This was like her recurring nightmares. The ones where she was being chased. She'd hide, and they'd find her, but she'd get away and hide again. She'd learned in college that they were normal stress dreams, that a lot of people had them, and they were very different from the ones that had been based on memory and experience.

How ironic.

A loud rustle at the top of the hill startled her into stillness. Pat had followed her. He must have recovered his senses and gone stealth again, because she hadn't heard him after she went over the ridge. She could almost feel his laser gaze on her back and fought the urge to press closer to the ground. It was movement that would give her away, not location.

Elation seeped away as Pat stood up there, surveying the woods. Gone went the clear thinking and easy breathing. Her spine tingled between her shoulder blades, and she was certain the knife was going to plunge into it any second. She struggled not to pant, squeezing her eyes tightly closed, listening so hard all she could hear was a loud, internal ringing.

Cool it, Zoe. You *have the knife, you moron.* The ringing faded a little. Her palm throbbed and fingers ached where they clutched the knife so hard it shook. But she relaxed them too much and the blade scraped on rock.

Pat heard it. She could tell.

And she had no fucking idea what to do next.

Natalie J. Damschroder

Chapter Twenty

Through everything that had happened over the last few days, Kell would have said he'd hit "worst nightmare" several times. He'd have been wrong.

Nothing came close to watching that madman drag Zoe into the woods at knife point. Or the look in her eyes, a sorrowful goodbye that turned the similar look when he left her at the airport into an obvious lie.

He yelled to Grant as he lurched after Zoe, ducking around one of Neely's team and pushing off into a run and then *wham*. An arm bar slammed into his collarbone and knocked him onto his back. One of Rhomney's stupid fucking followers stood over him, laughing. Kell couldn't even wheeze, the lack of air making the rest of him weak. Another moron joined the first, and Kell flailed at their feet and fists, as effective as grass waving in a breeze.

Then his lungs unlocked and he sucked in hard, coughing, and managed to curl into a protective ball. Once his head cleared, he could tell the blows were half-hearted. One of them kept glancing around, as if putting on a show and wanting to make sure they were—or weren't—being watched.

He grabbed a raised foot near his head and pushed, knocking the kicker off balance. That gave him enough space to allow him to struggle back to his feet.

"Not fully committed to the cause, huh?" He glared at them, upper body heaving. He raised clenched fists and balanced on the balls of his feet. "I'm not letting him take her. Try to stop me."

"Fuck that!" Grant appeared holding some kind of assault rifle. Kell's opponents muttered and backed up a few steps, right into a cop with a handful of zip ties. "Are you an idiot, or what?"

"He took Zoe," Kell growled. It gave him some satisfaction to see panic flash across Grant's granite face. "He dragged her into the woods. He cut her. I'm going after her."

"Hold on." Grant surveyed the clearing. "We can't go alone."

"I'm going! The longer we wait, the further he gets! It's still dark, and if we don't pick up the trail—"

Grant glowered at him. "I know how it works. But if you go charging after her, he'll just kill her. Look what we did to his plans." He waved a hand at the table. "We have to be smart about this."

Kell clenched his fists, barely feeling the slice in his palm, and stared hard at the trees Zoe had slipped between a couple of minutes ago. Grant was right, dammit, and he *did* have experience with this shit. But God, Zoe. He couldn't stop the images of gushing blood and empty eyes, couldn't stop hearing her screams while Rhomney tortured her. And he knew they were nothing compared to reality if Rhomney did start carving her up. What if he had a vehicle somewhere on the other side of the woods? Kell had no idea where they were or what was around them, but he bet Rhomney did.

"What's the plan, then?" he ground out.

"We need help."

But even though the chaos was contained, everyone seemed to have their hands full. Trying to mobilize the FBI or gather Grant's scattered team would take too long. They had to get on their trail now.

"We can't wait," he told Grant, who finally nodded.

"All right. Let's go."

An hour later, Kell was ready to howl. Grant was sure he had the trail, but they moved way too slowly for Kell's sanity. He got the logic—don't provoke Pat into acting, wait until they had an advantage—but the passing minutes throbbed like a heartbeat, surging blood through knife wounds onto the ground. Zoe's wounds, Zoe's blood. Zoe's death. He couldn't take it anymore.

"Neely."

Grant stuck his fist in the air, tight and fast. Kell froze. His hearing sharpened as he focused, and he heard tiny rustles. The kind you'd attribute to animals, except slightly more rhythmic. Footsteps.

He strained to see through the early dawn light and the second-story trees that waved in a light breeze. Grant slowly pointed toward the left, and Kell twisted his head to look. Brown, boxy, bigger than trees—it was a shack of some sort. Dark inside, he saw when he tilted right and glimpsed a gaping doorway.

Now everything was still. Grant eased to their right, uphill. Kell followed but kept his distance. He knew the high ground was an advantage, but it also made them a bigger target. Let the merc take point, draw fire or whatever. If Rhomney was out here alone, and he engaged Grant, that would leave Kell free to rescue Zoe.

Not that he cared who rescued her, just that she was safe. *Please let her be safe.*

Then suddenly Grant was running along the top of the ridge, full out, and Kell's heart decided to leap up and choke him. He dashed up the hill and paused. About a hundred feet down the ridge, Grant charged fast enough that his silence was eerie. Kell couldn't see past him, didn't know what he was running toward. Rhomney? Zoe? Both? A body? He picked up his pace to follow, braced for some kind of impact. Physical or emotional, he didn't know what to expect, but it was obviously coming.

Then it did, but not at him.

Grant suddenly dodged left, and Kell saw something snap up off the ground, flinging dried leaves everywhere. Grant's speed and the slope of the hill made his left foot skid, but it didn't save him from the spike that hit his shoulder. Kell bit back a yell and ran harder, trying to scan the ground and trees for other booby traps. Grant had already run this way, so at least the ground on this side was clear.

Kell dropped to his knees next to Grant, not

knowing what to do first. Grant blinked, so he was conscious. Kell needed to know if there were other imminent threats. He peered through the camouflaged, spiked, hinged, trellis-like thing that had flown up and now stood still, bristling lethally. He could see a light-colored splotch against the tree trunks and squinted to make out a man standing at the top of the hill, looking down the right-hand slope, away from them. Rhomney?

Kell turned to Grant, keeping half his awareness on the other guy to make sure he didn't come closer. Grant's black jacket was wet with blood, the hand he held to his shoulder covered with it.

"Leave it," Grant ground out when Kell tried to peel back the cloth. "It didn't go all the way in. That's Rhomney down there, and I think Zoe is down the hill."

"Shit. Is he armed?"

"Probably. He didn't see me until I sprung the fucking trap. Saw the trigger too late." He lay back and glared at the sky. "You need to get down that hill and circle around below Zoe without Rhomney seeing you. Look for wires and odd shapes in case he has other shit out here. The way he was moving, though, I think this might be it. You only need one to slow down pursuit, because they don't know there's only one. Fucking bastard." He grunted and pressed harder on the wound.

"Okay. Then what?"

"Then wait and watch."

Kell didn't like that. It meant Grant wasn't going to

lie here and let Kell dispatch Rhomney and rescue Zoe, then drag him out of the woods to medical care. "You can't—" he started, knowing it was fruitless.

"I can," Grant growled. "Go." He hauled himself up to sit, then rocked to his feet, blocking Kell's view of Rhomney and therefore, hopefully, Rhomney's of him. Kell cursed silently and backed up, low to the ground, until he reached a row of brush that zigzagged down the hill. He slid behind that and flattened himself to the ground, where a gap between branches gave him a clear view. His heart sank.

It *was* Rhomney standing down the ridge. He didn't have the knife he'd held to Kell's throat, but that wasn't good news. He'd replaced it with a mechanical crossbow, the kind that fired small but still deadly darts. Where the hell did he get that? He was aiming it down the hill, toward a boulder that covered his target—Zoe.

There was no way Kell was going to be able to come up on Zoe's position without Rhomney seeing him. Not without going way out into the woods at the bottom of the hill. And even then, his movement would draw attention. In this area, the tree trunks were narrow and sparse, and even the shorter trees and underbrush were low.

"Hey, Pat!" Grant called, and Kell's time was up. When Rhomney swung around to face Grant, Kell shoved himself down the hill, sliding as fast as he dared. Grant yelled nonsense about the FBI and the rest of his freelance team being on their way, covering the rustle and clatter of Kell's descent. He almost cheered when he reached the bottom and barely stopped himself from sliding into a gully. A broken ankle would have been a disaster. But the dark groove in the earth, probably a seasonal wash now mostly dry, went in exactly the direction he needed to go.

In seconds he was in the gully. Heart pounding, he crab-walked as fast as he could along the bottom, trying to keep his head low and estimate how far he'd come. He could still hear Grant shouting. Fuck, what if Zoe decided to go up the hill to help him? He scuddled faster, wondering if he imagined a *ping-swish-thunk* that was the crossbow. *Let him be aiming at Neely.*

He didn't want to overshoot Zoe's position. He stopped, his back against the gully wall closest to the hill, and listened. He could make out Rhomney's voice, almost directly above him but not facing this way. Probably. Grant still had his attention. Kell risked rising a tiny bit, tilting his head back to make only his eyes and the tip of his nose clear the edge. He couldn't breathe at that angle, and spots danced in his vision for a second. But when they cleared, he saw Zoe hunkered behind a boulder, holding Rhomney's wicked knife. Thank God. Now if he could just get her down here without catching Rhomney's attention.

"*Ssst.*" She didn't move. His right calf cramped, and when he shifted it, his head bobbed higher. The movement drew Zoe's attention. Her eyes widened when she saw him, gratitude and relief flooding her expression. She made an abrupt move, halted immediately, but it was enough. Kell dropped flat on his back just as a crossbow arrow zipped past him and buried itself in the opposite bank.

"She's not for you!" Rhomney shouted. He was so furious Kell could hear spittle, spraying from his lips and spattering the dry leaves. For a moment he lay paralyzed, listening. "She's always been mine, Kellen Stone! Even when you loved her, lavished her with your riches, developed a life with her, she didn't tell you about *me!* I've left an imprint on her psyche and her soul that you can't even *hope* to match!"

The words were meant to burrow deep into Kell's heart and ruin the rest of his life. They only pissed him off. He raised his head just a bit and spotted a big rock embedded in the dirt by his right foot. He kicked at it.

"You've got it backwards, Rhomney!" The rock shifted, but barely. He kept kicking. "I've given her the peace she needed to leave you behind! She never told me about you because you don't *matter*!" He slammed the heel of his boot against the rock. It pulled almost completely out of the moist dirt, showering the leaves around it with little clumps. He dragged it up next to his hand and hefted it. Yeah, that would work. Or not. Rising up a little, he heaved the rock to his left and surged upright. The rock sailed further than he'd hoped, and *yes!* Rhomney tracked it. Even better, Zoe dashed across the twenty feet between them and in seconds was in the gully, in Kell's arms.

"Oh, God, Zoe. Jesus Christ." He clutched her to him, rolling to bury her under his body in case Rhomney fired again. But no arrows struck. "God, I was scared. Are you okay?"

She nodded and squirmed. "We've got to get out of

here, Kell. And Grant—"

"I know. Come on." He grabbed her hand and started them crawling back the way he'd come. She twisted her hand out of his, sending a different kind of fear panging through him, until he realized she still clutched the knife in her other hand.

"Leave it," he told her.

"No." She looked grim but picked up her pace.

Kell led her back to the point where he'd slid into the gully. "A little further," he told Zoe. He glanced upward, but could see and hear nothing over the noise of their movement. After a couple dozen more feet, they crouched in the gully and listened. Silence.

"Grant." Zoe's whisper cracked, and Kell winced.

"He'll be okay." Though Kell had his doubts about the merc's ability to come back from two should-be-fatal shots in a day. They hadn't seen Rhomney shoot him with the crossbow, but why wouldn't he? "Let's just concentrate on getting up that hill. Then we'll help him—"

She was gone before he finished his sentence.

"Dammit!" He scrambled up the hill after her as she scrambled behind the row of underbrush.

Grant was still standing.

Rhomney was no longer in sight.

The sun had risen high enough so the breeze cast dancing shadows, several of which Kell thought were attacking Zoe before he realized what they were.

He barreled after her. This chasing crap was getting old.

"Zoe, stop!" he risked calling, but she ignored him.

Grant turned, and the sun glistened on his sleeve where the blood from his shoulder wound had saturated it. Kell knew once Zoe saw that, there'd be no stopping her.

What happened next had an inevitability that sank down to Kell's heels.

His feet slid in wet, dead leaves as he tried to make it up the hill. Zoe was alone when she reached the top. She raced along for only a few steps, toward Grant, and skidded to a stop when Rhomney loomed up in front of her, out of nowhere Kell could see. She fell and scooted backwards on her butt. The knife she'd been holding tumbled down the hill, straight to Kell's hand. He scooped it up and ran, hearing the echo of Grant's shout in his ears, seeing the glint of sunlight on the mini-crossbow in Rhomney's hand, the horrible finality in his grin as he aimed it at Zoe's heart.

Kell was too far away. Grant was too far away. Zoe was helpless. Rhomney was going to kill her. There was only one thing Kell could do. He threw the knife, as hard as he could.

And missed.

He choked but kept his legs pumping, and thank God, because even though the knife didn't hit anything, it startled Rhomney enough to raise the crossbow. Kell launched himself at the man, half aware of Zoe doing the same thing. He hit him high, she hit him low, and the three of them tumbled down the far side of the slope.

Leaves and sticks battered Kell's face as they all hit the ground, bounced into the air, and hit again. He struggled to hang on to Pat and took a flailing hand in the chin. Three-toned grunts filled the air. His knee dug into something soft. Hopefully Rhomney's gut and not Zoe's.

They came to rest in a tangle at the base of a tree more than halfway down the hill. Before Kell could orient himself and know which body was whose, black boots pounded after them and a long arm dragged Rhomney upright before Grant plowed a fist into his jaw, knocking him out and about six feet across the forest floor.

"Zoe." Kell twisted and helped her sit up. Blood glistened at the corner of her mouth, and he cursed. "Where else are you hurt?"

She shook her head. "I'm fine. Is he—?" She twisted until she saw Rhomney, and relaxed. "Thank you." Her hands tightened on Kell's forearms, fingers curling into his sleeves so he couldn't have moved away if he tried. Something inside him loosened at the same time.

"Where the hell is everyone else?" Zoe asked Grant.

On cue, the cavalry arrived.

* * *

After hours of conferring with his team, being debriefed by the FBI and threatened with charges for interfering in a federal investigation, and being forced to go to the hospital to get his shoulder patched up, Grant dragged himself to the hotel Henricksen referred him to. The agent had intervened to keep him from being charged—at least for now—and kept him apprised of Zoe and Kell's status. They'd both been treated on site for their minor wounds and questioned by a battery of agents and cops.

He'd just gotten out of the shower when he heard the knock on his door. He threw on a pair of fatigue pants and even buttoned them, but didn't bother with anything else when he went to let Zoe in.

Surprised the hell out of him to see Stone at the threshold instead.

"Hey." He looked into the empty hall and then turned away, rubbing a hand towel over his hair and listening to Stone coming in, closing the door, and following him into the room, which was much smaller than the suites they'd had in Utah. "How's Zoe?"

"Fine. Generally speaking." Stone stopped at the corner that closed off the bathroom area, folding his arms and leaning one shoulder against the wall. He eyed Grant's injured shoulder. "You?"

Grant shrugged despite the wave of pain that created. "Showering's a bitch. No major damage." Generally speaking. He went across the room and dropped into a chair by the window, ignoring the towel clenched in his good hand.

"I wanted to clear the air," Stone said.

Grant made a "go ahead" motion. As far as he was concerned, their objective had been met. They didn't need to act like partners anymore.

"Thank you." Stone shook his head a little, as if in disbelief. "For everything. Zoe wouldn't be alive if it weren't for you, and probably neither would I."

"Just doing my job," Grant lied. "Where is she?"

Stone shouldn't have left her alone. Not yet. His hand gripping the towel turned white.

Kell shifted and ran his hand through his hair. "She's still sleeping. Had a nightmare last night."

Of course she did. They probably all did. "How bad?"

He lifted a shoulder. "Not bad, I suppose, given what happened. She didn't wake up from it."

"That's probably good." Kell looked worried, so Grant added, "She's strong. She got through worse as a kid. She'll get through this."

"I know. I just wish she didn't have to."

Grant inclined his head to acknowledge that and waited. Kell seemed lost in thought for a moment, but spoke directly. "Your world is a lot like what went down last night."

Shit. "Look, Stone, I know—"

"No. You don't." His jaw tensed. "She loves you."

Curse the friggin' joy that statement force-fed. "She—"

"Just shut up and let me talk."

Grant clamped his mouth closed, not at all interested in hearing it, but hell, he'd endured worse. Maybe.

"She's loved you since the beginning. Seeing you again has brought all that back, which is why she didn't let me back in when I showed up. Why this turned into a battle over her."

Grant knew how this conversation was going to end, and he just wanted to get there. He shoved to his feet. "She doesn't want me."

"The hell she doesn't." Stone's laugh held no humor. "Or I wouldn't have slept on the floor last night."

Grant halted in his tracks. "She made you sleep on the floor?"

"No, I volunteered."

He scowled. That wasn't the same thing. "She doesn't belong with me."

"Do you love her?"

"Hell, yeah." The words came out a growl, a threat, but Kell only nodded. He tilted his head to look at the floor, then back up toward the ceiling, and blew out a massive breath.

"She'll choose me," he said. "And I'm not sure she should."

And with that honest, broken admission, everything fell into place for Grant. The fight was over, and a metric ton of tension he'd been holding since Stone showed up just…released.

"You said it yourself," he told him. "Last night wasn't an aberration for me. I run scenarios far worse than that on a weekly basis. She's not going to want to live with that. She *shouldn't* live with that."

His heart cracked open and bled, but the wound wasn't fatal. Not sure he could keep it off his face, he walked the few steps to the bedside stand and grabbed his water bottle, using the time to open it, drink, and twist the cap back on to hide his feelings. He'd been so fucking short-sighted. He fit with Zoe's goals and dreams even less now than he had before. Nothing had changed. Yeah, okay, if he really wanted her, he'd retire from the world he worked in. But then what? Become a city guy, living a white-collar life and mingling with people who worked hard so they could be pampered? He'd hate it, and then Zoe wouldn't be enough. She'd hate him for that, and he'd hate himself even more.

When he turned back to Stone, the man was slumped against the wall.

"Can you get past what she did? The lies and secrets, and contributing to your sister being a target?"

Kell shook his head. "After all this? I know she'd have died before putting Olivia in real danger. She thought she was making the right choice. Sure, we have to rebuilt trust between us. But I can convince her to share everything with me." He shrugged. "She already has, really."

Grant thought he was minimizing the challenge, but that wasn't what really bothered him. "You don't want her if her feelings aren't completely yours," he guessed, but again Kell shook his head.

"If she chooses me, she'll stick with it. That's who she is. But if that's not what's right for her, if she won't be fully happy—"

"I'm not going to chase her away." Satisfaction had an interesting healing effect when Grant noted the absolute rage that flickered across Kell's face. "Her choice has to be hers, and you're right, I do love her, and I'm weak enough to want her in my life if that's where she wants to be." He kept all expression off his face, knowing he was balls-out lying now. "But I'm not going to be her choice," he continued. "Love isn't absolute. It doesn't require honoring. She loves you as much as or more than she loves me, and for different reasons. More importantly, she doesn't want my life, never did. She wants what she can be with you."

Kell's mouth quirked up on one side. "Not what I can give her."

"Hell, no, she can get all that crap on her own." Both men laughed. "She hid her past because she didn't want to be ruled by it," Grant explained. "Not because you couldn't handle it or because she was ashamed of it or anything. Now that you know the truth, it just means she can be her whole self with you."

"She can be that with you, too."

Goddamn the man. Why did he keep pushing? Grant closed his hands into fists. "No, she can't. Because she'd live with fear, and that would keep all this shit alive in her. She doesn't have to bury it, but she can still get past it. And not with me."

Silence rang in the room. Then Kell laughed. "Which one of us do you think she'd kill first if she heard all this?"

So it was over. Grant moved to usher him to the door, but Stone went on his own. He paused with it open but didn't look back.

"For what it's worth, I'm sorry."

"Me, too, man. Me, too."

Chapter Twenty-One

Zoe woke alone and empty. Bereft. Aimless.

It would pass. She only felt that way because the quest was over. Pat was back in jail, and this time there were far too many people to testify against him. He'd never get out of prison. The totems would go into evidence with the FBI and probably never come out. Everyone was safe, so she didn't have to rush to get on a plane or dig into research or plan out an operation. She could go home and start again.

Soon. There was one thing left to do, and she dreaded it.

She dragged herself out of bed, showered, and dressed before finding the note Kell had left:

> *Room 412. I'll be in the café in the lobby*
> *when you're done. Don't worry. Everything*
> *will work out the way it's supposed to.*

She sighed and rubbed her forehead. Time to choose. The fight between the guys had become more of a debate. Both had made their cases — without actually making their cases—and now it was up to her.

Before she made a move Henricksen called and asked her to come to the hospitality suite the FBI was using for its out-of-town agents. She gratefully took the reprieve and headed straight over there.

He handed her a mug of tea and a Danish and had her sit on the sofa.

"Where is everyone?" Ravenous, she took a big bite of flaky pastry, tangy cherry goo, and bitingly sweet frosting.

"Field office. I'm headed over there soon but wanted to talk to you first. You know they might need you in DC when—"

"Yeah, they went over all that last night." Had spent hours questioning her and explaining her options and obligations. "How are Amelia and Will?"

Henricksen smiled. "Both okay. Amelia is already back with her family and Carling should be released from the hospital this morning. That one's gonna need therapy."

"I bet." Guilt wouldn't let Zoe laugh. "His injuries?"

"Superficial, physically. I don't think he'd be happy to hear from you," he cautioned.

"I know. What about Rudy and Ozzie?" After they'd found out about Ozzie's assault, she'd never heard if Rudy was okay.

"Checked on 'em this morning. Rudy was never approached. Ozzie'll be okay, too." He cocked his head. "You find out about Olivia?"

That was the first thing Kell had done as soon as he

had a cell signal. "She's coming home tomorrow. Her parents have talked to her every day, and she texted Kell that her eyes are stuck in a permanent roll of annoyance that they thought she needed protection from some lame scandal." She was able to smile a little, imagining the girl saying that with dramatic demonstration.

She took a breath. "Grant's team. Will you…" She wanted to know if they'd be going Guantanamo on them, but Henricksen shook his head.

"The local guy would have his head, but Neely's too valuable to the government. His kind of moral compass is hard to come by. So his involvement is being reported as ancillary."

Tears pricked her eyes, but she nodded and blinked them back. "Good. I guess that's it, then?"

"Mostly." He studied her with his Fed stare. "How are *you*?"

Her laugh was short and shrill. "Oh, peachy." She cleared her throat. "Actually, not bad. Pat's staying in jail, I hope?"

Henricksen nodded. "The parole violations are solid. He'll be arraigned on the new charges and held without bail until the trial. Carling confirmed his presence in California and is prepared to testify to Thomashunis's involvement in his involuntary cross-country trip. The rest will take some time, but it will come. You'll be safe. All of you."

"What about the totems and key?"

"The key was destroyed. One of Rhomney's guys. You called him PB? Pretty Boy?"

Zoe looked up sharply at his careful tone. Was PB an agent? Knowing she couldn't ask or at least wouldn't get an answer, she nodded.

"He set it on fire. As far as the legend goes, the totems are worthless without the key. And that detail, much to our frustration"—he winked—"made it into the news report about the raid."

So no one else would ever have a reason to try to obtain them. That was it, then. It was all over. Except for a long-overdue conversation with her parents. The thought of how her mother would react when she saw the news made her wince.

She stood. "Thank you so much, Shaun. Without you, all of this could have been…"

"It wasn't. That's what you have to focus on." He held out a hand, but when Zoe took it they both tugged and landed in a laughing, friendly hug. "You call me any time, for anything. You have my contact info, right? Keep me posted on your life." He winked. "Wouldn't mind a wedding invite, should it come to that."

She smiled. "We'll see. A wedding isn't only up to me."

"Go to it, then." He patted her on the back and let her out. "Room 412."

Zoe rolled her eyes but gathered her courage and headed over there. Grant opened the door before she even knocked.

"Morning." He examined her, head to toe, and she rolled her eyes again as she pushed past him.

"I'm fine."

"Of course you are."

She looked at him sideways, not sure if she'd heard a sardonic tone or not. "I am."

"Good." He stood in the center of the room, feet braced, arms folded, looking hot and so delicious and everything she'd expected him to grow up to be. She found herself blinking back tears again.

"Are you?"

"Of course."

He said it so quickly, Zoe knew he didn't mean physically. She pointed to the bandages around his arm, visible below the hem of his T-shirt sleeve. "I meant that."

He looked down and lifted his folded arms a little to see the bandage. "Oh. Yeah. Fine. Spike missed the arteries and stuff. Didn't go too deep."

"Good." She slid her hands into the back pockets of her jeans and tried not to rock on her feet. Her gaze traveled around the room of its own will, until she sighed and forced it back to Grant. His mouth shifted, as if he'd been smiling at her and didn't want her to see.

"We need to talk," they said at the same time, then grimaced together.

"Sit down." Grant indicated the chair next to the window, but Zoe shook her head. Her throat closed up, because they really *didn't* need to talk. They both knew all that was going to be said. Sorrow and loss squeezed her heart, burned her dry eyes, and she saw answering torment in Grant's. She lunged forward and he wrapped his arms around her, holding her tight to his chest. A few tears burst and splattered on her cheeks.

"Ah, Zoe." His hand stroked down her hair, down her back, then came up to cradle the back of her neck. With a subtle press, he moved her back and tilted her head, and his mouth came down on hers.

The kiss rocked her. Filled her heart with love and trust. Made promises, that he would always be there if she needed him, that he understood, that he agreed. And it said goodbye.

The only thing it didn't do was make her question her decision.

When the kiss ended they held each other for an immeasurable amount of time.

Let go.

She couldn't. Releasing him meant breaking away from a part of herself she'd just discovered. A strength she didn't know she had. Gratitude for everything he'd done for her, everything he'd let her be, rendered her immobile.

"Zoe," Grant finally said, moving his hands to her shoulders. "He's waiting."

Her heart cracked. "I know." She wanted to go to him. As soon as she crossed the threshold, her body, heart, and mind would make the shift. But part of her didn't want to leave here. It was the part she'd buried and ignored for so many years, awakened by her renewed friendship with Grant. She wanted to embrace that part of her, become whole—who she might have been if she hadn't left so much behind.

But if she stayed, if she chose Grant, she would be doing it out of fear. Because it would be easier than rediscovering herself as a whole person. It was so tempting to revert to who she used to be—but it wasn't possible to be that Zoe anymore.

Grant didn't push her away. He was leaving it to her, somehow understanding that it had to be her move. Finally, she pulled back. Not fully away from him, but enough to see his face. "Thank you, Grant. For everything. I—"

"No." He didn't want to hear it, and as much as it hurt to keep it in, Zoe didn't blame him. There was so much. He'd helped her face the past without getting lost in the horror of it. Let her be what she needed to be, follow the path she'd needed to follow, and supported her, helped her, without pushing her to the background and taking over. But she knew saying any of that would be rubbing salt in the wound.

"Okay, then. I'll keep in touch. Kind of." She wouldn't do anything to threaten her fragile relationship with Kell, but she didn't want to break fully from Grant. She wanted to know he was okay, even if they weren't part of each other's lives. And he understood that, too, nodding.

"Give my love to your mother," was the last thing she said before she left the room.

She knew he'd know what she really meant.

* * *

Zoe couldn't go straight to Kell in the café downstairs. It wasn't that she didn't want to see him or wasn't ready. Everything *had* kind of clicked as soon as she left Grant's room. She was already in a new frame of reference, inhabiting her new life.

But when she went back to her own room to pack, her movements slowed with every item she set into her bag. She didn't doubt her decision, or her choice. But she only had control over herself. She had no idea what Kell meant by "Everything will work out the way it's supposed to."

She sank onto the bed, not really seeing the shirt she folded on her lap. He had every reason to refuse her. She'd run out on him. Lied to him about the secrets she'd kept for years. Broken a fledgling engagement, put him and his family in danger, then almost got him killed in the woods. Multiple times. Even though he'd chosen to be there, none of what they'd just been through was real life. The Zoe Kell had seen over the last few days was not the Zoe he'd proposed to. Nor was she the Zoe he'd be going home with.

Admit it. You're not just afraid. You're freaking terrified.

Once she thought the word, it blossomed like a mushroom cloud in a confined space, filling every bit of her, weakening her muscles, telling her she should call her mother, check in, reassure her, make plans to visit—and do it right now, because of course Kell could wait.

Of course she could put off his rejection forever.

Nuclear fear had nothing on the spear of loss that pierced her heart. And that was just *worrying* that he might say goodbye. Could she survive the reality?

"Only one way to find out, moron." She pushed to her feet, dropped that last shirt in her bag, zipped it, and set it by the door, next to Kell's. Solidarity in luggage products. Symbolic.

Right.

Kell was where he said he'd be, leaning over a folded newspaper on a small round table in the lobby café. Two tall paper coffee cups sat in front of him, one emitting a tiny curl of steam. Her fear and pain unfurled and drifted upward, as if drawn by that steam curl.

He glanced up as she approached, and his blue eyes dazzled her the way they had the first day they met. Her lips lifted, and his answering smile went all the way into those awesome eyes.

"Hi." He stood and leaned to kiss her cheek, one hand curving lightly around her elbow. "You okay?"

"Sure." They sat, and he nudged the hot coffee toward her.

"They were out of hazelnut, so I did caramel."

"Thanks."

He folded the paper, his movements casual and easy, but his tension hummed like electronic equipment in a quiet room. Her pulse skittered. He was no more sure of her than she was of him.

"So," he said, "how did it go?"

"With Grant?" When he nodded, she caught herself looking down at her coffee and forced her head up. "It went fine. It was sad. Hard." *Honesty forever. Even if it kills you.* She caught a flare of jealousy, maybe, behind his eyes, but he didn't react otherwise.

"It was bound to be difficult," he said. "Tell me why?"

She would have preferred to flay herself open—emotionally speaking—in the safety and privacy of their own home, but she knew this couldn't wait until they got back to Boston. She took a deep breath and let it out slowly. Her scalp eased, and she was able to pick up her cup with loose fingers instead of crushing it and splashing coffee everywhere.

"Grant's special to me," she began, and Kell's nod encouraged her to continue. "I didn't know how much when I first came down here. I thought it was just nostalgia, old connections, you know." She picked at a tiny crack in her plastic lid, but kept half her attention on Kell, braced for a negative reaction. "But he's grown into a man I can respect and trust." She swallowed any references to attraction and love. She could have loved Grant if she didn't love Kell so much, but saying so seemed to take honesty a *little* too far.

"He's a good guy," Kell agreed. He pulled the heat sleeve off his empty cup and rolled it into a tight cylinder. "More than anything, I want you to be happy."

Tears sprang to her eyes and she reached across the table to put her hand on his forearm. His rope-tight forearm. She'd better move on to the other stuff before she broke him.

"Grant can't make me happy, Kell."

His head came up, his blue eyes blazing. "He could."

She shook her head. "No, he can't, because he's not you." She cleared her throat and found it even harder to look at him now that she was talking about him instead of Grant. "When I found out about this whole thing"—she waved a hand to encompass, well, everything—"I didn't want it to taint you. I didn't—" She had to take another deep breath. God, this was hard. "I didn't think you could handle the sordidness. I was so, so wrong. You're so much stronger than I gave you credit for." His arm settled a little, became slightly less tight. He let go of the curl of cardboard and rested his hand rest. Something inside Zoe loosened, too, allowing a little bit of confidence to join hope.

"More importantly," she said, "*I'm* stronger than I believed." His smile allowed her to offer one. "That was what really held me back before. I didn't tell you about Pat and Freddie and all of that because I was too scared of what it would make me, how it would undo me, if I let any of it into the life I'd built."

Kell cleared his throat and sat forward on his chair, putting himself a little closer to her. "When you left, and I started to get an inkling why, it hurt that you didn't want my help. That you were protecting me—protecting my family—was an insult."

"I know. But I wouldn't change it, Kell. I have to be honest about that." Her confidence waned. "I could only see things a certain way, and I couldn't let something happen to you because of my past. My secrets. I understand that you might not be able to see it that way, that you can only see the danger I might have caused your sister and the rest—"

"You didn't." He wrapped his hands hard around hers, as if stilling their motion would shut her up. "I was being unfair. You *absolutely* should have told me everything. But you didn't leave her vulnerable, and you never put her in danger. Pat did. It was always him. You get that?"

She nodded, because she really did. "So…"

"I don't ever want it to happen again."

She laughed, a gurgle of tangled emotion. "That sounds like we have a future."

He eased his grip and threaded their fingers. "We'd better."

"I did a lot to you. Even after I told you everything. The airport—"

"I've never been so furious in my entire life." He shook his head. "It will be our most famous grandparents story. 'The time Grandma fooled Grandpa.' " His brow wrinkled. "I guess we should talk about kids and stuff."

Her laugh came much easier this time. She rubbed her thumb over his fingers. "We'll get there. We have time." The reality of those three words swept through her, banishing all the remnants of darkness and anxiety she hadn't realized were still there. "We have time."

Kell smiled at the wonder in her voice and stood, pulling her to her feet. He dug into his pocket and pulled out her engagement ring. A piece of fuzz had caught in the setting. "Crap." He released her to pluck it off, then wrapped an arm around her waist, as if hand-holding wasn't nearly enough. "This is less romantic than the last time, but—"

"Hell, yes." She snatched the ring, wrapped it fiercely in her fist, and planted her mouth on his. With a burst of joy she flung her arms around him, and he wrapped her tight, answering joy reverberating through his kiss, his body against hers, and even the air under her feet as he lifted her off the ground.

When he finally set her down, his smile was freer than she'd ever seen it. For the first time in her life, everything felt completely right.

"Come on," she told him, turning to leave the café. "Let's go home."

Natalie J. Damschroder

About the Author

Natalie J. Damschroder grew up in Massachusetts, and loves the New England Patriots more than anything. (Except her family. And writing and reading. And popcorn.) She writes romantic adventure (sometimes paranormal) as well as YA paranormal adventure as NJ Damschroder. When not writing, she does freelance editing production management. She and her husband have two daughters they've dubbed "the anti-teenagers," one of whom is also a novelist. (The other one prefers math. Smart kid. Practical.) You can learn more about her and her books at www.nataliedamschroder.com.

29868316R00236

Made in the USA
Middletown, DE
05 March 2016